# SHATTERED INNOCENCE

*Welcome to the*

# BLACK ROSE AUCTION

In **SHATTERED INNOCENCE** by Sara Cate, a Cinderella remix, a woman is being auctioned off even though all she wants is her stepsister. Desperate, the two hatch a plan to have an old flame bid on her behalf…only for him to decide he's playing for keeps and wants them both.

In **ROYAL HEART** by Nana Malone, a Beauty and the Beast remix, a woman must work with the thief she blames for her father's death to steal back a priceless royal necklace. But the dark depths of the auction is no place for unwary hearts, and soon she may be the one stolen after all…

# ALSO BY SARA CATE

**SALACIOUS PLAYERS' CLUB**
*Praise*
*Eyes on Me*
*Give Me More*
*Mercy*
*Highest Bidder*
*Madame*

**SINFUL MANOR**
*Keep Me*

**THE GOODE BROTHERS SERIES**
*The Anti-hero*
*The Home-wrecker*
*The Heartbreaker*
*The Prodigal Son*

**AGE-GAP ROMANCE**
*Beautiful Monster*
*Beautiful Sinner*

**WILDE BOYS DUET**
*Gravity*
*Free Fall*

**BLACK HEART DUET**
*Four*
*Five*

**COCKY HERO CLUB**
*Handsome Devil*

**SPITFIRE DUET**
*Burn for Me*
*Fire and Ash*

**WICKED HEARTS SERIES**
*Delicate*
*Dangerous*
*Defiant*

*The*
# BLACK ROSE AUCTION:

# SHATTERED INNOCENCE

# SHATTERED INNOCENCE

# SARA CATE

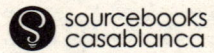

Copyright © 2024, 2025 by Sara Cate
Cover and internal design © 2025 by Sourcebooks
Cover illustration and Design © Elizabeth Turner Stokes
Internal design by Tara Jaggers/Sourcebooks
Rose frame art © Marek Trawczynski/Getty Images
Header illustration and design © Azura Arts

Sourcebooks and the colophon are registered trademarks of Sourcebooks.

All rights reserved. No part of this book may be reproduced in any form or by any electronic or mechanical means including information storage and retrieval systems—except in the case of brief quotations embodied in critical articles or reviews—without permission in writing from its publisher, Sourcebooks.

No part of this book may be used or reproduced in any manner for the purpose of training artificial intelligence technologies or systems.

The characters and events portrayed in this book are fictitious or are used fictitiously. Any similarity to real persons, living or dead, is purely coincidental and not intended by the author.

All brand names and product names used in this book are trademarks, registered trademarks, or trade names of their respective holders. Sourcebooks is not associated with any product or vendor in this book.

Published by Sourcebooks Casablanca, an imprint of Sourcebooks
1935 Brookdale RD, Naperville, IL 60563-2773
(630) 961-3900
sourcebooks.com

Originally self-published in 2024 by Sara Cate.

Cataloging-in-Publication Data is on file with the Library of Congress.

The authorized representative in the EEA is Dorling Kindersley
Verlag GmbH. Arnulfstr. 124, 80636 Munich, Germany

Manufactured in the UK and distributed by Dorling Kindersley Limited, London
001-352804-Oct/25
CPI 10 9 8 7 6 5 4 3 2 1

# FOREWORD

When we set out to create the Black Rose Auction series, we knew we wanted it to be luxe and dangerous and sexy! The premise is that there's an annual auction, presided over by the mysterious Reaper, where anything can be purchased for the right price. It's a place to make statements, to auction off the services of some of the world's most exclusive sex workers, to find priceless artifacts that the general public has only heard rumors of. Within these six books, you'll find dangerous men, powerful women, and a heist or two! Be sure to check out read.sourcebooks.com/blackroseauction or scan the QR code  to get an introduction to all six authors and their work!

Sara started by telling us she wanted to do a Cinderella remix for her book, and we grinned enthusiastically. Then she told us Cinderella would be in love with her stepsister, and we gasped with excitement. Then she told us it would be a ménage between Cinderella, her *very wicked stepsister, and her stepsister's former flame… and we about fell out of our chairs with glee.*

*In Sara Cate's version of the fairy tale, they enlist Prince Charming to win Cinderella's hand in marriage in the Black Rose Auction to save her from being sold off to someone else, but he makes things deliciously complicated when he refuses to let either of them go once the auction is over. It's no exaggeration to say this is very possibly the most gloriously filthy thing Sara Cate has ever written.*

*Jenny Nordbak and Katee Robert*

# CONTENT GUIDANCE

**TROPES:** Arranged marriage romance.

**TAGS:** Dubious consent, FFM romance, primal play, auction, virgin bride, impact play, exhibitionism.

**CONTENT WARNINGS:** This book contains dubious consent, violence, abuse from parent, domestic violence, mention of murder, and explicit sex.

# PLAYLIST

Throughout *Shattered Innocence*, you'll find footnotes referring to songs that inspired a scene, might be playing in the background of a scene, or may otherwise enhance your reading experience. We encourage you to cue up these songs so they're ready to play whenever you see them referenced. For a handy Spotify playlist  tailored to each book, go to read.sourcebooks.com/blackroseauction or scan the QR code and search for *Shattered Innocence*.

**I HATE IT HERE**–Taylor Swift
**VAMPIRE**–Olivia Rodrigo
**PICTURE YOU**–Chappell Roan
**MONSTER**–Shawn Mendes and Justin Bieber
**TOO SWEET**–Hozier
**CROSSFIRE**–Stephen
**THEY OWN THIS TOWN**–flora cash
**LIKE U**–Rosenfeld
**APOCALYPSE**–Cigarettes After Sex
**EASIER**–Mansionair
**FIRE MEET GASOLINE**–Sia
**BIRDS OF A FEATHER**–Billie Eilish
**ON MY KNEES**–RÜFÜS DU SOL
**RUN**–Joji
**FIRE FOR YOU**–Cannons
**DADDY ISSUES**–The Neighbourhood
**LOVE IS A BITCH**–Two Feet
**BANG BANG (MY BABY SHOT ME DOWN)**–Daniela Andrade
**VIGILANTE SHIT**–Taylor Swift
**I'M YOURS**–Isabel LaRosa
**DESIRE**–Meg Myers

# BIRDIE

One more chapter. Just one more chapter, and then I'll get back to work.*

It's a lie I like to tell myself when I'm alone in the house. Rain pelts against the windows as I sit curled up on the floor in front of the cold and empty fireplace. Even with the rain, it's hot outside; what I wouldn't give for winter weather, when we're allowed to turn on the fireplace. There is nothing better than reading to the sounds of rain and the crackle of the fireplace.

A car door closes outside in the distance.

*Shit.*

After quickly climbing off the floor, I run to the window and see my stepmom's car pulling up to the front of the house.

"Shoot," I whisper, my breath fogging the glass. The rain must have postponed the horse race, so she's home three hours early. In a sprint, I hurry up the stairs to my room. Going first to

---
* I HATE IT HERE–Taylor Swift

my closet, I climb the shelves to discreetly shove my paperback on top, safely out of view. I refuse to lose another one to my cruel stepsister Luna, who seems intent on destroying everything I love.

Then I dash down the hall to where I left the vacuum sitting unplugged and silent in Luna's room. Just as I hear the front door close, I switch on the machine, and it whirs loudly as I start running it in straight lines across the floor.

There's a commotion downstairs, but I ignore it. With the sound of the vacuum, I can't make out what they're saying anyway.

I'm minding my own business when someone jerks hard on my hair, and I let out a shriek. Spinning around, I stare daggers at Luna. Reaching out, I grab a handful of her bleach-blond waves and tug hard.

"You fucking bitch!" she screams, and I can tell by the slur in her voice that she's drunk. I guess she and my stepmom had enough time at the track to get trashed.

"You started it," I reply quietly.

Her hands fly toward me in a violent shove. I trip over the vacuum but catch myself before falling on my ass. When I gape back up at her in shock, I see she's wearing a smug expression on her hideous face.

She's always hated me, so it's easy to hate her in return.

I don't shove her back, no matter how much I want to, only because I won't play her games. And because I know which of us will pay for it in the end anyway.

But nothing stops Luna. When I roll my eyes at her, she lifts a hand to hit me. I cover my face, preparing myself for the blow.

"Don't," barks a feminine voice. When I open my eyes, I see my other stepsister, Violet, holding her sister by the wrist, sneering at her angrily.

They stare at each other momentarily before Luna tears her arm away. Then she glares at me.

"Get the fuck out of my room," she snaps.

"Gladly," I reply with a condescending bow. Then I brush past Violet as I storm down the hallway. Before I can reach my room, I'm cut off by my stepmom reaching the second floor. As soon as she sees me, she makes a face of disgust.

"What is going on up here?" she says with a snarl. "Birdie, what the hell are you up to now?"

"Nothing," I mutter as I try to move past her to my room.

She snatches my arm. "Where do you think you're going? Did you finish your chores?"

I roll my eyes. "Yes," I lie. She's too drunk to know the difference anyway. We have cleaners who come twice a week, but my chores are a form of torture. And her way to manipulate me.

She claims it's my way of earning my keep since I'm nineteen now. But it's not like being an adult means I'm free to leave and live my own life. Ever since my dad's heart attack two years ago landed him six feet under, leaving my stepmother a wealthy widow, she's made it her mission to make my life hell.

And what choice do I have? I have rights to my inheritance, but she keeps that under lock and key. With no car, skills, or connections of my own, I have no way out.

Not until this weekend, when I'll be forced to trade one prison for another.

My stepmom yanks me toward her, putting her vodka-scented breath in my face. "You're an ungrateful little bitch, you know that? And I've put up with you long enough."

"Only until Saturday though," I reply, my head held high.

"That's right. Then you'll be someone else's problem."

"You're not concerned about who might win my hand in marriage? It could be a murderer or a monster, and you don't care."

She snickers with an evil smile. "I hope it is. Then you'll finally get what's coming to you after the way your father treated me."

I swallow down the acid rising in my stomach from the thought of my father, as if I had any control over how awful he was to her. He made all our lives miserable, but she seems to think I was his accomplice instead of another one of his victims.

"Or you could just send me off on my own. I'll take exactly what's owed to me and leave forever."

Her grip on my arm stings. "And miss out on the payout I'll receive? Men will pay a lot of money for a pretty virgin bride like you, Birdie. Besides," she adds with her chin held high. "You agreed to this, remember?"

"Only to get away from you," I mutter under my breath.

And it's true. I did agree to this ridiculous auction—even had to sign some asinine contract stating I was doing so consensually. But honestly, what choice did I have? I could either agree to be married away to the highest bidder or live out the rest of my days as the dirt under my stepmother's shoe.

Nothing could be worse than this hell.

My nostrils flare as I fight the tears that want to spring to my eyes. How did my life get like this? I know my own mother loved me and wanted a beautiful life for me. I may not remember much, but I remember the love I felt from her. It was always supposed to be me and her forever. Then, a drunk driver took her life when I was only six years old.

And my father turned into a violent jerk who married another violent jerk.

"The best you can do now," my stepmother snarls in my face, "is get your beauty sleep and pray you land a generous husband at the auction this weekend. And if you try anything sneaky before then, I promise I will make the rest of your life hell, Birdie. You'll wish you were in that car with your mother. Understand me?"

When I blink, a tear slips over my lashes and down my face. "I already do," I mutter angrily before snatching my arm away.

She sways in place as I rush off to my room, slamming the door when I'm safely inside. Then I stifle a scream that I can't let out. It's bad enough I slammed the door—if she hears me throwing a fit, it'll only make her want to punish me more. My face is red with anger as I snatch a pillow off my bed and toss it against the wall in my rage.

Then I drop to the floor and pull my knees to my chest. I hate it here.

I hate her. I hate Luna. I hate my life. I want to rewrite my story and somehow give myself something happier than this.

When the door opens, I wince, hiding my face in my hands. Through my fingers, I watch as someone steps closer, looming over me.

I know without even opening my eyes, it's my stepsister Violet. I don't want her pity, and I don't want her to see me crying like a child. Tearing my hands away from my face, I defiantly gaze up at her through my tear-soaked lashes.

Regardless of what I want, pity washes over her features. Her brows fold inward, and her mouth presses into a straight line.

"Don't say anything," I mutter through gritted teeth.

"Oh, Birdie," she replies. Then she drops to her knees and throws her arms around me, gathering me into a warm embrace.

"I hate her." I sob into her neck.

"I know. I do too," she replies. Her arms hold me tight, stroking my back and then my hair. "It's okay," she whispers, letting me cry out my frustration. "I'm here."

As she squeezes in closer, my legs part, allowing her more room, and my arms wrap around her middle.

After my tears have subsided, she pulls away, taking my face in her soft hands. She gently brushes my hair from my face and wipes my tears with her thumb.

"I'm so sorry," she whispers.

When I gaze into her eyes, I feel like I'm no longer in this hell. Violet makes this house bearable. She is everything my stepmom and Luna aren't. She's warm, gentle, and she looks into my eyes with love, not disgust.

When she leans forward, brushing her lips against mine, I let it erase everything else in this house. Her touch is hypnotizing, making me forget the rest of the world. And when her tongue slides into my mouth, I forget my own name.

"I love you," she whispers once the kiss comes to an end.

Our foreheads are resting together as I cling to her body. "You promise you can get me out of that auction?"

"I promise," she replies, her hands squeezing my arms.

Violet is the one person I care about—the only person who truly sees me.

What started as a friendship five years ago, when my father married her mother, slowly morphed into something more. It was a montage of quiet nights in the same bed and whispered secrets under the covers.

Violet has always been the one bright beacon in my life. But just last year, when she finally confessed her feelings for me, she became even more so. Whispers became kisses. Secrets turned into touches.

Now, Violet is everything to me.

"I don't want you to worry, Birdie," she mumbles softly as she kisses my cheek again. "I'm going to figure something out, okay? I won't let her marry you off to some monster."

"What are you going to do?" I whisper with a sniffle.

"I don't know." She grabs my hands with hers and links our fingers. It's intimate, and my heart starts to beat faster. "But if I can find a way to get you away from her, then you and I can take care of each other. We'll move so far away that she'll never bother us again. You'd like that, right?"

She glances up through her lashes so our eyes meet.

The erratic beating of my heart is overwhelming now. This plan she's been talking about feels like a dream. It's the only thing I live for now.

"More than anything," I reply. The corner of my lips tugs into a crooked smile.

Violet pulls me in for another kiss. We don't let it get heated because we don't have enough privacy for that right now. If her mother or sister found out about us, they'd ruin us.

"Just trust me, okay? I'll make sure no one else can take you away," she whispers.

"Okay," I reply. I'm putting my future in her hands, but I do trust her.

Violet would never let anything happen to me.

## VIOLET

"I'm here to see Alaric Stone," I say to the guard at the gate.* His brows pinch inward as his eyes rake over my body in the front seat of my car. I hold my shoulders back and let him check me out. He thinks I'm here to fuck his boss, and once upon a time, I was.

But that was over a year ago, and that ship has sailed.

Tonight, I'm here for more important business.

"Your name?" he asks skeptically.

"Violet Scarrow."

He turns his back to me and mutters my name into his earpiece. After an excruciating wait, he finally opens the gate and ushers me in. Driving down the long narrow road that leads to Alaric's sprawling mansion, I swallow down the anxiety that keeps creeping up. The only reason I didn't text Alaric first is because I didn't want him to turn me down over text message. If

---

* VAMPIRE–Olivia Rodrigo

he looks into my eyes and sees my desperation, I might actually have a chance.

I have to do this. I would rather die before I let some asshole take Birdie from me.

Alaric is the only friend I have, and at this point, he's hardly a friend at all. I haven't spoken to him since our fling ended, but there was a time when we were close. Besides, he's my only option. I just hope he'll be able to help me.

When I reach the front of his house, there are men there to open my door for me and usher me inside. Alaric is the guy people call when they need a mess cleaned up—whether it's a political scandal, a personal vendetta, or a business negotiation. Alaric has a way of making people's problems go away. I know this from experience.

We met at a party my mother hosted a couple of years ago. I was a rebellious twenty-one-year-old, and he was a broody thirty-eight-year-old. Alaric was the only down-to-earth person I knew. He wasn't like the rest. He didn't try to charm me or get me into his bed. But after some deep conversations and a bottle of wine, I ended up there anyway.

On multiple occasions over a few months.

I could have loved Alaric, but I was too love-drunk for someone else. And the moment Birdie admitted she felt the same way… it was over with him.

As the door to his house opens, I see Alaric standing in the entryway waiting for me.

"Hello, Violet. What a surprise. I wasn't expecting you," he says with a glass half-full of amber liquid in his hand. His tone and expression are not as welcoming as I'd like. He's on guard and skeptical of my unexpected visit.

"Hello, Alaric," I reply, crossing the entryway toward him. The click of my heels against the hardwood floor echoes through the giant house.

When I reach him, I stop about a foot away and stare into his eyes. I nearly forgot how handsome he is. For a man now in his early forties, he's still as sexy as ever. With jet-black hair and haunting blue eyes, he has a rugged appeal and distinguished allure. From what I learned during our short fling, he came from nothing and clawed his way to the top. I have no doubt that while he lives a life of luxury, he'd be more than able to thrive with nothing at all.

Which is also why he terrifies me. That sort of survival instinct comes from being cunning, ruthless, and not doing favors for others.

"To what do I owe the pleasure? Did you come here to seduce me?" he asks with a mischievous smirk.

"No. I...need a favor," I reply, trying to appear genuine.

"I don't do favors, Violet," he replies coldly.

My shoulders fall, and my face starts to soften with desperation. "Will you just hear me out? I do have something to bargain with," I say in a pleading tone.

His jaw clenches as his eyes narrow. For a few moments, he just stares at me in contemplation.

Finally, he nods and turns away, walking toward his office. "Fine. Follow me," he calls.

I quickly step in line, following behind him. When we reach

his office, one of his men closes the door behind us, shutting me in with Alaric. Then he sits behind his giant mahogany desk, gesturing toward the extra chair for me to sit. I clutch my purse in front of me as I keep my spine straight as an arrow.

After Alaric lights his cigar, he nods at me. "Go ahead then."

This is all so formal and different from the way we used to be. I'd come over, and we'd get drunk on his leather couch before getting naked and fucking in nearly every room of this giant place.

I hate how odd things feel between us now. I clear my throat and swallow down my nerves. "This weekend is the Black Rose Auction, and I know your name is on the list."

"How do you know that?" he asks curiously.

"I overheard my mother gossiping to my sister, and she mentioned you."

"What exactly were they gossiping about?" he asks.

"Possible suitors for my stepsister."

Alaric laughs with his teeth around his cigar. "I'm not interested in finding a bride or being a *suitor*."

"I know," I reply flatly. My fingers grip the bag tighter. I need to frame this the right way, or I could lose all hope of this working. "I want you to bid on her, and I want you to win."

"I just said—"

"I know what you said," I reply, cutting him off. "I want you to bid on my stepsister, and I want you to win her, but I don't expect you to actually marry her. In fact, once you win her, she will be free. We will *both* be free."

He stares at me for a long time, his brow growing more and more furrowed with each second. Then he rests his cigar on the marble ashtray and leans forward. "Why would you want me to win your sister's hand in marriage but not marry her?"

"Step," I say, sitting straighter.

"Excuse me?"

"She's my *stepsister*. And she's not entering this auction by choice. My mother is forcing her to in order to receive a hefty payout and be rid of the burden at the same time. I care about my stepsister very much, and I don't want to see her get sold off to some rich asshole who will only abuse her and force her into something she doesn't want. So I'm asking you to help me."

"How old is she?" he asks with concern.

"Nineteen," I reply.

"Then why doesn't she just move out? She's an adult now."

"Because my mother has done everything in her power to control Birdie. She's limited her access to the outside world so that Birdie has no way out. It's twisted and wrong, and if I thought I could get Birdie out of there without my mother coming to find us, I would have already. But my mother is conniving and evil. And she would never let us have a shred of happiness at her expense."

Alaric leans back in his chair and stares at me as he picks up his cigar and takes a puff of it. "So you want me to bid on your sister—sorry, *step*sister. Bring her back here, away from your mother. And then you and she will run off together forever?"

I force myself to swallow. "Yes. Basically."

"What's in it for me?" he asks with a raised brow.

Taking a deep breath, I open my purse and pull out the blue satchel. His attention is glued to the thing in my hands as I open it and pull out the gold chain with the glistening sapphire encased in shimmering diamonds.

"A family heirloom," I say as I pass it to him.

Holding the pendant in the palm of his hand, he inspects it carefully. Then he gives me a reassuring nod. "This is beautiful."

"It will cover whatever you have to bid on Birdie."

As he passes it back, he gives me a skeptical glance. "I assume you weren't invited to the auction as a bidder then."

I take the necklace and place it back in the blue velvet satchel. "Correct. So, I need someone who was."

"And you can't just offer your mother this necklace in exchange for your sister's freedom?"

"She doesn't know I have it. Besides, my mother does not show mercy or empathy. The only happiness and prosperity she cares about is her own."

His face remains in a skeptical grimace as he stares at me. He picks up his cigar and takes a puff in contemplation. Then he stubs it out in the ashtray as he stands up and fixes his tie. "I'll think about it."

My jaw drops. "What?"

"What you're asking is no small task, Violet. I'd be putting my neck out for you and your stepsister. I'll need to think this through."

"But... I thought you were my friend," I plead.

He lets out a haughty chuckle. "We were never friends, Violet."

My lips set in a thin line as I let his gaze pierce this impersonal air between us. His words hurt, and not because I am still pining for him, but because it would appear that he is holding out hope for me. He seems bitter and jaded. Did I leave too abruptly last year? Did he really care that much? Is this some form of payback for ending things like I did?

When he tries to pass me by, I grab his arm and stare into his eyes. "Alaric, I'm desperate. Please."

"I said I'd think about it."

No matter how much my lip trembles or how hard I squeeze his arm, his answer doesn't change. When I feel as if all hope is lost, my grip loosens. He ushers me to the door, where his men escort me back out to my car.

Before getting in, I turn back to stare at him. Once upon a time, Alaric and I shared something special. Even if I did end things too abruptly, I thought he cared about me—at least enough to help me. I must have been wrong.

With a simple nod, he looks me in the eye as he says, "See you tomorrow, Violet."

# BIRDIE

It's past midnight when I hear Violet creeping down the hall.* She always waits until the house is dark before she comes crawling into my bed, but tonight, she's later than normal.

"Where were you?" I whisper as she silently closes my door.

She doesn't answer as she tiptoes across the room. I pull back the covers, allowing her to climb into my bed next to me. Once she's settled, I ask again.

"Violet…where did you go?"

I hear her swallow. "I went to see Alaric Stone."

My mind swirls at the mention of that name. Violet has seen him before. It was just last year that she would go to his house, staying until the early morning hours. I know they've slept together, and it makes me sick to think about it.

"Why?" I whisper.

"Because if anyone's likely to help us this weekend, I was

\* PICTURE YOU—Chappell Roan

hoping it was him," she answers. I can barely make out her warm green eyes in the darkness of my room, lit only by the moonlight cascading through the windows.

"Help us how?" I ask, wary of what the answer might entail.

She takes a deep breath. Then I feel her hand as it strokes my long blond hair. Normally, I welcome her comforting touch, but tonight, I'm afraid she's doing it to settle my worries when all I really want are answers.

"Vi," I say in a colder tone.

Immediately, she speaks. "I thought if he could win you at the auction, it would be our chance to run away together."

My mouth goes dry. "He and I wouldn't have to…"

"No," she answers quickly. "It would be a front. After the auction, you'd go live with him, and from there, you and I would be free."

I can't keep my hand from her waist now. Just the thought of being with Violet forever has me feeling bold and needy.

"Just you and me," I say, repeating her words.

She brushes my hair from my face, curling it behind my ear. "Always," she whispers.

I tug her closer, and I hear her breath escape with a quiet gasp.

"Birdie."

"Yeah?" I reply softly.

"I want you."

The next sound from my mouth is a whimper because I've never heard three better words in my entire life. She wants me. It reminds me of the first night she crept into my bed—the first time she touched me. The thrill of that night and the way it awoke something electric and consuming inside me lives with me forever now.

"I want you too," I say as my hand tightens on her waist.

Slowly, her face inches closer, and when her lips finally touch mine, I stop breathing. They are soft and gentle as they part, delicately sucking on my lower lip.

My mouth opens wider, and Violet deepens the kiss, licking her way into my mouth and tangling her tongue with mine. I slide my hand up her waist and tug her lightly toward me. She takes that as her cue to roll on top of me.

I let her take control as she kisses me and gently grinds her body against mine. I'm lost in her touch. Not a single thought enters my mind, only sensations—like the way she feels in my arms and on my body.

"God, Birdie, you feel so good," she whispers against my mouth as she trails down my jaw to my neck, and I let out another whimper when she sucks on the tender skin there. Everything feels multiplied by a million. Every touch. Every kiss. Every breath. It's infinite and ethereal.

And I never want it to end.

My heart is hammering in my chest, and moisture pools between my legs. As her hand travels down my body, she first stops at my breast, squeezing it gently in her palm. It sends a bolt of lightning to my core.

"Does that feel good?" she whispers as she hovers above me.

Nervously, I nod. "It feels so good," I whisper.

She kisses me again as she pinches my nipple, making me

hum against her lips. When her hand leaves my breast and travels lower, my body erupts in shivers and goose bumps.

Violet is the more dominant one in our relationship. I constantly feel as if I'm just waiting for her to take the lead, to tell me what to do, or to make me feel good. I want nothing more than to be the one to initiate. Hell, I'd love to be the one to ravish her, but something is always holding me back. Maybe it's fear or nerves or insecurity. I just keep telling myself that one of these days I will get over it and show her just how much she means to me.

Softly her fingers dance over my belly, lifting my shirt to touch my stomach. Then she looks into my eyes as she inches her fingers along the thin waistline of my panties.

"Is this okay?" she whispers.

I gasp as her fingers slip under the cotton. My hands are holding her tightly at the waist as I nod again. "Yes."

"Good," she replies as she slides them lower. When I feel her fingers brush the patch of hair above my clit, I shudder.

My hands tighten their grip on her waist. Staring into my eyes, she applies pressure to that sensitive spot, almost as if she wants to watch the look on my face when she makes me feel good.

"Is this mine?" she whispers, pressing harder on the nerves that light my entire body up.

I nod. "Yes."

Her finger slips lower, leaving my clit and gliding across the pooling moisture. "Tell me it's mine," she says.

She's hovering there, and I can hardly breathe. I nod again as I cling to her for dear life. "It's yours. My body is yours."

When she eases her finger inside me, I gasp loudly.

"Shhhhh…" she warns, sliding her finger out and then back in.

"I'm sorry," I whisper, my voice strained as I struggle to keep my moans in check. Her finger fills me, hitting a spot inside me that makes me feel euphoric and needy for more at the same time. With one finger, Violet can drive me wild, making me feral for her.

"You are so tight. Does this hurt?"

I shake my head. "Feels…good," I croak, letting my head hang back.

"You're so fucking wet," she replies. After pulling her finger out, she uses the moisture to stroke my clit again. The warmth and wetness create a perfect combination that makes me feel so filthy and horny. My hips start moving, grinding against her hand as I chase the release I need.

"What do you think about when you touch yourself?" she asks with her mouth against my cheek. She's still massaging my clit, going back and forth from fingering me to covering that sensitive spot in my arousal. "Do you think about your stepsister fingering you in your bed?"

"Yes," I cry out in a needy whisper.

"Yeah? Do you think about your stepsister licking your little pussy?"

"Yes," I say again. My body is on fire, and the need growing between my legs is now painful.

"Do you want me to make you come, little sister?"

I let out a groan as I bury my hand in her shoulder-length brown hair. "Yes, please," I beg.

Her finger slips back inside me and pulses while her palm rubs hard against my clit. Reaching down, I grip her wrist to hold her there.

This feels so dirty and wrong, but I love it. Violet with her hand down my panties, stroking me in secret while calling me her little sister. What is wrong with me, and why do I find this so hot?

"You're so beautiful," Violet whispers against my neck. "Do you have any idea how much I love touching you? All day it's all I can think about. And God, Birdie. You are so, *so* tight."

I let out a gasp as the pressure builds. Violet grinds her palm harder as I hold on to her wrist. Finally, pleasure explodes throughout my body, and I seize up as the orgasm takes over. Clutching tight to her body, I silently ride out the rapture as it hits me with intensity at first, then slowly starts to fade.

"That's my girl," she purrs. "Come on my hand."

"Don't stop." I groan silently, wringing every ounce of sensation out of this climax. All too soon, it comes to an end, and I'm left panting in postorgasm bliss with my eyes still clenched tightly and my heart thumping wildly in my chest.

"Jesus, that was beautiful," she moans against my ear.

My breathing is loud as my body starts to come back down. My pulse is still thrumming loudly in my ears as my limbs fall lazily at my sides.

"That was the best orgasm of my life," I whisper, making Violet chuckle.

"You say that every time. After we're free of this house, I will gladly give you one every day of your life." Her voice is low and sultry as she peppers my face and neck with kisses.

The thought of this weekend makes my heart stutter in my chest. "Are you sure Alaric will really go through with it?" I ask.

She hesitates. "If he doesn't, then I'll smuggle you out of there myself."

I wrap my legs around her hips and my arms around her waist. "But he said he would?" I say, framing it like a desperate question.

Her jaw clicks as her molars grind. "He said he would think about it."

With that, my heart drops, and my blood runs cold. "Violet," I whisper in a panic. "What am I gonna do if he doesn't?"

She frames my face with both her hands and puts hers close to mine. "You're not going to worry because I've got you. You are *mine*, Birdie Windsor. And if I have to burn that mansion to the ground this weekend, I swear I'll do it. This is not just some fling to me. You are my forever. Do you understand?"

Tears prick my eyes as I stare at her. My next breath shatters into a sob. I nod obediently as I pull her close. Her head falls to my neck as she holds me back. The two of us stay in that embrace until I fall asleep, replaying her words in my head over and over.

I am hers forever.

And she is mine.

# 4

## ALARIC

God, I hate things like this. I'm supposed to enjoy it.* The show of wealth and exclusivity. Being part of the rich crowd and welcomed only for my bank account and power and not the merit of my personality or humility.

But growing up poor as I did, these sorts of engagements feel more like a hit of my favorite drug than something I'd attend willingly. I need this. This validation that everything I've worked for and sacrificed has not been for nothing.

I *earned* this.

"Your key, sir?" the man at the door says with a cold, lifeless expression. I reach into my pocket, retrieving the skeleton key sent with the invitation. Handing it over, I watch as he inspects it briefly before stepping inside and welcoming me into the dark sprawling space.

* MONSTER—Shawn Mendes and Justin Bieber

It's already crowded with guests, most of them mingling in their secluded groups and pairs. I came alone, as I always do.

But for some reason, my mind flickers to Violet. There was a time last year when she made her visits to my home somewhat frequent. I enjoyed it. Not just the sex—although, who at my age would complain about a beautiful twenty-one-year-old spreading her legs for them? But it was her company too.

Violet is bold and fearless. You have to be to survive in our world. I appreciate that about her.

I knew her stepfather briefly, enough to know he was a selfish, cruel, abusive man. He had four women under his thumb, and as harsh as our society can be, no one I work with condones that sort of shit. If you hurt women, children, or innocents, you're not worthy of our business.

What a pity he had that heart attack.

I sleep better at night knowing he got what was coming to him, and I hope his last moments were painful.

If that makes me a monster, so be it.

I do a turn of the room, grabbing a flute of champagne off a server's tray as he passes by. It's a party full of show-offs, people flaunting their treasures up for bid, some objects, some humans.

"Mr. Stone," a pretentious feminine voice calls haughtily from behind me. I turn to see Clarissa Windsor standing with a beautiful, albeit terrified, young girl at her side.

"Mrs. Windsor," I reply in a frigid tone. My eyes scan the space behind her for a sign of Violet, but I don't find her anywhere. Then my gaze settles on the young blond beauty in Clarissa's clutches.

"This is my stepdaughter, Bernadette Windsor. Her hand in marriage will be up for auction tomorrow," Clarissa preens. "Isn't she lovely?"

The young woman's eyes meet mine, and I'm surprised to find something more than innocence in her expression. There's defiance there too. And a hint of fear.

So this is the girl Violet came to see me about. The one worth stealing that beautiful heirloom. She is lovely.

"Yes, she is," I reply, still staring at the girl instead of Clarissa. "Lovely to meet you, Bernadette," I say, bowing my head.

"It's Birdie," she replies with confidence.

Her hair is long, down to her waist, and it's as gold as the sun. Her dress is a soft blue, hugging her waist tightly and cinched around her bust to create cleavage in the V-shaped neckline.

"Well, it's nice to meet you, Birdie," I reply with a hint of a smile.

By the way she's staring at my face, desperate and intense, I'm willing to bet she knows why her stepsister came to visit me last night. This girl is literally relying on me to save her this weekend, and I hardly know her. The only thing I do know about her is that she means a lot to Violet.

"She's only nineteen years old," Clarissa adds. "And a virgin too."

My brow furrows as I glance harshly at the woman. This poor girl is being paraded around and spoken about like she's not standing right here. Like an animal headed to slaughter.

Birdie's eyes are still clinging to my face as I take a quick scan of the room. What I see are a lot of men, mostly old ones. Rich, power hungry, and ravenous. They will eat this girl alive with no consideration for her or her feelings.

I don't know this young woman, but I don't have to. It makes me sick to think of what they'll do to her. No one deserves a nightmare like that.

"Birdie, would you like to dance?" I ask, putting out my arm.

The corner of her mouth lifts in a tiny smile. "Yes. Thank you," she murmurs as she sets her hand on my elbow. It's oddly relieving to get her away from her stepmother.

As we reach the dance floor, I pull Birdie close to my body and hold her hand in mine. When her fingers brush my neck, something hopeful and intimate thrums in my chest.

We move slowly to the rhythm of the music. "I'm not usually one for dancing," I admit.

Her head slants as she blinks. "No?"

I shake my head. "I never really learned," I reply with softness.

"Well, you're doing just fine." Her voice is sweet, like honey. And holding her in my arms makes me feel more rough and coarse than normal, as if she's a delicate feather I could crush without meaning to.

"Didn't you learn to dance as a child? Or growing up?" she asks.

I take a deep breath. "I didn't grow up like this," I say, my eyes traveling the room. "Where I lived, we didn't dance, at least not how you and I are right now."

"Where did you grow up?"

"Sometimes in shelters. Sometimes on couches. Or on the streets for short periods of time if we had to."

Her brows pinch inward. "That's awful." Her hand inches closer to my neck.

"We don't need to talk about that anymore," I say. "Tell me about you."

Just then, I spot Violet's watchful eyes from across the gala. As Birdie speaks, I give her half my attention as she tells me about how her mother died when she was young and her father remarried. The entire time I just keep glancing back at Violet's eyes on me.

There's something about her expression that seems odd. I'd think she'd be happier to see me dancing with the girl she begged me to save. But her jaw is tight, and her eyes are narrowed. And she's staring at Birdie as if the girl might disappear if Violet takes her eyes off her.

Judging by her reaction, I'm willing to bet there is more going on between these *stepsisters* than they'd like us to believe. Which certainly complicates things, doesn't it? Did Violet really come to my home to ask her old flame to save her new one? A bold request if you ask me, but Violet is nothing if not bold.

"You will help us, won't you?"

I blink, tearing my eyes away from Violet to stare down at Birdie, who seems to have stopped with the small talk and dived straight into the business portion of our interaction.

When I don't answer her for a moment, she adds, "I know my stepsister spoke to you last night. So you know how much we need you. We're begging you."

I swallow, furrowing my brow and straightening my spine. I don't like to feel cornered into things. Every decision

I make is one I make on my own, not coerced or pleaded for or bribed.

But suddenly, I feel as if I'm in a choke hold with two pretty pairs of hands wrapped around my neck.

# BIRDIE

Alaric is handsomer than I expected. He has gentle creases around his eyes and a weathered texture to his skin.* For a man old enough to be my father, I still find myself incredibly attracted to him. Maybe it was the way he spoke to my stepmother and pulled me away from her for a dance. Or maybe it's because I can see something soft and kind beneath that rough and broody exterior.

I find something comforting in the roughness of his hands and the delicate way he holds mine.

"Please," I whisper, staring up into his cool blue eyes.

"I told Violet I would think about it," he says weakly.

"And have you…thought about it?" I ask.

He takes a deep breath before giving me a sympathetic expression. "It's complicated, you know. What you're asking could be risky for me."

* TOO SWEET–Hozier

"Riskier than being sold to a cruel or disgusting man?" My tone has grown cold. "Riskier than being fucked by a stranger or sold like property?"

"Yes, as a matter of fact," he replies. "Deceiving your father's widow could bear serious consequences for me. What happens when she finds out I was an accomplice in your little scheme? Your stepmother still has very powerful connections, you know. I do just fine on my own. I don't need complications from a desperate little girl too afraid to face the music."

My eyes widen as I tear myself out of his grasp. "You have no idea what my life is like," I whisper angrily. "And I am *not* afraid. Just because I'm choosing to fight back against the cards that were dealt to me does not mean I'm a coward. If anything, you're the one who sounds afraid."

With that, I spin away from him, leaving him on the dance floor as I march toward where I spot Violet near the door that leads to the large balcony overlooking the grounds.

When I reach her, I don't stop. My stepmother wouldn't let me stand around and speak to her anyway. I need to just disappear for a moment, so I rush out the door straight to the large stone railing.

As soon as my fingers grasp the edge, I take a deep breath, willing my tears not to well in my eyes. It only takes a moment before I feel soft hands brushing my hair out of my face and rubbing my back.

"Are you okay?" she whispers.

"He won't help us. No one will help us," I reply.

"So we have to help ourselves," she says matter-of-factly.

Turning toward her, I wrap my arms around her waist and bury my face in her neck. "What are we going to do?" I cry. "It's not like we can just walk out of here."

She rubs my back to console me, but she doesn't speak. Probably because she doesn't know what to say. There is no good way of getting out of here. We're trapped. We don't have a car. We're too far away from anything to walk. Besides, the moment we go missing, my stepmother would send someone after us. It would be a lost cause.

Violet takes my face in her hands. "I don't want you to worry. If Alaric doesn't pull through for us and some monster wins you in that auction, I swear I will burn this place to the ground. *No one* will touch you. Understand? No one."

I sniffle as I stare into her eyes. Then my gaze falls to her lips, and on my next breath, she closes the distance and presses her mouth to mine. Her tongue is soft as she sucks on my bottom lip. We grasp at each other desperately, and I feel her putting as much desperation and passion into this kiss as I am.

Suddenly, the click of heels on the stone floor echoes closer. Out of the corner of my eye, I see someone pass through the light shining from inside. Violet and I quickly tear away from each other and turn together to see my other stepsister joining us on the balcony.

"Mom is looking for you," Luna says with bitter disgust in her voice. I don't know which one of us she is talking to, but at this point, it doesn't matter. We're both doomed.

"Come on," Violet says to me as she takes my hand in hers. Slowly, we walk together toward the door.

I feel Luna's judgment-filled eyes on us as we pass by her, but when she mutters something quietly to us, Violet snaps. After pulling her hand from mine, she slams her sister against the exterior wall and presses her forearm against her throat.

"What did you say?" she snarls in her face.

"I said you make me *sick*," Luna replies with a sneer. Her face is turning red as she struggles against Violet's hold.

"Violet, let her go," I cry out in a low whisper, so we don't draw attention from the other guests.

"The only thing sick around here is you and how you seem to have your head so far up our mother's ass, you've practically become her."

"Violet, please," I beg as Luna's eyes begin to bulge.

"What kind of sister are you, anyway?" Violet asks, and I hear the raw emotion in her voice. She's hurt. "You may not care about Birdie as much as I do, but you're a monster if you think she deserves any of this."

"After the way her father treated us," Luna mutters breathlessly.

Violet's head tilts as she stares at her sister in confusion. "And the way you're treating her now…"

Finally, she lets her sister go. Luna sucks in a big breath, bending over and holding on to her knees as she forces air into her lungs.

Violet glares down at her with contempt. "You're no better than he was."

Then she grabs my hand, and the two of us rush inside.

The rest of the evening is spent at my stepmother's side. Various men come and go, each of them talking about me as if I'm not standing right here. They make disgusting remarks about my body, my age, and how *pure* I am. It's like these people only see *one* thing as sex, but little do they know I've had plenty of sex—just not with a man. But they don't seem to care about that.

According to them, if it's not a dick penetrating a vagina, I'm still a virgin. What a bunch of Neanderthals.

Violet stands on the other side of her mother, glaring insidiously at each of them.

Alaric is lingering across the room, staring at me most of the night with a look of contempt on his face.

Part of me regrets fighting with him in the first five minutes we met. I never argue with anyone, except for Luna. It's not like me to speak up to someone like Alaric the way I did. But he brought something out in me.

The way he seemed to protect me from my own stepmother brought out a sense of strength I didn't know I had. As twisted as this sounds, he did what I think most men should do for their daughters. My father never instilled strength or confidence in me. When he wasn't completely ignoring me, he was shouting at me to go away, be quiet, and do what I was told.

Feeling protected by Alaric was oddly nice. And as I glance at him across the room, I wish he'd do it again.

A short man with scars on his face and a ring through his ear steps into my line of vision so I can no longer see Alaric. He smiles at me with a grotesque and creepy grin that makes me take a step back.

"What a peach," says the man in a raspy voice and thick British accent. "Is she ripe?"

I make a repulsed face and try to back farther away from him as he leans closer. My stepmother presses a hand to my back, shoving me toward the disgusting man.

"She'll go for a pretty penny tomorrow," Clarissa says with pride.

"No doubt she will," the man replies as he drags a finger down my arm.

I shudder, trying to move out of his grasp only to be shoved closer again.

"How about a test drive before the auction?" he asks. "I'd like to see how it feels behind the wheel before I place my bets, if you know what I mean." As he lets out a disgusting laugh, I feel my stomach sour with terror.

My eyes scan sideways toward my stepmother. She wouldn't let me be dragged away by this stranger, would she?

"I'll keep her in mint condition," he says with a wink as he glides his hand up the side of my body. I let out a whimper and notice Violet growing restless on the other side of her mother. Then, the man reaches out and pinches my nipple through my dress. Pain radiates through me as I let out a yelp and bat his hand away.

"Don't you touch her!" Violet shrieks as she puts herself between me and the man.

"I'll touch who I want, cunt," he snaps in return. He tries to push her away, and panic rises up my chest. I can feel the attention of those around us, and that's the last thing I want. My stepmother will just find a new way to torture me if I embarrass her.

Out of nowhere, the man howls in pain. I look up to find that Alaric has him by the back of the neck, snarling in his face. "Did she say you could touch her, fuckface?"

"Jesus, Ric. Calm down," the man replies with a wince. "You know violence isn't allowed at the auction."

"I don't give a shit. If you even think about looking at her again, I'll make sure your next trip home to England is in a body bag."

"Got it." The man puts his hands up in surrender, and I notice the way they tremble.

"Get the fuck out of here," Alaric says, grunting as he shoves the man away.

Then he turns toward me and grabs my hand. "Mrs. Windsor, I'd like a word with Birdie." I yelp as he pulls me toward him.

"You already had your dance with her, Mr. Stone," she implores. I can tell by the look on her face that she's not happy, and when my stepmother isn't happy, I'm usually the one to pay for it.

Alaric doesn't answer. He's too busy dragging me away from the gala, down a long hallway.

"Where are we going?" I ask, but he doesn't answer. We don't stop as we continue up a set of carpeted stairs until we reach a guest room door that I assume is his. My stomach is in knots as I watch him use his key to unlock it. When it beeps and he opens the door, I simply stare at it in confusion.

"Inside," he barks, but I don't move. He lets out a sigh. "I'm not going to hurt you, Birdie, but I can't sit there and watch those fucking creeps paw all over you any longer. You'll stay in here until the gala is over. Then you can go to your own room."

A feeling of relief and warmth passes through me. He's protecting me. Again.

But why?

Without another word, I step into his room and he closes the door behind us. The moment I'm safely closed in the room with him, he relaxes. Taking a deep breath, he loosens his tie.

I clutch my hands in front of me. "You realize tomorrow night those creeps will bid on my hand in marriage, but it's too risky for you to help me. Remember?"

He grimaces as he crosses the room toward the wet bar, where he pours himself a glass of something amber.

"I said I would think about it," he grunts.

I march toward him. As he lifts the glass, I wrap my fingers around it, take it from him, and bring it to my lips instead. I swallow the shot of whatever that was in one hot, stinging gulp. It goes down like fire, and I start coughing immediately.

He chuckles as he pats my back.

"God, what is that?" I ask between fiery coughs.

"It's whiskey. Cheap whiskey because that's what I grew up on."

"You grew up on whiskey?" I ask with astonishment, making him laugh.

"You know what I mean."

"It's awful!" I shriek, which makes him laugh more.

"I could have warned you. Why on earth did you do that?"

I stand up, shaking off the urge to vomit. "Tomorrow may be the worst day of my life. Not only could I be forced to marry someone cruel and terrible, but the minute he gets me back to his room, he can literally do whatever he wants to me, and I'll have to endure it. So let me get a little drunk tonight, please."

"Jesus," he mutters. Then he pours another and hands the glass to me. "This time, don't take such a big gulp. If you want to shoot it, hold your breath. The air is what makes it burn worse."

Furrowing my brow, I throw the shot back, but this time, I make sure not to swallow a bunch of air at the same time. It still burns like hell, but I don't cough—as much.

He smiles proudly, and it makes my stomach flutter. He really is handsome. And almost kind.

"Good girl," he says softly, and that flutter turns into a hurricane in my belly.

I'm staring into his eyes for a little too long when we're interrupted by a knock at the door.

# VIOLET

My skin is buzzing with anxiety as I wait impatiently at the door.* I hear Birdie's voice inside and heavy footsteps on the carpet. I'm grateful Alaric took her from that gala, but it makes me anxious for reasons I don't understand to think of them in a room together alone.

Alaric opens the door and gives me a curious smirk as I shove past him and find Birdie with an empty shot glass in her hand near the large mahogany dresser. This was not what I expected at all.

"What are you giving her?" I snap as I march across the room and snatch the glass away from her.

"I didn't give her anything. She stole it right out of my hands."

"My mother is going to kill us if she goes back there drunk," I say.

Immediately, Birdie starts giggling, and I roll my eyes.

---

* CROSSFIRE–Stephen

*Too late.*

"She can stay here," Alaric answers as he grabs the bottle from her.

I tilt my head at him. "Over my dead body."

Looking offended, he huffs. "I'm not going to hurt her. Jesus, Violet. What kind of monster do you think I am?"

I don't answer him because I won't admit to Alaric that I don't think he's a monster at all. Sure, I know exactly what he's capable of, but he's always been kind when it counts.

He just doesn't want anyone else to know that.

But I still can't stand the idea of her staying in here with him overnight, unattended.

"My mother would never allow that. You're lucky she's letting you be alone with her this long. She can't risk her precious Birdie losing her *purity*."

Birdie screws up her face in disgust.

"Then take her to your room and keep her there until tomorrow. There are plenty of men out there who would gladly try out the merchandise without taking her *purity*."

"Will you please stop!?" Birdie shouts. "Everyone talks about me like I'm not right here. I'm so sick of this talk of my value and purity. It's disgusting! If they're so obsessed with this idea of *virginity*, I wish someone would just take it right now, so then they'll think I'm worth nothing. Then maybe she'd let me go."

Tears spring to her eyes, and I run to her, taking her face in my hands. "My sweet Birdie. You're right. It is disgusting and wrong. You know how much you're worth to me." I kiss her on the lips, not caring that Alaric is watching.

There's a bang at the door that startles us both. I pull away and stare at Alaric in panic.

"Lie down," he whispers to Birdie. "Look asleep."

She throws herself onto the bed, her back to the door, and does her best to look passed out. With the drunken state she's in, it shouldn't be hard.

Alaric gestures for me to come to him, and I rush to his side as he slowly opens the door. My mother is standing on the other side, her long black hair hanging over her shoulders in loose curls. Her eyes dance back and forth between Alaric and me.

"Clarissa, how can I help you?" he asks in a flat, disinterested tone.

"Where's Birdie?" she snaps.

Alaric steps out of the way to reveal Birdie lying face down on the bed.

"What on earth happened to her?" Mother says with a gasp.

"She had too much to drink, I suppose. You should really keep a closer eye on your daughter."

Her attention turns to me as a scowl paints her features. "And what are you doing here?"

I step closer to Alaric. "I was *trying* to have some alone time with Alaric, but Birdie couldn't handle her liquor and passed out in his bed."

My mother's brows scrunch together tighter. "What did you pull Birdie away for then? You wanted to speak to her."

"About me," I answer for him. "He spoke to Birdie to find out if my feelings for him are real."

"And are they?" she says through gritted teeth.

Holding her gaze, I reply, "Yes."

She pulls in a deep breath and presses her lips together. "This whole night, Alaric Stone has stolen her attention from other men in order to talk about *you*?"

Alaric speaks up. "You are aware your stepdaughter does not want to be in that auction tomorrow, correct?"

Glaring at Alaric, she replies, "I don't care what she wants. She's been my burden for years, and now she has the opportunity to pay me back, so she can either take it or spend the rest of her life working it off. Which do you think she'd prefer, Mr. Stone?"

"Children aren't normally indebted to their mothers," he replies coldly.

"Then it's a good thing I'm not her mother."

If I could slap her right now, I would. I'll never understand how my own mother could have so much hate in her heart. She only loves those who have something to offer her, like my sister, whose only contribution to my mother has been her loyalty and obedience. The moment I started to pave my own path in life, my mother basically cast me aside as useless.

Even as a child, I never truly felt she had compassion for me. My father loved me. He showed me affection and made me feel seen, and maybe it was that attention from him that caused her to resent me so much, but the day he died, my mother made it very clear to me that the love in our household died with him.

"I'll look after Birdie tonight. I'll make sure she's ready tomorrow," I say boldly.

"You better," she says, looking right at me.

I hold her stare for a moment, hoping I might see something

that shows that my own mother cares about me or loves me. But there's nothing.

"Good night, Mother," I whisper.

"Bright and early tomorrow," she replies. "No excuses. And, Mr. Stone..." she says, turning her evil glare toward Alaric. "Don't lay a single finger on Birdie."

Alaric lets out a low growl before slamming the door in her face. His eyes meet mine, and he lets the corners of his mouth lift in a delicate smile. He's never looked sexier to me than he does in this moment.

"Your mother is a real piece of work."

I roll my eyes as I cross the room to where the whiskey is. As I pour myself a glass, I let out a huff. "You have no idea."

"Is she gone?" Birdie whispers.

"Yeah, she's gone," I reply as I carry my glass over to the king-size bed. Crawling onto the mattress at Birdie's feet, I lean my back against the high ornate footboard and take a sip. She smiles at me as Alaric raises his hands in disbelief.

"We're not all going to fit in that bed," he says.

"You can sleep on the floor," I reply snarkily over my glass.

"It's marble!" Birdie shrieks with a gasp. "You can't make him do that."

"Thank you, Princess," he says, dropping onto the mattress next to her.

"Don't call her that," I snap, but he only chuckles in response.

"So why does your stepmom hate you so much?" he asks.

"She's just a bitch," I reply, taking another sip.

"Now you can see why we're so desperate to get away from

her," Birdie adds, looking down. I can hear the slight slur in her voice from the whiskey.

Alaric takes a deep breath. "Does she know about you two?"

Birdie glances at me before biting her bottom lip.

"She knows that I love my stepsister, and that's all she needs to know," I reply, staring at him coldly.

"Don't let her find out," Alaric replies. "Never show your weaknesses to your enemies."

I glance back at Birdie, feeling a sting of guilt and fear. If my mother knew how much I care about Birdie and how much I'm willing to do for her, she could definitely use that against us.

Because he got one thing right—she is my weakness.

# BIRDIE

It's still dark out when I wake up sandwiched between two warm bodies.* I'm lying snugly against Violet in a way that's not entirely uncommon for us. We've cuddled in the same bed for years. Of course, no one thought anything of it, assuming we were just sisters. And at first, we were.

But today is different because aside from her warm body behind me, there is someone else's hand resting on my hip. Without peeling my eyes open, I reach down to find Alaric's fingers gripping me.

Peeking my eyes open, I stare at him sleeping on the next pillow. Even though his face is relaxed, his hold is tight, and I can feel the tension radiating through his touch. His arm trembles, and his face morphs into fear. With eyes still closed, his brows pinch inward and his nostrils flare.

It takes me a moment to realize—he's having a nightmare.

* THEY OWN THIS TOWN – flora cash

Gently I rest my hand over his. In his sleep, he lets out a whimper, so I inch a little closer to him.

"Shhhh…" I whisper, gently stroking his hand. Then his arm. Rubbing him all the way up to his shoulders and then his face.

He lets out one last violent shudder before his eyes pop open. He's staring at me while my hand still rests delicately against his cheek.

"You had a nightmare," I murmur.

His eyes are still frantic as if he's trying to reconcile his dreams with reality.

"I'm right here. You're okay."

Suddenly, he blinks, and his eyes return to normal. "Did I wake you?"

I shake my head.

Then he looks down at where his hand is on my hip, and he swallows. Clenching his jaw, he relaxes his grip. "Sorry," he says, pulling his hand away.

And I know I shouldn't, but I quickly grab it and pull it back to my side. I'm not doing anything inappropriate. Violet is right behind me, and I'm just trying to console him.

And yet, I feel a hint of guilt as I softly whisper, "Leave it there."

Our eyes meet, and we simply stare at each other through the moonlit space between our pillows. I just met this man today, and already, I feel so drawn to him. Maybe it's because he could be my savior, my knight in shining armor. Or maybe it's because I know Violet trusts him, which means I trust him.

Or maybe it's because I can already tell that there is a genuine man under this tough attitude he exudes. With his hand on my hip and my fingers resting on his, I let my eyes drift closed.

A feeling of safety and comfort washes over me, and I quickly drift back to sleep.

---

"What kind of lush gets drunk on two glasses of wine and passes out in a man's room?" my stepmom snaps from behind me. Violet is curling my hair, and we make eye contact in the vanity mirror as she rolls her eyes, making me laugh.

"You owe Alaric and Violet an apology. You were an embarrassment last night. Tonight, you will behave."

My stepmom is scurrying around the room, getting ready for the auction tonight. We've spent the entire day *prepping* me, which feels a bit excessive. I've had my makeup done, my hair curled, my legs waxed (right along with everything from my belly button to my asshole), and my nails painted.

There are three dresses hanging in the closet. They are all dark blue and sleek, but I don't know which one is mine. I'm not sure if they are for me and my stepsisters or if one is my stepmom's and mine is somewhere else.

"I apologize, Violet," I say with a wink when my stepmom isn't looking.

My mood is unexpectedly good today. Alaric, Violet, and I were up late talking, and I could easily tell that she has chemistry with him. But oddly enough, I'm not bothered by it. I could also tell that he's not as hard or as cruel as he lets people believe.

Considering what I'm being prepped for, I feel optimistic. I believe Alaric will step up for us tonight.

And every time Violet's fingers brush my scalp as she curls my long strands, I think about the prospect of our future. My heart skips a beat as I picture it.

"Get dressed, girls," my stepmom barks from the bathroom. Judging by the slur in her voice, she's already finished a bottle of wine. "I have to meet with Reaper before the auction. Be downstairs and ready in fifteen minutes."

"Where's my dress?" I mutter when I see only Violet's blue gown left hanging there.

"You're not wearing a dress," my stepmother replies casually, as if I should have known.

I'm almost afraid to ask. "Wh-what will I wear then?"

"What you're wearing now," she replies with a bite in her tone.

My eyes catch Violet's in the mirror, and she's wearing the same confused panic that I am. I glance down at the thin short white robe I'm wearing with nothing underneath.

"But I'm not...wearing anything," I mutter.

*Don't be stupid, Birdie*, I tell myself. *Of course, you're not wearing anything.*

My breathing starts to grow erratic as the entire situation becomes more and more real and dire. I'm being *sold* tonight. My hand in marriage. My future. My body. Me.

Tears prick my eyes as my gaze grows fuzzy and unfocused. The door to the room slams closed as my stepmom leaves. In a rush, Violet turns me toward her and wraps her arms around me.

"Don't panic, Birdie. It's going to be okay." Her words are soft and soothing, but it's not helping much.

"I can't...I can't do this," I stutter in desperation.

"I'm not letting you go down there in this," she says, stroking my head.

On a sob, I cling to her arm like it's my only lifeline.

I feel like I've done nothing but cry for days. And what good has it done me? My tears haven't saved me from a damn thing. The only thing they do is ruin my makeup.

I'm so fucking tired of being helpless and meek. People do nothing but stomp all over me and treat me like I'm not even a person. I'm sick of it.

But what can I do about it now?

Wiping my eyes, I sit up and pull away from Violet. Then I stare into the mirror at the beautiful girl staring back.

She looks like a doll. Fair and blond and delicate.

"Are you okay?" Violet whispers.

My mouth is set in a thin line. For the first time, I feel nothing.

"I think it's time we come to terms with the situation, Violet. I'm getting on that auction block. Someone we don't know could win, and I will have to leave with him. I will become his wife, and I will have to have sex with him."

"Don't say that," she says darkly through clenched teeth.

I turn toward her with a huff. "Why not? I'm just being realistic. It could be worse, right? Forced to fuck some rich old guy? You don't think I'm tough enough to endure that? After everything I've been through, I can handle it."

"I know you can handle it," Violet replies with fury in her eyes. "I'm the one who can't handle it."

"Oh, I'm so sorry you have to endure *me* being fucked by a stranger." My tone is cold and spiteful. I don't mean to fight with Violet, but I'm desperate and angry, and I don't know what else to do.

"I'd take your spot if I could," she replies softly.

"I know you would." I can't meet her eyes as I stare down at my perfectly manicured nails.

It's silent between us. I wish I could stop time and stay in this room, but I know we need to face the music now.

"You should get dressed," I say.

"You wear it," she replies. "I'm not letting you go down there in nothing."

"I can't—"

"Wear it," she snaps, shoving the dress in my direction. "I have another one. What is she going to do? Rip it off you?"

I force a smile as I take the dress. "I'm sorry for yelling," I say quietly.

She leans down to where I'm still sitting and presses her lips to my forehead. "I wish you'd yell more, Birdie. I like it on you. Scream, fight, do whatever you have to."

For now, I'm going to fix my makeup and put on this dress. Then I'm going to walk down those stairs and face whatever awaits me. Just because I'm complicit doesn't mean I approve. But if this results in my freedom from my stepmother, I'll do it.

Violet puts on the same gown she wore last night, and once she has hers on, she zips mine. Hand in hand, we walk out the door and down the hall toward the staircase that leads to the main level. Then we walk to the grand hall where the event is being held.

I can already hear the charismatic Reaper calling out bids for whatever—or whoever—is up right now. My throat goes dry, and my palms start to sweat.

*I can do this.*

Violet squeezes my hand as we approach my stepmom and Luna, who are waiting for us near the door. When she turns, her eyes widen with shock as she rakes them over my body.

"What the fuck are you wearing?" she snaps.

"I wasn't going out there in that paper-thin robe," I argue with my shoulders pressed back and my head held high.

"You sassy little cunt," she spits. Then her hand comes flying, slapping me hard across the cheek. I let out a gasp as I hold my hand there to soften the sting.

"Mom!" Violet shouts, putting herself between us.

Behind my stepmom, Luna laughs in a drunk, amused giggle. "You're such an idiot, Birdie. You were never going out there in the robe, you nitwit."

My eyes widen as I turn to stare at my stepmom. "Naked?"

"Take…it…off," she growls.

My hands instinctively cling to my body as if I have any chance of stopping her.

"The men deserve to see what they're bidding on," she adds.

At this point, I know she's doing this to torture me. It's not about the money or finding me a rich husband. It's about making me pay for whatever my father put her through. The violence. The humiliation. The torment. His sins are now my cross to bear.

And it doesn't matter how unfair that is.

I'm too focused on my stepmom's evil expression to realize Luna is now behind me. "She said take it off, Birdie," she says insidiously as she tears down the zipper, scratching my back as she does.

I let out a scream as I move away from her. Violet pounces on her sister, but one of my stepmother's goons is quick to hold her back.

My stepmom takes a step toward me, latching her claws on the front of the blue silk gown, tearing it down in one violent motion. The ripping at the seams echoes louder than my screams and the muffled voices of the crowd cheering just beyond the door.

It's the sound of my dignity being shredded by her hand.

"Mom, stop!" Violet shrieks, but she doesn't.

They just keep ripping. My stepmom in the front, and Luna in the back. Until the dress is lying on the floor in strips of blue satin, and I'm standing between them, shivering and exposed.

I've never felt more vulnerable and afraid.

And alone.

Clarissa laughs when she's done, staring at my face and the tracks of tears running down it.

"Don't wipe those away," she says, getting so close I have to fight the urge to punch her. "Some of them will like that look on you."

I clench my teeth to keep my lip from trembling. Then I force my face to reveal nothing. I won't give her the satisfaction.

Just then, the door to the auction room opens, and a man steps out. "Windsor. You're up."

"That's you," she says to me, and I turn to stare into her eyes. There is no life there. No soul or humanity. There is just evil and hatred.

Without a word, I step over the pile of shredded dress on the floor. With nothing but my long hair draped over my shoulders and my high heels on my feet, I walk through that door and into the auction.

# ALARIC

I swirl the whiskey in my glass as my eyes scan the room.* In the dark, it's hard to see faces in the crowd. I can't help but peer around, wondering which of these men—or women—might bid on Birdie. And more importantly, who will win her?

It doesn't matter to me.

It *shouldn't* matter to me. I just met this girl yesterday. I don't know her, and I will effortlessly go back to my regular life after tonight, unbothered by what happens here this weekend.

Or at least, I should.

There's a haughty laugh from the table to my left. Peering over, I narrow my eyes as I stare at the bloated, sweaty drunk mess of a man as he drags an unsuspecting server onto his lap. She fakes a smile before forcing her way out of his arms.

I level a glare of disgust in his direction.

* LIKE U–Rosenfeld

What if *he* wins Birdie? Will I be able to sleep tonight?

Can I live with myself?

She showed me tenderness last night, and normally an act of kindness doesn't sway my decisions, but this girl is too sweet to ignore. She's so innocent. So pure. Someone like her would bring a light to my life that would only make me a weaker man. Weaknesses are targets.

There are a lot of very powerful men in this room tonight. Many of them were made enemies by Birdie's father through bad business deals and millions of dollars lost. If I align myself with her, does that put the target on my back?

I haven't prospered this long by forming bad alliances. I work alone. I live alone. And if I'm smart, I might be able to squeeze another forty years out of this miserable existence.

Just as the crowd quiets, Reaper returns to the stage with a charismatic smile. "What a lovely treat we have next. Come on out now, sweetie," he murmurs to someone offstage.

Emerging from the dark corner is a pale naked figure. My eyes land first on the supple pair of breasts and soft pink nipples, pebbled tight in the cold room. The crowd whistles and cheers at the display of nudity as the girl ambles across the stage.

When she meets Reaper in the center, he turns her to face us.

My whiskey glass lands on the rich carpeted floor with a *thunk* as I burst out of my seat and stare in shock at Birdie standing onstage without a stitch of clothing on her body.

"This lovely little thing is Miss Birdie Windsor. Only nineteen and a *virgin*. But bid wisely, my friends. It's not just her innocence you'll be winning, but her hand in marriage as well. There's a sturdy contract to be signed for this pretty little bird."

I can't tear my eyes away from Birdie standing up there, stark naked. Her face is set in an obstinate expression, but I can see the tremble in her hands from here. She's shaking like a leaf, and it makes my molars grind just to see it.

"Turn around and bend over, sweetie! Let us see how pretty you are," a lewd voice from the dark crowd yells. Birdie doesn't budge, staring straight ahead as the crowd reacts to the outburst with cheers and whistles. I let out a growl.

"Sit down," someone hisses at me from behind, but I don't move. My eyes quickly scan the room, but it's far too dark to make out much past Birdie illuminated like porcelain onstage. I wish she could see me, but I know with that heavy spotlight on her face, she's practically blind.

"The bidding starts at five hundred thousand for this sexy little virgin bride."

"Five-fifty," someone angrily shouts, and it takes me a moment to realize the voice that uttered that bid was mine.

"Can I get six hundred?" Reaper responds, slinging an arm around her shoulders as if they're close friends. She holds her stoic, emotionless expression.

"Six hundred," the grotesque man beside me shouts.

"Seven-fifty," I reply.

All sense and rationale are gone. I know I should sit down. I should rethink this. But my eyes are glued to her sweet form, remembering how those very hips felt in my hands last night.

Waking up from a nightmare to the feel of her touch and the warmth in her eyes is etched in my memory.

"Eight hundred," another voice calls.

"Nine," I grunt.

I'm determined now. I don't care about alliances or money or prosperity. Rushing that stage to carry her off in my arms will get me killed and do her no good. But emptying my bank account will, and I don't care if that's what it takes.

"Nine-fifty," the beast to my left calls.

"One million," I say before he's even had a chance to finish.

Reaper smiles menacingly. Birdie squints as if she's trying to find me. Can she recognize my voice?

*I'm here, Princess. I'm here.*

"I didn't know you were in the market for a wife, Mr. Stone," Reaper croons. "Or is it the promise of fresh pussy rousing your bids?"

At the mention of my name, Birdie's expression changes. Her features soften, eyebrows leaping upward as she lets out a gasp. I find myself stepping toward her.

"I've clearly won, Reaper. Call it!"

"One-five," the disgusting man next to me calls.

I sneer in his direction. "Two million." I growl. Turning back to the stage, I shout, "Call it!"

Reaper chuckles with a sinister smile. "Two million going once…"

My fists are clenched so tight I'm surprised my knuckles haven't snapped yet.

"Going twice…"

"Goddammit, Reaper," I mutter lowly. He's drawing this out to toy with me.

I've never been a hothead. I make cool, calm, and calculated decisions. I don't throw two million dollars at an auctioneer in a fit of caveman-like territorial rage. My vision is littered with red flags because none of this behavior is like me, and I know it's all *her* fault.

She's too beautiful. Too innocent. Too sweet and perfect. And she needs *me*.

I'm a fucking fool to fall for this, but it's too late now.

I'm a fool with a new wife and two million dollars lighter.

"Sold! Congratulations, Mr. Stone. You'll have fun with this one," Reaper says as he carefully leads Birdie off the stage, muttering something else to her I barely hear. I'm too busy shrugging off my jacket and rushing across the room to where she's standing.

When her eyes meet mine in the dim light, I notice the way they sparkle with excitement. I quickly throw my jacket over her shoulders, which only reaches to the middle of her ass, but it's better than nothing. Then, I hoist her into my arms and usher her out of the room.

We slip out into the brighter hall of the house. "Let's get the fuck out of here," I mutter darkly as I walk with her cradled against my chest toward the stairs leading to my room.

We make it halfway across the grand space when two large men in black suits step in front of us.

"Get the fuck out of the way. You have my money already," I spit at the men, but they don't move.

"Mr. Stone." A woman's voice echoes through the massive hall from behind us.

"What do you want?" I reply with a snarl as I turn toward Clarissa Windsor. She's wearing a smug expression. There is a young woman at her side that might as well be her clone but with bleached hair. Then there's Violet, who looks so tense someone could probably snap her in half. I hate seeing her by that woman's side as if she truly wants to be there, which I know she doesn't.

My jacket isn't long enough to cover Birdie's lower half. I can feel her fidgeting, trying to hide herself from these men and their wandering eyes.

"We have business to attend to," the woman says, causing my brow to furrow.

"I have no business with you," I reply with bitterness as I start toward the stairs.

"There are conditions of your winning bid, Alaric."

I stop and stare back at her, waiting for her to continue.

"Reaper mentioned them while Birdie was onstage. The guest with the highest bid complies with all the terms of the purchase, or the deal is nullified." Her voice is calm and playful, and it grates on my nerves.

"What the fuck are you talking about?"

Her patience wears thin, judging by the tense expression on her face. From under her arm, she produces a stack of papers. With a huff, she walks them to the center of the room, where a large glass table sits. There, she slams the papers down and points to a line on the first page.

"We don't have all night, Mr. Stone. Per the agreement of the bid, you must sign the contract and abide by all the terms within. One of which explains that the engagement be consummated by the stroke of midnight tonight."

The room goes silent as we all stare at Clarissa. It feels as if the blood is being drained from my face. Slowly, I lower Birdie to the floor, but she stays glued to my side. She presses herself under my arm and against my chest. I squeeze her tighter as I glare at her stepmom with rage boiling under my skin.

"What the fuck are you talking about?" I mutter.

"If you won't sign the contract, it's not too late to put Birdie back on that stage for another patron to bid on. Someone who will be willing to do what needs to be done."

"No!" Violet shrieks.

Clarissa gestures toward the two men behind us, both of whom take a step toward Birdie. She lets out a scream as I hold her closer.

"Stop!" I bellow. "Fine. I'll sign it."

Not once in my life have I ever signed a contract without reading it over with my lawyer in meticulous detail. But right now, the situation is a bit too dire for such formalities.

With Birdie still buried against my chest, I walk over to the table and stare down at the contract. Picking up the pen, I glance over the terms listed.

*Birdie will be my financial responsibility.*

*An official wedding ceremony must take place within thirty days.*

*Her debts and estate are transferred to me.*

*The engagement must be consummated by midnight with witnesses of the seller's choice.*

If Clarissa wants me to promise I'll make love to Birdie, I'll promise her whatever she wants. I have no intention of hurting this girl, but Clarissa doesn't need to know that.

"Why the fuck would you care if we consummate? What difference does it make to you?" I ask.

"I want to ensure that she becomes your burden and can't come back to me. What ties a woman to a man more than the prospect of a child?"

"I would never come back to you," Birdie says through her teeth.

I roll my eyes as I pick up the pen. "You're fucking sick."

Quickly scanning through the contract again, I read it quickly one more time.

*Birdie will be my financial responsibility.*

*An official wedding ceremony must take place within thirty days.*

*Her debts and estate are transferred to me.*

*The engagement must be consummated by midnight with witnesses of the seller's choice.*

Wait…what the fuck?

"Witnesses?" I ask as I lift my head to glare at Clarissa.

"You don't think we're just going to take your word, do you?"

"You're going to…watch them?" Violet asks in a soft, frightened-sounding tone.

"*We're* going to watch them," Clarissa replies.

My nostrils flare as my gaze dances from one woman to the next. I've encountered some terrible, disgusting people in my life, but what this woman is doing to these two is horrific on a different level. She must know her daughter is in love with her stepdaughter, and I'm convinced she's doing this to torment them both.

"Can we hurry this up, please?" Clarissa snaps.

I glance down at my watch. It's almost eleven. My gaze slides over to Birdie, who is still snugly pressed to my side.

I can't do this to her. I can't force her into this if it's not what she wants. There has to be another way.

"Let me offer you more money to take this out of the contract," I say, lifting my angry glare toward Clarissa.

"I don't want your money, Alaric. Sign the contract."

"There's no way Reaper would allow this," I argue, looking around for anyone at the auction to back me up on this. "It has to be consensual."

"It *is* consensual," Clarissa replies proudly. "Isn't it, Birdie?" Her cruel glare lands on the woman standing next to me. It's emotional manipulation. It has to be. This girl is so desperate to be out of this woman's clutches that she'd actually agree to this.

My blood practically runs cold as she takes the pen from my hand and quickly scribbles her name next to the space left for me.

"It's fine," her soft voice mumbles at my side. "Just sign it, Alaric." She drops the pen onto the paper and looks up at me expectantly.

"Don't you understand what this means?" I ask. There's no way she could want this.

"Yes," Birdie murmurs, staring into my eyes. There is so much grace and confidence in her gaze that it shatters something inside me. When she turns toward her stepmom, her expression hardens as she adds, "It means I'll be free."

# BIRDIE

Alaric's body is warm and comforting.* I feel like a fool for clinging to his side, but I can still feel the breeze on my bare ass and between my legs, something that makes me feel very, *very* vulnerable.

His arms provide safety and comfort.

I can't seem to look at Violet as he signs the contract. If I could, I would run to her. I wish I could pull her into this warm embrace, but she can't leave her mother's side. Not yet.

I know she wants to. I know she loves me and wants to be free of her mother too, but I also know how incredibly complicated this all is for her.

So I won't make eye contact. I won't let her see my fear, so she won't have to worry too much. It's the least I can do.

When Alaric signs the contract, he throws the pen down in anger and stares at my stepmom as he waits for further instruction.

* APOCALYPSE–Cigarettes After Sex

I find his obstinance in this situation endearing. It's nice to feel protected. Fought for. Cared for. I don't know how long it will last with Alaric or what it means, but I'll take what I can get.

"The clock is ticking, Mr. Stone." Clarissa's tone is frigid and cruel.

"Can we have a moment of privacy before you force me to defile this beautiful girl?" he replies with sarcasm.

My stepmom rolls her eyes. "By all means, Alaric. Take her to your room. You have fifteen minutes. And then we'll be knocking."

He scowls at her before scurrying me up the stairs and down the long hallway toward the room I slept in last night between him and Violet.

He mutters obscenities the entire way. When we reach his room, I feel a cold panic wash over me. *This is really happening.*

When we get inside, Alaric starts for the bottle of whiskey we drank last night. "This is some seriously fucked-up shit, Birdie."

"I know," I mumble in reply as I follow him.

"Did you know about this?" he asks as he pours two glasses, each a bit fuller than last night. He hands one to me, and I slowly shake my head. His expression is sympathetic.

"Drink up," he says before tossing his back with a wince, blowing through his pursed lips after the liquid goes down. In the distance, I hear the thunder roar outside. It matches the pounding of my heart in my chest.

I don't want to be drunk for this. I want to have my head about me, or else I'm afraid I might really freak out. But I would like to take the edge off and stop this incessant trembling in my hands. So, with a deep breath and following his instructions from last night, I shoot the whiskey back and hold my breath for a second before blowing out the way he did.

"Atta girl," he replies with a smile and a nod.

The next thing I know, I'm smiling softly.

After a second, his fades though. And I can tell he forgot for a moment what we're about to do. "Are you sure you want to do this?"

I shrug. "We don't have much choice. But I'm not afraid. I know you won't hurt me."

He huffs out a laugh. "No one has ever said that about me before." Then he reaches forward and brushes my hair from my face, tucking it behind my ear. "But it's true. I won't hurt you. Not if I can help it."

I force myself to swallow, something warm building in my belly. I'm afraid to ask my next question, but I have to know. "You do...want to, right? Because if you don't... You can imagine I'm someone else."

"Wait. Want to...what?" he asks, shaking his head with confusion.

"Want to sleep with me."

His lips part, and he freezes in surprise. Then he takes my glass and sets it on the counter with his. Crowding me toward the wall, he places his warm hands on my bare hips and brings his mouth close to mine that I can barely breathe.

"Want to..." he mumbles. "My sweet princess, you have no idea how much I want you. I'm just not as sweet or as gentle as you are. I don't want to sleep with you, Birdie. I want to *fuck* you.

I want to do filthy, awful things to you. But I know how scared you are tonight, so I'm going to do my best to be gentle. Please don't you dare take that to mean I don't want you. Understand?"

I let out a whimper as I stare into his eyes, feeling those words brew in my belly like a fire burning so hot my body aches with need.

I'm a terrible person for how much I want this. Just yesterday, I saw Alaric as a father figure. He protected me and cared for me. And now... I want to hear about these filthy, dirty things he wants to do to me. I want to hear every single one.

But what about Violet?

Just thinking about her and remembering her reaction downstairs make my insides feel hollow and cold. If we go through with this, I'm not the only one at risk of being hurt.

I love Violet more than anything, but I've never been more torn in my life. How can I love her so much and still want someone else physically?

But what choice do I really have? There are far worse men downstairs, who would not be as kind as Alaric. Even after the dirty things he just said, he still looks at me with tenderness. Not like I'm just a warm body to use.

I lean closer to him. "I'm not afraid of you," I whisper.

He lets out a grumbling sigh as his brows draw together. "You don't want to lose your virginity to a forty-year-old man, Princess."

I shrug. "I don't care about that. If you help me get away from my stepmom, the only thing I'll be *losing* is the nightmare I'm living in now."

After a moment, he pulls away and pours another two shots. As he hands one to me, there's a knock on the door.

"We don't have all night," my stepmom barks through the wood.

I look at Alaric, and we take the shots together. The whiskey burns, but it's already in my bloodstream, calming my nerves and loosening the tension in my body. Alaric slams his glass on the counter with a loud *thunk* before walking to the door. When he opens it, he does it with a scowl on his face.

I watch from the bar as my stepmom walks in, my stepsisters, Luna and Violet, behind her.

Luna is wearing a smug, almost giddy expression. She always did love to see my pain.

Violet looks despondent. There is evidence of her tears still streaked down her face. She won't look me in the eye, no matter how much I want her to.

Behind them, two security guards trail in.

"Is all this really necessary?" Alaric gripes from the door.

My stepmother takes a seat on the large chair while everyone else stands around her. "My late husband had a taste for sharing me with his friends while everyone watched, often against my will. I'm sure you and Birdie can handle this much."

Bile rises in my throat as tears sting my eyes. She really is trying to make me pay for the awful things my father did to her. And there's not a thing I can do to stop her or make her see how unfair that is.

Alaric looks me in the eyes as he tears at his tie with a reluctant jerk. He walks over to where I'm standing, frozen in fear. He leans in, and the scent of his cologne is already familiar to me. It calms my nerves, and for the first time all night, I'm able to take a deep breath. Instantly, my lungs are filled with him.

In a whisper next to my ear, he says, "I want you to lie down under the covers. Then I want you to close your eyes and pretend they're not here. Understand?"

With a gulp, I nod.

Then I do as he said.

Walking over to the bed, I don't look at the crowd of people standing across the large room. As I'm climbing under the sheets, I shrug off Alaric's jacket so I'm naked again. I pull the covers around me and close my eyes, anxious for the moment when I feel his touch.

I hear his footsteps and the rustling of his clothes. When I peek my eyes open, I notice the room is dimmer, almost too dark to see the ceiling.

Then I feel the bed dip with his weight, and I let out a gasp. My eyes close again. His warm body slides under the covers next to mine, but I stay still as I wait.

He brushes his fingers softly across my stomach and then my waist. They are soft and gentle as he drags my body closer to him, and then I feel his nakedness against me. His chest is hard with a tuft of hair tickling my arm. His legs are firm and against my thigh as is the unmistakable shape of his erection. I tense immediately when I feel it.

When he climbs over me, he places his legs between mine, and hovers so that I can no longer feel the intimate part of him. My hands are clenched into fists over my chest.

"Open your eyes," he whispers.

When I peel them open, I just see him—his perfect, handsome face and the tan skin of his chest and abs. He notices the way my gaze travels slowly downward.

"Touch me, Princess. Feel my body."

I have to force myself to breathe.

When my gaze finds his, the expression is sweet and encouraging. He wants me to feel him? Why?

Slowly, I open my hands and reach out to place them against his chest. The hair is curly, and his muscles are tight. Each of his hands is pressed into the bed around my head as he props himself up.

As I drag my fingers down over the ridges of his abs, I watch the way my touch affects him. He lets out a tiny gasp, and his breathing picks up speed.

I continue my trail downward, lower and lower until my fingers graze the patch of hair below his belly button.

"Keep going," he whispers.

I pause as I stare into his eyes through the darkness. It makes sense now why he's letting me do this. He wants me to have a moment of control. He wants to be the one being touched instead of the other way around.

I have to lift my head an inch to see the jutting length of his cock, aimed directly at the core between my legs. With shaking hands, I touch it. I wrap my fingers around his cock, surprised to find just how hard it is. It's unnaturally rigid and thick, like nothing I've ever seen or felt.

When my fingers brush the soft mushroom tip at the end, he trembles and makes a sound of pleasure. So I do it again.

I watch as his eyes roll with the stroke of my hands around him.

He clearly loves it when I play with the tip. I even toy with pressing my finger into the slit at the end, and his hips jerk as I do. I've never felt a dick before, hard or soft, and I'm fascinated by just how rigid and smooth it is.

I'm so enthralled with exploring his erection that I forget we have an audience.

I also realize, as I take in the size and girth of his cock, that it's going to hurt more than I anticipated when he puts it inside me.

He must read my hesitation, because he leans down, resting his length between my legs. Settling on his elbows, he brings his face close to mine. "I need to get you wet, Princess. It won't hurt as much if you're wet."

I drag in a deep breath. "How are you going to do that?"

"I'm going to touch you, and I'm going to put my mouth down there. Is that okay?"

Feeling instantly self-conscious, I clamp up. The only person who's ever touched me like that is Violet.

"Is that...what you want?" I whisper.

He lets out a deep chuckle. "More than anything."

There's a buzz of arousal from his words. So I give him a small nod.

Slowly, he travels his way down my body, kissing a trail from my neck to my belly.

"Let's get this over with," my stepmom barks, and I shut my eyes, trying to convince myself she's not really here. "We don't need the foreplay."

"You said we have until midnight," Alaric bellows from where his face is lingering just near the apex of my thighs. "And every time you open that ugly fucking mouth of yours, it kills my boner, so I suggest you shut the fuck up."

I let out a laugh just as Clarissa gasps across the room.

Under the covers, Alaric gently pries my thighs open. My laughter quickly dies when I feel his breath so close to my delicate skin. When I feel the soft friction of his wet tongue lap through my folds, I let out an embarrassing whimper. One hand dives under the covers to hold the back of his head. The other clamps over my mouth to keep me from making that sound again.

I was quite sure when I climbed under these covers that I could never get aroused with my stepmother in the room watching me. But right now, I'm focused on Alaric, and only him…and at the moment, he's proving me wrong. I feel my body tightening and the blood in my veins growing hotter. To my surprise, I sense the building pressure of a potential orgasm—especially if he keeps doing that.

He licks and licks, coating me with saliva before latching his lips around my clit and sucking so hard my hips lift from the bed. I can't keep the sounds in anymore. I'm moaning through my hand and holding his head there so he does it again.

He sucks once more, but this time, he slides a finger inside me while he does it.

It's too much.

He thrusts it in and out as he continues to suck. I feel like a balloon slowly being filled with air, ready to pop at any moment.

It's a mixture of pleasure and pain as he forces my body closer and closer to something I didn't see coming.

When he crooks his finger, I reach the pinnacle of this sensation. Writhing on the bed, my thighs fidgeting around his head, I finally feel the balloon pop, and my body erupts in a seizing tide of pleasure. It courses through me, wave after wave.

I don't realize I'm now biting my hand to keep from crying out until the orgasm crests and I start to feel the pain of my teeth around my own flesh.

When Alaric pulls away, I open my eyes and lift the blanket to find him wiping the moisture from his mouth. I reach for him in desperation.

As he climbs back up my body, I wrap a hand around his neck and haul his mouth to mine. I taste my own sex on his lips as I devour him in a passionate, bruising kiss.

When I feel the head of his cock prodding my entrance, I don't feel fear or hesitation.

I pull away and look into his eyes. "Alaric," I whisper. "I'm ready."

## ALARIC

Birdie is trembling beneath me.* The taste of her cunt is still on my lips when she whispers, begging me to fuck her.

I've done despicable things in my life. I've killed, cheated, stolen, and lied.

But taking this perfect angel's innocence feels like the worst.

I should be prouder of making her come on my tongue, but I only feel like a monster. I enjoyed that far more than I should have. To be honest, I'm enjoying all of this too much. Fucking a sweet virgin who happens to be Violet's girlfriend does not make me a good man, but enjoying it this much makes me a despicable one.

As I drape my body over hers, my cock leaks at the tip with anticipation. Brushing her hair out of her face, I look her in the eyes. "Just look at me, okay, Princess?"

With her lips pressed together tightly, she nods.

* EASIER—Mansionair

"She's doing this to hurt you, but don't give her the satisfaction of letting her see your pain."

"Okay," she whispers.

"It's going to hurt, but only at first," I say lowly.

"You have fifteen minutes, Mr. Stone," Clarissa snaps from the other side of the room.

My molars grind as I hold Birdie's gaze. "It's just me and you," I mumble.

"What if it doesn't fit?" Birdie chirps with fear.

I give her a soft, reassuring smile. "It'll fit, Princess."

She gulps and tightens her grip around my neck.

"Now, hold on to me," I say in a raspy whisper.

When I line my cock up with her cunt, it's still so soaked, my cock slips easily in just an inch before I feel resistance. She tenses in my arms.

"Just do it," she murmurs.

"Relax, angel," I reply. "This part will hurt."

"I can take it," she says confidently.

I smile down at her, proud of her strength. Leaning in, I kiss her on the forehead.

Then I drive my hips forward, breaking through the barrier and sliding all the way in. Her pussy is tight, and she screams in my ear from the pain. It makes me hate myself for how good it feels.

"I'm so sorry, Princess," I whisper against the side of her head.

"It's okay," she replies. "It's not your fault. It just…burns."

"I'll give you a moment. Once I start moving, I don't know if I'll be able to stop."

Lifting up on my hands, I rise to see her eyes. With my cock buried deep inside her, I feel like she's an extension of myself. I've never felt like this with a woman before, but the urge to protect and care for this one is like nothing I've ever experienced.

I would murder every person in this room for her. I probably should.

After only two days, she has stolen my heart straight from my chest. It's hers now, and I don't even care. She can have anything of mine.

"Alaric, are you okay?" she breathes.

I must look like a deer in headlights, staring at her in shock as I realize I'm falling hard for this girl I've just met.

Pulling my cock out to the tip, I slowly thrust back in. A moan claws its way up my throat at the sensation of her body choking the life out of my dick.

She winces in pain, so I shut my eyes tight so I don't have to see the way I'm hurting her.

I pull out and thrust in again, and again, and again. Picking up my speed, I know the best thing I can do for her at this point is to get it over with quickly.

*God, I'm so disgusted with myself.*

Then I hear her whimper beneath me. A grunt escapes my lips, and I open my eyes to find her face no longer frozen in pain but bordering on pleasure. Suddenly I'm thrusting harder, working at different angles, desperate to hear her make that sound again.

"It feels…better now," she mumbles in a gasping response.

"It does?" I ask.

"Y-yes. Right there," she says, adjusting her hips to find a spot that feels good to her.

It's so hot and beautiful that I might explode already. "Use my cock." I grunt. "Find what feels good."

"Go slow," she murmurs. "But a bit...harder?"

Her sweet voice making requests is almost too much. When I slam into her, she whimpers again, and I nearly come.

"Oh fuck, Princess. You feel so good."

Her face morphs into euphoria at my words, clearly loving the praise.

"You are so fucking perfect," I mutter between thrusts. "And you're all fucking mine, understand?"

She gasps, her mouth hanging open as she struggles to breathe between each violent impact of my cock impaling her. Reaching down, I grab her right leg and hold her under the knee so I can plunge even deeper.

"Yes," she cries out, throwing her head back.

"That's right. You love my cock, don't you?"

"Yes," she repeats, higher pitched this time. I know we're loud enough for our audience to hear us, but I don't care. Right now, she is the only person who matters.

Forever—she is the only person who matters.

My balls start to tighten, and I know I'm close. "Tell me you want me to come inside you." I growl into the crook of her neck.

"Please," she says on a whimper. "Come inside me, Alaric. Make me yours."

"Oh, you're fucking mine, Princess."

With that, I pound in one last time before pleasure explodes behind my eyes, coursing through every inch of my body. My dick shudders inside her, filling her up as I groan out my release.

The sensation lingers so long that I refuse to pull out. Even after the orgasm ends, I rest my pounding heart on hers. We breathe the same air. She is mine in every way that matters.

I have never felt changed by sex before, but Birdie changed me. It's like she crawled inside my chest and buried herself against my heart.

When her eyes find mine, I swear she can feel it too.

"Congratulations, Mr. Stone. You've won yourself a wife. She's yours now. Your burden. Do with her what you will." Clarissa's voice is like a harsh buzzing sound somewhere in the distance, but I'm too focused on Birdie to care.

I hear footsteps and the door opening. Then, a cold "Come on, Violet."

That's when I turn around to see Violet's tear-streaked face. She's seemingly surrendered to her grief as she shuffles out the door behind her mother.

The door closes with a thud, and just like that, I'm alone with Birdie.

I finally ease my cock out and stare down at her in concern.

Brushing her hair back from her face again, I whisper, "My sweet princess, are you okay?"

Her next inhale is a shuddering sound. Then she nods. "Yes."

"Let me get something to clean you up," I say as I rise from the bed. When I reach the bathroom, I see the streaks of blood on my cock. I'm a vile piece of shit for how much that turns me on. My dick is already hardening again at the sight.

I dash to the sink and wash it off in a rush, disgusted with myself. I won't let her see that. Then I grab a washcloth and soak it in warm water before taking it back out to the room to find her curled up on her side, waiting for me.

"Let me, darling," I mutter softly as I peel back the blankets. She's such a good girl for me, spreading her legs and letting me wipe her clean of the blood and leaking cum. Her eyes stay on my face the entire time, watching me with a perplexed expression as if she's studying me.

"Thank you," she whispers.

I pause and gaze into her eyes. "Don't thank me."

"You got me away from her. You saved me," she replies.

"I'm no hero, Birdie," I reply darkly.

"You're my hero."

I only grunt in response. Then I toss the washcloth back in the bathroom and cover Birdie back up with the blankets.

"What now?" she asks innocently.

I know she means for us, for her, for her future. But I don't have those answers. And I don't want to scare the poor girl when I tell her that I meant every word. She belongs to me now. She is my burden—my beautiful, perfect, sexy-as-fuck burden.

I can't let her go.

So I keep that part to myself for now.

"Now you sleep," I reply, clicking off the lamp next to the bed.

"Sleep next to me," she whispers.

"I will," I say, but I can't sleep yet. I can't rest until I go take care of something.

"Where are you going?" she asks.

When I don't answer, she bites her bottom lip.

"You don't have to tell me. I don't need to know, but if you see Violet…" Her voice cracks on the name. "Tell her I'll be waiting."

I let out a heavy sigh as I nod. "I will."

Leaning down, I kiss her forehead and watch as she flutters her eyes closed and falls asleep.

For a while, I don't move. I can't look away.

It's like I'm standing at a crossroads. After all the bullshit my life has given me, it decided to drop this angel in my life like I'm supposed to know what to do with her. The last time I felt myself falling in love with someone, it was Violet, and she left me high and dry for nothing. I don't know if she fully grasps the pain I felt from her absence.

And now I feel the same thing again with Birdie. Who is in love with Violet.

What a mess.

All I know is I can't walk away. I'm in too deep. I care too much. If I get in my car tomorrow and drive home without her, I won't be able to resume my life the way it was.

But she's not mine to keep. Not yet.

All I know is that Birdie is not leaving this mansion without me.

# VIOLET

The vodka doesn't burn anymore.* It doesn't hurt. It doesn't betray me. Or break my heart.

At the moment, vodka is my best friend. The love of my fucking life.

I sniffle as I take another numbing swig from the bottle. The cool breeze tickles the bare skin of my shoulders, but thanks to the vodka, I can barely feel it.

What a fool I am.

I'm supposed to be smarter than this. My sister, Luna, is the senseless one of the family, but right now, I feel like it's me.

I literally talked the handsomest and most charming man in the whole city into marrying the person I love most. I deserve this. I deserve to lose her because I was too fucking weak to come up with a better plan.

Of course, if I had any idea my conniving, cruel, evil fucking

---
* FIRE MEET GASOLINE—Sia

mother had planned to force them into fucking in front of my very eyes, I never would have sought this plan out. I thought he would just take her to his house where I would meet up with them, and Birdie and I could run off together into our blissful, perfect future.

My feet sink into the wet grass as I amble through the labyrinth of this massive garden behind the mansion. I lost my shoes hours ago. Tossed them into the bushes. Or was that just a few minutes ago?

Who the fuck knows?

And it doesn't matter.

Nothing matters anymore.

Birdie is gone. My Birdie. The only thing on this lonely fucking planet that I care about.

Just the mention of her name in my brain drags up the sound of her whimpers as Alaric fucked her. The way she *loved* it. The way she begged him to come in her.

Suddenly, I'm retching into a hedge. My vodka bottle tumbles into the grass, spilling what was left inside. After my stomach is emptied, I collapse onto the ground, crying into my folded arms.

When I hear footsteps, I freeze.

The last thing I need right now is for some asshole from the auction to harass me out here in the hedge maze in the middle of the night. Reaching for the vodka bottle, I grab it by the neck and watch for whoever is about to turn the corner and find me here.

It's not a stranger from the auction, but I tighten my grip on the bottle nonetheless.

"Violet," Alaric calls as if he's searching for me.

The next thing I know, I'm launching myself at him, swinging the bottle as a sob escapes my mouth.

"I hate you," I cry out. Just when I'm expecting the bottle to crash against his skull, he snatches my wrist in his hand and overpowers me.

"Crazy fucking bitch," he mutters as he yanks the bottle from my hand and pulls me to his chest, tightening his grip on me. "I've been looking for your drunk ass for the past two hours. Why the fuck did you come out to this godforsaken maze?"

"Why does it matter?" I cry. "You want your fucking jewel?"

"No, I don't want the fucking jewel," he replies in a harsh tone. His lips are next to my ear, and I hate myself for the way my body reacts.

I'm supposed to want to kill him, not fuck him.

"Then what do you want?" I groan, big warm tears sliding down my cheeks and over my lips.

"I want to fucking talk to you," he replies, gritting his teeth as he continues to fight me for control. I struggle to escape his grasp, and even though I no longer have the empty bottle in my hand, I'd still like to claw at his stupid, handsome face and pummel my fist against his perfect cheekbones.

"I don't want to talk to you," I reply drunkenly. "I hate you."

Thunder roars overhead as a light sprinkle starts to rain down on us.

His grip tightens around my body, forcing me to focus on the hard, muscular plane of his chest. Then he puts his mouth next to my ear. His voice comes out in a sexy, raspy grumble. "I'm sure you do, Violet," he says. "I just fucked your girl, and I'll do it again."

I let out a sobbing shriek as I fight his strength to no avail.

"But I care about you, you wild little bitch, so I want you to listen to me."

"Care about me?" I scream. "If you cared about me, you wouldn't have jumped into bed with the woman I love."

His hands are rough as he grabs my face under my jaw and holds me tight. I can feel his frustration and anger with me, and it only fuels mine in return. "What the fuck are you talking about, Violet?" he snaps. "You asked me to do that for you."

"You clearly enjoyed yourself," I reply spitefully.

Suddenly, I'm being hoisted off the ground. Alaric's strong arms carry me off the gravel path and into the dark abyss behind the bushes among the trees and flowers of the garden.

"Let me go!" I scream.

His hand quickly clamps over my mouth. "I should leave you out here," he says with a groan as he lowers to his knees, taking me with him so we're hidden behind the shrubs. "You want these thugs around here to hear you screaming? You'll get us both kicked out, and then what happens to Birdie? So keep your fucking voice down while I talk, understand?"

I whimper behind his hand as I struggle to calm myself down. I know he's right. I know I'll only cause more trouble by making a scene, but I can't help it. I'm full of so much rage and anger I don't know what else to do with it.

I rest back on Alaric's kneeling body, and that's when I feel the prodding erection in his pants against my ass. Just the feel of his hard cock makes my blood boil again with fury.

Tearing his hand away from my mouth, I turn my head

toward him. "You get off on forcing women to do something they don't want, don't you?"

When I try to swing my hand at his face, he snatches my wrist again and forces me face down into the grass.

"Dammit, Violet." He growls. "I knew you had fire in your blood, but I had no idea you were this fucking crazy."

"I'm not crazy," I spit back at him.

His voice is near my ear again. The weight of his body on top of mine is infuriatingly comforting and arousing. The length of his cock rubs through the crack of my ass, and I let out a humiliating whimper.

"That's what I thought," he mutters in my ear. "How can I be turned on by women who don't want me when you so clearly do?"

"No, I don't." I growl, my face tickled by the grass.

He grinds himself against me again, and I let out another guttural moan. "You sure about that?" he replies.

"So what? Are you going to fuck me out here only hours after fucking my stepsister?"

"I'm *not* fucking you out here," he replies. "I'm trying to talk to you, but you're struggling against me so much it has my dick confused."

Suddenly, I'm out of energy. My limbs fall to the ground, spent and exhausted. And still drunk. Just then, the sky opens up and the drizzle turns into hard rain. Lightning flashes in the distance, illuminating the dark maze for a split second before it goes dark again.

I let my tears fall into the dirt and grass with the rain while Alaric waits to be sure I'm not going to swing at him again. Then he finally climbs off me before sitting on his ass with his arms draped over his knees.

After a few minutes of sobbing like a child and feeling sorry for myself, I slowly get up. He watches me cautiously as I move into a seated position.

"You look like shit," he mumbles, and I give him a scowl and the middle finger.

"Well, today was the worst day of my life, so forgive me for not being pretty enough for you."

"I didn't say you weren't pretty. I said you look like shit," he replies, shaking the rain from his head.

"What do you want me to do about it, Alaric?" I wipe the makeup from under my eyes, but it's caked on so heavily, it's not helping much.

"Come to my room and shower. Let's get some rest, and then we can talk. Assuming you're done trying to kill me." He puts up his hands in surrender, and I roll my eyes.

"Fine," I mutter.

When he stands up, he puts out a hand for me. Hesitantly, I place my fingers in his, and he hoists me to my feet. Suddenly, I'm standing an inch from him, staring up into his eyes.

That memory of potential love for Alaric Stone comes flooding back. If it hadn't been for Birdie, I probably would have let my heart get attached to him, but because of her, the roots of our love never had a chance to grow.

She came first. She *always* comes first.

"Let's go," he whispers after a long moment of charged eye contact. "We're getting soaked."

With his arm over my shoulder, he leads me to his room. The mansion is dark, but I hear movement in the halls and rooms. Whatever is going on behind those doors and walls is more than likely wicked.

But there's only one room I care about.

And when Alaric opens the door, I lay my eyes on Birdie's sleeping form in his bed. I wish I could say it doesn't hurt. But she's still naked, and her hair is tousled in a post-sex knot of tangles. The memory of watching her give herself to him so freely still burns like my heart is pumping acid through my veins instead of blood.

"Come on," he whispers.

I'm too drunk and heartbroken and exhausted to face her at the moment. He must be able to tell because he gently guides me to the bathroom. Once we're in there, he starts the giant shower and pulls out a towel for me to use.

But I don't move. I stare into the mirror at the mess of a woman in the reflection. I can hear my mother's words in my mind.

*You're so weak, Violet.*

*You only care about yourself, Violet.*

*You think you're so much better than us, don't you, Violet?*

*You'll never leave, Violet.*

*You're too afraid.*

Without a word, Alaric drags the zipper of my dress down, and I blink away from my reflection to watch him carefully undressing me. It doesn't feel sensual or charged. It's nurturing.

The blue silk dress falls to the floor, and with his help, I step out of it. Then he unclasps my bra and tosses it to the floor. I don't even flinch when his fingers slide under the elastic band of my underwear, easing them down my legs until I'm completely naked.

As he opens the shower door and guides me inside, I realize at some point, I'm going to have to snap out of it and start taking care of myself. But my arms feel like they're filled with lead, and my head aches with the thought of any effort at all.

I simply stare at the white marble shower wall for a long time. The water is scalding, and it burns my skin, but I don't care. I lean into the burn.

When the shower door opens again, it takes me by surprise. I glance up to find Alaric standing a foot away from me, the hot water cascading down his naked chest.

"You know what I always liked about you?" he says as he slowly spins me around so the water hits my back. Gently, he tips my head back and runs his fingers through my hair. "You never played by their rules."

"What are you talking about?" I mumble. My voice trails as he squirts shampoo in my hair and begins to work up a lather on the scalp. My eyes flutter closed, savoring his relaxing touch.

"I've always been an outsider. A self-made man. I didn't grow up rich like you did, or anyone else in this twisted fucking community. So I never felt like I could connect with anyone. Until I met you."

My eyes pop open. "Me?"

"When I met you, I knew you were an outsider too," he says as he continues to massage my head.

"How could you tell that?" I murmur.

"Everyone around here has a motive. They play for themselves. People only sleep with others for power or money. Relationships are schemes. And I'm sure your mother tried to set you up with powerful men who would further your family's prosperity, but you didn't. You came to me."

"I liked you," I whisper.

"I liked you too, Violet. A lot. We could have had something amazing together. But you left."

His words land heavily on my chest. Guilt blossoms there, and it's impossible to ignore.

"Why didn't you try harder to get me back?" I ask, remembering the last time I saw him romantically and the last text he sent that went unanswered.

"I figured it was for the best. In my line of work, a happy man is a man with weaknesses. I make other people's problems go away, and sometimes that puts me in compromising situations. I've made enemies, Violet. Being a discreet nobody with nothing to lose is what has kept me alive and wealthy for many years."

I don't respond as he rinses the shampoo from my hair. I start replaying the encounters Alaric and I shared before. Did he really like me more than I thought? Was I a liability to him?

"What about Birdie?" I whisper, turning around to face him. "You're not going to let her go, are you?"

"No," he replies solemnly. "I can't let her go now."

I wince, the pain of the truth stabbing my chest like a knife. "Will she be safe with you?"

His expression grows serious. "I won't let anything happen to Birdie."

"You barely know her. How can I trust you? How do I know you'll really care for her after only meeting her yesterday?" I ask, my tone growing cold, but there's a tremble that I can't help.

"I wish I could understand, but all I know is that she's mine now, Violet. And I will care for her."

I squeeze my eyes closed, letting a tear slip through my lashes. "What about what she wants? How do you know she'll stay with you?" I whisper.

Alaric brushes the water from my brows. Then he leans in and presses his lips to my forehead. "Because you'll tell her to," he replies with confidence.

My eyes pop open, and I lean back and stare at him in shock. "I will not."

"If you care about her, you will," he says in a dark, matter-of-fact way that chills my bones. "Does she know the truth about you, Violet? Does she know what you *did*? What do you think she'll do when she finds out?"

I let out a gasp as I lift my hand and let it fly, slapping him hard across his cheek. He doesn't stop me this time, even though I know he could. Maybe he knows he deserves this one.

"Are you threatening me?" I ask in a whispered shriek. When I lift my hand again, he grabs it in a swift motion and shoves me against the wall, covering my naked body with his. Then his mouth is an inch from my face as he speaks.

"I'm not threatening you. I'm being sensible. Think about it, Violet. Birdie could be carrying my child as we speak. Your mother is clearly crazier than I expected. Did you honestly think that the two of you could just ride off into the sunset together and no one would care? She will find you, and she will make you pay for trying to outsmart her. And if Birdie does have my child, your mother will use that child against all of us."

"You're wrong. My mother will be glad to be rid of us," I argue.

"What money are you using, Violet?"

My lips press together as I stare into his eyes because I don't have a good response for that. "We'll—" I start, but he cuts me off.

"You honestly think Clarissa will let you have a dime of either of your inheritances? Just like before, Violet—you make the plans, and I execute them. Remember? Just admit it. Birdie would be safer with me, and you will tell her so."

He buries his hand in my hair and tilts my head back so I'm forced to stare upward at him. Then, to my surprise, he licks along the seam of my mouth.

I let out a gasp, my hands gripping the wet skin on his sides, unable to gain purchase to push him away.

"See?" he murmurs. "I like the way you fight with me. You're not afraid of me, Violet, and I love that about you."

"Alaric," I breathe out before his mouth crashes against mine. At first, it's just his lips pressed to my lips, and I do my best to fight him off. I do my best to hate him.

But when I gasp, he slides his tongue inside, and I'm helpless. My hands stop clawing at him. My body stops trying to get away. I don't understand anything; honestly, I stop trying. I melt into his arms and let him kiss the life out of me.

It doesn't make any sense.

I hate my body for the way it responds to his touch, warming at the core and wanting more.

I hate my heart for the way it calls out to him, wishing for a moment he'd let me in.

I hate myself for letting him kiss me while Birdie sleeps in the next room.

When his lips trail hungrily from my mouth to my neck, I whisper, "Stop."

But it's a weak attempt. Because *I* am weak.

After all this time, I made Birdie believe she could trust me. That I could take care of her. But I can't do anything. My mother was right. I am a disappointment. I promised Birdie I wouldn't let anyone touch her, and I failed. I promised I'd get her out, and I failed.

Maybe he's right—she is better off without me.

"Alaric, stop!" I bark louder, pushing him in earnest now. He takes a stumbling step backward and stares at me in surprise. Without looking directly at it, I can tell his cock is hard and protruding toward me.

What would have happened if I didn't stop him? Would he have fucked me right here in the shower? I'm humiliated just thinking about it.

I'm tired of being weak and helpless. And I won't do it anymore.

"I'm not going to just let you take what you want," I say, feeling sober and determined. "Not me and not Birdie. My plan might not have been perfect, but I'm just as capable of taking care of her as you are. So if you plan on keeping Birdie, you better plan on keeping me too. Because where she goes, I go."

With that, I turn off the water and step out from under the spray.

When I turn back to glance at him, I'm surprised to find him wearing a haughty smirk.

# BIRDIE

When I blink my eyes open, I'm staring at a mess of dark strands on white sheets.* My forehead creases with confusion. Before moving, I replay the events of last night through my mind.

The auction. Alaric. The whiskey. The room. The audience. The sex.

I had *sex* with a man last night.

It's not that being with a man is really so shocking. Until Violet, I sort of assumed I would end up with a man. But then she changed everything.

Just a few days ago, I thought I was about to get everything I ever wanted. Violet had a plan—a plan that meant I would finally be hers, and she would be mine—for real this time. Forever.

Then... Oh *God*, she had to watch. She had to watch him

* BIRDS OF A FEATHER–Billie Eilish

touching me, making me feel good, making me say those things during sex.

Fuck, what did I say?

*Come inside me.*

*Make me yours.*

I let out a groan as I cover my face with my hands. My poor Violet.

I was so caught up in the moment—desperate to cling to anything to escape the reality of what was happening. I made myself believe it was just him and me, and nothing else existed.

In the dimly lit room, I scoot closer to Violet. As I touch her arm, she shivers. Just past her sleeping form, I can see Alaric. His back is to her, wearing a tight black T-shirt, and his hair is tousled from sleep.

"Violet," I whisper.

I can tell by the way she tenses that she's awake. Quietly, she turns toward me. When her eyes meet mine, it feels like a thousand bricks landing on my chest. Her eyes are swollen, most likely from crying. Her expression is despondent, and it breaks my heart.

"I'm so sorry," I whisper, tears welling in my eyes.

She forces a sad smile on her face. "Don't be sorry, Bird. It's okay. You didn't do anything wrong." Then she leans closer and presses her lips to my forehead. I rest in her arms, my head lying softly under her chin.

Violet has always been my soft place to land. With her, I'm safe and comfortable and home.

What is going to happen to us now?

It's the question I'm too afraid to ask.

We lie together like that for a while. Neither of us speaks or addresses the elephant in the room—or the man sleeping next to her.

The important part is that I don't have to go back to my life at Clarissa's. I'm free.

"Are you in pain?" Violet asks in a low whisper.

I shake my head. "Just a little sore."

My hand snakes down my naked body and slides between my legs. It doesn't feel any different, although it is tender to the touch.

Violet's hand caresses my back and hip. "How about a shower?" she says quietly.

I nod. "Yeah, that would be nice."

Slowly, we both climb out of bed. Alaric fidgets but stays asleep. Violet takes my hand and leads me to the bathroom.

I wish I had some clothes. I know there's nothing at that house worth going back for, but I'd really like to have some of my things. My laptop. My clothes. My stepmother said she was having it all packed up while we were gone, but I don't trust her word at all.

Violet turns on the shower and tests the water before pulling off what I assume is one of Alaric's T-shirts and climbing in first. I follow close behind. The moment we're alone, I fall into her embrace. Her breasts are soft against mine. I've missed this. The beat of her heart. The scent of her hair.

"What are we gonna do now?" I whisper.

She strokes my back, hesitating before she answers. "We're

going to take it one day at a time. We know we can trust Alaric, so for now, we'll go stay with him."

"Both of us?" I ask, my brow furrowed.

She pulls away and takes my face in her hands. Holding it close so I can stare into her eyes, she says, "You're not going anywhere without me. Understand?"

Swallowing the lump in my throat, I nod.

"Where you go, I go," she says.

"Where you go, I go," I repeat.

"If he tries to take you from me, I'll kill him," she says in a low mutter, and I can tell by the expression on her face that she's serious.

Leaning in, she presses her lips to mine, and I wrap my arms around her neck to hold her close. I need Violet like air. During the worst days of my life, she was there. When I found my father's lifeless body on the floor. Whenever my stepmother would get drunk and take it out on me. Whenever Luna would bully me so bad, it made life feel like a burden to keep living.

Violet was the sun when it felt like morning would never come.

Then, now, and forever, I know it's me and her. She will protect me the way she always has. She will love me when no one else wants to. She will never leave my side.

My heart expands in my chest at the thought of how much she means to me. So I pour that passion into our embrace. Our kiss deepens as she presses me back against the wall.

Her mouth trails from mine down my neck, and I gasp for air when her teeth close over the tight bud of my nipple.

"Quiet," she whispers.

"I'm sorry," I reply breathlessly.

Taking my breast in her hand, she squeezes it and sucks at the other eagerly, making my core grow hot with need. Her hands and mouth are rough, but I know Violet—this is her way of reclaiming me. I just wish she knew I was always hers. I will always be hers.

When her hand drifts down between my legs, I suck loudly through my teeth, and she pauses. Looking up at me, she whispers, "Is my sweet girl sore?"

Holding her hand by the wrist to keep it from touching the tender spots, I nod.

I watch as she drops to her knees in front of me. "Let me kiss it better for you then."

Sucking my bottom lip between my teeth, I bite it as I watch her bring her tongue to my clit. My fingers claw at the tile as I soak in the warm, soft touch of her mouth against my most sensitive spot.

It's unreal how good it feels. Unlike Alaric's mouth last night, Violet's is gentle. Without the scruff of facial hair, her skin is delicate against my thighs. Her tongue spears me, and I let out a moan. My head hangs back as she slowly drives me to the brink of insanity.

Licking, nibbling, gently prodding. It's like she's toying with me.

"Violet, please," I whine as I drive my hips toward her.

"What do you want, baby?"

"Make me come," I whisper in a needy drawl.

"Come here," she says with a grunt as she jerks my hips

farther away from the wall and dives in closer, using the suction of her lips to detonate a surreal explosion of pleasure inside me.

"Don't stop," I cry out. "I'm so close."

There's no way Alaric's not hearing this. I'm clearly unable to keep it down when her mouth is between my legs. Most of my weight is leaning against the wall as I find myself careening toward my climax. My legs want to give out beneath me, but Violet helps to hold me up as she sucks eagerly on my clit and drives two digits deep inside me.

When I do finally come, a guttural, raw noise claws its way out of my chest.

My spine curls, and my body shudders. How can one person bring another so much ecstasy?

After my orgasm rolls through my entire body, lingering with aftershocks, I grab onto Violet by her arm and haul her to her feet. Once she's standing in front of me, I attack her lips with my own. They are soft and lush and taste like my arousal. It drives me wild with need.

Shoving her back against the wall, I feel as if I'm suddenly coming to life. Sex with a near stranger last night and getting off in the shower from my stepsister's mouth. Who am I? What is happening to me?

I don't know, but all I can think right now is that I need to show her the same tempest of pleasure she just showed me. I don't have enough confidence in my own oral skills to return the favor, but I do know how I normally get off in the shower. Turning toward the showerhead, I smile wickedly when I see that it's detachable.

After grabbing it from where it's mounted against the wall, I bring it down between our bodies. She lets out a yelp when I aim the high pressure at her clit. Then I kiss her again, driving my tongue into her mouth as I press the showerhead closer and closer. She's squirming against the sensation, but I hold her in place, swallowing her cries with my kiss.

"Oh my God, Birdie," she sings, letting her head hang back and moaning so her voice echoes throughout the entire bathroom.

"God, you're so sexy," I say with a hum. My kisses dance from her mouth to her jaw and along her neck. Going even lower, I get a taste of her breasts, licking the tight bud of each nipple before teasing it with my teeth. She cries out even louder.

Slowly, she starts to fall apart, losing composure with each passing second.

When I feel her grip my scalp so tightly, it makes my eyes sting with tears, and I know she's about to come. I'm swelling with pride as she seizes up in my arms, crying out loudly so damn near everyone in this whole mansion can hear it.

I watch it all unfold, and it's the most beautiful thing I've ever seen. I've dreamt of this moment for years, and while I had some help from the water pressure, I just made Violet come for the first time in my life. And it was incredibly hot. So hot, I want to do it again.

"Well, that was something." A deep voice interrupts my thoughts.

I drop the showerhead with a yelp as I turn to see Alaric's blurry figure through the foggy glass of the shower. I turn back to Violet with wide eyes. "Did you know he was there?"

She shrugs. "I saw him walk in," she replies, still breathless from the orgasm. "I wasn't about to stop you."

"How long were you standing there?" I shriek.

"Relax, Princess," he replies, opening the shower door and getting a good long look at both of us. "You got fucked in front of a crowd last night. Letting me watch you get your stepsister off is nothing."

Violet slams the shower door closed and hangs the sprayer back on its mount. I'm still dumbstruck while she helps me wash my hair and then my body.

There's something about what just happened that I can't shake. It was more than just being watched, but it was being watched by him…while I was with her. I probably shouldn't have loved that as much as I did.

# BIRDIE

"A party? What kind of party?" I ask Alaric from across the table in his room where he had his staff serve us lunch.*

"A play party," he replies casually while staring down at his phone.

Violet is sitting to my right, and she glances at him skeptically.

"What's a play party?" I ask.

He glances up from his phone. "Doesn't matter. You're not going."

"Why not?" I pout.

"Because it's too much for you."

I huff in my seat as I scowl at him. "Excuse me? Isn't that for me to decide? Since when did you become my father?"

Alaric gives me a warning glance. "Will you just trust me? It's not a regular party or any party you've ever been to. And I

* ON MY KNEES–RÜFÜS DU SOL

promise you're not ready for what may or may not happen to you at that party, so drop it."

My lips purse as I let my imagination take over, conjuring up images of exactly what this party could be like for things to happen *to* me there. "So, you're going...without us?"

He drops his phone in frustration. "The only reason I'm going is because I promised Reaper I'd go, but I don't plan on participating if that's what you're worried about, Princess. I'll drop in, show my face, and leave."

"Alone?" I ask.

He swallows, glancing sideways at Violet. "Come to think of it, it would probably be impolite of me to show up without a partner. So, I'll take Violet."

"Nice try," she snaps. "I'm not leaving Birdie."

"Fine," he replies with a grimace. "I'll go alone."

I watch the two of them, wondering what on earth he meant by that. Was he considering taking her to this...party to try and have sex with her? That doesn't make sense.

Glancing back toward Alaric, I try my best to appeal to his sympathetic side, although he still claims he doesn't have one.

"You do realize my stepmother never let me go to any parties. No social life."

"Like I said, Princess. This isn't that kind of party," he replies flatly.

"So keep me by your side all night. You'll protect me. I know you will. But don't shelter me the same way she did. At least let me see it, and then we'll leave. Promise."

Giving him a soft, delicate smile, I try to look as angelic as possible. He lets out a disgruntled sigh and glances toward Violet, who only shrugs.

"I'd like to see it too, if I'm being honest."

"Fuck." He groans to himself. After a moment, he points an authoritative finger at me and then her. "We'll go down for ten minutes. That's it. Neither of you will so much as look at anyone else in that party. Don't touch anything, and don't speak a word. As for the main event…"

His expression grows serious, and my interest is piqued.

He slams a hand down on the table as he adds, "Don't even think about joining that."

Swallowing, I nod obediently. Violet does the same. And I don't bother asking what the main event is, although I do hope I find out.

---

Violet lets me borrow a dress for the party. It's a short A-line gown that only reaches past my ass, but it flows outward, so I find myself spinning my hips in it to make the fabric look like an umbrella. Alaric takes one look at me as he comes out of the bathroom, and with a sigh, he shakes his head.

"You look far too sweet for where we're going."

I force a smile on my face as I twirl my dress again.

"Stop it," he mutters.

Violet buckles her shoes and chuckles to herself. Once she's ready, the three of us make our way downstairs to where the party is being held. The mansion is so different today. It's quieter and has an ominous feel that makes the hairs on the back of my neck stand up.

I clutch Alaric's arm tighter. As long as I'm by his side, I'm safe. I have nothing to worry about.

As we enter the room, I watch as he nods at the man who put me up for auction yesterday. He's incredibly handsome and alluring, but I can't help but feel a bitter resentment toward him after the hand he played in the worst moments of my life.

Tearing my attention away from him, I get a good look at the room. And my jaw drops.

There is normal furniture scattered around the room as well as some *not-so-normal furniture*. Things I can't even begin to describe or name. There's a bench that I can't quite imagine how anyone would sit on. A rack near the wall that looks as if it's meant to hang things—or people—by leather cuffs and chains.

Then, I get a look at the people. Some formally dressed. Others...hardly dressed at all.

I feel Alaric's mouth near my ear. "Told you it would be too much for you."

I straighten my spine. "I don't know what you're talking about. I'm just curious. That's all."

"Curious?" he replies haughtily. "Anytime you'd like a lesson, I'd be happy to teach you."

"Stop it, Alaric," Violet mutters. "Leave her alone."

Ignoring her, I look at him. "Is this...what you like?" Remembering the way he spoke last night about wanting to fuck me has my blood scalding my veins. Moisture pools between my legs as I hear those words in my ear again.

"From time to time," he replies casually.

My mouth goes dry as I notice that people are not holding back. There is a couple most definitely having sex in the corner.

How much of life have I missed out on? My internet searches have been far too safe because it feels like I've barely scratched the surface of what's possible. The moisture feels like a flood at this point. I'm so aroused, it almost hurts.

Is it wrong that I want him to show me? Would Violet be angry to know how curious I am? And did she participate in stuff like this too, with him? How naive am I?

Just then, the blond man Alaric nodded to stands at the front of the room and makes an announcement.

"Time to play, friends," he says enthusiastically with a sinister smile. "The game tonight is a hunt, but we're doing things my way."

A hunt?

"What is this? A game of hide-and-seek?" I ask quietly, to which Violet chuckles.

"No, Bird. Not quite."

I glance up at Alaric, who only clenches his jaw. "I said no," he mutters quietly. It confuses me what makes him so strict about this game. That is…until the man called Reaper continues.

"Participation is not required, of course," he says. "But those who want to play will choose to be predator…or prey. Prey flees. Predators pursue. And if a predator catches their prey, they can have their filthy way with them. For this game, we'll follow the tried-and-true safe words. 'Red' means stop. 'Yellow' means pause. Understood?"

My jaw drops, and that warm brewing need in my belly starts to feel like an inferno. The thought of being chased and then *caught* does something I did not expect to my insides. It shouldn't be as arousing and enticing as it is, but I can't help it. My thighs squeeze together as I imagine it.

Running for my life. The thunderous sound of their chasing steps behind me. Being caught and forced and—what is wrong with me?

I scan the room, watching as the *prey* begin to line up near the arched doorway, grabbing a red wristband from the attendant standing nearby. I see the anticipation in their eyes. The excitement. The promise of sex and fun and something deliciously naughty.

Not because they're being forced to, but because they *want to*.

These people, as far as I know, haven't been imprisoned, sheltered, hidden away as a form of torture. They weren't sold against their will or bullied for having a voice. They are standing independently at that starting line, doing something because they crave it. And no one in this room is daring to tell them they can't.

"Prey will get a five-minute head start. If you want to play foxes to our hounds, come to me now." Reaper's voice feels like a beacon, a siren song of freedom and excitement and *rebellion*.

I feel myself slipping away from Alaric's side. He's speaking to Violet and hardly notices my stepping just a few inches away. Those inches alone fuel that spark.

I can do whatever I want now.

But I'm not seriously thinking about doing this, am I? Any one of these predators, practically drooling at the players near the archway, could catch me. And they could have their way with me. Unless, of course, I change my mind and use the safe words Reaper said.

"It's time," Reaper announces, and I take another step. Just then, Alaric turns his attention toward me with a worried arch in his brow.

"What are you doing?" he mumbles.

"You both want me, right?" I ask, glancing between the two of them.

"Birdie…" Violet says in warning as I take another step toward the archway.

"Prey, your five-minute head start begins…now."

The people behind me start their sprints as I give Alaric and Violet a smirk. "Guess we'll see which one of you catches me first."

And with that, I turn on my heels, grab a red wristband from the attendant, and take off in a mad sprint into the mansion. Behind me, I hear Violet and Alaric screaming at me to come back at the same time, and for the first time in my life, I don't obey.

## ALARIC

"I'm going to kill her."* Violet is pacing angrily back and forth as we wait the grueling five minutes before we can leave this room to find Birdie.

I've pleaded with Reaper and explained that Birdie just isn't cut out for this, but he wouldn't budge. I just pray she was listening when he explained the safe words. She just has to utter the word *red*, and they can't touch her.

That's if I don't murder every single one of these assholes first. It would undoubtedly cost me my own life, but it wouldn't be the first irrational thought I've had this weekend where this girl is involved.

When Reaper finally calls for the predators to start their hunt, I barely register anything in the chaos. The sounds that fill the halls chill me to the bone, and normally, I'm unbothered by these animalistic displays, but I can only think about her. Her fear. Her innocence. Her safety.

\* RUN—Joji

Violet and I watched Birdie run to the right, so that's where we both sprint. When we reach a staircase, it's like a fork in the road. Would she go up there? She'd be cornering herself. But if she stayed downstairs, there's a chance she'd go into the garden, and there's no telling what would happen to her in that hedge maze.

Violet is clearly thinking the same thing. She gives me an intense glare.

The screams and sex can already be heard in the recesses of the mansion, and my molars grind at the sound.

"You go up, and I'll look down here," she calls frantically. For a moment I hesitate, staring into Violet's eyes with uncertainty. As much as we both care about Birdie's well-being, I know we're thinking about her last words before she ran from the room.

*Guess we'll see which one of you catches me first.*

We're not really competing for Birdie, are we? I certainly feel the buzzing tension of competition under my skin.

"Fine, go," I mutter as I stomp up the stairs. Violet takes off in a sprint down the main hall in the opposite direction.

The halls upstairs are winding and intricate, and I stomp through each one in search of Birdie, looking closely at each person being roughly fucked in nearly every corner of this mansion. None of them are her, but I can't seem to feel relieved.

Instead, I'm starting to feel aroused. When I find her, I can't promise I'm going to be nice about it. A feral need to claim her starts to take over. The very thought of another man putting his ugly hands on *my* woman has me wanting to kill them and fuck her.

When I enter the main hall upstairs where the gala was held, I see the balcony and rush out to get a look at the grounds from a higher viewpoint. I can't see the entire maze, but I can see enough. I notice a flash of dark hair below and see that it's Violet running from the house toward the garden.

"No sign of her?" I call.

She glances up at me, finding me on the balcony before shouting back, "Nothing. But I had to tell more than one predator to fuck off." She holds up her wrists defiantly to show she's not wearing a red wristband, something I guess the predators didn't notice when they approached her.

A subtle possessive urgency to protect Violet during this play party seems to climb up from out of nowhere. The thought of someone else touching her has me gripping the balcony even tighter.

"Use your safe words," I warn her.

"I know, I know," she calls. "Keep looking!"

Just then, I see a glimpse of something out in the hedge maze. Squinting in the drizzly moonlight, I see that fucking blue twirling dress Birdie had on.

"The maze!" I bellow, pointing toward where I saw her. Violet rushes toward the garden as I turn and sprint off the balcony.

I may have just given my competition the upper hand, but winning is hardly the priority right now. I just need Birdie to be safe.

Then, I'll make her pay.

My feet move faster than I've ever moved them before as I pump my legs down the stairs and toward the door that leads to the garden. Before I know it, I'm at the entrance of the hedge maze, but I have to stop in my tracks to listen for the girls.

"Birdie! Where are you?" Violet calls from my right.

She hasn't found her yet.

My heart is pumping wildly in my chest as I take off to the left, hoping I'll find Birdie in this direction.

"Birdie!" I bellow, but the only response is a breathless giggle somewhere in the dark. The rain picks up, and just like last night, we're getting soaked.

Even over the pitter-patter of rain, I hear the delicate footfall of Birdie, so I pick up my speed and turn the corner to find her standing in the clearing, soaked to the bone, with a wild smile on her face.

In the corner of my vision, I notice Violet entering the clearing at the same time, but I can hardly see anything but Birdie at this point. That carnal need takes over, and I'm running toward her.

She lets out a scream as I rush toward her, wrapping my hand around her throat. I don't squeeze tight enough to cut off air or hurt her. Dragging her face to mine, I sneer at her with anger. "Did anyone hurt you?"

Fearfully, she shakes her head. "N-no."

"What the fuck is wrong with you?" Violet adds from my side.

"I w-wanted t-to have fun," she stammers, staring at me in elated fear.

"Oh, you want to have fun?" I ask with a wicked smile. Using my hold on her throat, I force her to her knees. "You want to know how we play, Princess?"

She stares up at me with confusion.

"Take it out," I mutter through clenched teeth.

Birdie's eyes scan over to Violet as if she expects her lover to save her, but Violet is just as drunk on the chase as I am. She doesn't utter a word, but I see the heaving of her chest as she struggles to catch her breath from the chase.

Instead, Violet leans down to her stepsister. "You want to be bad, Birdie? Then you pay the price. Take it out," Violet whispers.

Birdie's eyes widen in surprise. This is what the hunt does to us. It makes us defy rationale and sense. We are fueled by lust and adrenaline.

As Birdie shakily unzips my pants, Violet moves behind her, quickly lifting her dress. I see the tense, frustrated expression on her face. We're both frustrated, and there's only one person to take it out on.

Birdie pulls my cock from my pants and stares at it with curiosity and apprehension. It's already throbbing hard and leaking from the tip.

Last night, I was gentle, but I'm not right now. Grabbing Birdie by the jaw, I look down at her as I mutter, "Open up."

Obediently, she does.

"Hold on to my leg, Birdie. If you need either of us to stop, tap it, okay?"

"Okay," she whispers. After she opens her mouth again, I force my cock in, and she gags immediately.

Just then, Violet smacks her hard on the ass. Birdie lets out a whimper in pain.

I thrust in again, hitting the back of her throat and feeling the way it constricts around me.

"You want to run from me again, Princess?" I growl as I fuck her mouth. Her hand rests firmly on my thigh as Violet continues to spank her hard on the ass. Even in the rainy moonlight, I can see the red marks starting to appear.

Saliva drips down Birdie's chin and over her soft white neck.

Tears stream down her face, but she holds her tongue out like a good girl, breathing through her nose as I keep up my thrusts.

I can tell the exact moment Violet roughly forces her fingers inside Birdie because she squeals loudly, followed by a guttural moan of pleasure. Her hips start to tremble as Violet keeps up the rhythm of her hand.

"You don't deserve to come," Violet barks at her stepsister.

My balls start to tighten, and I feel the growing orgasm as I fuck Birdie's mouth harder.

Before I can reach my climax, she's ripped from my arms.

"Mine," Violet mutters.

With a hand in Birdie's hair, she yanks back her head, forcing her mouth to open. Violet spits ruthlessly into her lover's mouth, and Birdie barely even reacts.

Then, Violet yanks up her own dress and shoves Birdie's mouth to her clit. I can see the tightness in Violet's clutching grip on Birdie's hair and the force in which she uses to hold Birdie's face against her cunt. It's hot as fuck to see her be rough with her, especially since I know Violet is feeling the same frantic energy I am.

Stroking my rock-hard cock, I move behind Birdie and admire the red welt of handprints on her ass. Licking my lips, I rear back my hand and land one of my own.

"That's for putting yourself in danger."

Birdie screams against Violet's wet pussy as I smack her ass again. I rub my hand over the red marks left behind, and Birdie keeps up her moans. She loves the pain. I can tell.

Sliding one finger through her pooling arousal, I find the answer I need. Yep, she fucking loves it.

The moment she feels my cock at her core, her little ass pushes higher in the air.

"What a dirty little princess you are," I mutter as I force my cock inside her. She screams against Violet, who has now moved into a lying position with Birdie's face still shoved forcefully between her legs.

After two rough thrusts of my cock, Violet yanks Birdie's head away. "Give me a color," she barks.

"Green," Birdie cries out. "I want more."

Then, Violet looks up at me. "Rougher."

Violet slams Birdie's face back down, and I pound my cock hard inside her, practically jostling her whole body against Violet's. We are all moaning, screaming, crying, careening as one toward our climaxes.

It's Birdie who gets there first. I feel her body tense up in my hands. Her legs tremble, and her spine stiffens. Her cries are muffled by her stepsister's cunt as Violet quickly follows her with her own orgasm. By the time the two of them are done, my balls tighten, and my cock unloads inside Birdie while I roar out my own release.

After a few moments of catching our breaths, I collapse into the wet grass and stare up at the dark sky as the light misty rain soaks me to the bone.

"I hope you're happy," I say with a grunt.

Birdie giggles, curled up against Violet as they intimately kiss each other slowly. "Yes, I am."

"You could have gotten seriously hurt," I add.

"I knew the safe word. Besides, maybe I wanted to be caught." She says it so innocently it grates on my nerves.

Letting out a growl, I stuff my cock back in my pants and zip them up. Then, I climb off the ground and hoist my new bride-to-be to her feet. Grabbing her face, I force her to look at me.

"If you ever do something like that again or even mention another man touching you, you're going to find out how bad of a man I really am. Are we clear?"

I expect her to quiver in fear. Instead, she gives me an innocent smirk. "Yes, sir."

Those words go straight to my cock, and that's when I realize how seriously fucked I am.

# 15

# BIRDIE

The mansion slowly disappears through the car window as we drive down the long gravel road.* Rain pelts the window, and I stare at the raindrops as they drizzle down the glass, trying not to think too much about the question of my future. Violet is sitting across from me in the back of Alaric's limo. He's beside me, looking at his phone. Her eyes are on me.

Memories of last night flood my mind. The thrill of the chase and how incredible it was when they both let loose on me. I know I made them mad and stressed them out, but the sex was amazing, and well worth it.

"I made sure to have them pack your things. They'll be delivered to Alaric's tomorrow," she says softly. Maybe she can read the forlorn expression on my face.

"Thank you," I whisper.

While I stare out the window, I play back my life like a movie

* FIRE FOR YOU–Cannons

reel, looking for the moment when it stopped feeling like a normal life and became this. It doesn't even belong to me anymore. I'm a pawn. I'm property. I was sold away from my own home like a piece of furniture, and the only person who will actually collect my belongings because they matter to me is Violet.

The family I was born into might not have been perfect, but it was mostly normal. My mother was kind, compassionate, and warm. My father, before the drugs and alcohol kicked in, was loving and attentive. Our lives were suburban and boring.

Then my father started to grow wealth and power in his business. My mother went to the store and never came home one day. From then on, it felt like the sun never rose again.

I kept my head down. I stayed quiet and did what I was told because I felt like if I could just weather the storm, I'd make it to the shore. But the shore never came. The day my mother died, my father was never the same. He might as well have died that day too.

He finally remarried, and I knew from the moment I met my stepmother that she was not like us. She didn't grow up in the suburbs or bake cookies or tuck her daughters in at night. I heard the whispers of shady business dealings in my own home. I saw drugs lying around in our living room. I watched my loving, grieving father morph into a monster, who only wanted more money and power and less of me.

I kept my head down for too long. I stayed quiet when I should have spoken up.

My life slowly spiraled into a nightmare, so when my stepmother offered to put me up on the auction block like a *thing*, I let her.

How could I let this happen?

This isn't how normal people live. I'm only nineteen. I should be going to college and parties and living my own life.

What's to become of us now? I already know Alaric won't just let me leave, but I'm not even sure I want to. I feel more than just safe around him. I feel cared for and protected—something I haven't felt from a man in a very, very long time.

And even if I did want to leave Alaric's house, I have no money, no place to stay, no one to help me.

I have these two, and that's it.

My heart feels like it's being torn in half. I love Violet more than anything, but something about this man draws me to him. He does care about me. He wants to take care of me.

I'm not ready to *marry* him, but I'm also not ready to leave him either.

Am I a terrible person? How can I have feelings for someone else when I have the love of my life sitting right in front of me? She would hate me if she knew.

"I have my staff readying your rooms," Alaric says without looking up from his phone.

"Rooms?" Violet replies as her head snaps in his direction.

"We can share a room," I softly mumble.

He gazes at both of us, licking his lips and giving us a stern glare. "You and I can also share a room," he says to me in the tone of a threat. "I'm being fair. Until we figure this whole thing out, we sleep separately."

I swallow and look down. Lifting my gaze, I stare through my lashes at Violet, who's giving him a death glare.

I should be flattered. This morning Alaric told me that he would be taking us *both* home with him until we were all sure I wasn't pregnant or Violet decided I was better off with him (his words, not mine). Honestly, the thought of staying at Alaric's house doesn't sound so bad. At least it's not with my stepmom.

"What is there to figure out?" Violet asks, sounding angry. "The plan was that Birdie and I would leave together after the auction."

"That's not the plan anymore," he replies. "And you know it."

He looks back down at his phone.

When Violet looks at me, I feel a spike of guilt and shame because I don't want to leave Alaric yet. It's not that I don't want to be with Violet, but... What if I am already pregnant? What if we leave and Clarissa finds me? I'll be safe with Alaric. It seems like the only option.

Violet leans back in her seat and goes quiet. None of us talks for the rest of the ride.

---

When we pull up to Alaric's house, there are serious-looking men waiting there to open the doors for us. Alaric gets out first, then helps me out of his side while Violet climbs out the opposite. He places a hand on the small of my back and leads me toward the house. I can tell he's softly pushing me away from her.

So I plant my feet and wait until she's at my side before I start to walk in.

"My housekeeper will show you to your room," Alaric says to Violet as we step inside the grand entryway. His hand stays on me the entire time.

She gives him a narrow-eyed expression. When I give her a small nod, she relents and allows the woman in black to show her to the staircase that leads to the second floor.

"Come with me," he says, guiding me down the hall to the left.

"Where are we going?" I ask.

"My room is just at the end of this hall. Yours will be here, just next to mine." He pushes open the door that leads to a simple bedroom. It's crisp and white and smells of clean linens.

"Did you have this room made up just for me?" I ask, stepping in and letting my fingers drift over the cashmere blanket. He shrugs in response, and I have to fight my smile. "That's very sweet."

"I'm not a sweet man, Princess."

"You're sweeter than you think," I reply. My eyes drift from the hard expression on his face to his muscular chest and over the soft bulge in his tight gray pants. I force myself to swallow and turn away from him, facing the feminine room he somehow had put together in the last twelve hours.

"Don't mistake my affection for kindness," he replies. "I'm doing this because I want you to stay. And until we know there's not a baby growing inside you right now, you leaving is out of the question. You understand that, right?"

Silently, I nod.

My feelings are all jumbled. I'm confused. My life has been flipped upside down. I don't even have a home at the moment, let alone any idea of where I want to go or who I want to be.

I just know two things for sure, and I'm clinging to them both as the only true things I know.

One—I love Violet more than anything, and I won't let her go.

Two—I will never go back to my stepmom's.

Everything else floating around in my brain is muddled and confused, including my feelings—and *desire*—for Alaric.

"You do want to stay, don't you, Princess?" he asks, taking a step toward me.

Without looking at him, I shrug. I *do* want to stay, but that's just how I'm feeling at the moment. It would be too impulsive and careless to say so.

"I need to hear you say it," he says a bit louder as I hear him step closer behind me.

"I don't know what I want right now," I murmur.

His hard body presses up against mine from behind, and I let out a gasp at the warm, comforting feel of it. His hands are soft and gentle as he grinds himself against me.

"I know what you want, Birdie," he whispers in my ear. "I know you secretly want me to fuck you again the way I did last night. Don't deny it."

"I can't," I reply, failing to hide the wanton need in my voice.

"I know you can't. I know you belong to her, and you won't betray her."

He grinds himself against me again, the hard contour of his cock wedged between my ass cheeks. The only response I can manage is a pitiful whimper.

He lowers his mouth to my ear again. "Over the next few weeks, your stepsister and I will be fighting over you. You know that, don't you?"

I nod.

He kisses hungrily at my neck, and I lose my sense of what

is up and down. I am nothing but a body made of nerve endings and designed for pleasure. And right now, it answers to him.

"Make no mistake, Princess," he mutters. "I'm going to win."

Then his hands and body are gone, and I'm left feeling cold and empty without him. I'm gasping for air as I turn to watch him disappear out the door.

My body is still buzzing as I throw myself on top of the bed. Lying there, I slowly wait for my brain to catch up. When it does, there is only one thought circulating inside—this is going to be a very long few weeks.

# VIOLET

"Oh, there you are," I say, leaning against the doorframe that leads to Alaric's sprawling library.*

Birdie is curled up in a ginormous blue velvet chair, reading something on her lap. She looks up at me and gives me a warm smile.

"Oh, sorry. Were you looking for me?" she asks.

I shrug as I enter. "Not for long. When you weren't in your room, I figured I would find you here."

I lean against the arm of the chair opposite her and cross my arms, taking a mental picture of her curled up in that chair like that. She looks so peaceful and in her element.

When was the last time I saw her like this? Her last home was a prison, but here, she could be truly happy. It's been six hours since we arrived at Alaric's, and Birdie has grown more at ease with every passing hour. If we leave together, it won't be like this.

* DADDY ISSUES–The Neighbourhood

It will be a struggle. No money. No place to stay. Is having each other truly enough to make up for all that?

The guilt gnaws away at me.

"I just realized something," she says sadly.

"What?" I reply, not liking the worried look on her face.

"I'll never find out how my book ends," she says.

I let a smile creep across my face, remembering the way I'd buy her books while I was out and she'd hide them around the house so my mother and sister wouldn't find them. She was smart. They would immediately take them from her, throw them away, or destroy them. They loved to rip everything she loved to shreds.

"I'm sure we can get you another copy. Do you remember the name?" I ask, pulling my phone from my back pocket.

She screws up her face. "Honestly…no. I'm terrible with titles. The cover was blue, and it had flowers on it."

I laugh. "I don't think that's gonna narrow it down, Bird."

"Oh well," she replies with a shrug. "I'm sure it was a happy ending."

"They usually are, right?" I ask playfully.

"In the books I like," she replies, turning back to the one in her lap. "Not in real life."

"You don't know that," I say, walking toward her. "Your story could have a very happy ending."

She looks up at me, and I touch her affectionately under the chin. "What about yours?" she whispers.

"If it's with you, it will be very happy," I say, brushing my fingers through her long blond hair.

"If?" Her expression twists with uncertainty.

I don't respond, at least not right away.

"What's going on, Violet?" she pries. "You're not going to leave, are you?"

I jerk my head back like she just slapped me. "I would never leave you, not like that."

"Then tell me what you're thinking."

I wish I could tell her. But the truth is there is so much Birdie doesn't know, and even if I could compete with Alaric and his big mansion and billion dollars, what will happen when Birdie learns the truth of what I've done?

"He's going to fight for you, Birdie," I say, gently caressing her jaw. "And I'm afraid he has so much more to offer that I'd never be able to win."

She looks offended. "You think I care about his money?" she asks.

"No," I say, shaking my head sadly. "But… Look at all this. He'd be able to keep you safe. He's a powerful man, Birdie."

"I don't care, Violet." She snaps her book closed and stands from the chair. In a fit of frustration, she walks to the shelf and slams the book down before turning back toward me. "We made a plan, and that plan worked. Just because Alaric and I had sex or because he seems to want me to himself now doesn't change that plan."

"And what if you are pregnant?" I ask.

"Then I'll take care of it. We will cross that road when we get there. I mean… Has anyone even bothered to ask me what I want? Does anyone ever take *my* desires into consideration?"

"Yes, of course—" I start, but she quickly cuts me off.

"I'm so *sick* of my life being decided for me, Violet. Don't you start too."

My mouth closes, and I swallow a flood of rising shame. She's right. I was trying to control her because I really thought I was the one best suited to do so. What is wrong with me?

"I'm sorry," I whisper.

She lets out a huff of frustration. "I know Alaric will be fighting to keep me, and I know you will too. But all I can think right now is that I'm finally free. I can *read a fucking book* without worrying about what they'll do if they find me. I can start thinking about my life. Maybe I'll go to college. Or maybe I'll get a job. I don't know, but all I do know is that I'm *not* trading one prison for another. I finally have my life back, and I'm sure as hell not going to let someone else decide my future for me."

With a sigh, she snatches the book back from the shelf and walks out of the room with it. She stops with one foot out the doorway and lets out an irritated grunt before brushing past Alaric, who peeks around the corner to find me standing here in stunned silence.

When he casually walks in, I give him a furrowed expression. "So you heard that?"

"Oh yeah, I heard it," he replies.

"She's right, you know," I say, meandering toward him. "We have no right to try and decide her fate for her."

"Who said I was deciding anything?" he says, putting his hands up in surrender.

Tilting my head, I roll my eyes. "You went a little caveman on us." Then I lower my voice and do my best Alaric impression. "*She's mine, and I'm never letting her go.*"

He smiles to himself. "I meant every word. I'm not letting her go. She'll decide to stay on her own though, when I convince her to."

Pressing my lips together and stretching them into a half grimace, half smile, I shake my head at him. "You're impossible."

He lets out a smug laugh, and I hate him for how good-looking and charming he has to be all the time. It's not a fair fight when I'm constantly distracted by the sharpness of his cheekbones or the allure of his eyes.

Leaning on the large desk, he nods toward the ladder attached to the floor-to-ceiling bookshelf. "Remember that?"

Immediately, I blush. "How could I forget?" I reply, biting my bottom lip to keep from smiling.

"I was afraid we were going to tear it from the wall that night," he jokes.

"Stop being so charming," I argue. "You're trying to steal my girl, and I hate you, remember?"

Ignoring me, he walks to the ladder. As he touches the rungs, I distinctly remember what they felt like digging into my back as he buried his face between my legs.

"You don't hate me," he mutters quietly. "We've been through too much together."

That last part is sobering, and the smile instantly melts from my face.

"If I remember correctly, that was the last night you came to see me," he says casually.

"My debt was paid," I reply flatly.

His eyes find mine, and I swear I spot a hint of regret in

them. Letting out a sigh, he clenches his jaw and looks away. "Yeah, it was."

"She can never know about that," I say, keeping my voice down.

"I'm pretty sure she knows we've fucked, Violet," he replies, taking a step closer to me.

"I mean the other part, Alaric. What we did. She can never know."

When I glance back up at his face, he's standing so close, and his eyes hold so many secrets, I have to look away. Facing my sins is like staring at my own death. I'd rather pretend they don't exist.

"I would never tell her that," he whispers quietly. Reaching out, he brushes his fingers over my arm, and I flinch, pulling away. "You did the right thing, Violet," he adds, and I feel a panic rising in my chest. I can't talk about this. I can't face it.

"I don't want to talk about it," I snap. When he reaches for me again, I quickly turn and march toward the door. Whenever this comes back up, I have to fight the urge to cry, scream, and vomit at the same time. All I know is that I can't be in a room with Alaric right now. I can't face him.

I'm nearly out of the room, only two steps from the door, when he calls for me, and I stop in my tracks.

"Violet," he says in a delicate command. As I turn toward him, he gives me a somber look. "Your debt was paid long before that, and you know it."

When I try to swallow, it feels like needles in my throat. I give him a quick nod and then rush out the door, eager to be alone.

It's not until I get to my room and shut myself inside that I let his words flow through me, absorbing exactly what he was trying to say.

I paid him with sex. And if my debts were paid, but I kept sleeping with him, then what did that make us?

# ALARIC

There are two women living in my house.* I've never lived with women before, not since I ran away from home at sixteen, but even before then, my mother was barely present and never attentive.

So I don't exactly know what I'm doing.

Birdie and Violet have been here less than eight hours, and they're both either mad at me or avoiding me. I've been hiding in my office, but there are no pressing issues to keep me here. Which means I have to walk out there at some point.

My house staff has dinner ready at seven every night, and when I glance down to see my watch displaying half past, I know I can't avoid them forever.

I'm supposed to be convincing Birdie to stay, but after that short interaction with Violet, I'm feeling like shit about it. I care

\* LOVE IS A BITCH—Two Feet

about Violet. So actively trying to take away the only person she cares about feels too cruel, even for me.

Having a conscience doesn't suit me. It's getting in the way. Maybe I should just give them both a parting gift of a few hundred thousand dollars and be done with this.

But deep down, I know what I want. It's just not easy expressing it.

Rising from my desk, I slip my phone into my pocket and head to the door of my office.

"Dinner is ready, Mr. Stone," my housekeeper says politely as I step into the hallway.

"Thank you," I mutter in response. "Where are our guests?" I loosen my tie as I stride toward the dining room.

"Miss Violet is still in her room, and Miss Birdie is...taking a bath."

I turn my head toward her. "Why did you say it like that?"

My normally coolheaded housekeeper looks a little uneasy. "Because she took two bottles of wine in there and shut the door."

With a growl, I halt in my tracks. Ripping my tie from around my neck, I spin around and storm toward the main bathroom, the only room with a soaker tub. As I burst into my bedroom, I pause when I see a pair of light-pink lace panties strewn on the floor next to a black bra.

I don't bother knocking.

Tearing open the door, I scowl at the girl up to her nose in bubbles. She lets out a yelp and then is lost in a fit of giggles.

"I found the wine," she calls out before taking a long swig straight from the bottle.

"That is over a thousand dollars a bottle," I say, shutting the door behind me. I step farther into the warm, rose-scented bathroom.

"Add it to my tab," she replies with a slur. "Two million, one thousand dollars."

Shaking my head, I undo each button of my shirt and slip off each of my shoes.

When she notices my actions, she slants her head. "What are you doing?"

"I'm getting in," I reply.

Emphatically, she shakes her head. "No. You can't. I have a girlfriend."

I hang my shirt on a hook and start on the button of my pants. "I didn't say I was going to fuck you. I'm just getting in my own bathtub, Princess."

"She's going to kill you," Birdie replies with a hiccup.

"I'd like to see her try." With a chuckle, I slide my pants down. And when I pull my boxer briefs with them, I watch the way Birdie's eyes catch on the length of my cock, hanging half hard between my legs.

Her eyes don't leave my dick, even as I slide into the large soaker tub across from her.

"Are they all that big?" she mutters to herself.

My brow furrows. "Are *what* all that big?"

She bites her lip, and her cheeks turn red. "You know…" She giggles again, and I can't help but smile in return.

I know exactly what she means, but I can't resist the temptation to mess with her a little. "I don't know what you're talking about. Can you be more specific?"

She widens her eyes before glancing down. After a moment of struggling, she finally stammers, "P-penises."

Leaning my back against the tub, I can't help but stare at her with affection. I've never met anyone like Birdie before. So innocent, and yet so curious. I'm torn between wanting to protect her innocence and shattering it beyond repair.

"Cocks," she adds so quietly I barely hear her. "Dicks. Wieners. Shafts."

"Are you done?" I ask.

She tries to hide sheepishly under the bubbles as she nods.

"To answer your question—I don't know," I reply with snark. "This is the only one I've seen up close."

"Me too," she says before taking another swig. "I've seen pictures and videos on the internet, of course, but it's different seeing it in person."

My eyes lift at her casual admission that she occasionally watches porn, but I don't press it because I don't want to embarrass her.

"Would you like to touch it again?" I ask with a tilted smirk.

She shakes her head. "I told you no."

"For now," I reply. Leaning back, I drape my arms over the side of the tub.

"Forever," she adds weakly.

Leaning my head back and letting the steam relax me, I smile. "Sure." I snatch the bottle of wine and take a long drink. It's a sweeter white wine, and honestly, I'm glad she's drinking it. I don't even know why I have it. I like my wine red and dry.

"I think my housekeeper bought this for special occasions," I say before taking another drink.

"What could be more special than spending two million dollars on a wife?" Birdie says as she reaches over me to take the bottle back.

"I did that to save you." I give her a furrowed-brow glare.

"Did you though?" she asks, leaning her back on the opposite side. "You seemed awfully eager to save me. *'Two million!'*" she bellows in a low, raspy imitation.

I growl with a grimace. "I had to get you away from those fucking monsters parading you around like cattle at the market."

She's biting back a smile. "Careful, Mr. Stone. You're starting to sound a little heroic again."

My brows pinch even further together. I'm not a good guy. Can't I just care about this sweet girl without all the name-calling?

Her eyes study me for a moment before she speaks up again. "That night…before they came in to watch," she starts. Then she takes another swig in the middle of her sentence. "You said you wanted to fuck me. And that you would be sweet and gentle, even though you didn't want to be."

My cock twitches at the sound of her saying that phrase: *fuck me*.

"Yeah?" I say, trying to keep my cool.

"Well, for what it's worth… You were very sweet and gentle with me that night."

"And? That took a lot of restraint, but I told you I wouldn't hurt you."

She's staring at me with fuzzy focus, her bottom lip pinched between her teeth. Leaning forward, I snatch the wine from her hand again and bring it to my lips. As I sit back, I keep it with me.

"What's on your mind, Princess?" My leg brushes hers, and she leans into the touch instead of pulling away.

When she doesn't answer, I laugh to myself, lifting the bottle again. After pulling another swig, I look at her with a lazy grin. "You're thinking about me fucking you, aren't you? Or... You were thinking about last night when I was rougher with you."

She scoffs. "I am not!"

With a chuckle, I shake my head. "You clearly are."

When she tries to fight her laughter, she fails, and it slips out through her perfectly full lips. When she launches herself toward me to grab the wine, it takes me by surprise. I lift the bottle out of her reach, and she falls forward, landing straight in my lap. Her hand comes down to catch her fall and lands directly on my cock.

She squeals and immediately tries to climb off me, acting like my dick could kill her. Instead of letting her get away, I snatch her by the hips and haul her onto my lap, each of her legs straddling me.

"Alaric!" she gasps in a sultry whisper.

Her weight settles on my thighs, her legs parted, and her cunt just inches away from my thick erection. And just like that, her fight to escape my clutches dies.

Her eyes meet mine, and her lips part, breathing heavily as she stares down at me. Slowly, I bring the wine bottle to her lips, feeding it to her. Her gaze never leaves my face. Wine dribbles over her lips and down her chin, landing in the bubbles.

Her hair is pulled up in a messy bun on top of her head, her cheeks red from the heat. And her features are so perfect and sweet, it distracts me from the fullness of her tits in my face.

"You like it rough, Princess? Want me to remind you how it can be?"

Unconvincingly, she shakes her head. "I can't."

There's something about the sincerity in her response that stops me from trying to convince her. If I wanted to have her panting and stuffed full of my cock, I could have it. I know it.

Something is stopping me, and I'm not stupid. I know exactly what my holdup is.

I can't do this to Violet.

Noticing my hesitation, Birdie climbs off my lap and takes her spot on the opposite end of the bathtub.

When the bathroom door bursts open, Birdie squeals and covers her breasts.

"What the fuck," Violet barks when she sees me and her girlfriend soaking together in a hot bath.

"Wine?" I reply, holding up the bottle.

She scowls at me and then at Birdie. "Is she drunk?" Violet asks.

I hold the wine bottle to my lips, taking the last swig left. "Yes, but in my defense, she was already drunk when I got here."

Violet snatches a lush white towel from the counter and walks toward us, holding it out for Birdie. "Get out. You need to eat something."

Birdie scoffs. "You are not my mother."

"You're goddamn right I'm not, but I'm about to spank you anyway," Violet snaps through gritted teeth.

My smirk deepens. "Can I watch?"

"You shut up," Violet yells at me.

Birdie crosses her arms and sinks deeper beneath the bubbles. "I'm not getting out, Violet. I'm perfectly fine in here, and you know Clarissa never let me relax like this. And she rarely ever let me have wine."

She reaches for the other bottle and the corkscrew on the shelf next to her. I watch as she fumbles to screw it in, and I wince at how poorly she's doing.

Violet is wearing a sympathetic expression but lets out an annoyed sound. "Give it to me." Birdie hands over the wine and corkscrew with a soft, drunk expression. Violet screws into the cork correctly and yanks it out with a pop. "Here." She hands the bottle back to Birdie, who smiles up at her with a cheesy grin.

"Thank you," she murmurs before taking a drink. "Two million, *two* thousand dollars," she adds, looking at me with a wink.

My heart swells in my chest. Why must she be so cute?

Violet stares down at both of us for a moment, her lips pressed together in irritation. Then, with a groan, she reaches for the hem of her black shirt and tears it over her head. I can't steal my eyes away from her as she undresses, remembering how every inch of her body felt under my touch and my tongue.

Once she's completely naked, she scolds us with a harsh command. "Move over."

"Yay," Birdie croons as Violet slides into the bath next to her.

The water rises with her body added to the tub, nearly spilling over. Not that I care. It fits the three of us easily. My legs are outstretched, trapped between their bodies.

Violet snatches the wine bottle from her stepsister and takes a swig. When she brings it down, she stares at me with narrowed eyes. "I bet you're really loving this."

I can't help but smile. "I'm not hating it."

"Do you want to watch us kiss, sir?" Birdie says with a drunken slur. She gives me a waggle of her brows, and it makes me laugh. She's playing with me, using that title for me again.

"No, Birdie," Violet says with a shake of her head. "You are too drunk, and we are not playing that game."

"It sounds like a dangerous game," I reply in a low, sarcastic tone.

"Don't start." Violet points a black-painted nail in my direction.

"Hey," Birdie murmurs. "We've had sex," she says to Violet. "And we've had sex," she says to me. "And you two have had sex. We're like a sex triangle."

I watch as Violet manages to laugh a little but quickly bites it back.

"I don't think Violet shares well though," I say, draping my arms over the back of the tub again.

Birdie shakes her head with her brow furrowed. "She doesn't share well at all. She wants me all to herself."

Violet clenches her jaw as Birdie rests her head on Violet's shoulder. I watch as Birdie's eyes flutter drunkenly. She's going to pass out at any minute.

"You should learn to share, Violet," I say softly as I watch Birdie fall asleep.

Violet licks her lips as her eyes stay glued to my face. I can almost see the wheels turning in her head. Am I a shameless asshole for even suggesting this? Probably.

But I am only a man. In a tub with two beautiful naked women.

And judging by the way Violet is staring at me, she's thinking about it too.

Just then, Birdie's head slides off Violet's shoulder, landing face-first in the water. She's so drunk, she barely even wakes up.

"Let's get her to bed," I say as I stand from the bath and reach for the towels. Climbing out, I quickly dry myself off and wrap a towel around my waist.

Leaning over, I slide my arms under Birdie's naked body and hoist her out of the water. Violet quickly follows, draping a towel over Birdie before grabbing another towel for herself.

Once Birdie is dry, I carry her out of the bathroom and into my bedroom. Setting her on the bed, I ease her warm, naked body under the covers. She turns on her side and mumbles something before falling asleep on the pillows.

Standing up, I find Violet giving me a harsh glare.

"If she's sleeping in here with you, then so am I," she says, climbing in the middle. She's still wrapped in her towel, but she obviously doesn't trust me alone with Birdie long enough to even go put on pajamas.

I shrug before switching off the light and climbing into the bed behind Violet.

She faces me, curling her arm under her head. "Don't get any ideas, Alaric. We're not both staying forever."

"Don't *you* get any ideas," I reply, brushing a drop of moisture from her shoulder. "You're not both leaving."

## VIOLET

When I open my eyes, there's a soft light cascading through the space between the curtains.* I stretch my arms and legs, enjoying the warm and familiar scent of Alaric's bed.

Alaric's house is comfortable. After only a day here, I suddenly find myself wanting to never leave. Birdie is happy here. I can hear her laughter coming from somewhere in the living room, and it makes me smile as I roll off the side of his large bed, my bare feet landing against the hardwood floor.

I'm still naked from the bath last night, so I tighten my towel around me. It's bigger than I remember, swallowing me whole and nearly touching the floor. It's heavier too.

As I walk down the never-ending hallway of Alaric's house, a familiar but cruel voice replaces Birdie's comforting laughter.

Realizing my mother is here, I pick up my speed, trying to

* BANG BANG (MY BABY SHOT ME DOWN)–Daniela Andrade

run down the long hall, but this stupid towel is making it hard to sprint as fast as I want to.

She's here to hurt Birdie. She wants to take her from me.

Birdie screams, and I kick my feet harder, begging them to carry me faster.

When I finally reach the living room, I stop in the entryway and open my mouth to scream, but nothing comes out.

Birdie is on the floor, crying over the dead body of her father. His lifeless eyes stare at the ceiling, and she's weeping with grief. My mother stands over her with a blank expression on her face.

"Oh, get up," she mutters at Birdie. "He deserved it." Then my mother looks up at me. "Didn't he, Violet?"

When her eyes meet my face, I realize they are sunken and hollow. How have I never noticed before how dead she is inside? My body is trembling now, but when I try to pull the towel around me to keep me warm, I realize it's gone. I'm standing in the living room naked, and the woman I love is in pain, but I can't move.

"I-I—" I stammer, unable to form any coherent words.

"Tell her how much he deserved it," my mother barks at me. Her voice is lower than normal and has a weird deathly tone, like she's speaking from beyond the grave. It sends a chill down my spine. I need to get the fuck out of here.

"What did you do, Violet?" Birdie screams. "What did you do?"

My eyes scan back down to where she's lying on the floor, holding her dead father in her arms.

But it's not her father anymore. It's Alaric.

"He's not dead," I mumble, although my lips will hardly move. "I didn't kill him."

"Yes, you did!" Birdie shrieks. "You killed him!"

"No," I say, shaking my head. "No, no, no, no, no."

Grief and pain swarm my heart, and it hurts so much I can hardly stand. Alaric can't be dead. He can't. It hurts too much.

"Violet," a deep voice growls in my ear. Spinning around, I look for Alaric, desperate to know he's still alive, but he's not there. It's just a dark, empty room, and it looks like the auction room back at the mansion.

Turning back toward Birdie, I realize she's naked now too. And Reaper is there, trying to drag her back on the auction block.

"Violet." The deep voice bellows louder this time.

A large hand grasps the side of my face, and Alaric's voice sounds so close now, I swear it's in my mind. "Violet!"

I let out a scream, and my eyes fly open. Instead of a bright sunlit living room or the dark hall of the mansion, I'm lying in Alaric's dark bedroom, staring at his face only inches from mine.

"You're alive," I whisper, relief pouring through me like warm, calming water.

"You had a nightmare," he replies.

I cover my face with my hands and stifle the urge to cry. His hand is on my hip, and he massages my side, pulling me closer. Without thinking about what I'm doing, I nestle so close to him, my face is in the crook of his neck.

"Shh…" he says, comforting me. "Birdie is still sleeping."

"Good," I mumble.

His scent is familiar and arousing. Spice, musk, and rose from the bubble bath fill my nostrils as I put my body as close to him as I can.

"Did you have a dream I was dead?" he asks. His voice is quiet, but the question is deafening.

I nod.

"You sounded pretty upset about it," he whispers, and I can hear the humor in his voice.

"Shut up," I reply.

When he chuckles, the deep vibration of his voice engulfs me. My fingers brush through the tuft of hair on his chest, and I press my hips closer, feeling the shape of his cock against my naked stomach, noticing the way it's hardening between us.

I don't know why I do it. Maybe it's because a moment ago, I thought he was dead. I saw his lifeless eyes, and I can't get the image out of my head.

So perhaps that is why I part my lips and kiss the tender skin of his neck. He freezes.

My tongue darts out and licks the spot where his pulse beats against my mouth. He hums softly, and his hands tighten their grip on my hips.

We are two naked bodies pressed together, and I can't stop myself. My kiss grows hungrier, sucking harder.

"Violet," he groans, drawing my name out like a chant. I slide closer, creating friction against his cock. It twitches from the touch. "What are you doing?" he whispers.

I pull away from his throat and stare into his eyes. Grabbing his face in my hands, I put my lips up to his. "I don't know."

Then I kiss him. His lips part, and he sucks tenderly on my lower lip.

We move in perfect harmony, kissing, biting, sucking. His hands move possessively over my ass and between my legs, growling into my mouth as he grinds me against his erection.

This is crazy. Birdie is sleeping right next to us.

But at the moment, I'm not thinking. I just need his touch. It feels like I'm claiming him, reminding him who touched him first.

It's that feeling of territorial ownership that has me crawling down his body, kissing my way across his chest and stomach. When I wrap my hand around his rigid length, he gasps. And when I reach his cock, licking around the tight head, he throws his head back with a hiss.

Birdie is facing the opposite direction, but she lets out a cute little growling snore, and we both freeze. What would she even think of finding me with Alaric's cock down my throat? Would she be mad at me? She was the one who pointed out how we're all so connected. Part of me thinks she'd be more likely to join in than yell at us.

Which is why I don't feel shame as I coat his cock with saliva, bobbing my head up and down fiercely. His hand grips my scalp as he pushes me down and thrusts up into my mouth. I gag and let a string of saliva stretch from my lips to his cock. Doing it again, I stroke his dick with my lips and tongue, loving the way he reacts.

"Fuck, Violet," he whispers with a groan. "Come here."

Reaching down, he grabs me under my arms and carefully

drags me up, careful not to jostle the bed too much. With a hand in my hair, he hauls my mouth to his, kissing me ravenously as he lines up his cock with my moist core.

With a rough grip on my hips, he slams me down, filling me as we both gasp for air. His hard length stretches me, and I immediately start moving up and down.

"Tell me you missed this cock," he whispers against my mouth. "Because it missed you."

I have to swallow my cries of pleasure as his dirty talk makes my body sing with need. With my hands on his chest, I grind myself on him. My eyes cast sideways to Birdie's blond hair cascading over the pillow. She's still fast asleep, and here I am... giving my body to someone else.

But I can't stop now.

I am a liar and a cheater and a...

"F-fuck," I stutter in a breathy cry as my body lights up with pleasure. Reaching down, I strum my fingers on my clit, riding the waves of ecstasy.

"That's my girl," Alaric mumbles. He brings my mouth to his again, claiming my lips in a bruising kiss. "Let me feel you come."

My hips keep up their grinding through my climax, and when I've grown exhausted, he pulls me down, and I fall onto the pillow beside him. With my back to him, he tugs me closer, and I let out a yelp as he thrusts inside me from behind. My face is just inches from where Birdie sleeps.

His lips find my neck as he fucks me. "I know you love her," he whispers. "You'd do anything for her."

I bite my lip to keep from answering. Being in his arms, feeling him move inside me, his voice and his words in my ear—it all feels so good. And like a betrayal at the same time.

"Stay with me, Violet. Both of you…stay." He thrusts harder on a groan, and I turn my head to see him. Our eyes meet as he picks up speed.

"Okay," I whisper just before his lips crash into mine.

He groans into my mouth, and I swallow his pleasure. His hips shudder and still as he comes.

For a while, we just lie in that position, letting our hearts catch up.

"I'm serious, Violet," he mutters.

I pull back to look into his eyes. "I know. I am too."

His mouth quirks into a small smile, and I quickly kiss it again.

"Violet…" Birdie cries with a groan as she turns over, her hair draped over her face.

"I'm here," I reply, quickly turning toward her. Alaric slips out of me, and I feel his cum leak between my legs. But I ignore it.

Brushing Birdie's hair from out of her face, I kiss her forehead. "What's wrong, Bird? You gonna be sick?"

She shakes her head. "I just want to hold you."

"I'm right here," I whisper, wrapping my arms around her. "I'm not going anywhere."

She nuzzles her face in my neck, and I squeeze her tight. My eyes drift over to Alaric, who watches us, and those familiar feelings of shame and regret rise to the surface again.

Is what we just agreed to really possible? Could I stay with both of them?

Deep down, I know it is. I know we could be happy. But if we do this, then I know what has to be done. Birdie needs to know the truth.

# BIRDIE

My head is pounding.* When I woke up this morning, it was a little alarming to find Alaric and Violet both in bed naked next to me. My mind immediately panicked, replaying everything I could remember from last night.

The fight with Violet in the library. Taking two bottles of wine into the bathroom. Alaric climbing in with me, followed shortly by Violet.

Everything after that is hazy.

If we'd had a threesome…I'd remember it, right?

God, I hope so. That's something I'd want to remember.

And now, a threesome is all I can think about. Having both of them at my fingertips. Feeling just how rough and hard Alaric likes it. Watching them touch each other.

I'm dreaming if I think either of them will lighten up enough

* VIGILANTE SHIT–Taylor Swift

to let that happen. They're both so angry all the time. *I* was the one paraded around at an auction completely naked.

But I'm the only one who seems to realize that if we stopped fighting over who I should stay with, the three of us could have a lot of fun together.

Sitting at the dining room table alone, I push around my breakfast with my fork. I'm not in the mood to eat much right now, and it's not about my wine hangover. I can't help but feel like something is going on that I'm missing. Normally, Violet is honest with me, but she has been avoiding me all morning.

"Are you finished, miss?" One of Alaric's housekeepers steps into the dining room. I think her name is Alexis.

"Yes, thank you," I reply with a smile. "I can take it to the sink though," I say as I pick it up.

"Let me, miss," she says, taking the plate from my hand.

My lips press into a tight smile. "My stepmom always made me do everything," I explain.

She nods. "Well, Mr. Stone gave us strict instructions to take good care of you."

"That was sweet of him," I reply.

She chuckles a little before turning toward the kitchen. I get the feeling that hearing me call Alaric sweet is what made her laugh.

Just as I move to leave the dining room in search of Violet, she steps into view.

"Hey," I say softly. "I was just coming to find you."

It only takes a split second for me to tell that Violet is tense about something.

"What's wrong?" I ask.

"Can we...talk?" she mumbles.

I freeze, the blood draining from my face. My first instinct is that she's about to tell me that she's leaving. Whether she thinks it would be best for me or she's decided she no longer loves me, I can't stand the thought.

"Of...course," I stammer. "Let's go sit down."

Leading her into the living room, I take a seat on one end of the large leather sofa, and to my relief, she sits next to me. I don't want her putting space between us.

I reach for her hands and interlock them with mine. "What's going on?"

Every feature on her face is tense. But she stares into my eyes and takes a deep breath.

"Alaric and I...had sex."

My lips part, and I stare at her, waiting for the rest. "I know..." I mumble.

"Last night," she adds.

Oh.

*Oh...*

I don't move. I just keep my eyes on her face, letting this news hit me. My mind is reeling with questions. *When? Where? Why? What does this mean?*

Is this rising anger inside me because I'm really angry or because I feel like I *should* be angry?

When I don't move for a moment, she continues.

"It just happened. I initiated it, and I don't know why. I feel terrible about it, and you have every right to hate me for it. In fact, you really should yell and scream at me. I'm the worst—"

"Stop," I say, pulling a hand from her grasp and holding it up. "Where was I?"

"You were sleeping," she answers.

Of course, I drank too much and passed out, leaving those two to do whatever they wanted.

"Alaric woke me up from a nightmare, and it just... happened."

My eyes dash back to her face. "Wait... You had sex in Alaric's bed? While I was sleeping?"

She looks down in shame. "Yes."

I don't respond. I know I should, but I have no idea what to say. Normally, when I don't know how to feel about something, I ask Violet for her advice, but I can't do that now.

"Say something, Birdie," she whispers pleadingly.

"Did you do it to get back at me? For sleeping with him."

She flinches. "What? No! Of course not."

A crease forms between my brows as I stare at her. "Were you trying to make him want you more than me?"

She shakes her head. "Birdie, no. That's ridiculous."

"Then why did you do it?" I ask in desperation.

As she stares at me, her mouth opens, but Violet hesitates before speaking. She struggles for a second before finally answering. "Because I wanted to."

"You wanted to?" I question. "Do you still have feelings for him?"

She shrugs. "Yes, I must."

"Do you still...love me?" I hate the way I sound even asking that question. I sound pathetic and needy, but Violet just admitted that she has feelings for someone else, and I need some validation, even when I know exactly what she's going to say.

She scoots closer, squeezing my hands in hers. "Yes, Birdie. Of course, I still love you. I will always love you."

Her tone is genuine, and I believe every single word. With a sigh of relief, I throw myself into her arms, needing to feel her comforting embrace.

"Aren't you mad at me?" she whispers, hesitant to put her arms around me.

"I don't know," I reply with a shrug, still resting my face against her shoulder. Pulling away, I stare into her eyes. "I'm a little mad you didn't wake me up. I'm a little mad you didn't tell me you still had feelings for Alaric, especially when *I* had to have sex with him. And to be honest, I'm feeling a little left out. But really…"

I gaze downward, gathering the courage to express what I'm dying to say.

With a hefty sigh, I continue, "I'm relieved. Because what I really want is—"

"Ma'am, you can't just barge in!" one of the housekeepers yells from the entryway, and Violet and I both flinch at the same time.

"I told you I'm here to see my daughter, and I have every right to see her."

The sound of my stepmom's voice sends a cold chill down my spine.

"What is she doing here?" I whisper, holding tight to Violet. We both stand at the same time, and Violet shoves me behind her back as Clarissa marches into the room with Luna at her side.

"There you are!" she barks at us.

"What are you doing here?" Violet asks in shock.

"Where is it, you thieving little bitch?" Clarissa yells, pointing at Violet.

"Where is what?" she replies.

"The emerald! I know you took it. I knew you were a slut and a murderer, but I never took you for a thief."

Rage boils inside me, and I push Violet aside to step closer to my stepmom. "Don't you talk to her like that!"

My stepmom actually looks surprised for a moment. With her brows up in shock, she lets a crooked grin pull at her lips. "Well, look at who finally grew a backbone."

"What the fuck is going on in here?" Alaric bellows as he rushes into the room. He takes one look at Clarissa before muttering, "Get the fuck out of my house."

"Not until I get what's mine," she replies.

"No, you leave *now*," he growls in return.

"You don't scare me, Alaric," my stepmom says in a cold, cruel tone.

Hate boils in my bloodstream. Just seeing her here, in this place where I felt so safe and at ease, makes the hatred burn even hotter. I take another step closer to her.

"You need to leave," I say.

"Or what, Birdie? You always were weak. Like a little mouse. So easy to step on whenever I felt like it."

My fists clench with anger.

She steps toward me, and I can't help but fall back an inch. "You always were so stupid too. So gullible. Did you really think these two were going to save you? You clearly don't know what they're capable of."

"Shut up," I mutter.

"If I get you the emerald, will you leave?" Violet cries out desperately.

Clarissa's gaze lifts to her daughter. "So you did take it."

"Yes, I took it," Violet barks in response. "If I give it to you, will you leave?"

Her mother ignores her request. She looks instead at Alaric. "Is that what she offered to pay you with? Last time, she paid you with pussy, but not this time? What's wrong? All dried up?"

"What the fuck is wrong with you?" Alaric asks with a shake of his head.

My mind is reeling, trying to keep up with what's happening around me. "Last time?" I whisper.

When Clarissa looks at me, she lets an evil laugh slip through her lips. "Sweet, stupid Birdie. I thought Violet loved you so much, but she didn't bother to tell you the important things, did she?"

I glance back at Violet. Her eyes are on my face, round and full of regret. "I'm sorry," she whispers.

My brow furrows in confusion. "What is going on?"

Clarissa laughs again. "I love being the one to break this news to you, Birdie. But having your father killed wasn't free, you know?"

The blood drains from my face. I turn back to my stepmom with tears in my eyes. My skin goes cold, and my legs tremble with weakness. Suddenly, it feels like I'm alone, a single lamb alone in a room full of lions. They're all staring at me.

"What?" I breathe.

"The love of your life paid a hit man to kill your father, but instead of paying him money, she fucked him. Quite a few times to pay off that debt, I assume. How many times was it?" she asks, looking up at Alaric and Violet.

"Get out," Alaric barks at her.

"Not without my emerald."

I feel like I might throw up. Violet runs from the room in a mad sprint while the walls start to close in on me. I'm swaying on my feet as I stare unfocused at the window, letting my stepmother's words wash over me.

Violet had my father killed.

Alaric killed my father.

That's why she started sleeping with him back then.

Then why did she need the emerald?

I feel Alaric's presence behind me. His strong, safe hands rub at my back as I let a tear slip over my cheek onto the rug at my feet. Slowly, I turn toward him and face the apologetic expression on his face.

"You know he deserved it," he whispers softly. "She said he hit you once, and she almost killed him herself."

While staring at his face, I replay the day my father died. I remember the relief that washed over me. And I distinctly remember the last day he laid his hands on me, slapping me hard across the face after I made a harsh remark to him.

Violet had him *murdered* for that.

She slept with a man she barely knew multiple times to keep me safe.

And she stole a family heirloom from her mother to pay Alaric to help because she didn't want to sleep with him again...for me.

In return, she had to endure watching *me* sleep with him.

My heart shatters in my chest as a sob escapes my lips.

When I hear her running footsteps approach the room, I turn toward her, watching her rush into the room with a frantic expression.

"Here," she says, thrusting the satchel toward her mother. "Now leave."

"No!" I shout. Before I know what I'm doing, I lunge forward and grab the satchel from Violet before she can hand it to Clarissa.

My stepmother gasps. "You little bitch," she sneers at me. "That is mine."

"No!" I shout at her. "You don't deserve this. You got *two million dollars* from Alaric for me. You have manipulated me. Tortured me. Abused me. For years, I endured you, and now I will be keeping this."

When she lurches forward to grab it back from me, I rear my hand back and hit her hard across the face. She stumbles, and Luna is there to hold her mother up.

I take another menacing step toward the both of them. "Everything Violet has ever done has been out of love. Everything you have ever done has been out of hate. I don't care that she had my father killed, and I don't care that she slept with Alaric to do it. These two people actually care about me, but you don't understand that, do you? Because no one has ever cared about you that much."

She's holding her cheek in her hand and staring at me in shock. "You little—"

Out of nowhere, a hand wraps around Clarissa's throat. She stares in shock at Alaric, who is snarling at her with anger. "Call her one more name, and you'll be leaving my house with your head separated from your body."

"You're all fucking wild," Luna shrieks, her face contorted in fear.

"Get your mother and get the fuck out," Violet spits at her sister.

Luna snatches Clarissa's arm and tugs her toward the door. Alaric finally lets her go, and she takes a gulping breath, the color returning to her face.

I stand between Violet and Alaric, watching my stepmother rushing angrily toward the door with Luna by her side.

"Clarissa," Alaric barks at her. She stops and glances back with terror in her eyes. "Your husband made a lot of enemies, and I know every single one. Come near me, Birdie, or Violet again, and I'll make sure they all get their revenge. In fact, I'll carry it out for them for free. Understand?"

With a tremble, she nods. But as she turns to leave, he stops her again.

"In fact," he snaps, taking a step toward her. "You will give Birdie and Violet everything they are owed. Every fucking dime of their inheritances on top of the two million you got from me at the auction."

"But—" She tries to argue but he takes another menacing step.

"You're lucky I don't bury you and your daughter right now. Why don't you thank me for my mercy?" he says. His voice takes on a chilling, darker tone that makes my blood run warm and aroused.

"Alaric," she gasps. "You know I appreciate—"

"On your knees," I add, staring down my nose at her. "Both of you."

Their eyes widen as they glance back and forth between me and Alaric, who slowly reaches for the gun strapped to his back.

Shakily, my stepmother lowers to her knees. I find sick satisfaction in the fear in her eyes, the tremble of her hands, and the whimper in her voice. After everything she's put me through, I deserve this.

"Th-thank you," she stutters with her hands up in surrender. "You'll never see us again."

He takes a step closer, nudging her chin with the barrel of his gun. She winces. "Good," he mumbles. "Now get the fuck out of our house."

As I watch her disappear, my palm stinging from hitting her and a gemstone hanging in my other hand, I feel truly free for the first time. Not just free from her but free from the quiet, scared girl I felt I had to be.

I won't let her or anyone manipulate me again. I won't let anyone tell me how to feel. And I won't be someone else's burden anymore.

I am free.

# 20

# BIRDIE

The house is silent after the front door closes with a resounding thud.* My hands are trembling with anger as I stare straight ahead.

A warm hand rests against my arm.

"Birdie…" Violet whispers softly. "Are you okay?"

I blink, then turn to face her. She looks terrified.

"You killed my father," I mutter softly.

She swallows, tears brimming in her eyes. "I'm so s-sorry," she stammers.

The pain etched into her features breaks my heart. I lunge toward her, grabbing her face and kissing her hard on the mouth. I can tell it takes her by surprise because she tenses in my arms.

Pulling away, I stare into her frantic eyes. "You've always been there for me. You protected me and loved me when no one else would. I know deep down you think you failed me because

* I'M YOURS–Isabel LaRosa

of what happened at the auction or because you had my father killed, but you didn't fail me, Violet. You have *never* failed me."

A tear streaks down her cheek. I quickly wipe it away before kissing her again. She melts in my arms, wrapping hers around my waist as she deepens the kiss.

Before it can get too heated, she pulls away. "Wait... You're not mad?"

I shake my head. "Because of you, I'm out of that house. I'm here...and I don't want to leave."

"Oh, you're not fucking leaving," Alaric replies.

Without warning, he hauls me toward him. I tilt up to see his face, and he brings his mouth to mine, kissing me passionately. My knees go weak, and I fall into his arms.

I don't care that Alaric murdered my father. I don't care that he's a murderer at all. I know he'd never hurt me, and I have a night of gentle lovemaking to prove it.

Although right now...with the way he's kissing me, I sort of wish he would.

When I pull away breathlessly, moisture pools between my legs as I stare up at him. "Alaric," I whisper. "I need you. Both of you."

His response is a guttural growl. He buries a hand in my hair and brings his mouth to mine. "You just found out Violet and I conspired to kill your father, and the first thing on your mind is being fucked?"

I swallow and purse my lips at him. Instead of cowering in shame or embarrassment, I straighten my shoulders and stare at him defiantly. "Yes. I'll tell you the same thing I tried to tell Violet earlier." I touch his cheek and lift my lips in a crooked smile. "The only thing I'm mad about is that you didn't think to include me."

Wrapping my arms around his neck, I leap into his arms. He wraps his hands around me and grinds me against him. I feel Violet at my back, stroking my hair. She guides my face toward her, and I kiss her with as much fervor as I kissed him.

I hardly notice Alaric is carrying me anywhere until I realize we're suddenly in his room, Violet still glued to his side. The door closes with a slam, and he carries me to the bed, tossing me down. I bounce on the mattress and quickly move to my knees.

Reaching for Alaric, I pull his face to mine and kiss him again. His lips are rougher than last time, nibbling and biting. The hint of pain only makes me want him more.

When Violet touches my hair, I shift my mouth to her lips. We move together like a storm, tearing at each other's clothes and covering each other with kisses. I can't believe how much I want them both. How much my body craves them *both*.

Once the three of us are completely undressed, Violet and I both move our attention to Alaric. He's sitting on the bed with me on his lap, facing him. All I can think about is how much I want to put my mouth on his cock.

I push gently on his shoulder, making him lie down. Violet is next to him, kissing his mouth as I slide my way down his body. My body is buzzing with excitement as I reach his cock. It's so hard, it protrudes upward, lying flat on his stomach.

As I wrap my hand around the length, he sucks in air through his teeth. Gently I squeeze, moving my hand up and down, loving the sounds he makes as I do.

Violet appears next to me with a wicked smile. "Let me show you," she says sweetly.

She takes Alaric in her hand, and while keeping her eyes on me, she sucks him into the back of her throat. My thighs clench, and something warm buzzes in my stomach. The slurping sounds of her lips around him turn me on even more, and my mouth waters at the sight.

I watch the way she hollows her cheeks and curls her lips under her teeth. Her hand strokes him at the base, where her mouth won't reach. Alaric is a mess of groans and fidgeting movements on the bed. His head goes back and forth from hanging back to lifting up to watch her.

After a few minutes, she pops off his dick and looks at me. "Your turn, little sister."

Eagerly, I take his cock in my hand and run the tight head across the length of my tongue. When I come back up, I delicately slide my tongue into the slit at the end, watching him go wild as I do.

Then I see how far I can take him in my mouth, pleasantly surprised that I reach as far as Violet did before my gag reflex kicks in. I try again and again and again, going a little farther each time. Soon, his cock is coated with my saliva, and the head of his dick is tight.

"Get up here," he groans at Violet, dragging her up his body.

While working his cock with my mouth, I watch as he places her legs around his head, urging her to sit on his face. My eyes widen as he buries his face in the sweet spot between her legs. She leans forward, and I spot his tongue peeking out to lap at her clit. Facing me, she lets out a yearning cry of pleasure.

"Come here, Birdie," she whispers to me. Her eyes are hooded with lust as she reaches for me. I crawl up Alaric's body before finding her lips and kissing her ravenously. I'm straddling his hips, grinding myself against his rock-hard erection.

Between moans and whimpers, Violet urges my hips up, and I lift Alaric's cock, poising it at my soaking core. I'm nervous to be on top, but eager to try something new. I know they've got me.

So, as I settle my weight, swallowing Alaric's cock as I go, I take my time to allow my body to stretch around him. When I'm finally seated all the way, I let out a gasp. It's nothing like before. I'm so full but also in control. He's busy moaning and sucking at Violet's clit when I start grinding my hips, finding a position and rhythm that feel good.

There's still a slight burn, but I welcome it. The pain goes well with the pleasure. It intensifies it.

And when I find a spot that sparks with intensity, I continue rocking, hitting that spot over and over and over.

"God, you're so fucking sexy," Violet murmurs, watching me with arousal in her eyes.

I lean forward and grab her for a kiss again. As we're kissing, she reaches down and strums my clit with her fingers. Matched with the grinding of my hips, it makes me feel like my body is on fire.

Alaric is pumping his hips upward, meeting my thrusts. Violet is grinding her body on his face. He's sucking greedily on her, and she looks like she's ready to explode. I can tell by the tremble in her thighs that she's almost there.

Where one of us ends, the other begins. I feel my heart swell with their cries of pleasure. Violet slams a hand down on Alaric's chest as she screams out her orgasm. I rest my head on her shoulder as I build to the same level of intensity. I'm slamming my hips down on his cock, so in love with the sensation that I know I'll never get enough. As soon as we're done, I'll want them to fuck me again.

I'm hooked on them, on *us*. This thing we have together, after only a few days, is so perfect. I paid the price with nineteen long years of pain and strife, only to get here with two people who feel so right for me. We made this life together, and I hope we make so much more.

I never want to leave, and it might not be what any of us expected, but it's the most natural thing I can think of. More love. More connection. More happiness. More freedom.

I'm lost in my thoughts, slamming my hips down so hard now the sound of our pounding bodies reverberates through the room. When my orgasm hits me, it's like a tidal wave. My head falls back, and my body explodes with pleasure.

Alaric pinches my hips in his hands as he drives upward, coming hard with a deep growling yell.

My climax seems to last forever, and when it finally subsides, I collapse onto his chest, panting and waiting for my vision to clear. Violet is lying on the other side, her head on his chest too.

Alaric pulls my face up to his mouth, and I hungrily kiss his lips, savoring her taste on his tongue.

None of us speaks for a while. I'm too distracted by exploring his body with my hands.

After a while, I'm the one to finally talk first. "Can we do it again? I'll be a good girl."

Alaric chuckles first, and Violet looks at me with a smile. "Yeah, we can," she says softly. "But there's really no rush. It's not like we're going anywhere."

"We have all day," Alaric adds.

"We have more than all day," I reply.

He kisses the top of my head. "That's right, Princess. We have far more than all day."

# EPILOGUE

## ALARIC
ONE YEAR LATER

"Give me a color, Princess."\*

Birdie's beautiful pale ass is now covered in red strike marks from the paddle in my hand. She's writhing against the spanking bench, sweat covering her back in a thin sheen as she rests her forehead against the padded surface.

"Green," she replies with exhaustion.

My eyes seek out the woman sitting in the chair by the wall. She's watching the entire thing play out, biting her bottom lip as she toys with one of her own nipples, hardening it between the pads of her fingers.

"What do you think, my love? Does she need more punishment?" I ask.

Violet smiles. "Maybe just a couple more. Then she can get what she really wants."

I shoot her a wink before rearing back with the paddle and

---

\* DESIRE—Meg Meyers

smacking Birdie again, this time a little softer than last time. She squeals and screams all the same. Her flesh is probably so sore at this point anyway.

Technically, Birdie is being punished for disobeying me when she promised to be home from the bookstore by nine last night. She walked in that door with bags loaded on either arm at nine-fifteen. And she did it on purpose.

We've been setting these *rules* for the past few months. Birdie loves the predictability of obedience and boundaries, but more than that, she loves the thrill of rebelling against them. And then, of course, the punishment.

Which I happen to enjoy too.

After three more smacks with the paddle, Violet stands from the chair. Fully naked, she waltzes over to where Birdie is strapped down to the bench. Gliding her finger through Birdie's now shoulder-length hair, she grabs a handful and tugs softly to make her whimper.

"I think she's learned her lesson," she murmurs sweetly before leaning down and pressing her lips to the top of her head. "Well, almost."

That makes my lips pull into a wicked grin. "What else do you think she needs?" I ask as I move toward Violet. Brushing her hair from her shoulder, I kiss her neck, trailing my lips up to her mouth.

"I think we should show her what she's missing when she isn't home on time."

"Good idea," I mutter against her cheek.

This is Violet's favorite form of punishment for Birdie.

Quickly, I unzip my pants and pull out my aching cock, giving it a few strokes before I step behind Violet. Shoving her forward, she rests her hands on the end of the spanking bench, bringing her face close to Birdie's as I align my cock with her core.

Birdie bites her bottom lip and cries out as I thrust inside Violet.

"You guys don't play fair," she whines as both Violet and I moan in unison. Birdie struggles against her restraints, but it's futile. She knows they won't budge, and she likes it that way.

Roughly, I slam into Violet, hissing and groaning with each thrust. She's pushing back against me as I fuck her, and the whole time I'm watching the way it affects Birdie. She hates being left out.

"Are you going to break curfew again, Princess?" I ask in a strict tone.

"No, I promise! I'll be good."

Beneath that expression of pain and jealousy is a mischievous grin because, deep down, I know she loves this.

When Birdie first came to live here, she was ravenous for anything and everything she could learn about and experiment with. Her stepmother kept her so sheltered, Birdie was learning how to live on her own without the walls of a prison.

Once we knew for sure she wasn't pregnant, she started taking birth control. Someday she might want kids, but right now is about *her*. Living her life. Finding herself and what she really wants. I want Birdie to be Birdie's only priority. And Violet agrees.

So we spend our days spoiling her, doting on her, giving her space when she needs it and boundaries when she wants them.

I never saw myself as a romantic, relationship man, and yet here I am, in love with two women. Putting all of our focus on Birdie has brought Violet and me together more than I expected it to. Once we realized that she was our common ground, it made me love her that much more.

These two are my world, and I'd gladly burn everything to the ground to keep them safe.

I've already killed for them, and I would do it again without hesitation. There's not a life on this earth I care about above theirs.

There are days I fear my line of work could put them in danger, but I've just had to adjust some of my practices to accommodate their places in my life. I don't do anything that could land me any enemies. I don't take jobs as recklessly as I did before, and I never let anyone in our world know what these two mean to me.

Clarissa hasn't shown her face since that day we threw her out. She sent the money I demanded, not that any of us cared about it. And just to show her how much we didn't care about her, we sent her a photo of us at our private wedding between the three of us. I am a man of my word.

"Alaric, sir, please," Birdie whines again.

She knows my weakness. She calls me *sir*, and I melt into a puddle for her.

"What do you want, Princess?" I ask, still fucking roughly into Violet's warm, tight cunt.

"Fuck me, please, sir," Birdie begs.

"Will you be good for me?"

"Yes, yes, I promise. Please." She looks like she's in more

pain now than she was when I was walloping her ass with that paddle.

"Let me make your stepsister come, and then it will be your turn. Okay, Princess?" I shoot her a wink, and she smiles salaciously up at me.

As she tugs her lip between her teeth and watches with carnal interest as Violet erupts in a screaming orgasm, I remember the day I met Birdie and how innocent she was back then.

But maybe she was never truly innocent. Maybe this sexy, shameless, proud version of her was lying dormant, waiting for that night at the auction and the next night at the play party to awaken her true desires. To give her a safe space to explore them and someone she could trust to give her room to do so. If that's true, then maybe Violet and I did rescue her.

At the time, I remember thinking that it was our job to protect her innocence, but now I realize it was never that at all. In fact, it was the opposite. It was our job to shatter it.

# ABOUT THE AUTHOR

Sara Cate is a *USA Today* bestselling romance author who weaves complex characters, heart-wrenching stories, and forbidden romance into every page of her spicy novels. Sara's writing is as hot as a desert summer, with twists and turns that will leave you breathless. Best known for the Salacious Players' Club series, Sara strives to take risks and provide her readers with an experience that is as arousing as it is empowering. When she's not penning steamy tales, she can be found soaking up the Arizona sun, jamming to Taylor Swift, and watching Marvel movies with her family.

Website: saracatebooks.com
Facebook: SaraCateBooks
Instagram: @saracatebooks
TikTok: @SaraCatebooks

*The End of*

# SHATTERED INNOCENCE

*and the Beginning of*

# ROYAL HEART

Every book in the Black Rose Auction is meant to be read as a duology. Now that you've reached the end of *Shattered Innocence*, simply close the book, flip it over, and start *Royal Heart* from the beginning. Happy reading!

*The End of*

# ROYAL HEART

*and the Beginning of*

# SHATTERED INNOCENCE

Every book in the Black Rose Auction is meant to be read as a duology. Now that you've reached the end of *Royal Heart*, simply close the book, flip it over, and start *Shattered Innocence* from the beginning. Happy reading!

# ABOUT THE AUTHOR

Nana Malone (she/her) is a *Wall Street Journal* and *USA Today* bestselling author of bold, unapologetic romance and loves all things romance and adventure.

That love started with a tattered romantic suspense she "borrowed" from her cousin. It was a sultry summer afternoon in Ghana, and Nana was a precocious thirteen. She's been in love with kick-butt heroines ever since.

According to *Entertainment Weekly*, she writes in a lighthearted, contemporary style, effortlessly blending off-the-cuff dialogue that makes readers feel like they're in the midst of a fun and flirty gossip session with a close friend—one who just happens to wear a tiara.

Website: nanamalone.com
Facebook: @nanamalonewriter
Instagram: @nanamalonewriter
TikTok: @nanamalone1

it was time to hang up the gig. Besides, I was a prince now. I should concentrate on making my brother proud.

And I would…after this last job.

"Thank you. I still can't believe I managed to convince her to tie herself to me."

I wrapped up the tuxedo and shoved it into the dry-cleaning bag, then crawled out of my hiding place. "Why not? You've gone legit now. Not to mention the last time I saw you, you couldn't keep your eyes off her. I'm no expert on love or anything like that, but she seems like the real deal."

"Thank you. I appreciate you saying that. Which is why I feel the need to warn you: Ari is on her way to this fundraiser that some rich idiot Zion Sterling is having. She thinks the Silver Fox Gang is after a Wistell painting. If you have any friends in that crew, now might be a good time to tell them to pull out."

Well, shit. He had called to warn me. "Like I said, I don't really know the gang. But I'm going to see your fiancée tonight. I'll be at the benefit."

He sighed. "Lucas, I'm telling you, she's hell-bent and determined to catch them in the act. So like I said, if you have a friend in the crew, now is the time to tell them to pull out."

"I don't really believe in pulling out as a birth control method. Sometimes you just have to take your chances. Thanks for the warning, Damon. Make sure you enjoy that champagne I send you and Ari. And console her about the Silver Fox Gang. She won't catch them tonight."

I hung up, returned the jacket to its place in Sterling's closet, and got in the laundry truck with five minutes to spare.

I had always liked Ari Denton, but tonight, she would not get her man. But I did understand, if she was sniffing around, maybe

"No, yeah, he's fine. He's got a job working for Galen, so he's keeping his nose clean. This is about something else."

I liked Damon a lot, but now was not the time. I finished sewing the lining of the tuxedo jacket and admired my handiwork for a moment before sliding the protected and folded canvas in, then sewing it shut.

"It's Ari. She's been driving herself up the wall chasing this group called the Silver Fox Gang."

I froze.

The Silver Fox crew was decades old. The original members were either in prison, retired, or dead. So I'd had no qualms about temporarily resurrecting their name to pull off a few select jobs.

"Oh yeah? What about this crew?"

"You know Ari. She's like a dog with a bone. She couldn't figure the case out until I said something when I proposed to her about having to hide the ring on me so she wouldn't find it. And then suddenly she was off and said she knew exactly what she was looking for. You wouldn't happen to know anything about the crew, would you?"

A cold sweat ran down my back. The buzzer on my watch went off; I had twenty-five minutes to put this tux jacket back where it belonged: out of the crawl space. And then I had to get back with the laundry crew and off the property so I could go home, get dressed, change, and come back as a guest.

"That's really interesting. But I don't know the gang personally. So I can't give her any insight. Is it an active case or something? And don't think I missed that part about you two being engaged. Congratulations. I owe you both the best champagne."

"Just checking in on you, man. You all right?"

"Yeah, I can't complain. You know, or I could, but who would listen?"

I kept sewing. I knew I had a limited amount of time. In thirty minutes I would need to be off the Sterling estate. Zion Sterling had a renowned art collection. Including a Wistell painting.

Zion also liked to throw a party. What better way to show off your art than to display it to your other rich friends?

And I'd had the distinct displeasure of meeting Mr. Sterling with my brother just last week. He was a dick. Treated his employees like shit. And, well, he was very handsy with the waitress. Sebastian had been meeting with him about some art endowment. I'd told my brother I wanted to go but hadn't mentioned that I would be depriving Mr. Sterling of his most prized possession: the Wistell.

I hadn't lied when I said I was mostly retired. I wasn't running scams anymore. They were too risky. I certainly wasn't interested in anything violent—that carried real time. But the art and the jewels… Even though I was a prince now, that didn't stop the itch to *take*. Especially if it meant taking things from people who didn't deserve them. People who treated others like they were beneath them.

Sometimes I liked to think of myself as Robin Hood. Lord knew I didn't need the money now. So I made donations with the proceeds. In the case of the waitress, I planned to go back and leave her a very special tip. But mostly I stole to keep my skills fresh. You never knew. "Something tells me this isn't a social call, Damon. Is everything okay with your brother? He's all right now, yeah? No other problems?"

# EPILOGUE

# LUCAS

I held my flashlight in my mouth as I sat in the crawl space, careful not to move too much.*

My phone buzzed in my pocket, and I didn't risk stopping to see who was calling.

The thing was, when you were a newly crowned prince, the king apparently liked to call you at all hours to handle all kinds of things while he was on his extended honeymoon. So I had to answer. Just in case it was my brother.

"What's up, Seb? I've got my hands full right now."

But the voice that came back to me was not my brother's. And it was less disapproving and more amused. "Is it a woman or a piece of jewelry?"

I paused for a moment. "Damon Hunt. What's the matter? Do you miss me already? I didn't expect to hear from you so soon."

* BUBBA SAYS–Bubba Graham

is preferable to seeing you frustrated. Besides, I'm relieved. Do you know how many times I had to move your ring? You almost discovered it twice. I finally had to start carrying it on me at all times. Hell, you almost found it two days ago when—"

"Wait, what did you just say?"

He frowned. "That I had to move the ring several times?"

I shook my head. "No, what you said about keeping it on you. Holy shit, you're a genius!"

He chuckled softly. "Do I even want to know?"

I looped my arms around his neck. "Why don't you take me to bed? I'll tell you all about it."

"Now you're speaking my language."

entire room was decorated with candles and rose petals. A table was set in the center, complete with a bottle of red wine and two glasses.

Damon pulled out a chair for me, and I sat down, feeling like a queen. He poured us each a glass of wine and raised his in a toast. "To the most beautiful, intelligent, and capable woman I know." "This is beautiful, Damon."

He sat down across from me. "Anything for my angel."

We chatted and laughed over dinner, enjoying each other's company. As we finished, Damon got up from the table and walked over to me, holding out his hand. "Care to dance?"

I took his hand, and we swayed to the music that played softly in the background. As we danced, Damon leaned in close to me and whispered, "I have a surprise for you."

My heart raced with excitement. "What is it?"

He pulled away slightly and reached into his pocket before tugging out a small velvet box.

My breath caught in my throat. "Oh, Damon..."

He got down on one knee and opened the box, revealing a stunning diamond ring. "Ari, will you marry me?"

Tears welled in my eyes as I nodded, unable to find my voice. Damon slipped the ring onto my finger and stood up, pulling me with him.

"I love you so much," he said, holding me tight.

Searching his gaze, I whispered, "I love you too. This was not how I thought the night would go a couple of hours ago. This outcome is significantly preferable," I murmured.

Damon leaned down and kissed my nose. "Seeing you happy

team. Even though he's admin, he seems happy. I asked Taryn to keep an eye on him." Damon chuckled softly. "Well, I guess that's why they're the Silver Fox Gang, right? They're notorious for their stealth and cunning. But don't worry. You'll figure it out. You always do."

I turned to face him. "I hope so. These paintings are worth millions, and Galen won't be pleased if I can't figure it out. I've been over the last job for hours, and I know I'm missing something; I just can't put my finger on it."

Damon placed a hand on my cheek, his gaze steady. "You'll figure it out when you least expect to. If you need my help, I can take a look."

I sighed. I wanted his help, I just also wanted to figure it out on my own. Galen used Damon for consultations. If he was going to help, I wanted him paid for it. "No, it's okay. I'm just frustrated. I'll tap you in if I need to. Hell, between you and the prince, you might have the contacts I need. But it's a puzzle. I do love puzzles." And figuring them out was my superpower.

I'd decided that from time to time, I would go into the field, when a difficult safe was involved. I'd learned to have a more balanced outlook on fieldwork. And let's face it. It was fun. But I didn't thrive on it like some others did.

I leaned over and took a whiff, the scent of garlic and spices wafting from the kitchen. "What's going on back there?"

He shrugged with a wry grin. "Just a little something special for you." He took my hand and led me out of his study, then tugged me down the hall.

When we reached the kitchen, I couldn't believe my eyes. The

# ARI

### THREE MONTHS LATER

How the hell had they done it? I'd gone over this a dozen times, and I still couldn't figure out how the Silver Fox Gang had taken a string of paintings.

By the time I stood up over my worktable and rubbed my eyes, several hours had passed and the damned sun was setting.

Damon stepped up behind me, wrapped his arms around me, and kissed my neck. "What's troubling my angel?"

I sighed and gave up, ready to ask for his help. Normally we had a separation of church and state. He was mostly focused on the import-export business and consulted on a few jobs for Galen.

"I still have no idea how this gang stole these paintings. Unseen, undetected. How can I recover something when I don't know how they did the job?" I sighed. "How was your call with Max?"

"He's relieved to be trusted enough to be on a travel recovery winked and kissed her cheek. "We deserve it. You took that bracelet?"

"Yeah. It was in next to his Rolexes, like he planned to give it to someone as a gift or something. I slipped it into my hand before we started."

"Did you know we were going to need it?"

"No, I had no idea. But I'm so glad I took it."

"You, Ari Denton, are entirely too good at this."

"Let's just say it's in my blood."

One officer patted her down briefly and shook his head. "She's telling the truth. She doesn't have anything on her."

Lane screamed, "She does. She took it."

The other officer patted Lane down and pulled something out of his pocket. Something that looked like a diamond Bulgari bracelet. Lane's eyes went wide.

"Sir, may I ask what this is?"

"I've never seen that before in my life."

But I had. That bracelet was worth two hundred thousand dollars. It had been stolen two years ago. I'd suspected Lane had stolen it, and now there it was in his pocket.

Lane fought, making a whole drama, even as the officer put cuffs on him. "She set me up. She planted that on me."

Ari shook her head. "Officer, I have never seen that man before. My boyfriend and I were just lost. I was looking for Rocker's Restaurant. I went to ask the doorman for directions, and he said we were in the wrong place, and I had just come back out when this guy grabbed me."

The cop nodded. "It's around the corner. You're free to go."

Ari walked over to me, and I wrapped my arm around her shoulder. We deliberately walked around the corner toward Rocker's. We didn't speak or breathe until we were alone, and I hugged her tightly to me. "Holy fucking shit, are you okay?"

"I am now. Necklace and compass secure?"

I nodded slowly. "I parked a block away in the other direction."

"You know we're going to have to go to Rocker's now, right?"

"Yeah, why don't we get a drink and an appetizer?" I

under my breath. I'd parked a block away. They wouldn't find anything on us if they searched us.

Ari's brow furrowed. "You don't know who you're dealing with."

"Oh, I think I do, little bird." He smirked. "I am always a step ahead."

The officers marched over. "We understand there's been a disturbance at the property."

"Yes, as a matter of fact, I caught this thief red-handed."

I chimed in immediately. "No, actually, all she did was walk out of the apartment building."

"I'm sure if you search her, Officers, you will find that she's holding something very valuable. A compass."

We should be clean. All we had to do was stay calm.

Lane scowled while gripping Ari tighter. She whined and cried, "Ow, that hurts. Oh my God."

The police officers shifted forward, and one said, "Sir, I'm going to have to ask you to let her go."

Lane growled at him. "No, you don't understand. She has my compass. I want it back."

Ari shook her head. "I don't know what he's talking about."

But Lane clearly wasn't letting her go. The other officer, the shorter one, grabbed him. "Well, now you're going to earn yourself a trip to the station for assault."

Lane tried to fight him off, shoving him back. "No, search her."

Ari had changed into a dress and flats. She threw her hands up. "I don't have anything on me. I swear."

"Ari."

"It's mine now," she said with a determination and grit I'd rarely seen until recently. The compass joined the necklace in our pouch.

With the safe door closed, we both ran back to the window and tied our pouch to a secondary line, then sent it down to the pool level. Then I ran for the door.

The plan was for Ari to head down to the pool level, change clothes, and tie the bags together while I took the fire exit to the main floor. Then she'd drop the bags down to me and walk out the front door.

My heart thundered as I escaped down the stairs and out the back door. There was no one waiting. Had we pulled it off scot-free?

The tied bags made it over. I picked them up, tossed them in the trunk, and then drove around to the front to pick her up. Then I spotted the one person I'd hoped we wouldn't see. Michael Lane.

I drove past the entrance and parked on the street a block away before running back for Ari.

She bumped into Lane as she tried to pass him nonchalantly outside the front door, and he grabbed her arm. I was on him within seconds, grabbing him by the lapels. "Let her go," I demanded.

"Absolutely not. I have already called the police to come search her."

Ari didn't panic. She was cool as a cucumber.

We saw the blue and red flashes in no time, and I cursed

"It's not my business how that man keeps his art. For him, probably just knowing he has it is all he wants."

Jesus. There was cash, which we ignored. Then I spotted a pouch, and Ari picked it up and looked inside. "Oh God, this is it."

We pulled out the necklace, and she took out her loupe, quickly assessing. There'd be no point in stealing something that wasn't real, and this might be bait. If we walked out with it and it wasn't the real deal, our efforts would be worthless.

"As far as I can authenticate it, it's real," Ari said.

"Holy fucking shit."

"Holy fucking shit," she repeated. And then Ari threw herself at me and wrapped her arms around me tight. "Oh my God, thank you."

A warm flush spread up the back of my neck. "Thank me for what?"

"Thank you for listening and believing that I could do this. Thank you for knowing I could find it."

"I always believed in you, Ari. You've always had the goods."

"Yeah, I guess. I just needed to believe it."

As we were about to close the safe door, she stopped. On the next shelf, there was a series of velvet boxes, including a large square one that piqued her interest.

"Ari, what's up?" I asked her.

She held up a finger as she pulled it out delicately. When she opened the box, a soft gasp escaped from her lips.

*The compass.*

"So this is what my father died for." Her brow furrowed, and she pursed her lips. "This thing was worth a man's life?"

though it was already slicked into the tightest of buns. She'd gotten that Afro under submission so we didn't risk leaving any DNA evidence behind.

The two of us took out our tiny stethoscopes. Ari lifted her wrist, set the timer, and took a deep breath. "Okay, ready? Our timing has got to be perfect."

"Yeah. You and me, we got this."

With a deep breath, we started turning the dials. Turn, turn, and on the third turn, slow it down and *click*. Right, sixty-two. We took three measured breaths together and looked at the time. On the twenty, we began together again. All the way to a slowed-down landing on forty-five. One more turn. We waited for the timer, listening carefully as we turned to the right. Ari called out, "Ten."

I spoke quietly, "Nine."

She frowned at me. "No, it's ten."

I lifted a brow. We couldn't be wrong about this. If we were wrong, we'd be out of luck.

"It's ten," she repeated. "Trust me."

And I did. "Okay, ten."

I shifted my dial. She shifted hers. Then we stepped back. She clicked the lever, and I held my breath.

When the lever gave way and she opened the safe, I breathed a sigh of relief. "Jesus fucking Christ."

Ari stood there staring. The safe was quite large, with several smaller art pieces lying down on the bottom.

She frowned at one. "Jesus Christ, is that a Picasso? It's a sketch, but still."

We found a massive bed made almost to military precision. There wasn't a single item out of place in the whole room. But that wasn't what made the place eerie. He didn't have a single photo. No books. Completely impersonal. Nothing that screamed that anyone used the place.

There wasn't much else in here. Honestly, it looked like a hotel room.

We walked into the massive closet, and that was where we turned on our flashlights.

Ari whistled low. "Wow. I mean, the douche is a real clean freak."

Every suit coat, shirt, and pair of pants was hung with a certain edge and crispness and was organized by color. There was a stand for accessories, which were also arranged by color, from silver to bronze to gold. He didn't play.

Over in the corner hung a painting, and we knew what we'd find behind it.

The two of us carefully searched the painting for trip wires and found a weighted one.

I held the painting slightly askew as Ari grabbed the adhesive from her tool belt and secured it.

With the painting down, she grinned at me. "It's a Maxine47."

I whistled low. "Oh boy. We can't force this." It had double dials, an intricate locking mechanism, and if you played with the numbers, you were screwed. I grinned at her. "We've got this though. Hell, we stole the Royal Heart from the Black Rose Auction. We can do anything."

Ari squared her shoulders and smoothed down her hair, even

We knew where Lane was. A charity event—of course, either scoping out something he wanted to steal or actively stealing something. By the time he came back, we would be gone.

I said a quiet prayer and went over the edge as well.

When I landed silently next to her, I gave her a nod. "All good?"

She yanked up her harness easily. "Yeah, all good."

We stacked our equipment into the bag we had brought with us, tied it onto a rope, and lowered it another ten stories to the pool level.

It landed with a *clank*, and we untied the rope.

Our bright exit idea was to walk out the damned front door.

Actually, if I were being honest, that was Ari's plan. She'd said people would never look for someone walking out the front door of the condo building. And I had to admit she was right.

It was dark inside the corner unit. According to the specs we'd obtained, the place was three thousand square feet.

The glass cutter worked like a charm. Ari put the tool back in her belt as we pulled the glass away. "I guess this is it."

"It is. Be careful, Ari."

"Always."

We began searching for the safe. The most likely location was the bedroom. People generally wanted to stay close to the things that were valuable to them.

We went through the expansive living room, down the hall to the left, past the bathroom, and then into the bedroom. I entered first just in case we'd gotten Lane's schedule wrong, but we hadn't. No one was in there.

# DAMON

There is no bigger fear than watching the woman you love rappel down the side of a building.

"Before you go over, Ari, I..." What the hell was I going to say?

She just grinned at me. "I love you too, Damon. Now, can we go get that damned necklace?"

I shook my head. "Woman, you are taking years off my life, do you know that?"

She shrugged. "I get that impression. Can we just do this thing? Close this chapter, okay?"

I nodded and pulled down my mask. "Roger that. Be careful, Ari."

She reached for my hand. "You be careful too. See you at the end."

As I watched her go over, my heart went into free fall. But I was the only one panicking. Ari had nerves of steel. She only had to go down three stories, directly onto the balcony.

back to my feet before bending down to scoop her into my arms.

She smiled lazily up at me. "I love you."

"I love you too. Now what will it be? Tub or shower?"

in plain brown wrapping. "After Lucas and I found Lane, I headed to one of my safe houses to get this."

Ari sat up and wrapped the sheet around her breasts. "What is it?"

"Open it." I couldn't help but chew on my bottom lip as she tugged on the twine ribbon. When was the last time I'd been so nervous giving a present?

She peeled back the wrapping and gasped. Her words were breathy as she asked, "What did you do?"

"After I left, I realized I still had all your father's tools strapped to me since he couldn't carry them himself. I couldn't bring myself to ever use them or to throw them away. You're one of the good guys, but I thought you should have them."

Her fingertips played over the safecracking tools and his glass knife, jewelry kit, and loupe. When she lifted her gaze to mine, her eyes were filled with tears.

"Shit. Ari. I didn't think these would make you cry," I said while wiping away her tears.

"No. It's...perfect. Thank you."

"I figured, if things were different, he'd have wanted you to have them."

She picked up the packaging and slowly set the tools aside before climbing into my lap and wrapping her arms around me. "Thank you, Damon. I don't know what to say."

"You don't have to say anything. C'mon, let's get cleaned up."

"I don't want to move."

"You don't have to. I'll carry you." I eased out of bed, then took a second to make sure blood had found its way me. Her muscles clenched, her legs quivered, her breath became choppy, and I growled as she tightened around my cock.

"Oh God. Damon."

"Help me, Ari. Show my fingers what to do."

Her fingers intertwined with mine, and we stroked her clit together.

"Fuck. Oh fuck. Oh God." She panted, and her muscles clamped down on me.

I roared my release, filling her with my come, and stayed buried inside her until my cock stopped twitching.

I dropped my forehead against her shoulder and struggled to catch my breath. Ari was shivering, her body trembling. I pulled out gently and kissed her shoulder. "You okay, angel?"

She nodded her head, then turned around. "I think after that, I'm a whole other level above okay."

I said, "Come on, sweetheart. Let's get us in the shower."

She groaned. "Don't want to."

I tucked her to me and kissed her shoulder. "Now you got me so carried away, I didn't get to give you your present."

"*I* got *you* carried away?"

"Yep. I was just going to break in here, give you a gift, and invite you on a heist with me. But you lured me into bed."

"Did I now?"

I nodded sagely. "You know I find it hard to resist when you start fighting with me."

"You're ridiculous."

"Maybe. But I got you something." My heart tripped as I reached for the bedside table and grabbed the parcel I'd wrapped

I held perfectly still, trying to let her get used to my size. Beneath me, she made these little mewling noises. I didn't want to decipher them incorrectly. "Talk to me, angel. Should we stop? I don't want—"

"What? No. Move." Her breathless command filled the room, and my eyes slammed shut.

This was it. I was going to lose it.

I took a deep breath, then another.

"Damon, please."

"Only if you tell me what you want."

"This. Please make me feel good."

I wrapped one hand around her hip and used the other to grab her hair and pull her head back. I nuzzled her neck and trailed a line of nips and nibbles over her shoulder to her neck.

I pulled out slowly, then thrust forward, and she screamed, "Yes. Oh God. I feel so full."

I kept up a steady rhythm, and she whimpered and writhed beneath me. "So tight…" I said.

With my hands on her hips, I pulled all the way out for a long moment, then dragged her back onto my cock, hard and deep. She gasped, and her muscles started to quiver around me. She was close, so close, and I thrust harder and deeper into her.

"Damon."

"You want to come, angel?"

"Yessss," she whimpered.

I gasped and reached around her hips, seeking her clit. When I found it, I stroked with one hand. She started to fall apart around

She did as I asked, and I let my fingers slide down the crack of her ass again before I teased her opening with the tip of my finger.

"Ah, fuck, Damon."

I grinned and stroked her again. "You like that?"

"Yes. I like it a lot."

I pushed deeper, this time with two fingers, and she sucked in a breath.

"Just breathe, angel."

She tensed in my arms, and I stroked a hand up and down her side until her muscles loosened.

When her body relaxed again, I pushed a bit harder. I could feel the tight ring yielding to the pressure, and it was hard to resist sinking into her ass right then.

I moved my hand away from her hip and pushed in farther.

"Yessss."

I wiggled my fingers gently, then pulled out. I covered my cock with lube and then took a deep breath.

Ari looked over her shoulder at me, confusion in her gaze.

"I'm going to be gentle, angel, okay?"

She nodded, and I eased the tip of my cock into her tight rosette. I closed my eyes and took another deep breath.

Goddamn, she was tight.

She whimpered, and I stroked a hand up and down her back again. "Keep breathing."

I took a deep breath myself and pulled back out. I pushed in a bit more and heard her gasp. I kept my movements slow, deliberate even, until I was buried deeply inside her.

*Fuck. Fuck. Fuck.*

"I wanted to try something if you're up for it. Do you have lube?"

Ari bit her bottom lip and nodded as she indicated the bedside drawer. She took one look at the length of my cock, her gaze trailing down every single one of my nine inches, but instead of seeming afraid, her eyes darkened, and she licked her lips. "You'll go slow?"

Christ, I was keeping her. "Of course. Just tell me if you don't like something, and we'll stop. I'll find other ways to make you come, okay?"

"I don't think I can come again."

"Why don't you let me worry about that?" I grabbed the lube from the drawer.

After I eased a pillow under her hips, I leaned down to plant a kiss on each ass cheek. Ari, being Ari, teased me by wiggling her ass back toward me, giving me the perfect view of her pussy and tight rosette.

I uncapped the lube, then drizzled some directly on her tight hole. I knew she was nervous because her muscles were tight, and my fingers glided over her asshole. "Shhh. Relax, angel." I slid the tip of my finger inside her.

She drove her hips back against me, and I pushed deeper into her body. "Oh," she whispered.

I withdrew my finger, and her muscles clenched around nothing. I spread the lube on my fingers again before adding another to her ass. I started to stroke in and out in a gentle rhythm.

I pulled all the way out, stroking a hand up her back to relax her. "Easy, angel. I've got you. Just relax for me."

I pulled out of her with a groan, not wanting to lose it just yet. It seemed like I had waited fucking forever for her, and I wasn't ready to finish yet.

She whimpered, and I stilled, then said, "Shhh. I'm not done."

With that, I pulled her up to her knees and steadied her so her back was pressed against my chest. I buried my face in her neck and started to thrust into her from behind.

I planted one hand on her hip and slid the other between her thighs. She was still swollen, so I went easy, using my fingers to stroke lightly over her clit, and she rocked back against me.

But a jolt of electricity barreled down my spine. "Oh, damn it." I grabbed her shoulders and pulled her back against me. Her head dropped back onto my shoulder. I used my fingers to tease her nipples and continued to stroke her clit.

"Harder, please... Oh God... Harder."

"You need a harder touch, angel?" I timed every thrust with a brush against her clit, and she started to flutter around me again.

"Yes," she hissed. "Fuck, yes."

I cupped her breast in my hand and fondled her nipple, then hardened it with a pinch.

"Oh, please, please." She arched back again, pressing her ass against me. I bit down on her neck and stroked her harder and faster until she came again, whimpering, and her muscles rippled around my cock.

Her back arched once more as she fell forward. I eased out, my cock still hard and glistening from her.

Braids cascading on her pillow, she turned her head to face me. "What are you doing?"

her clit. Her head fell back against the pillow, and I took the opportunity to kiss her neck.

Her moans were sending me over the edge.

"Please, please, please," she begged.

I shifted again, this time dragging my dick over her sweet spot before rocking against her, using my hips to rub my dick against her clit and her pussy.

"Damon, please."

I drove home in one swift stroke, gripping her hips tightly to hold her still.

Who the hell was I kidding? I was trying to keep from coming too quickly as her pussy gripped my cock and she screamed my name.

I thrust forward again, and she moaned.

"I won't last if you do that, beautiful."

She moaned again as she palmed her breasts and pinched her nipples. My gaze glued to those perfect tits, I increased the speed and force of my thrusts.

I needed her to come. Right the fuck now. Or I was going to lose it. I eased a hand between us, then stroked my thumb over her clit in a slow, deliberate circle.

Her gasp had me chuckling against her skin.

"I'm going to come," she whispered.

"Come for me, angel."

She shook her head. I brought my mouth down on hers and slammed my hips into her.

Ari screamed, and her inner muscles fluttered around my cock as she came. Her body felt like it was on fire, and I had to grit my teeth as she pulsed around me.

When she moaned, I smacked her other cheek before diving back in to lick her with the flat of my tongue.

She moaned louder and started to move her hips again, fucking my face. I inserted another finger into her ass and kept going until she thrashed in my arms, her legs trying to choke me out.

Instead of stopping to worry about breathing, I sucked her clit harder into my mouth.

I smiled in satisfaction as I sucked while she screamed my name and then came apart with a shuddering arch, her whole body quivering around my fingers and tongue.

I eased out of her gently before kissing her inner thighs. "You are so fucking sexy when you come, Ari. One day soon, I'm going to spend the day making you hoarse from screaming my name."

I shifted our position so I kneeled between her thighs again. After smoothing my hand down her leg, I lifted her leg gently before pressing my cock against her slick flesh, letting her feel just how hard I was and how badly I wanted to be inside her.

One of her hands fisted in the sheets as I thrust forward, rubbing against her center.

"Oh, God."

"You're so wet, angel."

She dug her nails into my back as I drew back and thrust forward again, a little harder this time.

"You want this, Ari?" She didn't say it, but she nodded enthusiastically. "Say it, angel."

"I want you."

I shifted my position a bit so I could thrust my cock against my fingers, but I wanted to take it slow. I didn't want this moment to end too quickly.

"Please," she begged, her voice trembling with desire.

"Just relax," I whispered, leaning down to kiss her lips softly. "We have time, angel."

I could see the frustration... I drew my fingers out of her, and she whimpered.

"Shhh, I'm not done yet." I used my hands to splay her wide and lift her hips a little, giving me access to the pretty rosebud.

I gave her a long, leisurely lick, and my angel screamed and tried to scramble away from me.

"Tell me to stop, or quit squirming. What will it be? If you don't tell me to stop, but you still squirm, I'm going to give you a spanking."

To my surprise, that only made her wetter. "Damon."

I used my fingers to open her and lick her again.

"Oh God."

"Mine," I rumbled against her pussy. "All mine." I pushed a finger into her ass, and she started to shake. "Tell me to stop."

She shook her head and shoved her hips at me, trying to take my mouth.

"If you don't tell me to stop, you're going to get a spanking unless you quit squirming. Nod if you understand."

"God, Damon. Please," she pleaded as she writhed.

"Nod."

Instead of nodding, Ari grinned wickedly. "I want a spanking."

With a raised brow, I flipped her over, gave her a quick swat on her ass, then flipped her back.

Plump breasts half covered by a lacy red bra. I pinched one nipple through the lace, and she sucked in a shaky breath.

"Jesus, Ari." I hooked my fingers into the straps of her bra, and I dragged it down her arms, until her luscious breasts popped free.

She arched into my hand as I circled her nipple with my thumb. I turned my head and took her breast into my mouth, sucked and nipped at the sensitive skin. "God, I need you, Ari."

She said nothing, but her hands tore at our clothes. In the fray, I heard some ripping of fabric, some sharp gasps, and a muttered curse.

But then she was naked beneath me, and fuck, I wanted to eat her whole. Kneeling between her thighs, I pushed her legs wide and used my shoulders to hold them open. "There is my beautiful angel. Now lie back. I've missed you and I'm hungry."

I spread her to get better access, and she whimpered.

I licked and sucked until her fingers were tangled in my hair, tugging. She was moving restlessly under me when I slipped a finger inside her. She was slick and hot, and I had to have more.

I continued pumping my finger in and out of her, feeling her muscles clench around it. She moaned and whimpered, her hips pushing against me in desperate need.

I added a second finger, stretching her gently as I curled them to hit her sweet spot. Ari's moans turned into cries of pleasure, and she grabbed on to the sheets tightly.

I added a third, and she came. Her head fell back, and her body undulated.

I could see the frustration and need in her eyes as I removed

# DAMON

We were a tangle of lips and teeth and tongues as I fumbled blindly toward the bedroom.*

Once we were inside, I kicked the door shut behind me, our mouths still locked together. My hands roamed over her body, tracing the curves of her breasts and hips. She moaned into my mouth as I palmed her curves.

My thumbs found her nipples easily enough, and one stroke had her whimpering.

I broke the kiss and moved to her neck, nipping and licking at the sensitive flesh there. She tilted her head back, offering me more access, and I took full advantage. My hands moved down to her thighs, pulling her tighter against my straining dick.

I unzipped her jacket, letting it fall to the floor before I yanked the hem of her shirt out of her jeans, needing to feel her skin. She lifted her arms, and I tugged her shirt over her head.

* MURDER–Justin Timberlake feat. Jay-Z

"If you're really going through with this wild plan," I said, "you do it with *me*."

I slammed my lips on hers again, and this time, she kissed me back, our tongues sliding over each other's.* I released her hands and slipped mine down to her hips to pick her up and hoist her to a better position.

She wrapped her legs around me, and all bets were off.

---

* LOVE, SEX, MAGIC—Ciara feat. Justin Timberlake

"I'm not answering you. After everything that happened?" She lifted her chin. "I don't need you."

That was a direct hit. Center mass. It felt like she'd left me bleeding out on the floor. "You're mad. I understand, Ari."

"*Mad* doesn't even begin to cut it. You abandoned me."

"I *didn't* abandon you, Ari. Can't you see? If you'd have given me four damn hours, we could have come up with a plan together. Can't you fucking see? I care about you. I've loved you forever, and now I have a second chance, and you expect me to let you walk into danger alone? Stop it? You expect me to let you stop danger alone? There is no part of me that is comfortable with you doing something that's going to get you killed. I'm sorry."

She struggled in my grip, trying to wrestle me. She lifted a knee swiftly, but I deflected by shifting my hips aside.

"Ari, behave yourself, right now."

She scowled at me, her eyes narrowed. "I hate you."

"I love you."

She struggled in my grip, a tear rolling down her cheek. "Let me go, Damon."

"Not until I'm certain you're not going to hurt yourself."

"If you don't let me go, I'll—"

I slanted my lips over hers. She went perfectly still for a moment, and I pulled back just a bit, giving her space to decide what she wanted.

I knew it took mere seconds, but it felt like a lifetime as our gazes locked. It was subtle, but the answer was there when her gaze dipped to my lips and her tongue peeked out to moisten hers.

had. The one that had made me restless, itchy. The one that had made me want to break out.

Taryn sighed. "I know you've made up your mind. Just be careful, okay?"

"Thanks, Taryn."

I hung up with her and double-checked all my tools again before I zipped up my fitted jacket and turned to go, only to find a shadow in the corner.

"Where are you going, Ari?"

# DAMON

I crossed my arms and watched her warily. She really thought she was going to go after Lane herself. Anger and fury coursed through my veins. She was going to get herself killed, and she didn't even seem to care.

If she had just fucking waited a few hours, I could have fucking told her that Lucas had a lead on Michael Lane. But she was ready to run off half-cocked and likely get herself killed.

Which would piss me off even more.

"I asked where the hell you think you're going."

Ari headed for the door, and I stepped out of the shadows, grabbed one of her wrists, and pulled her toward me. I backed her up against the wall, and she tried to hit me with her other arm, which I caught easily and joined to the one above her head.

"Answer me," I demanded.

of understanding. But I guess not. Which is fine. I spent the past eight years without him. I don't need him now."

Taryn sighed. "Oh, shit. If we had more time, I would want every damned detail of the mission. Because, oh my God, from the redacted version of the report, all I know is that you were stuck in an antechamber. What happens in the vault, stays in the vault, except between us, right? Because I *neeeeeed* to know," she whined.

I laughed. "Yeah, sure. I'll fill you in."

"Ari, you seem sad. Are you okay?"

I dragged in a deep breath, roughly blinking to stay the tears. It had been one thing for Galen to tell me no. One thing for my boss to look at his liabilities for this case and choose the safe option. It was a whole other thing to have Damon look me in the face after everything that we'd shared this past week and tell me no. Like he didn't believe in me. Like he didn't trust that I could do this. It hurt. The pain settled into the grooves of my soul, making a permanent camp.

"It never would have worked out with Damon. I need to forget him. I'm just going to even the score and move on."

Taryn sighed. "God, I was really hopeful that you were finally getting something that you wanted."

"I'm fine. I'm perfectly happy. My life is good. Maybe it's not that exciting, but it's been great." My brain tried to force itself to remember how I'd felt about my life before Damon came walking back into it. I had been content. Happy.

*Had you?*

I tried not to think about that kernel of dissatisfaction I'd to deal with Galen. I'm worried you're going to walk into an ambush and get yourself hurt."

"Taryn, do you have his location or not?"

"Well, yeah, thanks to the photos from your pendant camera, which I accessed, I have partial facial recognition, and I have a location of your nemesis."

My heart pounded against my ribs. "Okay, let's rock and roll."

"If you don't report back here tomorrow morning, I'll kill you myself."

"It's going to be fine."

"You need to check in with me hourly. Text me, okay? If you don't, I'm sending Galen."

"Taryn…"

"No, Ari. This isn't like you. And this is very dangerous. Do I have full faith that you can do this? Yes. Do I think you should? No. So be careful, okay?"

"Always."

"I know that this is important to you, Ari, so do what you need to do, but come back in one piece, yeah?"

"Taryn, I've got this. Have faith."

She snorted. "Right. Because as the analyst, you're so good at having faith."

"You know, that's a solid point."

"What about Damon? Is he going to help you?"

I scowled at that. "No, he's not. He agrees with Galen. Some bullshit about it being too dangerous. I don't know. I thought on the mission, we'd…" I tried again. "I thought we had some kind

# 27

## ARI

I shoved my tools into a bag.

Taryn was working on the information I needed. Michael Lane had killed my father, and everyone was acting like I was from another planet for wanting to go after him. I wasn't. For once, I refused to sit on the sidelines, hiding. I could do something. And the fact Galen didn't trust me to do it? Well, that one really stung.

*And if you fail?*

Well, then at least I wasn't sitting on the bench. At least I was doing something about it.

*Okay, if you say so.*

My phone rang, and I dove for it. "Taryn, do you have anything for me?"

"Just so we're clear, I am doing this under duress because I love you, and I want you to have what you want. However, and that's a big *however*, I think this is dangerous. I think you need

"Don't do this. I'm not abandoning you."

I knew it would be better for her if I could walk away, finish the job, and stay gone. But I didn't want to. I wanted to do this with her. Just in the way that was safest for her. Lucas and I might need to kick over a few hornet's nests to find the prick.

She turned abruptly. "See you around."

"Ari—would you wait!"

But she kept walking, and I knew she was going to do something reckless. Watching her walk away from me hurt worse than that moment when Lane had pulled the trigger on her.

At least when he'd fired the gun, I'd had hope that she was okay.

in a stalemate. I *didn't* work for him. Technically, I worked with Lucas, so I could do as was necessary, per Lucas.

"I know you don't work for me, but like you just said, it isn't wise to go after him with no backup."

"Lane and I have a history. So, you know, this is personal, and I'm still going after him. Let me know when you have a plan. In the meantime, I'm going to head out of here."

I walked out of Galen's office with Ari hot on my heels. "So, what, that's just it? You barged into my life, got me to do this, and now you're just going to abandon me?"

I tugged her down the hallway. "Keep your voice down, Ari. You know Galen doesn't want you on this. It's dangerous. You have already been shot. I know you want to go after him. But at least wait until Galen has a team ready. I'm going to get in touch with Lucas and see if we can locate him."

"Not without me."

I scrubbed a hand down my face. "Ari, be smart. Let me locate him. Then we go in."

"That's just it? I know what that means. You're going after him alone. Without me. I wasn't a liability in the field."

I frowned. Her shoulders were stiff, her arms were crossed, and I could see it in her eyes: not anger. "Ari, that's not what I said. I'm just saying I agree with Galen a little. We need to be smarter about going after him. Don't attempt this on your own. Just wait."

"I don't want to. I don't trust that you all won't bench me."

"You're being unreasonable, Ari."

She shook her head, backing away from me.

character killed your dad. I get it, but I can't put you back out in the field. You've been shot."

And that was a point for Galen. I was worried about her. When we had finally made it out of the woods, we'd had a doctor look her over and patch her up. The shot was through and through, in and out of her tricep. She was a little lightheaded and tired, but otherwise, not too bad. The worst part for her had been Lane escaping.

I could see it on her face. Galen's message was not sinking in. She was going to go after Lane. "Ari, I see your brain churning. At the very least, you need a team. You can't go it alone. Let's wait and regroup."

Galen had other ideas. "There is no regrouping. I'm sorry you got shot, Ari," he said. "I heard there were some other odd occurrences at the auction anyway. You got lucky. Reaper isn't after you. You have to be smart. Going after Lane isn't smart." Galen turned to me. "And you, where is Prince Lucas?"

"Doing what you won't do and trying to track down Lane." For Lucas, this still wasn't over. And for me, well, I didn't like getting what I wanted on a technicality. While the deal had been to steal the necklace, not deliver it, this still felt like unbalanced scales.

Galen shook his head. "I want everyone off this. I will put together a secondary recovery team. I'll speak to the prince myself, Damon."

I smiled at him. "You recognize that I don't work for you, right?"

Galen cocked his head and met my gaze, the two of us locked

To his credit, nothing rattled Galen. He was a chilly motherfucker, that was for sure. "How I feel about my employees is none of your business. And how you feel I should be running things is none of mine. But rest assured, I will do what's best for Ari. Which, in case you're interested, includes keeping her safe."

Feeling pissy, I muttered, "That's my job."

"I see you've been doing a bang-up job. Or are you just doing the bang part?"

Ari had apparently had it with both of us. "For fuck's sake. I need you both to listen. I don't need to be kept safe. I need to go back out there and get Lane. Which one of you is going to help me?"

I wasn't going to endanger her again. Not for anything. In that split second when Lane shot her, I thought I'd die a million deaths. But I knew she needed to do this. She just needed to do this with a shadow. I wanted to give her what she needed. But I was going to make sure she was safe.

"Listen to her, Galen. She wants to be involved and won't give up. If that fucker hadn't held a gun to my head, we never would have handed over the necklace."

Galen shook his head. "I thought you were a master of this. Emotions just get you killed."

"Yes, but in this case, emotions can be useful. Besides, I think you can judge by the look on Ari's face that she's going to go after Michael Lane and that necklace whether you want her to or not."

Ari slid her gaze over to me and nodded. "I am."

Galen shook his head. "Ari, you are my most levelheaded analyst. This isn't like you. Focus. I know this Michael Lane

entry pad at some point during the weekend. According to Penny, after a guard turned up dead near one of the exits, Reaper got suspicious, so his team went over everything with a fine-tooth comb and discovered the print and the forgery. He is currently under the assumption that Michael Lane is responsible for the necklace. His people will find Lane soon enough. Time to let it go."

Ari glowered at him.* "Bullshit, I'm on ice. That lunatic is responsible for my father's death. He *shot* me. He threatened to *kill* Damon. He took something from me. Correct me if I'm wrong, but isn't it our job to recover things? We are the recovery team, are we not? I'm not usually one for revenge, but he killed my father. And now he's taken more from *me*. I am going to take something from him."

Galen put up his hands and nodded slowly at Ari. "We will go after him. But the how and when are in question. And when we do, I'll send other people in. Not you. Lane has powerful allies. Hell, Hunt has gone after him before and failed. Think about it. He'll expect retaliation. Going at these things head-on is not always the best option. You know that. We don't know where he is yet. Besides, you are emotional. And that's never a good combination."

I pushed away from the wall. "We have to fucking do something. That fuck shot at Ari. We owe him blood."

Galen lifted his brow. "I'm sure in your line of work, you've already heard this: don't make it personal."

"She's your employee. Do you even care?" I spat out, getting in his face.

* WALLS COULD TALK—Halsey

# 26

## DAMON

This was my fault. I'd come back into her life like I belonged in it, and I'd almost fucking gotten her killed.

I paced Galen's office, my eyes on Ari. She was steaming. She didn't say anything, but her features were set with grim determination. Lips flat. Eyes slightly narrowed.

Galen leaned back against his desk, looking as cool and bored as a well-fed lion. Something told me his lazy stance belied something more lethal though.

Ari was the opposite, the waves of tension making her coiled muscles practically vibrate.

"How are you recovering, Ari?"

She shrugged. "I'm fine. When do we go after him?"

Galen shook his head. "No dice. You're on ice, kid. As far as I'm concerned, we got lucky. Despite the disintegration of the plan, you got off clean thanks to us being prepared. Same can't be said for Lane. He was sloppy and left a half fingerprint on the antechamber least we weren't sitting in a jail cell or dead. But twice now, Michael Lane had come for my family, and twice he'd walked away the winner. As Damon started the car, I vowed that as soon as we were patched up and safe, I was going after Lane.

"I thought you were worried about visibility."

"I am. But use your ears. Guards are coming. We're not going to make it around on foot. Get in, Ari."

The water was choppy, and rain and waves began to fill the boat as we shoved off from the makeshift shore. I held on tight to the side as water sloshed in and the waves tipped us from side to side.

When Damon had finally rowed us to the opposite end, he jumped out and reached out to me. "Take my hand, Ari."

Without even thinking, I placed my hand in his, knowing I was safe with him. We weren't dressed for the rain, and with our clothes soaked through, a chill started to set in as we tried to move quickly to the tree line.

Without any of our gear, the trek through the woods felt treacherous with the downpour. The little light there was, was diffused and hazy in the rain.

In the distance, we could hear dogs.

"Fuck. Are they seriously sending dogs after us?" Damon said.

Twigs snapped around us, and branches whipped us in the face. I knew my hair was a sodden mess. The clips I had used to secure it were long gone, and my braid was unraveling. My hair soaked up the water like wool, curling into big fat clumps.

I didn't know how long we'd roamed around in the woods, but eventually, we came across the Jeep nestled right where Lucas had left it for us.

God, this was not the way I thought we'd be leaving. Not at all.

This definitely wasn't the worst of the worst scenarios. At

with me at a dead run. It wasn't until we hit the lake that he put me down. "Can you run?"

I smacked him. When he didn't move, I tried to shove him hard. "You did this. You brought me into this and made me care, and now you're letting him get away."

Damon took both my hands.* "Ari, don't you get it? You're more important to me than the necklace. *You*. My only goal is to get you out of here safely. That's all I care about. I don't care about the necklace. I'll find another way to repay Lucas."

I scowled at him. "No, we said we could do this. I can't fail."

He cupped my face, the rain making it hard to see as the droplets and their close cousins, my tears, clung to my lashes. "I know, Ari, but let me take care of you. When that's done and you're up to speed, we can get retribution or whatever. But for now, let me make you safe."

My head was starting to spin. I glanced back toward the mansion. I could see the guards on the top levels, flashlights ablaze, looking for people hiding.

There really was no going after Lane right now. I'd failed. To make it worse, I'd almost lost Damon. What would I have done if Lane had killed him? My heart cracked in two as I thought about not having him. He'd only been back in my life for a short time, but I loved him.

Losing him now... I wouldn't survive that.

With a groan, I followed Damon, taking his hand as he dragged us around the lake through the soft marsh to the boat hidden there.

* BANG BANG—K'naan feat. Adam Levine

men finding us. We have to get out of here. You two leave the property. I have to find Penny and tell her what's happened."

I shook my head. "We can't leave. We have to go after Lane."

Damon hauled me to his side. "You're bleeding. You're not going to make it if Reaper's men are coming. We need to focus on getting out."

I glowered at my shoulder, hating that he was right. "I think our best egress route is that way," I said, pointing to the south, around the lake, in the opposite direction of where Lane had gone. "We have to go get him. We can't just wait."

Damon tugged me behind him. "I've got her, Lucas. You get out of here. We'll have to regroup."

Lucas nodded, eyeing me carefully. "Get her to a hospital."

"A hospital?" I argued as I fought Damon's grip. "Seriously?" I tried to shake him off, but he easily tugged me behind him. *Think, Ari. Think.* If I didn't get Lane now, I'd never get him. I had to go after him.

"You've been shot, Ari," Damon shouted, and I could hear the fear in his voice.

Water was running down his face, soaking his hair, matting it to his forehead. He brushed the sudden curls out of his eyes. "You're shot," he said more quietly. "We're done."

I shook my head and fought his hold. "We can do this. We just need—"

Before I knew it, Damon picked me up and flipped me over his shoulder. I was already wet and soaked through, and my arm was killing me now.

Lucas stepped back into the shadows, and Damon took off

## 25

## ARI

The rain kept coming down hard, stinging my skin.

"Damon, stop him before he gets away," I groaned as my arm started to throb. I had to move. He was escaping. Why wasn't Damon doing anything? I struggled in his arms, forcing him to put me down.

Damon shook his head. "Are you joking, Ari? You've been shot."

I slipped and stumbled in the mud as I tried to start in the direction Lane had gone. "But he's getting away."

Damon wrapped his arm around my waist. "No, sweetheart. Stay with me. You're hurt. This is my fault. Let me get you to safety first."

Before I could argue my case, Lucas came running back, all the while shaking his head. "I think Lane did something to trigger an alarm. More guards are coming. I disabled the cameras back here, so we have a moment, but the last thing we want is Reaper's

While Lucas ran off, I continued to roll on the ground with Michael; then suddenly, the gun went off, a bullet pierced my left arm, and I felt like I'd downed molten heat with a pain chaser.

I screamed, tears welling in my eyes, as Michael rolled to his feet, snatched up the Royal Heart, and took off running.

Damon was on me as soon as he stopped trembling. "Oh shit, Ari. Fuck." He wrapped his arms around me. "I've got you. Shit. Ari. I'm so damned sorry."

"He's getting away," I croaked.

He shook his head even as he scooped me into his arms. "Doesn't matter. You are what's important here," he yelled over the howling wind.

I clutched my wounded arm, trying to stop the bleeding, but the pain was too much. I'd done all this and failed him anyway.

Damon growled, "Ari, run, damn it. Take the necklace and run."

But I couldn't. I couldn't walk away from him.

I stood frozen for only a moment, clutching the necklace in my hand, as Michael pressed the gun harder against Damon's neck. The rain was pounding down even harder now, turning the dirt to mud beneath our feet. In the distance, I could hear guards getting closer. But they wouldn't be here in time to save us.

Michael's grip tightened on the gun, and I could see the feverish gleam in his eye. He was enjoying this, reveling in the power he held over us. I knew I had to act fast before something terrible happened.

In one swift motion, I tossed the necklace just over his shoulder, and when he whirled to look at it, I dove right for him, knocking him off-balance. He stumbled backward, the gun firing wildly as he fell to the ground and dropped it.

I threw myself at him even as Damon and Lucas rushed for me. Damon tried to pull me loose as I attempted to whale on Michael. Michael pulled something out of his pocket and hit Damon with it. He fell to his knees, jerking.

*Christ, a Taser?*

Michael crawled toward the gun, and I screamed, "No," landing on him before he could grab it. He turned me over, but I managed to bite his arm.

"You bitch," he spat.

At the same time, we heard one of the guards' footsteps on the pebbled gravel in the maze.

"Shit, I'll deal with it," said Lucas. "Damon, are you good to deal with him?"

it wasn't yet dawn, and with the rain and the dark clouds? No fucking way.

Lucas was busy packing away our harnesses. "Lucas, can we steal a car? Maybe one of the diplomatic ones?"

The rain came down in heavier splats as thunder rumbled above us. "Reaper will notice if you take a diplomatic car. But maybe one of the staff ones. Let's go."

We headed around the house to the staff parking lot, but before we could see if any of the cars were viable, I heard a clicking sound.

Lucas and Damon stopped immediately. I turned around slowly to find Michael Lane holding a gun with a silencer on Damon. How the fuck had he smuggled a weapon in here?

"Gentlemen, Ms. Denton, as if I didn't recognize you. You're famous to me, darling. Your father was a worthy adversary. You'll hand over the Royal Heart now, won't you?"

Lucas stepped forward. "If you looked, you'd find that the Royal Heart is in the vault. But that shouldn't matter, because it's not yours."

"Hand it over," Lane gritted out as he pointed the gun at Damon.

My throat constricted, and Lucas sighed. "Hand it over, Ari."

I went to pull up my top, but Damon shouted, "No, Ari, you and Lucas get out of here. Go. He won't shoot me. It's a bluff."

I shook my head as I peeled the necklace and body tape from my skin. I opened the pack for Lane. "Put your gun away. I have what you want. Leave him alone."

He levered the gun even higher this time and pressed it to Damon's neck when I hesitated.

worrying about who to call for a lawyer. I'd let my guard down and showed my true feelings because I hadn't thought I would get another opportunity.

Meeting Damon's eyes on the outside was going to be tricky, especially if he didn't still feel the same way. I heard his muttered curses as we worked our way through the vents and eventually to our original escape tunnel. The route popped us right back out where we'd expected, and I inhaled deeply, relishing the fresh air.

Above us, thunder cracked, and the sky opened up.

Around the bend a quarter mile into the woods, we'd be home free. The rain pelted in hard fat drops, stinging my skin. Behind me, Damon bellowed, "Wait for us."

What was taking so long? Lucas was still welding the gate shut when Damon caught up to me and shouted something that I couldn't hear over the howl of the wind. Eventually, Damon took my hand and tried to drag me back.

"What are you doing? It's this way," I said.

Lucas came running up. "You missed the checkpoint. Guards discovered that car a couple of hours ago. They assumed a drunken guest parked like an asshole. It's not an option. We need to try for the boathouse."

Just as he said that, a shifting cloud obscured the moonlight.

"Fuck," Damon cursed as rain spattered the ground around us. "We're not going to make it on a boat with the rain, with no light, and then through the woods."

I turned back toward our original egress. Tiny pellets of rain fell rapidly enough to partially blind me. It was hard enough to find the way through the woods in the daylight, but

The relief hit me so fast that my knees gave out, and I slumped against Damon's back. "You just saved our lives, bro."

"When you two missed your checkpoint, I figured I needed to come in for a rescue. We don't leave teammates behind." Lucas eyed the knife. "If you two don't mind, I figured you wanted to get out of here before anyone came looking for you and asking questions."

When Damon still didn't sheathe his knife, Lucas put his hands up and turned around slowly, showing Damon he had nothing up his sleeve. All I cared about was that he'd come to get us and there was hope of not getting arrested.

"You can see my tool kit from here," Lucas said. "I just have the ropes and rappelling equipment to get us all up and out of here. I'm unarmed, Damon. I'm your friend."

Suddenly I could feel the tension ease out of Damon. He cleared his throat and then nodded, tucking the knife back into his boot. "Thank you, Lucas."

The prince nodded.[*] "Did we get the necklace?"

I lifted the top part of my shirt where I'd taped it back to my sternum as Lucas put a harness on me, then clipped something to the rope. With the gloves Damon had given me, the climb up was pretty easy, but I was also helped along the way.

Up at the top, Lucas had left glow-in-the-dark markers showing the path. It was a tight fit, and I worried about Damon making it through. But if Lucas had, Damon would. At least I hoped he would.

I had been thinking about never seeing daylight again and

[*] MONEY ON THE DASH—Elley Duhé feat. Whethan

"You're impossible."

"Yeah, but you love me."

When he'd said he loved me earlier, I hadn't been able to process a response. The slow smile that spread over his lips now was catching as I said it back to him, "Yes, I love you."

He took my hand before kissing it. "It's going to be okay, you know." He pulled me into his big body, and I knew he was trying to shield me from the coming horror that was going to be our lives. He knew what to expect, but I did not. And I was scared.

I checked my watch and saw it was four-thirty in the morning. Still at least an hour from discovery. After the festivities last night, everyone was probably completely hungover.

In that moment, the big vent grate above us creaked, and Damon immediately tucked my face into his chest and backed me up against the wall. He turned his back to me, his arms splayed behind him, and I noticed a knife in his palm.

"Damon, you promised, for fuck's sake."

"Just let me make sure you're safe; then you can lecture me."

I kept my gaze trained on the door, but no one was coming that way. The sounds were definitely coming from that grate overhead, and shortly, a pair of feet dangled, then gave way to calves, thighs, and a tool belt, all in black. My heart hammered against my ribs. Damon's whole body went stiff, ready to pounce. I could feel the tension as he leaned over slightly onto the balls of his feet. The person who dropped down had a black mask over their face.

I wished to God I had a weapon now too. I wasn't going to let Damon fight alone. Then the thief grabbed his mask and tugged it off, revealing Lucas Newsome.

# 24

## ARI

Damon brushed his hands along my edges, trying to smooth out my hair while we dressed, but it had a mind of its own. I'd tried to knot the massive braid into a bun, aware that some of the puffs had made a break for it and were trying to unravel. As I pulled my clothes back on, I glanced around. "Damon, where is my underwear?"

The corner of his lips lifted into a smirk. "I don't know. We were in a very big hurry to take them off."

I scowled at him. "Now is not the time for jokes. Seriously where is my underwear?"

I was forced to slide back into my slacks without them, and I sat there uncomfortably until he pulled them from his pocket.

"Oh, these things?"

I tried to snatch them from his grip. "Give them to me."

He kept them just out of reach. "No, I think I'm going to hold on to these," he said as he stuck them back into his pocket.

I barked out a laugh before I could even think to hold it back. "You, woman, are after my virtue. I knew it." The trill of her laughter was a sound I wanted to bottle and keep with me forever. "Can we get back to my perfect date now?"

"By all means."

"Well, you see, I was going to turn up with a clichéd helicopter ride."

She nodded her head, grinning. "Now you're just showing off." Her eyes crinkled at the corners as they danced.

"No. If I were showing off, I'd mention that this is all taking place in Paris."

Ari shook her head. "Of course it would be. I think I would've liked that date very much. Any date."

I wove our fingers together. If I could rewind the clock several weeks and never have dragged her into this, I would. We were here because of me. "It's just you and me, okay? None of the rest of it matters. Even if this is the only time I get with you, it was perfect."

Tears filled her eyes before gently spilling down her cheeks, and I wiped them away with the backs of my fingers.

"Just so you know," I said, "all I've done—everything—was because I was trying to be better. To be deserving."

"You always been good enough." She kissed my palm before sitting up, wiping her tear-streaked face, then putting her Ari mask back on.

*Perfect.*

could be. I wanted to be the kind of person she could be proud to be seen with.

"I didn't count on getting arrested though," I muttered.

"I've been trying to figure a way out of here," she said. "But I can't visualize it. For once I have no solutions."

I rubbed a hand down her back as I felt her start to tense. "Shhh. We'll figure it out. So, on the off chance that we don't get arrested coming out of this, what does that mean for us?"

"I'm not sure. What do you picture happening?" she asked shyly.

I met her gaze. "Well, for starters, I take you out on a proper date. One that doesn't involve an auction. Maybe I could take you back to the drive-in. A little picnic just for us."

She giggled. "Not bad."

"That would only be the start. I'd take you to my favorite restaurant for dessert."

"You said the magic word. *Dessert*. My mom always let me eat dessert first. Though it was a trick—I'd get to eat a quarter of it first, then have to eat dinner to get the rest."

"She was devious. I think I would have liked your mom."

"I think she would have liked you too. She would have gathered you right up like a lost duckling. Fed you, clucked over you. That was kind of her thing."

I pulled her close and kissed her brow. From what I remembered, Ari had rarely talked about her mother. Paul had been the same. "I would have appreciated her clucking. Lord knows I needed it."

With a sniffle, she changed the subject. "Is dessert the end of our date? Or are we having another kind of dessert?"

Artistic, talented, bright. He has a similar story to mine. Bounced from home to home, couldn't seem to find a place to stick."

"That must have been hard."

"It was. I finally found him years after we'd been split up. He'd run away from his last place. By that point, I'd lost your father. I thought maybe if I could teach Max some things, keep him off the streets, that things would be better for him. I went so far as to adopt him and everything. But it didn't change much. He's still a magnet for trouble."

"You must really love him."

I shrugged, trying to distract myself from the way my eyes stung thinking about Max. "He was hanging out with the wrong crowd and kept getting in trouble. The problem is, now that I have money, the danger just shifts tax brackets. So now, instead of trying to keep low-life thugs from beating his ass because he owes them money, I mostly write checks to endowment funds."

"That's a lot to go through."

"What can I say? He's my brother. But this time he's bitten off more than he can chew, and even when I bail him out, it's going to cost both me and Lucas. It's a mess."

"Do you really think you *can* save him?"

"He deserves a shot. I got one, and without it, what would've happened to me? I'm just trying to do right by him. Give him a shot that most of us never get."

"You're a good man."

She meant it. Her eyes were shining, open, bright. She really meant that. She thought I was a good man. In that moment, I wanted to do everything in my power to prove I

adrenaline, the excitement. And in this case, we broke into this vault to do some good."

"I know that you and my father had rules about who you would steal from and who you didn't rob. And that idea is exciting. It's like being Robin Hood."

He shrugged. "I wasn't always Robin Hood. For a long time, I was trying to survive. But once I got more stable, I wanted to honor Paul's memory. Do some good with the shot he gave me."

I cocked my head. "Why *this* job?"

I could see that he didn't want to tell me, but he swallowed hard and gave me an answer anyway. "I took in my foster brother. The kid didn't have the same opportunities that I had. There was no Paul Denton there to pull him out of a scrape."

"What happened to him?"

"He's been working on getting his footing. He spent a lot of time in survival mode, so he's had a rough go finding his thing. Recently, he crossed a dangerous man, and now my brother owes him a debt. Lucas is going to help Max either way, but I feel like I owe him this favor. I vowed I would never, ever come back, that I'd stay out of your life, but I broke that vow to save my brother. And once I saw you, I couldn't walk away."

# DAMON

"Tell me about your brother," Ari whispered softly.

I lifted my head and kissed her nose. "He's a good kid, mostly.

"I spent far too much time wondering what you tasted like. I thought about kissing you so many times. Like that time you got ditched by your friends to go to the drive-in and I volunteered to take you instead."

"See, you weren't a total asshole at the time."

"Hardly. I'd heard Todd Strong wanted to ask you out. That idiot was known for being handsy. I didn't want him pawing at you, so I told him I was your boyfriend."

Wait, he'd done what? "What? Why?"

"He was a dick and tended not to ask for consent. You deserved better."

"I don't know. Talking to you, I realized that my dad was just trying to protect me. I've been angry with him for so long. It feels weird to not carry the weight of that, if that makes any sense."

He nodded. "I think he'd be very proud of you. He just had no idea of what to do with a young daughter who was obviously desperate to follow in his footsteps. He was proud of you but at the same time he wanted to protect you from this life."

"What about you? Who's going to protect you? I don't want you hurt like he was in the end."

"Losing your father changed me fundamentally. He saved my life. He taught me. He died on my watch. I wanted to be worthy of him saving my life."

"All I wanted was to *not* be like him. And now you are. I can see why you do it though," I whispered against his skin.

He brushed his thumb over my cheek and then down my jaw to lift my chin until I met his gaze. "There's a thrill to it. The

"I still can't believe you never said anything." All that time I'd spent pining after him, and he hadn't given me the time of day.

"What was I supposed to say? I couldn't very well tell Paul I had it bad for his daughter. That would not have worked out well."

"You could have told me." I lifted my head to meet his gaze. "Hardly seems fair."

He played with the end of my braid, and when he spoke, his voice was soft. "It's not fair. But regardless of what happens, I want you to know how I feel." He licked his lips. "How I've always felt."

I could hear the gravity in his voice.

"What, Damon?"

"Ari, I have loved you since we were young. It didn't take me long after that to *fall* in love with you."

My heart stopped, unable to beat. My breath was thin and reedy. "What?"

"I didn't know what it was then. I thought you were curious and cute and likely to get yourself in trouble. But mostly I wanted to look out for you. Not just because you were Paul's daughter. I loved your determination. I admired it."

"I wish I'd known how you felt. I think it would've made me a little less jealous of your relationship with my dad."

He shook his head. "It certainly would've distracted me more. God, what would we have done if I'd told you then?"

"Oh, I would've begged you very awkwardly to kiss me. Just like in the movies."

His chuckle was low, sending a vibration through my body.

of hair there. I didn't even know how I could laugh right now. If someone had told me a month ago that I'd be wrapped around Damon Hunt and know just how talented he was with his hands, I'd have told them they were high.

"That works. Except for that pesky problem of how we got into this room in the first place. No one could have accidentally figured out that code to get in the door. And no doubt we'll be searched, so they're going to find the necklace, discover that one of them is a fake, and we'll still go to jail."

"Hello? I'm just spitballing here. Remember, there are no bad ideas."

I laughed. "There are bad ideas. So many bad ideas."

His gaze searched mine as he lifted his head. "You okay?" he asked softly.

What a hell of a question. Was I? Physically, I was sore in places I hadn't even known could be sore. But I'd also had more fun than I'd ever had in or outside a bed. When it came to the heart stuff, I was less sure.

It may be easier locking the feelings away, but they were all out now. Not to mention, I didn't want to. This weekend with Damon… I couldn't go back on it. I didn't want to. I'd started out a completely different woman. Now I was someone new. And new Ari liked letting him in.

*But what if it hurts later?*

Well, then it would hurt, but I'd survive it.

"Yeah, I'm good."

"Hardly seems fair that I finally have you in my arms where you belong and I'll have to give you up."

## ARI

I woke up surrounded by heat, with Damon acting as my cushion. All that cushioned his back was the carpeting and our clothes.

That couldn't be comfortable. But I couldn't help but lie there for a moment, thinking. In a matter of hours my life would change. *Unless you find a way out of here.*

There had to be another way.

I tried to get up, and he mumbled, "Don't you dare move."

I flushed from head to toe at hearing the gravel in his voice. "I don't know how long we've been in here, but we do need to get dressed. That door is going to open at some point, and I'd rather not be naked when it does."

He shrugged and merely held me tighter. "That would be one way to explain what happened. We snuck off for a little personal time, got carried away, and accidentally got locked in here, where I had to ravish you."

I laughed into his chest, my fingers playing with the dusting

She hesitated, then slowly nodded.

"I'll be gentle." Slowly, I slid my finger into the tightness of her ass. I just brushed over it, making her breath hitch. "Mmmm. I love the way your pussy and ass feel around my fingers. Your little muscles are so tight. I can't wait to feel them squeezing my cock again."

"Oh God."

I thrust my finger in and out of her ass while I sucked on her clit and licked her clean. Her body trembled as I increased the pressure on her ass to match my rhythm on her clit.

She started to shake harder, and I felt her pussy start to pulse again.

"Come for me again, Ari."

"Oh...oh...oh hell! Damon!"

Her pussy clamped down on my fingers, and I felt her all the way in her core. She was so tight, I worried I was hurting her.

"Oh. My. God."

As she started to relax, I slowly withdrew my hands from her body. I pulled her into my arms and held her close. I liked the feel of her soft curves against me, and I thought I might want to keep her there.

Actually, I knew I would do anything to keep her there for the rest of my life.

Ari Denton had been made for me.

I pulled her braid back as I kissed her deep and made love to her, wanting to sit as deep as I could.

She fluttered around me again, and my orgasm hit me so hard, I came in hot, hard spurts, filling her tight pussy until she was overflowing. And I kept fucking her, making my permanent home. Fuck, I was never leaving. I was going to stay right here and come again and again. Maybe I wouldn't stop until I'd finally fucked a baby into her. And maybe not even then.

*Holy fucking Christ.*

Was I dying? I was pretty sure I was dying.

I was already coming down from my orgasm when I realized her pussy was still pulsing around my cock.

"Shit! Are you okay?"

She pulled back, panting. "Yeah. I just… My orgasms are different."

"You're still coming?"

She tucked her head into my shoulder, but I could feel the nod.

"Wow. I think I should definitely help you ride it out."

I felt more than heard her chuckle as her nails dug into the flesh of my shoulder. "H-how?"

"Let me show you." I eased out of her body, kissing patches of exposed skin as I went. I parted her thighs, smiling at how her pussy still fluttered. "I know just what my angel needs. Watch me, Ari." I slid my tongue over her clit.

Her eyes rolled back as she arched off the carpet.

I did it again and again until she was shuddering under me.

When her cries started to get higher, I swiped my finger through her slickness, then gently over her tight pucker. "This okay?"

I didn't even try to stop myself; I thrust forward and sank to the hilt inside her. Her slick pussy lips stretched tight around me.

"Oh God," I groaned, my vision going gray as the pleasure rolled through me.

She cried out, her hands digging into my ass.

I retreated until I was almost out, then sank back in until I bottomed out, making us both gasp.

I fisted her braid as gently as I could. "Eyes on me, beautiful. I want to watch your face when you come around my cock."

She gazed up at me, her eyes on mine. She opened her mouth to speak, but I kissed her hard, my tongue mimicking what my cock was doing.

I pulled back out and then thrust in again, and again, and again, loving the way she took all nine inches.

I could feel her tightening around my cock, and I started to pick up my pace, making her writhe beneath me. I wanted to make her come, and I wanted to see the pleasure on her face.

I kept my pace, determined to make her come apart before I paid any attention to the electric bolt wrapping itself around my spine. But my rhythm slipped and stuttered with each whisper of my name, each flutter of her pussy around my cock.

"That's it, Ari. Give me everything, angel. Come for me."

"Yes, Damon! Oh God!"

She cried out and buried her face in my neck as she started to come. Her pussy clamped down on my cock, pulsing as she rode out her orgasm. I could feel her coming around me, and my balls drew up.

my boxers. And now she was begging for my cock? "I know, sweetheart. I'm sorry. Next time. I'll take my time."

She shook her head. "I don't want to wait. I haven't dated anyone in over a year. I'm on the pill."

Oh God. I wasn't going to survive this.

"Ari. I don't ever have unprotected sex. Not ever."

She licked her bottom lip as she threw her head back. "Okay, maybe just the tip. I just want to feel you. Please, Damon. Just the tip?"

I sank my hand into her hair again before I kissed her deep and ground my cock against her pussy. "Do you know what you're asking me? Once I start fucking you raw, I'll never be able to stop. I will come inside you so deep, and every time, I'll pretend I'm fucking a baby into you."

"Damon…"

I didn't let her finish. "I will be an addict. I'll need to come inside you raw all the time—your pussy and your ass. I will take the greatest pleasure in watching that pretty pussy and that perfect rosebud of an asshole stretch around my cock, then dry with my come. You don't know what you're saying."

Ari's fingers tightened in my hair. "I do, Damon. I want it all. With you I want everything."

"Fuck me." My voice came out rough as I shoved my boxer briefs down, freeing my cock.

I couldn't help my groan when I pressed the tip of my cock through her slick folds.

I wanted to take it slow, but Ari grabbed my ass and pulled me forward.

with pleasure. Her lips were swollen from our kissing, her hair a wild mess around her head. I couldn't remember a more beautiful woman in my life.

I lifted my fingers to my mouth and groaned as I tasted her on my fingers again.

"That's a fucking beautiful sight," I murmured.

After sliding my hand up over her taut belly to her bra, I unhooked the front clasp, then pushed her bra down her arms, releasing her.

I watched her as she watched me, her breaths coming in pants. Her breasts heaved. Her nipples were dark and swollen. Her body was flushed with pleasure.

I trailed my fingers down her stomach before toying with her belly button. When I slid a finger into it, she giggled, and I grinned down at her.

I loved it when she laughed. "That's my favorite sound, Ari."

My fingers hooked the waistband of her underwear, before I tugged it down over her hips. Her pussy was flushed with arousal as I pushed between her legs.

"I need to be inside you."

Ari's pupils dilated as she reached for me, but I still hesitated.

"Fuck." How could I be so stupid?

She started to push into a sitting position. "What's wrong?"

"No condoms."

She groaned, her legs scissoring. "But, Damon, I need it. I need you to fill me. I'm so desperate."

"Fuck." As I kissed up her body, she rocked against me. At this point I was just trying to maintain control and not come in legs. I made quick work of my own clothes but left my boxers on as I settled myself between her thighs.

I flicked her clit over the fabric of her panties, and she arched her back, crying my name.

When I pulled her panties to the side and slid a finger into her wet heat, she writhed against me. Her pussy was so fucking wet. I had to have it. I slid my finger back out and sucked it into my mouth. "You taste amazing."

"More," she groaned.

I slid a second finger in and sucked on her nipple again as she rode my hand. She was so fucking wet and tight. I used my unoccupied hand to play with her other nipple.

"I want you to come on my tongue."

Her eyes widened as I slid my fingers out of her and then sucked her nub into my mouth.

I shifted my weight as I went for her knee and then pushed it back to open her up even more.

"Damon," she moaned, her breathing coming harder.

I slid my fingers back inside her, and she cried out as I licked at her clit. I set up a steady rhythm of fingers and tongue as she gripped my hair and writhed beneath me.

She gave a cry as I flicked her clit again, and then I felt the tremors start. Her orgasm was so fucking hot that I couldn't stop myself. I shoved my fingers deeper and used my tongue to lap her up.

She cried out, her body convulsing as she creamed on my fingers, her pussy pulsing as she rode out her orgasm.

I licked her slowly as her body calmed, and then slid my fingers out of her. I looked down at her face, which was flushed

She rocked against my cock again, and this time I gave in, sliding my hands down her sides and under the waistband of her pants to find her ass. While palming her with my big hands, I pulled her hard against my erection, moving her how I needed.

I groaned murmuring against her skin, "So fucking perfect, Ari. I've wanted you for so long."

I sucked her nipple in again, and she gave a moan of pleasure.

"I feel like I'm coming out of my skin," I said.

"I'm not doing anything."

"You know what you're doing," I groaned.

I slid my hands to her thighs. When I felt the edge of her panties under her pants, I groaned and pulled her closer. "God, Ari. You are so soft and so damned wet."

"It's because of you, Damon. I want to feel you. I want—"

"What is it, Ari?"

After licking her lips nervously, she added, "I want to come. You're the only one who's ever made me come before. I want you to feel it."

"Fuck," I moaned, knowing she felt how my cock was more than desperate to be free.

I slid my hands to the edge of her panties. Then I tried to push higher, but it was impossible with her pants in the way. "I want to taste you."

"Please, Damon…"

I shifted us around so she was on her back on the carpet in the antechamber, her tits spilling out of her flimsy bra. I hooked my thumbs in her waistband, then tugged her pants down her lithe bra, with the Royal Heart in the velvet pouch taped to her sternum.

Ari's eyes locked on mine as I brushed a thumb over a sensitive tip. When she moaned softly in response, my cock jerked against my zipper. Gently, she untaped the black pouch and placed it on the platform next to her bag of tools.

Licking my lips, unable to resist the temptation, I leaned in to kiss her nipples through her bra, first one and then the other, drawing the tight peaks into my mouth along with the lace. "I love your breasts, Ari."

She had the world's most perfect breasts. Cupping the high peaks, I teased her nipples, watching her closely. When I leaned forward again, sucking one of her delectable peaks into my mouth and pulling deep, she gave a sharp gasp.

I moaned, tugging her nipple harder. She tasted like honey with a hint of salt. Her hands slid from my hair to grip my shoulders as I sucked.

"Damon."

Her breathing was already coming harder, faster. I felt her hips shift on my lap. My cock twitched in response to the friction of her moving so deliciously against me. I wanted the sensation to last forever.

She threw her head back and slid her pussy against my cock, our clothes still too much of a barrier. Her fingers threaded in my hair once more, holding me to her.

I smiled against her skin when I released her nipple, and she gave a whimper of displeasure, only to moan again as I took the other tip into my mouth.

# DAMON

I leaned in and captured her lips with mine while lacing my fingers into her hair and pulling her closer.* Our tongues danced in a heated tango, exploring each other's mouths as if discovering them for the first time.

I shifted her so she could straddle my lap.

I moved my hand to her face and cupped her cheek. She was so damned soft and perfectly beautiful that it made me ache. I didn't know what I had done in my life to deserve her, but I was eternally grateful.

Deepening our connection, I sucked lightly on her lower lip. Ari slid her hands into my hair as she angled her body higher, bringing her breasts into closer range of my mouth.

Sliding my hands up her back, I gently eased her braid out of the way and went for her zipper. I tugged her black top up and over her head, leaving her in nothing but a gold-and-black

* NEW RULES–Dua Lipa

Ari watched me carefully, her dark eyes wide. "I wonder what would have happened if you'd kissed me back then."

I shook my head. "That would have been a disaster. Because then I would have been totally into this girl, known how she tasted, and inadvertently broken her heart."

"But what about now?" she asked quietly.

"Now I'm a man who selfishly pulled you into this mess."

"Are you going to break my heart?"

"Isn't it already broken, Ari? I've gotten you caught."

"Not yet." She grinned. "By my watch, we still have several hours until we're really caught. How are we going to use those?"

I was *obsessed* with you. I just wanted you to see me, for the love of Christ."

"Well, fuck, I did see you. I was trying to be cool. I was also trying to survive, but I was sort of fascinated by my mentor's nosy kid. Every time you snuck out, I knew. I could tell. You had this mischievous look on your face."

She laughed at that. "Oh no, I thought I was being so stealthy."

"You weren't. You were completely adorable. All I wanted was to impress you in that older-guy-who-knows-shit kind of way. You were cute, but you were too young."

"I was not too young. I was fifteen."

"Which was too young. I was eighteen, and I thought I was so much older. Honestly, I was just a clueless kid who didn't know anything."

"I wish I had known. I wouldn't have tried so hard."

"You were always my Ari. That's how I saw it in my head. It's why I never told your dad you were sneaking out. You know, I was looking out for you."

"Well, thank you for that, but now I feel like a fool."

"You weren't. Because what you wanted, I wanted. I just was in pure survival mode."

"And now?"

I swallowed hard. "Well, now you're my wife."

She laughed softly. "We can stop pretending here."

"I haven't been pretending since we got out of that limo. For me, this is a fantasy I've let myself live. One I never dared to hope for."

realized you were my last hope of feeling close to him again. So you didn't do this to me. I chose it myself."

"I need to feel like you're capable of making better choices than that."

She shrugged, then eased off her heels before rubbing her arches. "Well, sorry to disappoint you."

"You are a mystery, Ari Denton."

"Am I?"

"I don't know. I guess in my head, I always thought you would rebel against the old man. Against being the good girl."

She wrinkled her nose. "I really hated it when you called me a good girl."

"Did you? There's nothing wrong with being a good girl, Ari."

"Back then, I loathed it. I wanted you to *notice* me."

I furrowed my brow. "I still can't believe what you told me."

"What, that I had a crush on you? I still can't believe I *ever* told you. But I mean, hey, I was young. You were older and worldly. Also hot."

I laughed at that. "Was I worldly? I was a hot mess. A dumb kid your father had to save."

She shook her head. "No, you were his legacy. And I hated you for it. I wanted to be you. But I also wanted you to notice me."

All that time I'd spent watching Paul's daughter ignore me and wondering what I'd done to make her hate me, and she'd been watching me? "You were serious about that? When you told me, I thought it was bullshit that sort of tumbled out."

"Oh, I was serious. Come on, anyone with half a brain knew.

*Fuck.*

Despite all my promises to keep her safe, I was going to fail.

Something pricked the back of my lids, and I tried to drive back the emotion.

I took Ari's hand and pulled her to me so she stood mere inches away. "I know this wasn't the plan. And I know this whole thing is fucked. And I'm sorry. But I can save you. Let me save you. Hell, at least give you a fighting chance. Let me do what I couldn't do for Paul."

She watched me mutinously for a long moment, her eyes welling up with tears. "Why don't we focus on saving both of us?" She swiped her tears away with the backs of her hands. "Sit down. We can do this." She sat back against the wall and sat. "Let's work backward. How did we end up here?"

She really wasn't going to give up? "You're serious?"

"Yes. Damon. We're not giving up. We have some small explosives, right?"

What we had wouldn't do the trick. Not to mention, it would bring unwanted attention. We were stuck in here until the morning. "I'd rather not have the guards joining us for the moment. I want to at least spend the next six hours or so pretending everything is going to be okay." I eased myself down next to her. "Why did you say yes to this job, Ari?"

"Honestly? Even if Galen hadn't made me, I would have eventually said yes anyway."

I lifted a brow. "What?"

"I was so incredibly jealous of your relationship with my father. After a day or so, I would have come to my senses and

What was I supposed to say to that? No? That was bullshit because I didn't have a way out of this.

"Ari, I'm so sorry. You wouldn't be here if it weren't for me. In the morning when they come to let us out, you're going to tell them that I forced you into this. You didn't know what was going to happen. Do you understand?"

"In the morning…which means that right now, you are giving up on us?"

I sighed. "Ari, I'm not giving up on us. I just need you to see your way out."

"What you're telling me is you are giving up."

"Look around, Ari. We don't have a lot of options. When someone comes through that door in the morning, they are going to mean business. Your safety, your way out, is to insist I forced you into it. Lie and do it well. Practice now. You're going to need it."

"I'm not just going to abandon you."

Why was she being stubborn about this? "You'd better abandon me, Ari. After everything your father gave me, I would never forgive myself if you went to jail for this. For me. Absolutely not."

Ari shook her head and pushed to her feet, her determined expression plastered on her face. It was one I'd seen often. Furrowed brow, intense gaze, teeth tugging on her bottom lip. "So let's figure a way out of this."

I knew what she was trying to do. Ari Denton, my slice of sunshine. Unfortunately, I had dragged her down. There was no way out of this.

At least I really fucking hoped so.

I'd spent my whole life trying to avoid becoming like my father, and I could very well end up being the one Denton to ever be cuffed.

# DAMON

How could I tell her that she had risked her life and her freedom on a gamble that I couldn't fucking pull off?

Because that was what was happening. I knew no way out of here. The vents above us were sealed. Hell, were they even big enough? And worse, Ari was looking at me like I would have the answers because that was the lie I had told her. And that was who I was. A liar. A brute. Someone who didn't deserve love.

Except I didn't want to believe that. Being with her *made* me not want to believe that. Being with her made me want to believe that I could be a better man. That I wasn't that same kid her father had literally saved from the streets.

I kept trying to think my way out of the box.

Finally, Ari's soft voice filled the room, and she leaned her back on the wall. "We're trapped, aren't we?"

I swallowed hard. "No, we're not trapped. I just don't know a way out yet."

"Doesn't that usually mean *trapped*?"

*She has a point.* "Don't give up on me, Ari."

"I'm not giving up on you. But we *are* trapped, are we not?"

Until now. That little voice inside me wanted to shout, rail against the unfairness of it. But that wouldn't have done any good. And we'd still be stuck. "What do we do?"

"I-I don't know, Ari. I don't have a manual for this."

I paced back and forth in front of the door, trying to make my brain engage so that the fear and its bestie, rolling nausea, didn't overtake me. "So what, we just stay in here until this thing opens in the morning? With very angry security staring at us and wondering how we got in here in the first place?"

"I wish I had an answer for you, Ari. I'm focused on figuring out how the hell we're going to get out of here."

My panic was not helping. I knew that. I had to stay calm. "Okay, sorry."

"All right, look, at the very least, Lucas knows we're in here. If we don't show up, he will come looking. It's not ideal, but it's all we've got right now."

"Jesus. How did this get so fucked up?"

"We might have triggered something in the locking mechanism," he suggested.

I shook my head. "I went over the schematics a million times. This wasn't us. This door should open. Something else happened."

"We may never know. Come on, help me try and figure a way out of here. Let's walk the room again."

As I watched him pace, check the vents, and climb on top of the tables, I realized something: we were trapped, and I was scared, but he was still calm. Maybe not comfortable, but calm. He was going to get us out of here, one way or another.

We rounded the corner in the antechamber. Then Damon stopped us to help secure the necklace under the bodice of my clothes. I did a quick check of my appearance and gave him the nod when I was ready.

At the door, he tugged, but nothing happened. When he tugged again with still no budging from the door, my gut twisted and dread settled into my soul.

Damon's voice was soft as he tugged and tugged and tugged again. "No. No, no, no."

I tried to shove down the sense of impending doom threatening to envelop me. We would get out of here. We weren't stuck. We couldn't be.

*Fucking hell.*

But the sat phone didn't work, and as I knocked on the walls, I knew they were concrete. "Laser cutter won't work for this."

Damon wasn't listening. He'd already stopped tugging at the door. He took out his flashlight and inspected the hinges. When he apparently found them not to his liking, he meticulously checked the walls, then the vents.

When he turned back to me, he hung his head. "Fuck, Ari. I don't know what happened. There's no way out."

"What?" I gasped. "There has to be a vent or something."

He pointed at the corners he'd just inspected. "You see, there and there, too small. The only hope I had was an access vent in case something needed repairs. According to the blueprints, there should be one up there. But it's sealed from the other side." He pointed at the ceiling directly above the central platform.

A chill skated over my skin. Everything had gone perfectly.

The Royal Heart was spectacular. The centerpiece of it was a massive diamond pendant; that thing was nearly as big as a toddler's fist. It was one thing to have a replica in hand. It was another to know we were going to be holding the real deal in a minute. *Holy hell.*

Damon approached the pedestal carefully, and I handed him the replacement. I knew it was perfectly balanced and an exact replica of the actual necklace. We were going to be okay.

Damon found the weight mechanism, and I eased the lever down as he replaced the necklace.

My knees shook. Had we actually pulled this off? I couldn't even think. My mind was buzzing. And then he slowly eased back, and nothing happened. Damon nodded. "Right, let's pack it in."

I had to give Damon his due. He didn't even look at anything else in the vault. Not the vibrant orchid under glass, not the stacks of cash and gold bars on the shelves. He was only here for the job.

In less than thirty seconds, we were out of the vault. It took both of us to push the massive door closed behind us. With the vault closed, Damon pulled me in for a quick, hard kiss that took me by surprise. "Fucking brilliant, Ari. I couldn't have done this without you."

"Well, I'll never repeat this in front of Galen, but it was kind of fun."

"What is this? Are you flirting with the dark side?"

I laughed and shook my head. "No thank you, Anakin. But I certainly see the appeal."

"Fair enough. Let's get this to the prince."

found out I was the proud owner of an account in the Caymans and, thanks to a series of investments, a very wealthy woman. College had been a breeze to pay for, and I could have done anything I wanted.

I had a complicated relationship with that money. Just like I had a complicated relationship with Damon. And right now, in the antechamber of this vault, Damon was the one person I trusted above anybody. He was the one person I knew could get me out of this. So I followed his breathing cues. I listened, I relaxed, and then he nodded.

"Now do your thing. You've got your father's quick hands and his touch. You can do anything."

I nodded slowly. "You know he loved you, right?"

Damon's hands stilled. "Your dad loved *you*." He cleared his throat as he turned his attention back to his dial. "I was a messed-up kid. He gave me some direction."

"It was more than that, and you and I both know it. You were the one he could teach his craft to without any guilt. You are his true legacy."

As we both reached our final number, we let out a long breath, met gazes, then turned in time. The vault door opened. A sudden shot of relief and euphoria flooded through my veins, making me weak.

"Christ, we've done it," Damon said. "We have broken into the vault."

We were not out of the woods yet. We navigated the rows of items being held in safekeeping. All with pressure sensors. When we found what we were after, both of us gasped.

asked about my father or his career, obviously, I talked about the garage. I wasn't allowed to have friends or sleepovers. In case of emergency, I knew there was a go bag in the walls and how to get to our safe house without being seen. No one ever explicitly told me, but I figured out my family was different after a while. I'd known it was something dangerous after the fifth-grade art incident. I'd known that I had to keep secrets. For a long time, I'd thought my family was just weird.

When he went on jobs, of course, my father didn't leave me at home alone. Usually, my aunt was with me.

Though his activities hadn't gone completely unnoticed. Once, my teacher, Mrs. Davis, was an eyewitness to the robbery of a fancy jewelry store on Wilkins Avenue. She'd had car trouble and was waiting for a tow truck. She swore she'd seen my father and the getaway driver speeding away from the scene of the robbery.

That was the first time I learned to lie and lie effectively. I'd crafted a whole story for my friends at school about how my father and aunt had spent the night teaching me to play poker. I'd kept enough details real about my aunt's visit and the games of poker I'd watched Dad play over the years that it sounded like the truth.

I'd been convincing enough that Mrs. Davis had questioned what she'd seen and hadn't gone to the police.

As I got older, I got better at lying. But Dad was selective. He spread his jobs out. And as far as things on the books went, he did actually run a garage, and did brisk business too. The other money never showed up anywhere anyone could find it.

It wasn't until I turned eighteen and a lawyer appeared that I

Once inside, I slipped off my heels, then scooped them up to follow Damon to the vault.

Even I had to stare in awe. I knew what we were in for, but still, it was a thing of beauty. I dropped my shoes and had my tools out in seconds, taking my place next to Damon.

Damon had his scope out, his face set in grim determination. I had mine as well, and we both began on the vault. My heart beat a staccato pace against my ribs as I tried to stay focused.

Damon's voice was low when he spoke. "I need you to listen to me, Ari. You can do this. We'll do this together. But I need your breathing and your heart rate to slow down so you can hear what you need to hear. Just focus on the sound of the clock and my voice. Breathe with me. In, two, three. Out, two, three…" His voice was soothing. Despite what had happened in that maze, he was still my Damon. What I had said was true. I wasn't afraid of him.

Just thinking about how close I'd been to messing up this whole mission made my stomach turn. And if I were being honest with myself, there was a moment there when I had been worried I wasn't going to make it out alive. No way I wanted to meet Reaper and his minions in a dark room.

I'd thought I was in real trouble. And then Damon was there like an avenging angel, and it had been exactly what I needed.

His willingness and his capacity to hurt that man wasn't even a question; he hadn't hesitated to come for me. I wasn't used to anyone turning up for me like that.

After Mom died, things were hard, but I never wanted for anything. We had money, but there were funny little rules. When

## ARI

All these years, wanting to be like my father but *not* wanting to be anything like him. Wanting to be better.

*But now you need to connect to him.*

"Are you ready?" Damon asked when we reached the antechamber door.

I nodded as I double-checked our timing. Thank God we'd padded our planning time by several minutes. Only a minute behind schedule. "Let's do it."

I waited for him to start the secondary video loop from his watch and give me the thumbs-up before I quickly punched in the code Penny had given me and held my breath.

When the antechamber lock flashed green, we both breathed a sigh of relief.[*] We had the decryption key, but that would have meant using precious time we didn't have.

[*] GOLDENEYE–Tina Turner

"Yes, basics. Well, more than basics. Galen insisted we all have an intermediate-level belt in case we should get in trouble on an assignment. Although I have never been on an assignment, have I?"

"Ari, I just—"

I shook my head. "We do not have time for this. Whatever that was, whatever you were working out, that is not what we agreed to do."

"Ari, I don't want you to be afraid of me."

I stared at him. "I'm not *afraid* of you. There's just a part of you I don't know at all."

"He was going to *hurt* you. I couldn't let him."

"You wanted to kill him."

"But I didn't, Ari. I didn't kill him. I just needed to make sure that he can't hurt anyone else."

"We don't have time for this. We need to get to that vault."

I led the way, with him following. And all I could do was wonder what had changed him. Who was he now?

"Ari, it's me. Are you okay?"

"Where is he?"

"Slumped against a fountain in the center of the maze. I found a little bottle of booze they have in hotels on him. Poured it all over him. If someone finds him, they'll assume he's drunk. And he won't remember us."

"You told me no one was going to get hurt."

"Yeah, I said I wasn't going to hurt *innocent* people. But that guy wasn't supposed to be there. Which means either he was watching you specifically or he wasn't one of the security people. Which is a problem. Especially if Reaper suspects us of anything."

"Don't you think I know that? I'm already scared enough. You don't need to—" I swallowed sharply, trying to force the bile back down my throat. "You didn't need to—you were so good at that."

"Damned straight, I was. I've had to learn to be. In the field you only have your people. You look out for each other, or you're dead. He was hurting you. I needed to neutralize him. And I would do it again, immediately and without hesitation."

All I could do was stare down at my shaking hands. "Jesus. We need to get inside. We don't have time for this."

He reached his hand out to help me up, and I ignored it, tucking one foot under my bent knee and pushing myself onto my feet.

"You've taken martial arts?" he said.

I frowned at him. "What?"

"Your kick at fuck-wad back there and the way you just got up—you've taken martial arts."

gaze over her body again. There weren't any other bruises that I could see. I wanted to hurt the guard some more, but we didn't have time for this, and I had to think about Ari's safety.

We needed to get to the vault.

"Stay here. I'm going to secure him; then we'll move."

She wasn't looking at me though. She had her back toward me, and her shoulders were shaking. I knew she was crying.

*Fuck.*

---

# ARI

I couldn't breathe.

I used the precious moments Damon was gone to calm myself down. One moment that guy had been hauling me to Reaper; the next, Damon was there.

Damon had subdued him with the kind of brutal efficiency of someone who was well practiced. So how had he become so well practiced?

*You know nothing about him.*

He'd been scarily efficient. And I'd be lying if I said the cold efficiency didn't scare me.

*But in this case, it saved your ass. Get yourself together.*

We needed to get to the goddamned vault. But the adrenaline had hit me hard, and I couldn't breathe.

When I heard footsteps coming, I scrambled backward, unsure of who it was. I only marginally relaxed when I saw it was Damon.

I was on them in seconds. He'd been so focused on her, he hadn't heard me coming. I hauled him off her, dragging him by the back of his collar. Then I slammed him into a statue.

My arm barred across his neck. His eyes went wide and rolling, like a frightened horse. "What the fuck are you doing to my wife?"

He started to stutter, and I didn't like what he was saying, so I smashed my fist into his mouth.

Behind me, Ari gasped. "Simon, that's enough. I'm safe. That's enough."

While my eyes scanned the area, I pulled him into a submission hold meant to make him lose consciousness, and after several seconds, he sagged in my arms. He dropped to the ground, and I grabbed one of the syringes we'd been given and injected him carefully. This way, when he woke up, he wouldn't remember a thing.

Ari gave me a choked sob. "Did you kill him?"

"What? No. He's taking a nap. The last thing we need is for him to ruin everything." My gaze flicked to hers, and my eyes scanned her body. "Are you hurt?"

I heard voices coming from the other end of the maze and pulled him into a rendezvous spot for lovers.

Ari scrambled in behind us and shook her head. "I-I-I'm fine. You're sure he's alive?"

She thought I'd killed him? "Yes. Check for yourself. Sadly, still kicking. We'll tie him up."

"I could have handled that. You didn't need—"

"Yes, I did. No one touches my wife." I dared to flick my

"You should be at the auction," came the garbled response.

"Honestly, my husband is being a bit of a prick at the moment, so I needed some air, if you must know."

I coughed. *Good girl, Ari. Put him on the back foot.*

The guard blustered, "You shouldn't be out here."

"Don't worry about me. I'll be fine—" And then she squeaked. "Hey, stop that. Put me down."

I didn't even think. I didn't lock the final gate either. I just bolted straight for the opposite end of the property. Ari was in trouble.

I had her exact location from the tracker she wore. Instead of dragging her to the security office, that fucker was dragging her into the maze. I ran the fastest way back to the garden. Where was he taking her?

I could hear her struggling. "Let go of me."

"I'd rather you tell me what the hell you were doing. If you won't, I'm sure Reaper would like to speak to you."

"Put me down. I am a guest."

I hopped over a bench, running straight into the garden. I took a sharp left, then right. My blood was pumping, my heart galloping in my chest, beating a *rat-a-tat-tat* pattern against my ribs.

After rounding the corner, I found the fucker with Ari. His hand was clamped tightly around her wrist, and he was dragging her back toward the main house while she struggled.

A red haze slammed over my vision, and I reacted just as Ari kicked him in the knee and he cursed. She tried to force him to release her wrist by bringing her elbow up sharply, but he had her in an iron grip.

"I have the easy part. I just plant the Reaser on the video line. It's light work. I'll be fine."

"Make sure you hit me on the comms."

She tucked her hair behind her ears and said, "I'll meet you at the rendezvous. Then we'll break into the vault together."

She was taking this in stride, and God, I hoped I was doing the right thing. I was in a pickle, and I'd put her in a pickle. The difference was, if anything went wrong, she had people who would come looking for her. People who loved her and would risk everything for her. No one loved me like that.

"Be careful, Ari."

I walked around the grounds, taking my time, painting the cameras with infrared as I passed. It wouldn't take the cameras out, but given that the room was dark, it would make them think that I wasn't there.

If Lane was here, I knew what he was up to. He was here to steal something. And something told me that seeing me here had piqued his interest, which I didn't like. Not one bit.

*Ari is counting on you.*

I checked my watch. Making good time.

"Ari, in position?"

"Roger. I've placed the charges. Heading back. I'll see you at... Yes, I'm fine. I'm just having a bit of a walk."

My blood ran cold.

A guard. I checked my map. No one was supposed to be in that sector right now. I could hear his muffled speech. "Why are you out here?"

"Taking a walk."

"Personally, I think we all feel it. That moment when the risk outweighs the rush. Or at least we should feel it."

"How? I mean, hell. How have you avoided jail for this long?"

He shrugged. "You never hit the same place twice. And if you do, make it years apart. Stay smart. Trust your instincts."

"He taught you well," she whispered.

"Yeah, the rules he taught me have kept me alive. They also made me rich and careful."

She nodded solemnly. "I miss him so much."

I strolled over to her before cupping her chin with my thumb and forefinger. "I miss him too."

We still hadn't talked about the other night. There hadn't been time to lay it all bare. Maybe when this was over, there would be space for us to breathe, to hold each other and talk about what she knew now.

As we headed out toward the auction, we were alone this time. Most people hadn't wanted to be late. We'd given everyone a thirty-minute head start, so most of the guards would be at the auction house. Some pieces were out on display. The items of higher value were in the vault. Knowing some of the history between Lane and Paul, Lane was likely going to make his move tomorrow because that's when the confusion would be. All we had to do was stay out of his way and get the necklace before he knew we were after it. We had our objective.

There was an additional day of events for very special guests. Everyone else was leaving tomorrow morning.

When we reached the end of our pathway, I took hold of her hand. "Are you sure you have this?"

# DAMON

Ari watched me the next night as we got ready.

Tonight everyone would be paying attention to the auction room, to the pieces that were available and being sold onstage.

Ari was dressed simply. Long black slacks and a black shirt. I knew what she was carrying under there. She was hiding the fake diamond heart in her bodice. We were doing this.

I wasn't nervous. I knew what I had to do. Lucas was counting on me, so there wasn't really any backing out.

I watched her closely. "Are you ready?"

She gave me a grim but firm nod. "I stay ready."

"You know, for what it's worth, you would be excellent in the field, and GT Securities would be lucky to have you there."

"I know. You've said it before. But maybe you were right, and I would like it too much. How do you know when to dial it back?"

make him pay. And he will, but not right now. Not this weekend. He's not our target, okay?" Finally, I saw her tears streak down her face, and I gently swiped them away. "Ari, he doesn't deserve your tears."

"I know. And I know I am not going to change the plans, but can we please just make sure that whatever we do, that man does not walk away with whatever it is he came to take?"

"The only way that happens is over my dead body."

"I don't want to be this person who can't move on. This person who pretends her world is great. I don't want to pretend. I want to be able to move past this."

"I know, Ari. I know. I'm so sorry," I whispered.

"What am I supposed to do? I'm going to go in there and stab him."

"Well," I said as I stroked her back, trying to ease some of the tension out of her. "Leave some for me."

"Let me go and I will."

"I'm the rule breaker, not you. Besides, stabbing involves blood. You don't want to get any blood on that beautiful dress you're wearing, do you?"

"I thought you said everybody was ogling my tits."

"Well, they are. But so long as those tits walk into my room tonight, then everything is fine." I stopped, rethinking exactly what I'd said. "Oh shit, I'm sorry." But surprisingly, that made her smile.

"It's okay. I have nice boobs."

I snorted a laugh. "You know what I meant."

"I don't know how to do this. He's in there walking around, and my dad is gone. He's a horrible person and deserves to die."

"He is. Unfortunately, horrible people don't always get what's coming to them. We've got to stay focused, Ari. You and me against the world. Can you do that?"

"How do you do that? Not let the hatred eat at you? I can compartmentalize, but this feeling… This is something else."

"I've had practice. You're going to be okay, Ari. He's a horrible person, and I have been thinking up ways over the years to

"I'm so sorry, Ari. I'm sorry, I should have told you."

"Why would you keep this from me? All these years, I thought... You know what I thought."

"You thought I killed him?"

"No, not really. I thought you got shot at by the police or security. I didn't know it was someone else. Another thief. Someone determined to take something from him. You didn't tell me." She pushed me, and the gravel on the path shifted under me, almost causing me to fall backward. Ari stood and started walking.

"Ari, wait for me."

"I will not wait for you. I don't think I can do this."

"You can do this. You are stronger than you know."

"No, I'm not okay. I'm not. What am I supposed to do with this? The man who killed my father is at this event, and you expect me just to pretend I don't know?"

"What you're supposed to do is give me a part of it to carry. Talk to me."

She shook her head and broke into a run toward the lake. She was fast, but I still caught her easily at the edge of the water. I wrapped my arms around her again and tugged her close. "I'm sorry, Ari. I'm so sorry."

She shook her head as tears welled in her eyes and she tried desperately to hold them back, refusing to cry.

"Ari, let go."

She kept shaking her head. "No, I can hold it together. I have to hold it together."

I just kept holding her. "Not with me, you don't."

tell me who the hell he is and what he is to you. Because I need to know. Especially if he's going to interfere."

Damon swallowed hard. "You think he's going to interfere?"

"If he doesn't know who I am already, he's searching. He was far too interested. And I get the impression he knew my father."

There was something on Damon's face. A flicker of anguish. I only recognized it because it was an expression that I wore often and publicly hid behind a barrier. "Ari…"

"Tell me who he is. Because if he recognized me and wants to get that diamond before we can, we're in hot water, and Galen is going to kill me. So explain yourself."

"Michael Lane is the man who killed your father."

---

# DAMON

My gut churned and roiled. I'd known the moment I'd seen him that this was unavoidable. I'd had no plans to ever tell her. Hell, I had tried to take him off the board three times in the hopes of never having to.

I watched her warily as she absorbed the shock. The denial hit first; then the full weight of what I had just told her sank in. And then she collapsed.

Immediately, I unbuttoned my tuxedo and cocooned her in it, then wrapped myself around her. She shook her head. "No, please don't tell me this. Please don't tell me that man who stood there, smug and smiling in my face, don't tell me he gets to walk around the earth and my father doesn't."

"You are so full of shit. Who *I* am has nothing to do with who *you* are. You're hiding something from me, and I need to know what it is before we go into the field."

"God, woman, we are in the fucking field already. This is it. This is what it looks like. It's scary, it's terrifying, and hell, people might die."

"I told you, no one's getting hurt."

"You told me *I* couldn't hurt anyone. Which, by the way, I don't do, Ari. I don't hurt people."

"Yeah, sure you don't."

He winced as if I'd slapped him, and immediately, I wished I could take the words back because I didn't really want to hurt him.

At the same time, there was a part of me that wanted to explode, to lash out—a part that wanted him to feel the frustration, the pain, the anger. Because while he had gone on to become some kind of wealthy billionaire thief, I was still mentally stuck in that garage, unable to move on with my life.

"Who the hell is Michael Lane? Tell me."

He shook his head. "It doesn't matter, Ari. Knowing isn't going to change anything. It isn't going to make you feel better. It isn't going to make you better at your job or make you a happier person. None of it matters."

"Damon, tell me who he is."

He shook his head. "No, I'm not doing that."

"You have to. You and I are going to walk into a vault room tomorrow and try to pull off something impossible. So don't you sit there and tell me that you're not going to trust me enough to

away? Tuck them in a box and bury them? Like they never happened. That what you did with Dad?"

"Christ, Ari." He started marching farther into the garden and then whipped around. "God, you have spent your entire life judging his decisions. After your mom died, your dad did *everything* for you. He provided for you and protected you, yet you have no idea how good you had it. Some of us have no fucking choice but to bury the goddamn past. Instead, you whine that your father didn't love you enough. For fuck's sake, Ari."

I staggered back like I'd been slapped. "How dare you?"

Despite having our jammer on, he kept his voice low and tight. "How dare I? It's true. You've been so mad at him for leaving you, but he was doing the best he could, and he loved you more than you know. But you held on to that anger and resentment, and completely shut down your life. You push everyone away. You use him shutting you out as a reason to keep everyone at bay. You think he would want *this* for you? Sure. You're brilliant. Well respected. But you are hiding behind a screen. It's not the *real* Ari. The Ari I knew had a sense of mischief in her. When her father wouldn't teach her, she taught herself. Following behind him, using his tools, learning what every single one did. Now you're an analyst? Come on, Ari. You are just like me. You *want* to be in the field getting your hands dirty, feeling the adrenaline pull at you. But you shut down. And you're looking for a reason to shut down now. But I am not going to give you one. The real reason you stay out of the field is you're afraid you'll *love* it. You'll love doing this, and it could cost you your life. You're scared."

were only two guards in the vault room, which matched the intel we'd gathered. Our guard schedules were correct.

I took Damon's hand. "Can I talk to you outside?"

He pressed his lips together, knowing exactly what I wanted to discuss with him. We headed to the balcony, but there were a few people smoking, so I led him down the stairs into the hedge maze.

"What was that with Michael Lane? Do we need to abort?"

"I—what? No. We continue. And that was nothing. It's fine, but stay away from him. He's dangerous."

"Half the people in there are dangerous. Who is he, and what does he have to do with why we're here? He called you Damon. He obviously knows you. This is worst-case scenario."

He shook his head and tried to turn back toward the house. I grabbed his elbow, keeping my voice low, and dragged him farther into the gardens. "I'm your partner. You need to talk to me, or I can't help. He clearly is a problem for you. Start talking to me. All I want to do is help, Damon. He spooked you. Now tell me what's going on. If we need to abort, then we will."

He frowned. "We're *not* walking away. Besides, he won't say a word about me. If he does, then Reaper shuts down the auction. He's here for something. He needs this auction to go on."

"Did you steal something from him? Who is he?"

He shook his head. "No one. Let it go, Ari, for once in your life. This is the past. It has nothing to do with you. Focus on the mission."

Why couldn't he talk to me? "When he poses a risk to the plan? Is that how you deal with problems? Just pretend them

## ARI

"Talk to me, Damon."

"About what?" he asked as he forced me to mingle.

Was he really trying to pretend that something wasn't wrong?

Throughout the party in the reception hall, he'd essentially showed me off like a trophy. He kept an arm wrapped around me, and I could feel the tension ease from him as he moved through the crowd. The farther we got away from Michael Lane, the more comfortable he became. Unfortunately, for me, the more comfortable Damon became, the more *un*comfortable I became. I tried to rationalize his odd behavior, but the more I thought about it, the more I worried. The more I worried, the more my brain tried to make the pieces fit together.

We spotted Prince Lucas across the room. He brushed his brow with two fingers as he talked to some gorgeous brunette.

That was our signal. He'd just been outside in the hall. There

The night of my father's death, Damon had muttered, *What the hell was he even doing there?* Someone else had been there who wasn't supposed to be, and something told me that someone was looking at me now, smiling in my face. I couldn't explain why, but given Damon's protectiveness and the green pallor of his skin, he hated this man. And I needed to know why exactly.

He studied me like a bug under a magnifying glass. "Huh, well, how did you find this gem, *Simon*?"

Damon was stone next to me. With no choice, I kept to the script. "He found me. At an auction in LA." I squeezed Damon's hand conspiratorially. That seemed to snap him out of it.

"Michelle works for a collector. She was quite upset with me about a vase."

"Oh, my goodness, seventeenth century. Baroque design. Exquisite, honestly. He swooped in and stole it from me."

Michael's brows rose. "He *stole* it?"

"Yes. I don't know how he did it, but he somehow found out the max bid my client was going to pay and outbid it by a dollar. How rude is that?"

Michael seemed engaged in the rehearsed story. Damon, meanwhile, looked like he wanted to scream. However, he contained himself.

I shook my head and squeezed Damon's arm, which was rigid underneath his tuxedo. Who was this man? I'd never seen Damon act like this before. Generally, he was snarky, a pain in the ass, arrogant. And how did this man know him? Damon had been clear that he kept a low profile. I was missing the bigger picture.

Was he someone Damon had stolen from? I didn't think he was in law enforcement. He didn't have that edge to him. Plus, few cops could provide enough in escrow to get in the door. And if he wasn't law enforcement, that likely meant he was another thief or somehow related to Damon's business.

The moment that it dawned on me, my gaze flickered to Damon's and a chill enveloped my body, making my skin prickle.

sweat. We were so fucked. What was the right play, and who the hell had heard him call Damon by his name?

Instead of answering, Damon tried to tug me away. What was he doing? We had to deal with him. We had a plausible script for what to say and how to act. But we had to say something. If we ran away, wouldn't he alert Reaper?

"Sorry, Michael, we're needed over here."

"Oh, but your wife and I were just getting acquainted. Michelle, sweetheart, you bear a striking resemblance to an old friend of mine. I can't quite put my finger on it."

I froze. Something was wrong. Very, very wrong. Based on the way the man was staring at me and almost smugly smiling at Damon, this was someone who knew Damon from his time in my father's life.

I needed to catch up. They were playing a game I didn't recognize.

Michael kept asking me questions. "Where did you grow up?"

"In California."

"Could have sworn I hear New England prep school in your accent."

"You don't. I'm from California," I said, lying through my teeth.

"Interesting. I must have mistaken you for someone else. But what do I know? Accents are so hard. Whereabouts did you grow up in California?"

"Oh, you know, I'd like to say LA, but really what I mean is Pasadena. Not that entertaining. Far away from the glitz and glamour. Just your average girl with a father who was wise with investments."

"I see you have no intention of introducing us. I'm Michael Lane. Pleasure."

When I gritted my teeth, Ari stepped forward. "Hello, I'm Michelle Christopher. His wife."

---

## ARI

I was missing something. Some kind of nuance, a trick, an inside joke.

Except it didn't seem like a joke. Something about Michael Lane made Damon edgy, so much so that his grip on my side tightened. What was going on here?

The man's brows lifted. "You're married? I almost feel insulted that I didn't receive an invitation. After all, I was there during one of the formative moments of your life."

They knew each other? Our cover was blown. But I also had no other choice but to stick to the script we made.

"Well, with Simon so busy, it took a while for us to figure out how and when we were going to do things. But we finally got it together. When we got married, he took my last name. Ticked my father to no end."

As I spoke, I still got the impression that I was missing a whole thread of nuance.

He cocked his head, a derisive smirk playing on his lips. "Simon, you say? Fine, I'll play along. Young love. How did you two meet?"

My heartbeat thundered in my skull, and my palms began to

The last time I saw him was in Éze, this quaint little village between Nice and Monaco. I was actually off the clock for a Xander Chase exhibit with Jazz. He was her favorite artist, so I had to be extra and pay for her ticket to the event and make sure she got to meet him.

The gallery was robbed that night. I was outside on a call for another job when I saw a security guard leaving the gallery very quickly. I recognized him right away when the moon lit his face.

So I hopped in my car and chased him down. And yes, I might have nudged him with my car, but the son of a bitch had nine fucking lives. And a secondary, who shot at me until Lane could escape.

After that, Jazz begged me to cool it with Lane. Yet I'd kept track of him over the years. That hatred was always simmering. But he wasn't the kind of guy I wanted to take a swing at anymore unless I was sure.

He'd gotten lucky too many times. Next time, I'd better not miss.

If I could avoid introducing them and exposing her to him, I absolutely would. Unfortunately, there was no way to do that.

"Might I ask who your beautiful companion is?"

I turned to face him. "Hello, Lane."

"Damon, so formal?"

"It's been a long time," I said through gritted teeth.

He grinned at me. "It *has* been a moment. How are you? You've grown up since I last saw you."

That piece of shit. I was going to kill him. But I needed to get Ari out of here, as far away from him as possible.

Ari gave me a tight smile and tried for a save. "Simon, darling. You really must have a doppelganger."

I was beyond saving though. I clamped my mouth shut, my jaw ticking and an icy shiver snaking up my spine.

And when I turned fully, I came face-to-face with the only person I'd ever wanted to kill.

*Michael Lane.*

What the fuck was he doing here? His name hadn't been on the list. Had he used an alias?

*Doesn't matter. He's here. Think on your feet.*

He looked the same. Just under six feet tall, with blondish-silvery hair. He'd aged well enough for the average person to consider him distinguished. For years, he'd been that ethereal ghost in the night. Always haunting me at the edges of my sanity. After he killed Paul, I vowed to myself to make him pay. I tried three times. Once in Paris when he tried to steal a Samson Marks painting. I followed him for weeks. Tailed him. Knew his plan.

I called the police on him. Bullshit move, but I was trying to keep my hands clean, the way Paul would have wanted.

Michael got tipped off and managed to escape, sans painting, mere moments before the police arrived.

The next time I ran into him was the grand opening of a Westhorpe Hotel in Dubai. Princess Elise of Norway was there, sporting a massive rock from her fiancé, the football player Ryson Beck. The five-million-dollar ring was a showstopper.

Unfortunately, that son of a bitch Michael posed as a waiter and used a Taser on me midjob, leaving me in the hotel gardens while he made off with the ring.

"Come on, angel."

I let her lead me arm in arm, calmly taking time, double-checking guard placements as we headed down the path that led to the mansion.

I wondered what it would be like if this were real.

Other guests were also starting to make their way to the mansion as the sun kissed the horizon.

Once we joined the rest of the guests, I took in the splendor. Some guests wore masks. And the entire room was a flurry of tuxedos, brightly colored ball gowns, and some costumes. It was a spectacle. The glitterati were out to play. Ari had zero problems walking. I frowned at her. "Are you wearing heels under there?"

"Oh no. I'm wearing platform tennis shoes."

I lifted my brow. "Are you serious?"

She lifted the hem of her dress just so, and I chuckled when I saw that she was, in fact, wearing platform tennis shoes.

"Of course."

"You better believe it. It makes this job so much easier."

I managed to snag us two glasses of champagne from a passing waiter and handed her one. She clinked her glass with mine and gave me a sweet smile just as the hairs on the back of my neck stood at attention.

From somewhere behind me, I heard, "Do my eyes deceive me, or is that Damon Hunt?"

The chill of the voice struck me, and my back went ramrod straight. *No. Fuck no. No, no, no.*

No way in hell he was here.

And neither of them had seemed to give a fuck about her being on my arm. Not that I'd made it clear she was off-limits. I would have been happy to growl at anyone who dared to even look at her, but she hadn't needed me.

True to Ari form, she'd dismissed them both handily as if they bored her.

She started to fix my tie, her delicate fingers brushing my neck softly. And my cock was hard and ready to go.

I was convinced she could feel it. It was pulsing with need as the tension swirled around us. I could kiss her now. The curves of her lips were pink and soft looking, and something about the way she'd done the makeup around her eyes made her look like a cat. She was perfection with her textured braid swinging down her back. She wore cuff earrings and one delicate, though enormous, diamond around her neck, which doubled as a camera and matched the ring that I'd slid onto her finger when this all started.

When she was finished with my tie, she patted my chest and backed away. "There you go. You look handsome."

I nodded again, my gaze drifting down to her breasts. The urge to pop one in my mouth made me salivate. I wanted to climb out of my body. What would it take to peel back one of those golden pearls around her breasts? Would her breasts fall forward?

She took my arm, and I gave her a tight smile before we opened the door.

"Are you sure you're okay?" she asked.

"Honestly, I'm having a hard time focusing. That dress… You look incredible." That, and I wanted to keep her all to myself.

She gave me a shy smile and cocked her head. "This old thing?"

I coughed. I was pretty sure my mouth was hanging open. "You look…" I had to lick my lips and swallow again. "Stunning."

She turned around. "It's not too much? Penny insisted that it had to be this one, but I don't know."

I cleared my throat. "It's perfect, Ari. Don't change a thing."

Fabric swished as she strode forward, and I realized the long skirt was actually pants.

If I knew Ari, she had tools hidden in there.

"Pants?"

She grinned, kicking out one leg. "Pants. The best part is no one will know."

"Wow, genius. You'll be more comfortable that way, I assume?"

"Yes, and I have places to hide my tools."

I grinned at her. "Always prepared. That's my Ari."

She hesitated for a moment and then reached for me. My gut clenched, and every part of my body screamed to pull her close. She was reaching for me. She *wanted* to touch me.

Earlier today, we'd had breakfast, explored the grounds, gone over the plans, found our ingress and egress routes, and mapped everything to the letter. Then we'd deliberately made it a point to hang out casually by the pool, where she wore the smallest bikini I had ever seen in my life. Okay, fine. It wasn't *that* small, but her curves were lush, and I hadn't been the only person watching her at that moment.

Not that I blamed them. This was Ari, and she looked like a goddess.

Two of them had even made an approach. One had gotten so bold as to ask if she would be participating in the auction.

2. Never attempt to go for something that you couldn't afford to lose.

3. Never take something from someone you hate. The personal gets you in trouble.

It was that last rule that I sometimes tended to bend. When it came to power, it was *always* personal. But the rules had kept me alive. The rules had made me wealthy.

It had taken me years, but I'd managed to buy myself a seat at the power table. And I wasn't letting go.

Lucas had grown up like me, hustling, and like me, he'd somehow managed to do more than survive and came out on top. We'd both learned to be wary, and those skills would serve us well here.

We needed them to serve us well. Or somebody would get hurt.

*But still, you twisted her arm into doing it.*

I had. I needed her because it meant keeping Max out of trouble and not having to owe Lucas any favors. Lucas might not keep tabs. But I liked even scales. And she'd thrown herself into the work.

I looked up when the door to the bathroom opened, and out she walked. My breath hitched, and then I couldn't breathe. She wore gold in some intricate design that covered most of her breasts but still showed enough of her luminescent brown skin on the sides that you wondered how it was being held up. Her hair was pulled back into one long ponytail braid that looked like several connected Afro puffs hanging down her back.

The skirt of the gown was more concealing. It had these swoops and loops that matched the ones on the upper part of the bodice. She gave me a little twirl. "Well, how do I look?"

# DAMON

It was the first full day of the auction, and the telltale hum of adrenaline had buzzed through me all day.

*Easy does it. This is not playtime. Remember you're here doing this for Lucas.*

The viewing had happened earlier, and soon, the party would start.

There would, of course, be posturing. Everyone in attendance was beyond wealthy. They were the elite. The see-and-be-seens. The very same people I loved to steal from. There were a few here, though, who were like me: who were wealthy, with an edge of power, and loved control.

When I was a kid, Paul had made it clear that when it came to stealing, nothing was personal. He had all these rules for me to follow. There were three main ones.

1. Never lose your cool.

deeply, gave me a nod, and plastered a fake smile on her face. She put the armor back on, and that was the safest thing for both of us. Because the moment she was unguarded, all I wanted to do was kiss her, taste her, possess her. And since I couldn't have her, thanks to our past, it was better if she kept her distance.

into the room, Ari had the blinds open, soft morning light streaming in and a breeze wafting through.

She looked stunning. Her bright-marigold sundress with the slit up to her thigh showcased her mile-long legs.

"Are you ready?" I asked.

Her gaze snapped to mine, then traveled down my body. I kept my grin in check. I liked it when she looked at me. Her gaze was assessing, but it was also hungry.

"See something you like, Ari?"

She flushed, her cheeks growing slightly rosier, and the tips of her ears went a slightly darker shade of brown. Dead giveaway that she liked what she saw, but I was never telling her that.

*Try and focus. This is never going to happen.*

The likes of Ari Denton didn't fall for the likes of me. History or not, incredible chemistry or not, I was responsible for what happened to her father. It had been my job to protect him, to at least help him. But what had I done? Not enough.

And now, I needed her help.

*You need to suck it up. Ari Denton is not for you. She never was. Remember that. Remember why you're doing this.*

I reached my hand out for hers. "Are you ready, angel?"

She stared at my hand for a long moment as if it would bite her or attack her.

Did I want to fit my hand perfectly over her breast like I had last night, but this time without the tight catsuit in the way? Yes. Was I going to do that? No. "Like I said, you can trust me, Ari."

I could almost see her shoring up her courage. She inhaled

After seeing the way she'd bolted from that garden, I had known I should have gone after her. Should have told her it didn't have to mean anything that she didn't want it to mean. Should have said something.

Instead, I had let her run. I'd come back to the chalet after trying to force my erection down for a half hour and found her already in bed, and she hadn't budged as I'd gotten ready to sleep.

Sure, I was selfish. I tended to get what I wanted and tended to be willing to do *anything* to get it. However, with Ari, I hadn't meant to push her. But every time I saw her with her mouth tight and her back straight, all I wanted to do was make her relax just a little. She'd always been so serious. But before, there had been flashes of determination and a little bit of mischief. This new version of her never let go.

Had I done that to her? Was I the reason?

As I showered and scowled at my again-pulsing erection, I tried to keep my mind focused on the mission at hand. These feelings for Ari were only going to get more complicated.

Especially since kissing her always felt like coming home.

When she had said yes, that looming, buzzing excitement inside my body had exploded everywhere, making me high, light-headed, and exhilarated.

*But even if she wants you, she will never, ever forgive you. She blames you for Paul's death.*

If that couldn't get my cock to go down, nothing could do it.

Okay, at least it was only at half-mast now. I toweled off quickly and finished getting ready. By the time I marched back

If I could have scowled at my libido, I would've. She was not helpful.

Damon pointed at the black area we'd seen on our thermal scans last night. "So today we need to get over here?"

I nodded. "Yeah, the auction is taking place over here." I pointed to the right of the map. "I think if we walk the grounds on that side to get a good estimate, we might get lucky."

His arms wrapped around me as he pointed at the schematics and blueprints in front of me. "This will be our best spot. I want to at least scope it out. We'll take in the landscape from the outside and then come back and plan from here. We just need to see how much security is posted there. What they've got in terms of cameras, et cetera."

I nodded stiffly. "Yeah, sounds good. Um, why don't you get ready for breakfast, and we'll take a walk outside."

He turned and grinned at me. "Are we going to head back to the garden?"

I was certain he couldn't see my flush. My skin was too dark. But his grin told me that he sensed it. I must have been giving off heat in waves. Jesus.

He held his hands up. "I'm only kidding. Unless, of course, that's what you want."

"Jackass."

# DAMON

She was retreating. Last night had been…unexpected.

Frustrated, I threw the hotel notepad at him.

He blocked it deftly with a pillow. "Got to talk about that crackle between us eventually, angel." He climbed out of bed, and I got one hell of a glimpse at what he'd been hiding under the covers. He'd only worn boxer briefs to bed.

Jesus Christ, he looked like Adonis. Broad shoulders. Lean, tapered waist. And abs. So. Many. Abs. Fully defined. Flat. Taut. His leg muscles well-defined. Honestly, I was probably salivating. I forced myself to turn around and get back to the schematics.

I cleared my throat. "We're scheduled to 'run into Lucas' at breakfast shortly, and I wanted to make sure I was ready." The plan was to have him spill something on me, then invite us to join him as recompense.

"Are those the schematics?" he asked.

I jumped in surprise. He was right behind me, looking over my shoulder. His breath tickled my neck, making my body stiff.

All I could think about was last night. His nose running along my skin, his hands cupping my breasts, his thumb rubbing over my nipple. The way I'd begged him to make me come. Heat suffused my face, and I wanted to duck and hide.

Why had I said yes?

And honestly, just because Galen had saved me didn't mean I needed to do everything he said. If I had just said no, I wouldn't be here. So close to Damon Hunt. I wouldn't have let the man kiss me and certainly wouldn't have let him...

*Let him what? Give you a much-needed orgasm? Let's face it. You are uptight. You needed that.*

dressed before he was even up. After the shower, I'd started reviewing the security schematics.

"You're up early." His voice sounded like a growl.

I squeaked, whirling around as he sat up and the covers fell off him, baring his muscled chest and all that golden-bronze skin with a light dusting of hair. He looked delicious. Gorgeous. Like something to savor and delight in, something to lick all over.

*Oh my God, stop it.*

"Good morning," I said.

"When did you get up?" he asked.

I frowned at the time. It was seven o'clock. Normally by now, I would have left for a run, eaten, and gone over the day's clients and their needs. "Um, early riser, I guess."

He cocked his head and gave me a smile that was somewhere between smug and sweet. "You were in bed early too."

"We don't have to talk about this."

He sighed. "Ari, we *should* talk."

"Damon, can't we just leave it at *it's complicated*?"

"Don't you want to clear the air?"

I sucked in a sharp breath and held it maybe for a little too long, because I started to feel lightheaded. Oh God, what was I supposed to say? I didn't lose control. Not ever.

He watched me carefully. "Okay, we don't have to talk about it. But you know, next time you want to wrap your arms around my neck and rub those gorgeous tits on me, let me know. I'll make myself available. And I don't count you throwing your body over mine when you sleep. You weren't kidding about being a bed hog."

# ARI

What was wrong with me?

*Other than a really great orgasm?*

I'd run straight back to the room after our hot and heavy session in the alcove and basically dove under the covers like a coward after getting ready for bed and checking our jammer. Because that had been the only appropriate response. I'd never—and I mean never—had an orgasm with anyone before. Not like my sex life was some rousing success.

Damon had come to bed thirty minutes later and climbed under the covers, but he'd taken my lead and kept to his side of the bed. At least at first. Somehow, I'd woken up starfished over his big body.

I clearly had no idea what I was doing. A part of him scared me, but I was drawn to him. I'd been completely lost, diving headfirst into kissing him. That wasn't me. Acting without a plan.

In the morning, I'd peeled myself off him, showered, and

"Fuck, angel, you are so soft." My voice was low and husky, filled with need.

I ground my erection against her heat through my pants, and she gasped and whimpered my name in a raspy tone that made me want to forget the outside world in favor of slamming inside this angel.

"Please, Damon," she pleaded breathlessly.

"Angel—" Fuck, I couldn't think.

I gripped her thigh and pulled her leg over my hip, positioning her heat where we both wanted it. I slid my thumb in circles over her clit as her hips arched into my hand.

"Oh my...fuck," she whispered as my finger rubbed against her slit.

Christ, I was going to lose it.

"Let me feel it, angel. Let go, baby."

"Oh God, yes!"

She lifted her hips more, trying harder to grind into me, and I pressed her back against the wall, pinning her in place.

"Just a little more, angel," I begged.

She was about to come; I could feel her body tense and shudder. I slipped one finger inside her tight heat, then another, filling her up, and she clamped down around my fingers.

"I can't," she cried out when I hit her G-spot. I pressed deeper, and when my thumb hit her clit again, she came undone.

Wave after wave of pleasure swept through her, and she gasped, her back arching off the wall as my whispered name came tumbling from her lips.

tantalized, making her breath catch in anticipation and her hips thrust forward.

My hand curled tighter against her breast, gently rolling the nipple between my thumb and fingers, relishing in her muffled moans.

Her hands slid down my shoulders, and she tugged at my sweater and shirt with painstaking slowness until she gained access to my skin. Then her hands splayed on my back, and she arched her body into mine.

I returned to the kiss with full force.

Like a man possessed, I took what I wanted. *Mine*. The primal part of me fought for dominance. The man in me battled for control.

I tangled my hands in her hair and pulled out the tie that held it up, nearly growling in satisfaction at the sound it made when it detached from her hair.

Our moans mingled as she tried to rub herself against my erection, grinding against me like a little vixen. Smiling against her lips, I pried her legs wider and slid my hand into her leggings.

My thumb found drenched satin and slid under the fabric to meet with slippery wetness. Unable to control myself, I trailed down her slit and paused with my thumb pressed against her clitoris.

My dick twitched at the thought of taking her right here.

*Fuuuck*. My finger just hovered outside her sheath, slowly, purposely dragging her out to the edge of sanity and back to me.

When I pulled away from the kiss, she opened her eyes, which were unfocused with lust.

# DAMON

I deposited her on the small ledge in the alcove before stepping between her thighs.*

My dick tried to sound the warning bells that I was too far gone to tease her. I was holding on to my control by a thread. When I ran my tongue along her lips, she dragged in a shuddering breath before she gave me access.

God, what was she doing to me?

My erection pressed against the heat of her cleft, and all I could think about was how she would feel when I thrust inside. She gave an involuntary shiver, and I murmured against her lips, "You're so fucking beautiful," all the while stealing her breath.

My voice was raspy, the desire nearly choking me.

I slid one hand under her top and up over her rib cage to cup her breast. My other hand inched closer and closer to her heat. Fuck, her skin was so damned soft. Her fingers teased and

* I WANNA BE YOURS—Måneskin

stop. The right answer was to not get caught up in this madness. The right answer was the safe answer.

But I didn't want to play it safe all the time. And I sure as hell didn't want to play it safe right now. I wanted that edge of danger, and God... I couldn't think. I couldn't breathe.

The tingles all over my body were sending my mind into scattered longing and need. All I could think about were his hands on me, his lips tracing oh-so-delicately over my skin, and how I wanted more. So much more.

So when I opened my mouth to say no, to tell him to stop, what came out was "Yes."

I felt more than heard the growl that emanated from his chest, and when he dipped his whole body, sliding his hands down my back onto my ass, and lifted me against him, I had no choice but to wrap my legs around his waist. Then he pressed me back against the stone wall, angled his head to kiss me, and paused just before his lips touched mine. "Hang on, Ari."

I didn't even know what the hell that was called. But the idea that he'd just sniffed me turned my core into molten lava.

I cleared my throat. "We should go."

His lips brushed my neck, and I sucked in a shuddering breath. When he pulled away, somebody whimpered. I didn't know who that somebody was, but it wasn't me.

Okay, fine. It *was* me. Jesus. Why was he trying to kill me?

I cleared my throat again. "Maybe if you just…" I couldn't continue, because he moved his lips to that patch right behind my ear. His breath tickled that spot, and—what do you know?—somebody moaned again. I had no idea who, because there was no way in hell I was moaning for Damon Hunt. I wasn't.

*Okay, you just keep thinking that.*

He was cocky, arrogant, and brash, and there was a hint of danger around him that I wanted zero part of.

But as his lips moved to the shell of my ear, I shivered.

"Just say the word," he whispered, "and I can make that aching need go away."

*You should dive in.*

I had the urge to take him up on his offer. All I had to do was give in. All I had to do was just say yes.

I *never* said yes. I always played it safe, all the time. Just once, I wanted to say yes.

And he was right here.

He whispered again, "Say the word, Ari. Say the word, or I'll stop. I'm waiting."

I knew the right answer. The right answer *was* to tell him to garden would see us if we moved. The voices grew closer and then finally passed by, and we both relaxed and resumed breathing, our bodies replenishing their oxygen.

"Are you okay?" he asked.

"You mean other than you smothering me? Yes, I'm fine."

He rolled his eyes. "Okay, next time I'll just leave you exposed."

I frowned up at him. "While I appreciate it, it was unnecessary."

"If you say so. Question: Why did you kiss me back on the balcony? Was it because you were taking to your role? Because it kind of seems like you wanted to."

I swallowed hard and tried to deflect. "It—um." I cleared my throat. *Think, Ari. Think.* "We were emotional. It certainly didn't need to escalate like it did."

He smirked down at me then. "Oh, is that what that was? Our emotions? Okay. If you say so. Or maybe, Ari Sari, you *wanted* to kiss me. Maybe you've been thinking about me too. Maybe that kiss made it so you can't think about anything else."

My tummy flipped at the low timbre of his voice. "Absolutely not. I don't think about you at all!"

"Are you sure about that? I think you do. I certainly think about you. And that kiss wasn't for show. You're starting to feel something, Ari. Tell me I'm lying."

I rolled my eyes. "No, you're mistaken. It was fake, Damon."

*Liar.*

He leaned close, towering over me, and rubbed his nose against my neck as he inhaled.

# 15

## ARI

He clasped me tight as we both held our breath and pressed up against each other.* I could still feel his lips from earlier. The soft glide of them, the sureness, the skill coupled with the hint of teasing.

Teenage Ari would have killed for kisses from Damon Hunt but had only dreamed of them.

But now, his kisses were a distraction. A deviation from the plan.

*The plan is that you act like a couple.*

Not the point. The point was that he shouldn't have *kept* kissing me. He shouldn't have been pressed up against me now.

You *kissed* him *earlier.*

I had, and once again I'd lost myself. And this was no different as my mind played out all the possibilities now.

*Or maybe he's also playing the part. Keeping his cover.*

Either way, whoever was walking along the path next to the

---

* VEGAS—Doja Cat

I nodded. "Yeah, so that means that the other massive concentration on the opposite side of the house has got to be where we're going."

"Yeah, I think so too. If the Royal Heart is as big and as priceless as they say, then I am pretty certain that's going to get the most attention." She pointed at the map again. "And that is the vault room."

"Are you sure?"

"Yeah. See? That black spot right there, that's not the wall. It's a hidden room. That's a vault."

I frowned. "Huh, you're right."

"I know. It's called research."

We stood and started to move, but then I heard voices and we both froze in our tracks.

I dragged her to a space in the wall along this side of the garden, and we both held our breath, waiting. We tucked ourselves into the little stone alcove, my body covering hers, and the voices only drew closer.

Paul had taken me in and given me a life. No way in hell had I intended to cross that line. But, Jesus, back then, Ari Denton was all I thought about.

I was fascinated by how her skin always seemed to be glowing, how she seemed to be serious one moment, and then her father would make a silly joke or disarm her, and she would give you a smile that brightened the whole damned world.

God, back then, I would have done anything to make Ari smile like that. Sometimes I succeeded, but most of the time, she looked at the world with her serious face on—one that didn't budge. And while her father tried to keep her ignorant of his activities, whenever he had to go to work or was traveling for a couple of days, that was the look she wore. Concerned. Worried. Ari was no fool. She knew exactly who her father was, and I sensed her resentment toward me even then. Every time we went on jobs, she always said to me, *You look out for him*. And I had done my best.

*Except you failed.*

Except I'd failed.

Changing the subject, she said, "It's this way." She pointed me in the direction of the side of the house, where security had been stationed in large numbers.

We crouched by the lake, using our heat sensors to scope out how many guards were on duty. She pointed to the device. "See? That's the concentration at the main auction room right there. But over here, where that big cluster is, I think that's where most of the pieces are being kept. They've got three-man rotations. Nothing at the window, but some at the different entrance points in the room."

I knew what he was talking about, and I refused to discuss it. I was in work mode. This was easy, just recon. Nothing major to be done right now. Of course he would bring up what had happened earlier. He couldn't just let it go.

"So we're not going to talk about that kiss on the balcony?"

"I don't want to talk about it, Damon."

"Angel, you kiss me like that, and I think we have a lot to talk about."

---

# DAMON

Ari shook her head. "No, we don't."

"Don't be like that, angel. You know you want to talk."

"What are you talking about? You don't know me."

I knew her too well. I'd spent so much time watching her. I wanted her, but not just that; I wanted to steal every single one of her rare smiles. I wanted to be responsible for them.

"Oh, really? Ari, you forget how long ago we met. I know you. You chew on your bottom lip or play with your braids when you're preoccupied and worried about something or when something is really perplexing you. You're doing that right now."

What I didn't add was that I'd been obsessed with those tics since I was a teenager. I was used to her trying to hang around. I was used to her curiosity about what we were doing and her ceaseless questions. But one moment, she'd been just Paul's semi-annoying kid, and the next, I seemed to suddenly notice *every-thing* about her. Like once I'd *seen* her, I couldn't *unsee* her.

My watch beeped, and I lifted my gaze. "Time to lay the groundwork for part one."

We started our walk, shrouded by the tall shrubs, and turned left along the stone path before turning toward the house. Damon held my hand as we strolled in the moonlight.

The lapping waters in the lake provided us with some auditory cover as we worked on the electronics for the video feed.

At the mansion, we took the side stairs on the far side of the garden before slipping through the employee entrance. The areas of the grounds we needed to explore weren't easily accessible just by walking around the perimeter. Which was why going up and over seemed the best method.

From there, we followed the route to the rooftop and paused at the edge.

Damon hooked up our rappelling gear. Thanks to Prince Lucas and Galen, we had the best gear available. GT Securities prided itself on being on the cutting edge, but this stuff was next-level.

Damon handed me my gloves, which were as thin as latex and fit amazingly. The grip was strong, and they didn't slip.

Once we'd left the roof, rappelled down past the balcony, and landed, Damon loosened the rope and let it fall. We would be walking back in through the side entrance of the restricted area. I'd already identified our best route when we had explored the grounds after arriving. We pulled open the map that we had on his phone as we sketched out where we were.

"Are we going to talk about the thing?" he asked in a whisper.

## 14

## ARI

In a pocket of time that Lucas had managed to steal for us, we dressed in silence, fully aware that our room was bugged. We'd done a search and hadn't found any cameras, so at least that part was safe, but we knew there were auditory devices, so we could be heard.

The gala was in full swing, so everyone would be occupied.

As standard protocol, I turned on our jamming equipment and plugged it in by the bedside lamp. To the casual observer, it would look like a phone. The range on it was pretty tight, so it would cover our bungalow and balcony.

Our gear was all black, including a small bag for supplies like night vision gear and some tranq darts if we needed them. But we were going light. I was wearing a skintight but stretchy black suit. Damon went with a lightweight sweater and black joggers that looked like they could have been dress pants. If we were caught, we were just a fashionable couple out on an evening stroll.

Before I knew what was happening, our bodies crashed together and our lips drew together like we were magnets.

Our tongues met, then danced wildly, lips exploring each other hungrily. Damon's hands were everywhere, pulling me closer to him, his erection pressing hard against my thigh. I moaned softly into his mouth while tangling my fingers in his hair and kissed him back with equal ferocity.

When he cupped my face, he licked into my mouth, teasing me. I was lost in him, melting under his touch. His body was hard against mine, desperation clawing at me.

My hands moved from his hair to his chest. He groaned into the kiss, and his hands slid down my back to my ass.

I moaned into his mouth again; then he broke the kiss and trailed hot, wet kisses down my neck. He nipped and licked at my skin, sending shivers down my spine. I could feel his breath on my skin, his hands squeezing and kneading.

This time, before we could get too carried away, *I* pulled back, acutely aware of what we were supposed to be doing. "Wait."

His breath was coming in sharp pants. "Yeah?"

I cleared my throat, trying to stay strong. Kissing him was dangerous to my equilibrium and my sanity. "Um, I think…we need to stay focused. We should go get ready."

The muscle in his jaw ticked several times, but eventually he nodded. "You're right. We need to stay on mission. But after, we're going to have this conversation."

My brain oh-so-unhelpfully added, *In a bed*.

"You didn't think about how I would feel? You brought my father back to me nearly dead and then *left us*! I understood why. But you didn't come back. You didn't check on me. You didn't come to his funeral. I was all alone with Aunt Adele. And to know you were the one he loved the most… That killed me." I wiped my tears with the back of my hand. "And when you did come back, it was to hand me money and walk away. I needed more than that, Damon."

He dropped his head into his hands and scrubbed his face. "I fucked up, Ari. When I reached out to Adele, she said you didn't want anything to do with me."

My heart cracked in two. "Of course I didn't. You'd abandoned me. You'd abandoned *him*. Why would I want to see you?"

He nodded slowly. "I know. I was following protocol. Your father taught me well. I was to stay away from you if anything ever went bad. I did what I was supposed to do, but every damned day, I regretted listening to him. Every damned day, I regretted leaving the first stable family I'd ever known. But I always thought I was doing the right thing. Keeping you safe. You didn't need someone like me in your life."

"Right. And now?" I whispered.

"And now, I couldn't walk away from you if I tried. You deserve so much better. But the only way I'll go is if you tell me to. I walked away once. I'm not doing it again. Please don't ask me to tear out my heart again. I can't do it."

"I…" My voice cracked. It was too hard to keep the shields up.

His voice was more of a low growl than actual words when he whispered, "Ari Sari."

When the red light started flashing, I breathed a sigh of relief. I could safely be out here for a few moments. No one could listen in.

"I'm fine. It's just a lot," I said as I grabbed a glass of champagne from a passing waiter.

He nodded. "I know." He cleared his throat suddenly. "Angel, I know you don't want to talk about it, but I am grateful I'm with you in here."

I shook my head and sipped my champagne. "You sure you don't mean to say that to the *contessa*?" I said her title with enough malice to make his brow lift.

He took the glass from my hand and placed it on the stone balcony. "You know full well I was on a job. I barely remember her, and any part I do remember was for the job." He scrutinized me closely. "You look tense, angel."

"That's hardly fair. I-I *am* tense. I'm not like you. All these years, you've been honing this skill. I have not. And how did you not have a scar when she met you?" My curiosity got the better of me there.

"Scar-filling makeup. Hard to be anonymous with identifiable markings. But I learned to hide it."

"God, all those years, you never looked back, did you?"

He shrugged. "I thought about you a lot while I was gone. More than you know. I've missed you, angel."

Tears pricked my eyes. "I can't do this now, Damon. I just… I really can't."*

"Fuck. I get it. I walked away and didn't come back. I knew you would blame me for what happened to your father. I thought I was doing the best thing by staying away from you."

* ME AND THE DEVIL–Gil Scott-Heron

played that well? Are you kidding me? The woman was practically draped all over you. We, in case you have forgotten, are supposed to be in love."

"Easy, hellcat. She's not remembering that night well. I drugged her, took her to a room, and stole her necklace. I absolutely did *not* have sex with her. That's what she wanted and likely what she thought happened, but no."

"Wow, you are even more—"

Before I could say anything else, he kissed me so softly my heart ached. But true to form, like most things with Damon, it turned possessive and demanding. And then he pulled back just when I started to melt. "Let's not pretend you don't know who I am. But you can relax. Retract the claws just a little. I never fucked her. She was just trying to get under your skin."

I refused to admit she'd gotten her wish. "I don't want to talk about this."

I twirled out of his hold and headed straight for the balcony. I was jealous. This was the dangerous part. Somewhere between getting to know Damon even better, planning this mission, and sleeping in the same suite as him over the last few nights, I'd forgotten who I was, who *he* was. I'd started to believe that the kisses and the touches and the looks were real. I was jealous over someone who wasn't mine and was never going to be.

When I realized he was following me, I stopped abruptly, but Damon took my elbow and dragged me out to the balcony anyway. "You look like you need a break."

Once outside, he took the signal jammer from my clutch and flipped it on.

and an actor. Gorgeous. Except, obviously, Simon here has blue eyes. But I can see the resemblance. It's in the set of the mouth. The jawline, a little bit. But personally, I think he looks like the model David Gandy. Like a younger version. And also harder."

It was so helpful that Damon had added contacts as part of his disguise.

I gave her a wink and grinned as I lifted onto my tiptoes, asking for a kiss. Damon, of course, obliged, and his lips lingered, stealing my breath for just a moment but long enough to make my brain fog. When he pulled back, I was slightly dazed. It was like every time our breaths mingled, he somehow managed to intoxicate me. Then I turned to the contessa with a sweet smile. "How did you and this mystery man know each other?"

The contessa lifted a brow, her nose slightly wrinkled and her lips pursed. "Well, I see maybe I was mistaken. The man I knew didn't have a scar and had more refined taste."

Damon kept his arm around me tight, and he turned to the contessa. "I'm sorry for the misunderstanding, but it wasn't me. But then, my tastes are perhaps more discerning."

And with that, he turned me around and deliberately walked us in the opposite direction. I held myself stiffly, but he held me close and pressed another kiss to my temple. "Easy does it."

He pulled me to the dance floor, wrapped his arms around me, and twirled me around as somebody played the instrumental version of what sounded like a Beyoncé song, but I didn't make it easy for him. My steps were stilted as we danced.

"You played that well, angel."

Fury bubbled up at the thought of him with that woman. "I

up to him, disengaging her hand from his bicep. "Simon, sweetheart, I found the piece I wanted to show you. It's over here."

Damon's gaze snapped to mine, and I could have sworn I saw relief in it.

I turned to the contessa. "Have we met?"

She lifted a brow and eyed me up and down. When her gaze narrowed, I could see the malice in those beautiful clear gray eyes. "Who are you?"*

"I'm his wife, Michelle." I put my hand out, not expecting her to take it.

Her brows lifted. "Contessa Annabelle Bouchon. I'm sorry, I didn't know he was married."

"Oh, we just got married two years ago. We're sort of on our extended honeymoon."

I wrapped my arm around his waist, and he threw an arm around my shoulders while placing a kiss at my temple. His fingers danced over the skin on my shoulders. "Yes, I just met the contessa. Unfortunately, she thinks I'm someone else."

I could have given him shit. I could have thrown him under the bus. But despite the pang of jealousy, the twist of anger, the stab that he had been with this gorgeous creature, I knew we had a job to do.

"Oh, that's odd. Although, I will say, my husband does have one of those faces. There was once a woman in Paris who swore she'd seen him somewhere before. It turns out, she was thinking about that movie star. You know the one in that really dirty Polish movie? Ah, I forgot the title. That guy is a model

* HOLD UP–Beyoncé

After an hour, my feet were screaming for a break. I scanned the crowd to find my husband once again with a woman. One who looked far too familiar with him as she stroked his arm.

Why was this woman eyeballing him like she wanted to eat him alive? I approached slowly, only catching the latest part of their conversation.

"Gareth, don't you remember we met in Saint-Tropez six years ago?" the woman asked.

He frowned. "I'm sorry, my name is Simon Christopher."

Damon tried to inch away from her, but I could tell he *knew* her.

Panic gripped me for a moment as I tried to figure out just what the hell we were going to do about the fact that she recognized him. Or what I wanted to do about the fact that it appeared they'd had some sort of intimate relationship.

*Not your circus, not your monkeys. Stick to the role.*

We had a problem. And it was currently wrapped around my fake husband.

"Don't you remember? You used to call me *contessa*?"

He winced, as if trying to place her. "I'm so sorry. I don't recognize you."

"And here I thought I was impossible to forget. But you know, I've had a little work done, so maybe that's why."

He shook his head. "I'm sorry. I've never been to Saint-Tropez."

"Listen, I'm not trying to embarrass you here, but I just knew that I'd see you again. We said goodbye against the hotel wall."

And there it was. Fury unfurled in my gut, and I stepped right

his and easily passed him the comm unit from the tiny packet I'd gotten from Penny.

He leaned in and kissed my cheek again before brushing a hand over his ear and placing it inside.

Immediately, Lucas's voice came over the comms. "Mic check, one, two, one, two. Damon, if you can hear me, touch your belt. And, Ari, if you can hear me, touch your hair."

We both complied, and he breathed a sigh of relief. "All right, excellent. You have your assignments. If anything goes wrong, reach out. In the meantime, remember you are being watched. This has got to be as realistic as possible. We go in two nights. So tonight, scope things out the best you can, study your tablets, and maintain your roles."

With their status as royalty, Lucas and Penny weren't being as tightly surveilled, but they had to be just as careful. Smuggling communications equipment in must have been a feat.

This wasn't a joke. I knew it, and I was terrified.

As we talked and mingled with the other guests, I was doing a mental check through the guest list. There were diplomats, aristocrats, art collectors, vineyard owners, and more publicly famous people. I met an actor whose movies I'd seen and enjoyed thoroughly. For an action star, he was really short. Barely my height of five foot eight. And I was pretty sure he was wearing lifts.

I'd already caught sight of Reaper, and unlike the last time, he was in nothing but leather. Lord, that man was attractive. I also noted the woman he was speaking to. Juliet Bryson: petite, brunette, beautiful. The vibrant emerald dress she wore was cinched at the waist, giving her great curves.

them so tiny these days. Galen should be happy with the images it captured. Thirty seconds later, I followed behind her. I was meandering down the hall as if admiring the artwork but discreetly checking security checkpoints and rotations.

I needed to get as close to the main offices on this level as I could to verify that the information we'd been given was accurate, but I only made it about halfway before a security guard found me. "Can I help you, ma'am?"

"Oh, I'm so sorry. I'm looking for the reception. I think I got turned around. Do you mind helping me?" I gave him a broad smile.

He nodded briskly and pointed in the exact opposite direction.

"Oh, I think I turned the wrong way from the bathroom. Thank you." Then I walked briskly before pausing at a painting. "I'm sorry, who's the artist of this piece?"

He shrugged. "I don't know, but I can have the host find you and tell you."

"I would love that. It's beautiful."

He angled his head and gave me another nod that indicated he just needed me as far away from the direction I'd come as possible. Which told me there were things down that way that I would probably find quite interesting. Not my concern though. I had one target, and one target only.

When I located my supposed husband, he was surrounded by women. But immediately, his gaze landed on me and followed me across the room as I snagged a glass of champagne from a passing waiter.

He excused himself and found me, then planted a kiss on my cheek and wrapped an arm around my waist. I laid my hand over who I was working with…especially when they could get me killed.

I found my way to the bathroom, where Penny met me, sliding into her role. "Oh, hi. I love your shoes."

I grinned at her as our fingertips grazed and she swapped her midsized clutch with mine. A quick peek inside showed me additional tools they hadn't been able to camouflage, including the Taser and tiny communications units.

"Thank you so much. I have to say, your makeup is gorgeous."

She chuckled. "Thanks. I learned early on how to do my own makeup, especially when traveling."

I nodded conspiratorially as I placed a listening device in my ear. "I know what you mean. That color of blush is just stunning on you."

"Thank you. You're so sweet. What's your name?" Penny asked as though we were complete strangers.

"Michelle. Michelle Christopher."

"Well, it's nice to meet you. I'm Penny Walsh, soon to be Winston."

"Oh my gosh. I guess I should have noticed that massive engagement ring."

Penny lifted her finger and signaled the code for the antechamber that led to the Royal Heart: *5-2-3-7-4*. I nodded my understanding, and then she excused herself.

"Hopefully I'll see you around again, Penny."

"Thank you."

Once she was gone, I adjusted my pendant. It was a beautiful piece, and the camera was state-of-the-art. Technology made

Ari smiled. "Thank you. Do you mind showing me the facilities? I'd like to freshen up a little."

He smiled and pointed the way. Ari knew exactly where she was going, but she was sliding into her role.

She'd pinned her long, thick hair up. *What I wouldn't give to unpin it and sink my hands into her soft tresses.*

*No. No, don't. That is not what we're here for.*

The plan was for Ari to see how far she could go inside and scope things out while looking for the bathroom. I would head to the sunroom.

At the front door, Ari leaned in and kissed my cheek. Her lips were soft against my skin. I sucked in a short breath, not expecting the contact. "I'll be back in a tick, love," she said.

"Yeah, back in a tick." And I had just that amount of time to get my act together. Because this wasn't real. And if I lost sight of that along the way, Ari's life could be at risk.

# ARI

I was a fool.

Had I really thought I could do this? The last six days had felt like being on holiday. But tonight, we'd be in the same bed. Just the one.

That was ridiculous. I could still feel the skip of electricity through my body from when he took my hand. Damon was trouble. So much fucking trouble. And then there was the prince. I'd been doing a little digging into him. I liked to know

"Showtime?" she asked.

"It's been showtime," I whispered against the shell of her ear.

"Only sort of. Tonight, you get to find out I'm a terrible bed hog."

"I'm sure we'll be fine."

"I swear to God," she said, muttering to herself, then added, "Remember, avoid Contessa Annabelle Bouchon at all costs."

*The contessa.* She was the only person on the guest list who might recognize me, from a job in Saint-Tropez six years ago. My only access point to her safe, her husband, had died on his yacht from a heart attack. I'd taken the risk and chosen to seduce her to gain access. I'd covered my scar and worn a prosthetic nosepiece, but she was still a risk.

Though not one worth pulling out for.

"I know, my darling." I wrapped an arm around her waist. "We've got this."

She lifted her chin. "I know that."

I chuckled and released her, sliding my hand gently down her arm and taking her hand in mine. "Well, angel, shall we?"

She turned to me. "Why must you call me that?"

"Because you're adorable. And your eyes are mischievous. And you have secret claws you like to sink into me." I led her along the gravel path.

A butler in full regalia stopped us. "Mr. and Mrs. Christopher, welcome to the Black Rose Auction."

"Thank you."

"Your bags will be brought straight to your room. Feel free to join the reception in the sunroom."

were either staying in the mansion or in the miniature chalets that dotted the edges of the property. Ari and I would be in one of the chalets…with one bed.

Lucas had already reminded us that once we set foot inside the doors, we were being watched. Hell, we'd thought it was bad back in the city, but now we were in a fishbowl. All guests would be treated with deference and *suspicion*. We had to act extremely in love, and it would be unwise to assume privacy in our own rooms. Which meant every conversation, every touch, every moment that felt private would potentially be observed.

I strolled around the Rolls-Royce to open the door for Ari, and she placed her delicate hand in mine, the ring on her finger glinting in the late-afternoon light.

A zing of electricity snaked up my spine, worked its way back down, and finally unfurled in my gut. It felt like getting punched in the solar plexus.

Was she the same Ari I'd left behind? She certainly wasn't a teenager anymore.

*How's ignoring her working out for you?*

Not well. Because Ari Denton, or rather Michelle Christopher, was going to be the death of me.

She slid her leg out, and my gaze caught on her taut brown skin. For a second, I let my eyes travel up the length of her calf. The sky-blue ruffle of her dress shifted, giving me a glimpse of two more inches of leg.

*God. Get it together.*

She stepped out, the movement bringing her body against mine. I forced a grin onto my face, leaned in.

## DAMON

I knew what was at stake here. And I was complicating matters by wanting her. The last six days had felt like a six-day first date. Like when you are making sure to put your best foot forward.

It was all part of the role. But there was a part of me that was enjoying the time spent with Ari. Sometimes it was far too easy to forget it was pretend.

It wasn't just the Royal Heart, but our lives too. I'd dragged Ari into this.

She might have been all business, but on my end, there were feelings there that we didn't need floating to the surface.

The grounds where the auction was being held were spectacular. Lush green lawns led to the stone steps of a mansion that was gothic in nature, complete with gargoyles. The house itself was massive. Three stories and stunning. According to the blueprints, the place had fifty-seven rooms. And all the attendees wholeheartedly. There's no one else I'd rather be in the field with. Get some rest."

He turned and closed the door behind him. The worst part of it was that his words had hit me harder than the gift. As I stared down at the gloves, I couldn't hold back the tears anymore. I swiped them from my cheeks angrily. This was not real. A kiss, a gift, and a compliment did not make him my boyfriend. This was not real, and I would really be better off if I remembered that.

"What's a dare?"*

"You deserve a gift that you *want*. Not just something you need. One wish come true."

"I don't know. I'm hard to get gifts for."

"Ari Denton, you forget I also know your birthday is coming up in six months."

"Oh my God, please don't."

But he was already shaking his head. "Nope, now you've put my mind to it."

"Okay, fine. It's your money."

"That it is. And wouldn't it be funny if I never spent a dime?"

"This is ridiculous."

He cocked his head then. "Can I ask you a question?"

"Yeah, what's that?"

"Do you never want anything because you don't want to be disappointed?"

Well, he'd gone right for the jugular. "I don't know what you're talking about."

"Uh-huh. Sure, you don't. Well, in that case, challenge accepted."

"You're different than I expected, Damon."

"I know. In a couple of days, we're going to the field, Ari. You and me. We've got to make it count."

"Yeah, we do. Do you regret not trying to do this by yourself?"

He crossed his arms and leaned on the doorjamb, looking like sex on a stick. Did he have any idea how sexy that leaning was? "About that... I was mistaken, Ari. You commit

* BEGGIN'–Måneskin

"You use these?"

"I have before. They come in handy and have saved my life, and I wanted you to have a pair."

I stared at the box, my eyes stinging and dangerously close to welling. If I allowed that to happen, they would certainly leak.

I'd been given gifts before. Things people were expecting me to be excited about while they stared at me expectantly. I never had a great response. I always tried to smile and be appreciative, but usually the gifts had nothing to do with me. They were more about the giver. The glove had everything to do with me, and shit, was I going to cry?

I blinked rapidly. "Um, thank you. I don't think I've ever been given a gift like this before."

He shrugged. "I figured. No big deal."

Shit, why wouldn't the right damn words come out? "No, these are actually really thoughtful. They'll be useful. They're something I need."

"Um, right." He shifted on his feet. "You should, you know, always get gifts that you want."

"I don't usually want anything," I said with a shrug.

He looked confused. "What do you mean, you don't want anything?"

"I mean I don't really make wishes. I'm not the wishing-on-a-star kind of girl. If I want something, I get it myself. These are useful, and they're something I never would have thought of."

"Okay, you recognize that's a dare now, right? You're the kind of woman who should always make wishes."

"Come in."

When he opened my door, the dim light from the hallway illuminated his face. "Why are you in the dark?"

I reached over to the bedside table and turned on my lamp. "Sorry. I like to walk the plans through in the dark with a timer. Just to think through everything."

"Do you do this a lot?" He wasn't frowning, but his brows were lifted quizzically.

"Yeah. Not for me, of course, but for the field agents. It's part of my job as an analyst. It helps me see where the pitfalls might be."

He sighed. "Right. It's clever. You'd make a hell of a field agent if that's what you wanted."

"Yeah, that's not in the cards for me. It's a one-time gig."

"Right. Anyway, I was going through the supplies Jazz brought over, and I got these for you." He walked over to the bed and handed me a box.

I opened it. "Gloves?"

"Yeah. I know that Galen and Lucas provided some, but I like these better. The ones I use will be too big for you, so I had these made to fit. They make great climbing gloves, and technology allows them to stick to glass. You can also recharge them."

I lifted my brows. "Are you serious?"

"Yeah. They also have a great grip for rappelling. They work with kinetic energy."

"You're shitting me."

"Nope. They're military-grade design. They're not even on the market."

## ARI

Three days until D-day. Three days until we were going to be tested.

Hell, that wasn't true; we were being tested now. Had been since we'd met with Reaper. We'd spent the last three days acting in love. Spa days, exploring museums, restaurants. The funny part was, Damon fully took to his role. He was cultured, well-traveled. Knowledgeable about art. Charming, funny, and easy to be with.

And then every night, away from prying eyes, we'd been drilling the schematics and plans.

I was doing a final check of everything—running through the maps, the schematics, our options—making sure I'd memorized it all. I liked to sit in the dark and mentally walk myself through the plan.

A knock sounded on the door. I tried not to be irritated, because, after all, how was he supposed to know that I needed silence to work?

I shook my head. "Give your dad a little more credit than that, Ari. I wasn't stealing his love. He just saw a kid with nothing else going for him. He was proud of you. You should know that."

I turned to go, but I heard her whisper, "Maybe you have a lot more to offer than I thought too."

"Oh, he can get women," Jazz clarified, "but he fucks up so quick."

Ari laughed at that. "Wow, Jazz, I think I like you too."

My blabbering assistant winked at Ari, turned, gave me a knuckle tap, and headed out.

I hung my head as I closed the door behind her. "For fuck's sake."

"A crush on me, huh?"

"I didn't have a crush. I just thought your skill was unparalleled. I was so tired of your father training *me* all the time."

She frowned at that. "You were?"

I shrugged. "You have the magic touch. All the stuff you learned by yourself so easily, I had to work really hard at. I wasn't very good at first."

She licked her bottom lip. "But he chose to train you."

*Does she really have no idea that he was protecting her and instead think that he didn't love her?*

"Your dad gave me training for a reason; I wasn't good at much. Or he didn't think I would be. I was a scruffy kid with no prospects. He gave me a chance to be something else. You, though, you had prospects from the beginning. He didn't want to mire you down into this thing that he was. You might not know it, but he was ashamed that he stole for a living."

She frowned. "I didn't know. All this time, I thought he—"

"What? You thought he loved me more? That I was the son he always wanted?"

"A little. He always said he wanted to protect me. But that felt like an excuse."

I chuckled low. "Jazz, not in front of the guest."

"Oh, come on, it's Ari. She knows what you do. Hell, her father trained you."

I rubbed a hand over the back of my neck as Ari grinned and said, "This is fascinating. By all means, do tell me his secrets."

Jazz chuckled. "God, I like her." She turned to Ari. "I mean, you…know your dad's rules. Damon has taken them to heart. Hell, he's mostly legit now."

"Is that so?"

Jazz was more than happy to spill. "As it turns out, Damon's actually pretty good at the import-export business. But occasionally someone calls for a favor, or Damon runs into someone that maybe needs to be taught a lesson and be parted from their prized possessions."

Ari slid me an assessing gaze. "Is that so?"

I ignored Ari's question. Instead, I focused on Jazz and her loose lips, then said, "I don't like assholes. Assholes with Picassos sometimes get robbed. I listened when your dad said to have something that makes me legitimate, a way out. Anything else, Jazz?"

"No, I've got everything else covered."

"Then you can go now."

"Okay." She turned to Ari. "It was a delight meeting you. Maybe one day we can, I don't know, sit down and chat. I have Damon stories for days. But I would love to know what young Damon was like. Was he as stupidly hot as he is now? He's still completely useless with women."

Ari blinked in surprise.

"None of this is important. What do you need?"

She rolled her eyes. "Ugh, it's such a waste not to tell the person you fangirl over how much you admire her when she's right freaking here. Ari Denton."

I wanted to die. "I'm a guy. I don't fangirl."

"Oh, don't be a misogynist. Fanboy, whatever. The point is you're a huge fan."

I gritted my teeth. Ari had her arms folded, a hint of a smile playing across her lush lips.

I rolled my eyes. "Yes, I was quite proud of you and the fact I know you, okay? No big deal."

"It's funny. You never said a word."

"There was no need to. Jazz, what do you need?"

"Okay, a couple of housekeeping things. I checked on the Burmans for you. The IRS came sniffing around with questions about their last tax return. In the meantime I've convinced them to take cash, but you'll want to find another way to funnel them money."

"Shit. Okay, I'll think of something."

"What else?"

"The jewels from the Obsidian Crest. I've returned them to the family, per your request, along with the papers of authenticity."

"Excellent."

"I sure wanted to keep those," she muttered.

"No ill-gotten gains, remember, Jazz? They belonged to the family, and they deserve to have them."

"Yes, I know. We are the good guys. But, damn, they were gorgeous."

to pick up stuff so quickly. Is it true that you can break into a Caston lock in five minutes and eleven seconds?"

Ari's eyes went wide. "Uh, yeah, I've done it once. But it's been some time."

"Oh my God, he's right, you Dentons do walk on water."

I shifted uncomfortably. This was never going to end. Or it would end badly, with me humiliated. "That's enough, Jazz. Ask your questions and get out of here."

Jazz shook her head. "And is it true that you learned to break into the Jackson Double Spring on your own and in the dark?"

"Well, sort of. Dad wouldn't let me work on anything with him, so I kind of had to teach myself."

"Oh my God, but to learn by touch alone, that's... *Wow*."

"It's been a while. I haven't done that since I was a teenager." Ari gave a nervous laugh. "I didn't know I had a fan."

"I just heard all these stories about you from Damon," Jazz said, obviously completely starstruck. "So naturally, I'm extremely curious about you."

Ari turned her attention to me. "From Damon, huh?"

"Yeah. He was saying that your dad taught him everything but didn't want to teach you, you know, to prevent you from becoming a criminal and all that. But you were determined to be just like him, so you learned all that stuff on your own with no help. Damon's, like, your biggest fan. I'm surprised he hasn't built a shrine to you."

And there it was. I was praying for a hole to open up and swallow Jazz. Hell, I'd climb in with her just to shut her up. "Jazz, for fuck's sake, that's enough."

She grinned at me. "How come she doesn't know this already?"

But Jazz was not having it. "Who is this gorgeous creature?"

Ari gave her an uncertain smile. "Um, hi. I'm Michelle."

She was going with her cover. *Good girl.*

"It's all right, Ari. Jazz works for me. You don't have to pretend."

Ari let out a relieved breath. "Oh, thank God. Hi, I'm Ari."

Jazz grinned at her. "I like you."

"Do you? I haven't done anything yet."

"Oh, the key word is *yet*. And you seem to already have my boss on his back foot, so that means I doubly like you."

"Do I now?" Ari asked.

"Yes, he's already tried to get rid of me," Jazz said, giving me the side-eye. "Which means there's something he doesn't want me to see." Suddenly, Jazz's eyes went wide. "Oh my God, this is her?"

I shook my head. "Stand down, Jazz. Time to go."

"Oh my God, this is her. You're Ari Denton."

Ari shifted on her feet. "Um, yes."

Then Jazz turned to me, and I prayed: *Shut your fucking trap, Jazz. Say nothing. Say nothing.*

I tried to communicate those words telepathically to her as I glowered.

But Jazz was not having it. "Oh, my fucking God. You know, he talks about your father like the man walked on water."

Ari gave her a wan smile. "Really? I think we had different experiences with my father."

"That's right, you two knew each other when you were young. He said you were a pain in the ass. Brave, but so curious and smart. I think he was a little in awe of how you were able

# DAMON

I knew that Ari had *said* she was ready for this, but on the chance she wasn't, I had to prepare. So I needed a few of my things just in case. When Jazz knocked on the door of the hotel suite, I tried to stop her from entering. "Thanks for dropping off my tools. We're good."

But she barged right past me. "While I'm here and have your undivided attention, there are some things that I—"

Ari chose that moment to come out of her bedroom. "Oh, I didn't know we had a visitor, darling."

The word *darling* snaked around my spine, grasping me, pulling me into Ari's orbit.

*Just because she kissed you like you were the only man on the planet does not mean that shit is real. Get your shit together.*

For fuck's sake, I needed to. I wanted her. That was dangerous enough without taking her into the field.

"Thanks for dropping this stuff off, Jazz. You can go now."

"Then go, have fun, be amazing. Okay?"

"Yeah, okay. Hey, Taryn? Thanks."

"Anytime."

So all I had to do was be nonchalant. Probably a lot easier said than done with that insistent throbbing between my thighs. However, I had set out to prove myself, and that was exactly what I was going to do. I wasn't going to let Damon Hunt stop me. Doing this job meant pleasing an important client. That was the goal. And I could finally prove that I wasn't my father. So despite those oh-so-sweet tingly feelings Damon inspired, I had to shut that emotional shit down. The goal wasn't to find out all the awesome things about sex. And I had to keep my eyes on the prize.

I sighed. "I have zero experience at this. I've had sex with two people. And it was always boring. And honestly, every time I had sex, I stared at the ceiling and made my grocery lists. I have kissed people before, but I've never felt like *that*."

"Well, think of him as practice for how it *should* feel. Also, keep in mind that sometimes the people who are really good kissers are not the people we try and keep, okay?"

"Keep him? There's no way I'm keeping him."

"Good, just remember how he made you feel before, and it'll be easier to get over him."

"Frustrated. Annoyed. Angry."

"Exactly. But if he happens to be a good kisser, then the more practice, the better. Just remember that he doesn't have the ability to pull you off the mission. Only Galen does. You've got this."

"Yeah. Thanks, Taryn."

"Oh my God, I love you. You're adorable. Go out there and act completely nonchalant. He will not suggest taking you off the mission again."

"But I'm chalanting. Totally chalanting here."

"The key is to *act* like you're not. You know all those meetings where you sort of mirror other people's emotions so you don't have to feel your own?"

"Yeah."

"Kind of like that."

"Okay. I can do that."

"The auction is in a matter of days. There's no way Galen's changing the plan, right?"

"Right. I know that."

Ugh. She had a point there. "Well, what am I supposed to do about the other feeling?"

"Oh, the one where you think it's real?"

"Yes." The more time I spent with him, the more I started to see him differently. Like the man he was now. Not like the boy he'd been.

"Ignore it. Pretend you are not having those feelings at all. You're good at pretending. Or even better, use the feelings for the role. Think of it as going method. Those feelings are dangerous for you postmission. But we're not going to worry about postmission right now. Do what you need to do, come home, and then you and I will cry about it over ice cream before we get you on the dating market."

"What if I don't get over it when I come home?"

"You will. And if you felt something, he's definitely feeling something too. What happened after he kissed you?"

"Oh, he cleared his throat and said, *That's enough practice.* And then he squared his shoulders and walked away."

"Oh, that's a good thing."

"I don't know what that means."

"That means he likely had a very potent reaction to your kiss and went somewhere to calm down."

"Oh."

"There's no need to worry," she assured me. "You're doing great."

"So I shouldn't practice anymore?"

She chuckled at that. "Well, I personally say practice as much as you think is necessary."

"I have, you know, like tingly crush feelings. It's like I suddenly see what all the fuss is about. And oh my God…"

She chuckled softly. "Welcome to the gang. I'm so happy that you get to experience this."

Nope. That was the wrong response. "How do I turn it off?"

Another long pause from Taryn. "Turn it off?"

"I mean I don't want to *feel* like this." Certainly not in the field. It was distracting.

"Well, I'm sorry to have to tell you this, but you can't exactly turn it off."

"I don't want it. This is *complicated*."

Her laugh was a soft trill, like she was really enjoying my predicament. "Yes, the best situations usually are."

"What am I supposed to do with this feeling?"

"Well, how about you enjoy it?"

"I don't want to enjoy it. I want to make it stop."

She chuckled. "Okay, so the concern is that you enjoyed it?"

"Yes, because, oh my God, what if he kisses me in front of people again, and this time I faint or something?"

I could visualize her rolling her eyes. "You're not going to faint."

"Are you sure?"

She was silent for a moment. "Just how good of a kiss was this?"

"Good. Really, *really* good."

"Well, in that case, problem solved."

What the hell did she mean by that? "Taryn, focus."

"I don't see the problem, Ari. He makes you hot. You're pretending to be in love. If he kisses you in public and gets you hot, everyone will *believe* you're in love. Easy. It's for the mission."

She let out a long sigh. "I get the impression I know where this is going."

I hurried to finish so she'd get the full view of my mortification quickly. "So he was trying to figure out a way to pull off the mission without me."

"Idiot," she muttered.

"Exactly."

"So then what happened?"

"Well, I told him to kiss me. That we should practice, because when I practice things, I get more comfortable with them."

"Oh, right. That's very practical of you. It's like an inoculation."

I knew she'd get me. "That's *exactly* what I said. So then we practiced."

She was silent for a long beat. "And?"

Oh, she wanted me to dish. "Um, it was good. I don't know. I feel weird and tingly."

"You *have* been kissed before."

"I know that. Except this time, it felt… I don't know. Hotter, I guess."

"All right, that's not a bad thing. Honey, have you never been, like, fully aroused?"

What kind of question was that? I was an adult in possession of a vibrator.

*But you've had stunted development in so many ways.*

I was aroused plenty when I was on my own. But somehow I'd never really been able to connect to someone else that way. I'd tried to be open to anyone, regardless of gender. I'd assumed I was asexual. Nope. Apparently, I was just *Damonsexual*.

## ARI

Yes, I was in fact hiding in the bathroom of the hotel suite while I used the phone and called on the secure line. I needed the running water to muffle my voice as I made the embarrassing call.

Taryn answered with a cheeky "What's up, buttercup? How is our secret mission going?"

"Um, Taryn, I need help."

Immediately, her voice turned serious and flat. Red-alert mode. Full focus. "Are you hurt? Where are you?"

"No, I'm not hurt. It's not like that. Um, I-I kissed him."

She was silent for a moment. "Explain."

"Okay, here's the deal: Damon said that I was uncomfortable."

There was a moment's hesitation on the line. "What do you mean, *uncomfortable*?"

"When we were meeting with a contact for the mission, we had to touch a lot, and he said I was stiff. And we'll have to touch a lot during the auction to seem like a couple in love."

hands fisted in my hair now, and she kissed me back, her tongue tangling with mine.

A rumble escaped my lips as I picked her up, and she wrapped her legs around my waist and rocked her hips against me. She ground her sweet heat against my cock, and fuck my life, the tingling started at the base of my spine.

*Shit. Shit. Shit.*

Involuntarily, I grasped her, assisting her in rocking against my cock and torturing me. Fuck, this was a recipe for disaster.

I tilted my head down and started kissing her throat, inhaling her scent.

The animal in me growled.

She whispered my name while moving restlessly against me. I didn't know what was happening here, but I knew this couldn't continue. I wouldn't survive it.

*Too bad, because she's under your skin.*

I stilled, then set her down on her feet before stepping back. "You think you can handle that, angel?"

nervous, she stood stock-still. "Remember, Ari, you asked me to do this."

Was I reminding her or myself? Because I knew that when I touched my lips to hers, it would be a whole hell of a lot more than a kiss.

I closed the distance between us, backing her against the wall. Her eyes widened in surprise, and a small gasp escaped her lips. I leaned in and wrapped my hand gently around her neck, then tilted her head back slightly. Her pulse raced under my fingertips, and I couldn't help but smile at the effect I had on her.

I lowered my lips to hers, gently at first. But as I felt her responding, her arms wrapping around my neck, I deepened the angle, entwining our tongues together in a slow, wet kiss.

I could taste the sweetness of her mouth, feel her body pressing against mine, and it was like nothing else existed in the world except for the two of us in that moment.

My hand tightened around her neck ever so slightly, eliciting a soft moan from her.

I fisted her hair and changed my angle as I licked into her mouth. The trick of it was, as I pressed into her lush curves and my cock fought my zipper, it was she who was owning me.

I'd meant to show her just how intimate we'd be, to prove that she couldn't handle it. But when she'd kissed me earlier today, she'd definitely been holding back.

This Ari was all seductress and would have me begging for mercy any second now.

I reached down and grabbed her ass, pulling our bodies somehow even closer. Her breasts were crushed against my chest. Her

"It won't be if I'm prepared for it. I don't date because I don't have time. And it also requires small talk and being near people, and it just feels like too much effort for too little return. And for your information, the reason I'm an analyst is because it's easier and safer with numbers and patterns. People are more complicated."

"You're doing just fine with me."

"I knew you before, so maybe it's easier to manage with you. Or maybe I don't feel like I'm managing with you at all. Anyway, we should practice."

I stared at her. "Ari."

"Either you kiss me, or I'll kiss you. And that will be far more awkward."

She was *asking* me to kiss her.

This was potentially dangerous. How the hell would she not see right through how badly I wanted to kiss her?

"Ari, if we're going through with this, we're going to have to touch *a lot*. We're going to have to be in what looks like sexual positions. I need to do a lot more than kiss you in front of people."

She sighed. "You and I have a lot of problems that I don't *want* to work out, but I trust you enough to know you won't deliberately hurt me. So just kiss me already. I just need to get used to it."

She had no idea what she was asking for. That kiss earlier on the balcony had been for show.

*So show her.*\*

I stalked toward her, and even though she was obviously

---

\* HAVE MERCY–Chlöe

The reality of it all. I can do this, but I'm not used to trusting anyone. I don't avoid the field because I'm afraid of it. It's just easier if—I only have myself to count on. I need time to get used to you as my partner—as someone I can count on. With a little time and prep, I could be ready."

"Fuck." I scrubbed my hands over my face. "I shouldn't have kissed you, Ari. For some reason I thought it would help."

She cleared her throat. "Did that kiss have anything to do with the mission?"

"Of course."

"Okay, so we should practice then. I wasn't prepared when you kissed me. So practicing is the only way I'll get used to you touching me in public. Like an inoculation."

"What?"

"An inoculation. You expose someone to a virus, and then their body knows how to fight it. Not all vaccines are like that, but you get the idea."

"You think I'm like a virus? Like a foreign agent?"

"Sort of." She bit her lip again, and it was so cute, I had to bite back a groan.

"Ari, we can't do that. I won't be kissing you again until you ask me to. I'm not going to make you uncomfortable."

"I'm asking you to now."

I pushed away from the table. "Ari."

She licked her lips nervously. "Look, I just need to get used to you touching me, okay? The rest of the afternoon was okay; it's just a lot. But this is the job, and I can do it."

"This is a bad idea, Ari."

"Yes. I'm not trying to undermine you. Trying to crack this vault alone is a terrible idea. It's a two-man job at best. It'll take me three times as long alone. But that's not the point. This plan is making *you* uncomfortable. Reaper made you uncomfortable? The people there will be ten times worse, with no facade of civility."

She stuttered, "I–I can do this."

"Ari, look…" I reached for her, and she skittered back. "See? You're on edge."

She chewed on her bottom lip, unable to deny I was right. The action just made me want to kiss her again, so I forced my eyes back to the plans.

"I could certainly use a second set of eyes on how to do this with one man, but I'm not trying to cut you out. I'm not trying to undermine you. I'm not trying to run in and steal the necklace. Remember, I'm working *with* Lucas. I want the best outcome for this. And taking you in while you're uncomfortable with me touching you is not a good path to success."

I could feel her gaze on me for a moment. The side of my face was heating from its intensity. Christ. It was already hard enough, trying to keep all my focus and attention on the blueprints, but when she was standing there looking like the softest material I could ever touch, it was impossible.

*Eyes on the prize.*

Except Ari definitely *was* the prize.

"I…" She cleared her throat. "I think we should *practice*."

I lifted my gaze. "What?"

"I think we should *practice*. I was caught off guard today.

I hesitated. "What makes you say that?"

"I'm not stupid. That's a plan for a one-man version of the job."

"Ari, listen to me. That's not—"

She threw her hands up, stopping me midsentence. "God, I've been so tense and anxious, worried I'm going to put a foot wrong this whole time, and you're busy trying to figure out how to cut me out. Why pull me in if this is what you were planning?"

"Won't you just sit down and stop talking? That's not what I'm doing."

"Okay, then tell me, what *are* you doing exactly? Because to me, it looks like you're trying to do this job on your own. Which means you're double-crossing us."

How could one small woman be so damned frustrating? "Oh my God, three plus one does not equal ten."

"What?"

"Ari, you were clearly ill at ease today. You were freaking out every time I touched you. We have to be a couple madly in love. You're not comfortable with me, and I get it. You hate me, and I get that even more. You hold me responsible for your father's death. Extra got it. I don't want you to be afraid, for fuck's sake. Also, after lunch with Reaper, it struck me that you really are just an analyst. I'm coming up with a plan B in case you're not okay to do this."

She blinked at me slowly, and her voice was soft and breathy when she spoke. "What?"

I repeated, "Plan B."

"You're doing this because you think I'm uncomfortable?" she asked.

There was a chance I was going to have to go in and do this by myself.

*Or maybe you trust her to pull it together.*

No. Screw the invitation. I could make it work.

*It's a two-man job for the vault. And that's just for the vault. Getting out of there* with *the necklace would take everything and everyone you have.*

Lucas would just have to help me out. Because there was no way I was comfortable taking Ari in there. If she was on edge, that would put our cover under scrutiny.

Not to mention this wasn't exactly a learn-on-the-job gig.

The energy in the air shifted, and immediately my hair stood at attention. I knew she was there, but she didn't speak.

"Are you going to stare at me all night?" I asked.

She padded into the living room of the hotel suite wearing silky shorts and a matching tank. My gaze swept over her and immediately noted her nipples were hard, and I had to drag my eyeballs away.

"What are you doing?"

"Nothing." There would be no point in telling her. She'd probably object.

"You're doing *something*." She came closer, and one glance at my laptop made her brows furrow. "The blueprints? You planning on liberating something else from the auction? I thought we were on the same team."

I glowered at her. "What do you mean?"

"Those plans. You're going to try to break into the vault by yourself before I get there."

## DAMON

Ari was freaking out.

I knew it from the moment I saw her stiff shoulders and her too-wide eyes after Reaper left us at lunch. It was one thing to imagine being in the field. It was another to be here and face the stark realization that anything could go wrong at any moment.

Reaper had been unsettling. Like the man could peel back your skin and see all of your secrets. I especially wasn't fond of the way he'd been eyeing Ari.

I wasn't worried about our covers, but a guy like that could sniff out something being off. We couldn't necessarily risk it.

We'd spent the afternoon walking the city hand in hand. We saw *Six*, had dinner in Little Italy, did touristy sightseeing. She'd managed it well enough, but by the time we returned to the hotel, I could see the tension in her face.

This was going to take a toll.

see us being in love. Acting completely normal. Shopping. I have a stipend Lucas provided, so we might as well go and spend some of it. The rest is in escrow for the auction."

"Smart of him to make sure we at least have the funds."

"Obviously. So how about it? Let's go explore the city."

I stared at his hand. I had no choice, and this was my opportunity to prove myself. And all I had to do was go shopping with Damon. Galen believed in me, so I needed to shove down my trepidation and make this work. There was no going back.

Time slipped away as we kissed. As far as I was concerned, we were in a bubble—just the two of us. His drugging kisses were making me pulse between my thighs. All I wanted was more.

Damon's hands trailed down my back and drew me even closer so our bodies pressed together in a heated embrace as my hips rocked against his.

But all too soon, he was tearing his lips from mine. When he released me, his eyes were hooded and his lips swollen. He cleared his throat, then pulled me into a tight hug before whispering, "I think that's enough convincing."

My legs were jelly, and my brain was mush. I couldn't think of anything other than the press of his body against mine. I could still feel the steely pulse of his erection, but instead of drawing me back for another kiss, he released me and took my hand.

"Let's go convince them in a way that will be less dangerous for us."

I wasn't sure what to say, but I couldn't just stand there, so I nodded. But as I followed him out of the room, I was sure every eye was on us.

I felt the heat creeping up my face.

I racked my brain, trying to remember if I'd ever seen two people kiss like that in public. Not just because it was passionate, but because it was…real.

I followed him back into the restaurant, then into the lobby, my knees weak and body on fire. I wasn't sure I was strong enough for this.

As I stumbled along beside him, he spoke to me as if he hadn't just stolen my soul with that kiss. "The whole point is to let them

I stiffened. But I knew he was right. We were being watched. Everyone needed to believe the kiss. I tried to think of myself as an actress. One who was portraying a character.

*Who are you kidding? You've wanted to kiss this man for years.*

Damon slid his hand up to cup my jaw, then sank his fingertips into the hair at the nape of my neck. His other arm wrapped around my waist, pulled me close. But instead of going straight for my lips, he placed a gentle kiss on my forehead and then my temple before angling to my cheeks and jawline and then, finally, my lips.

*Holy hell.*

Not only were his lips shockingly soft, but the man knew how to kiss.

Not in an oh-he-must-have-dated-a-lot-of-women kind of way, but a the-man-should-be-giving-professional-lessons kind of way.

When his fingertips pressed the tight muscles at the nape of my neck ever so slightly, cuing me to angle my head, his tongue swept into my mouth, and every brain cell I had shorted out.

I moaned into the kiss, my tongue eagerly meeting his as my hands found their way to his chest, feeling the firm muscles beneath his shirt.

*You should pull back.*

This was convincing enough, right? But for some reason, when I could feel Damon retract, feel him lessening the pressure, I dug my fingers into the cotton of his shirt and tugged him closer.

Damon chuckled against my lips as his erection pressed into my thigh. "Christ, Ari."

He was enormous. Like *security* enormous. And his suit bulged around his muscles. While he might have just liked to work out, I'd learned early in life that just because you were paranoid didn't mean they weren't out to get you.

I'd known what this would entail. However, the reality of it had a way of hitting differently.

*Out here, mistakes mean death.*

"What do we do?"

Damon's fingertips continued to skim over the skin on my shoulder. "We sell our story."

When he took my clammy hands, I hesitated. "I just—I need a second."

How was he so calm? How could he just ignore the spikes of adrenaline or the knowledge that if we made one wrong move, that could mean our lives.

He smoothed a thumb over my knuckles. "Being scared is natural. It means your instincts are firing. Reaper is a dangerous motherfucker. Your body is responding to the perceived threat. You'll be fine."

He stood and pulled me to my feet. His fingers intertwined with mine as he led me onto the balcony. Damon made a big production of pulling out his phone and then showing me something on it, like he was pointing out where we might be going later that day. Meanwhile, he was really pointing out our other tails.

"Are we going to try and shake them?"[*]

"Nope. Like I said, we're going to put on a show. Brace yourself, Ari. I'm going to kiss you now."

[*] LOSE CONTROL–Teddy Swims

Reaper swept his gaze over me, lingering as he went, before very deliberately meeting Damon's gaze again. Damon, to his credit, didn't flinch or tuck me in closer, just kept his grin in place and stared Reaper down.

I could feel the silent posturing as the two of them mentally circled each other like lions.

Reaper finally eased back, in a way that said he wasn't conceding a loss but calculating that Damon wasn't an adversary he wanted.

"Simon, you haven't shared what you're most looking forward to at the auction. Anything or *anyone* your heart desires?"

*Oh, so you are a shit stirrer?*

"I already have everything I desire. But if I see anything I can't live without, you'll be the first to know."

"You make sure to let me know. Your wish is my command."

The rest of the meal passed without incident, but I couldn't shake that edgy feeling. After lunch, Reaper excused himself, and Damon and I were left on our own. I breathed a sigh of relief. Damon once again threw his arm over my shoulder, then gently rubbed circles into my skin.

I stiffened in his arms. "Show's over."

"Have you already forgotten what Lucas said? We are being watched. Every moment. Every movement. Case in point, the black sedan across the street. It circled the block three times. We, my darling, are under surveillance."

*Shit.* I grabbed my sunglasses and slipped them on surreptitiously while I did a light scan of our surroundings. Damon was right about the car. There was also a man in a suit at the bar.

It's supposedly cursed. It may be silly, but that dress comes with so much history."

Reaper leaned forward. "Yes, there are all manner of delights to be found. Anything you're looking for, anything that tickles your fancy, we can provide."

The way he said *tickles* made me wonder just how good the man was with his fingers. But then common sense prevailed. I had no idea how he did that—managed to have sexual chemistry with every single person he encountered.

The man was a menace. There was also a dangerous aura around him that had my senses on red alert and adrenaline spiking my blood.

It was Damon's hand on my knee that kept me grounded and tethered to him. "Well, that is quite the offer," Damon said in an icy tone. "Whatever she wants, I'll provide."

Reaper smirked at that. "Interesting."

The conversation stayed casual as we ordered and the food arrived. Though Reaper continued to flirt with everyone he made eye contact with. The waitress was so flustered when he pitched his voice low and asked for a Vieux Carré, she dropped her tray and notepad. When he stopped to help her and their fingers brushed, she banged her head on the underside of the table.

Next to me, Damon grumbled under his breath.

"What's the matter, darling? So used to being the only man women stutter over?" I whispered.

He turned that dazzling smile on me then. "Sweetheart, you're the only woman I care about." He pulled me close and kissed my temple just as Reaper sat back up.

Between him and Reaper, I felt like I was going to combust. Just burst into flames right here.

Though when Reaper dragged his gaze from me and pinned it on Damon, I watched as Damon hesitated for just a moment, then returned Reaper's direct stare. When Damon held it and didn't waver, Reaper smirked. "The two of you are going to be fun. I can tell that immediately." He broke contact with Damon and pulled out his laptop. "Mrs. Christopher, if you can just put your thumbprint here, then we shall go to the more enjoyable part of our afternoon—the lunch."

He and Damon chatted for a moment as I discreetly donned the thumb sleeve Lucas had provided under the table. I leaned forward and planted my thumb where he'd indicated, and sure enough, the laptop showed my photo with Michelle Christopher's ID. And Damon was Simon Christopher.

When I pulled my hand back, the three-carat princess-cut diamond wedding ring I wore glittered in the light. The thing was stunning—not to mention blinding. It looked at home on my hand. Correction: on Michelle's hand. A ring fit for an heiress.

Michelle and Simon were minor nobility, had lived a life of leisure their entire existence, and met and were married within just a few months. Completely mad about each other. Simon was looking to buy Michelle something special to celebrate their anniversary.

"And you, Michelle, what is it you are looking for from this auction?"

"I don't know. I've never attended anything like it before. I mean, obviously, we've all been to an auction, but nothing quite like this. What I'm really eager to see is the Bryson Blue Dress.

Reaper wore an excellently tailored Tom Ford gray linen suit and a pale-blue tie. The pale blue matched his eyes, which offset his white-blond hair. Immediately I knew the attire was wrong. This man belonged in leather.

He turned with what I'm sure he thought was a genial smile, and I stutter-stepped, needing Damon to steady me. When Reaper stood and approached us with what could only be described as swagger, I involuntarily clenched my thighs together.

It was only as he drew closer that I noticed the piercing in his lip and the one in his brow.

He shook hands with Damon, then kissed my cheeks like I was some sort of French socialite. "It's lovely to meet you," he said.

Holy mother of Christ, as my grandmother used to say. One thing for certain, two things for sure: Reaper was walking, talking sex on a stick.

And by the way he was eyeing up me and Damon, he was happy to devour both of us at the same time while everyone in the restaurant watched.

He eyed me intently, and I couldn't help but shift uncomfortably under his gaze. He watched me like I imagined a lion would watch a lioness carrying an antelope leg. You weren't quite sure which need was going to win out: the urge to fuck or the urge to eat. It was disconcerting.

Damon sank into the role more easily than I did, and he sat with his hand on my knee. His thumb pressed into my skin, the gentle caress making me slowly lose my mind. He had to know what that was doing to me. There was no way it was an accident.

never seen before. Of course, he was different now. Looser somehow, with more charm, which made him even more dangerous.

But as beautiful as Damon was now, eighteen-year-old Damon had been breathtaking. There'd been no one like him among the high school boys I'd known. He was gorgeous. He'd had enough of a dangerous edge that you knew to stay away from him, sort of. And the number of girls that I'd gone to school with who would try to get his attention had been too high to count. But now here I was, acting like I was his wife.

He easily threw an arm around me and kissed my temple. The contact made me shiver, but I plastered a smile on my face and tilted my chin up.

We were on display. Now was not the time to catch a case of feelings.

Per Lucas, we were meeting the Concierge today. We'd been told they'd meet us at the restaurant and what time, but not much else. We'd arrived at the hotel this morning and had just enough time to go over our roles again before we'd showered and changed.

When we got to the hostess stand, the hostess informed us there'd been a change of plans, and instead of the Concierge, we were meeting Reaper. We were led to the back of the restaurant, to a private booth overlooking the park, and Reaper was seated in the shadows, only his profile in view.

An immediate prickle of awareness tingled my scalp as we approached.* Damon was just as tense while he held my hand in a death grip.

* TOM'S DINER–AnnenMayKantereit feat. Giant Rooks

slid my gaze to Damon. "My beloved fake husband's face. Won't someone recognize him?"

Lucas's gaze darted between Damon and me. "She doesn't know?"

Damon pursed his lips. "We haven't had time for a lengthy catchup."

"I don't get it. What does that mean?"

Damon sighed. "No one knows my face. I only did one or two jobs in the early days out of desperation where I had direct contact with buyers or sellers. After my first big score, I figured it would be best to use intermediaries. Keep a low profile. My name might be known, but it's a rarity for anyone to see me. I keep a tight network. There have been one or two jobs from my past that might have some exposure, but it's been years. And even with those, I was using an alias."

"So what, you're the invisible man?"

He shrugged. "Something like that." He took the guest list from Lucas. "Let's see if my past is going to come back to bite me in the ass."

Right, and while he did that, I'd try and forget about the fact that there was only one bed.

---

If anyone had told teenage Ari that she would be holding hands with Damon Hunt as they walked into a hotel restaurant, she would have called bullshit.

Sure, I fantasized about him sometimes. At eighteen, Damon was extremely good-looking, with a kind of brooding intensity I'd

Penny interjected. "I will be in attendance, obviously, and I doubt there will be any problems. It's all very strict. But maybe instead of guns, we can use tranq guns to minimize the violence. It's an easy ask. I'll see what we can get in."

Damon glowered at me. "What the queen wants, the queen gets."

Penny shook her head. "No, it's just plain Penny right now. I'll be queen later. But for now, I'm just Penny."

His lips twitched, and he gave her a nod. "Fine, what the future queen wants. No violence."

Lucas flashed a grin, and his gaze landed on me, full of mischief. "Ari, are you good with that?"

I glowered at Damon. "Yes."

"Excellent. Is this a good time to remind you that the two of you need to get over whatever this is and act like a couple in love? Stupid love. These are not the kind of people we want sniffing you out. There are hundreds of millions of dollars at stake at this auction. Some of it is black-market money. I want to really drive this point home. You *two* need to get your shit together."

Heat crept up my neck, and I stiffened. "And we will. GT Securities provides you with the best recovery, and that's what we'll do. *Professionally.*"

Damon just grunted.

*Awesome.*

"Excellent." Lucas grinned again. "I have a guest list if you need to look at it."

I chewed my bottom lip. "That brings up another question." I

much, but he'd been watching me the whole time. "What do you need, angel?"

I furrowed my brows. "Angel?"

"Yes, angel. We should have pet names, of course," he said nonchalantly.

Nope. Pet names were for real couples. "Please don't call me by a pet name."

He laughed. "No, I think I like pet names. It'll be fine."

I ignored him and turned to the prince. "Lucas, you have to promise me there'll be no violence. I don't want anyone hurt."

Damon pushed away from the wall. "What are you trying to say, Ari?"

"You know what I'm trying to say, *Damon*. Sometimes the people around you end up dead. I don't want that happening to anyone. Least of all myself."

Lucas's voice was low. "This is a simple recovery mission. No one is getting hurt. Besides, anyone gets out of hand, and they need to answer to Reaper. No one wants that."

"Right. But it needs to be very clear."

"All my people walk out alive." Damon's voice was tight and clipped.

"All *your* people?"

I could see the muscle tic in his jaw. "Yes, all my goddamned people. But I will not hesitate to do whatever is required to protect people on my team. If it means your life or some asshole's and you're on my team, I shoot first and ask questions later."

I shook my head. "No. No shooting. Under no circumstances. That's my request."

"Interesting. And what about the jewels?"

Penny walked over and picked up the pendant. "The necklace has a camera in the connector, right here."

"Are you sure they won't search us? I mean how are we going to get my tools inside?"

She gave me a nod. "I will smuggle in your smaller items and tools." She picked up the glittering gold clutch on the side table. "In addition to getting you the code that'll get you to the vault, I'll swap out clutches with you. You'll have a duplicate. Everything you need will be in there. From what we've been told and what we can see on the plans, the vault area has an antechamber. Presumably to review items taken."

Okay then, so they really had been thorough.

I did have more questions though. "Lucas, are we supposed to know you or not?" I asked.

He reached for a folder and handed it to me. "You do not. But at breakfast on day two, we'll bump into each other, and I'll invite you to sit with me. Oh, also, here are your IDs. Ari, once you agreed, I had one of my people fill in your background. You are Simon and Michelle Christopher. You've been married two years, and you're still madly in love."

I squirmed at that, but I could manage. It was just pretend. "Okay, I assume you have background workups on us?"

Lucas nodded. "They're in here. You just need to study them."

I nodded back. "I'll memorize them. But I do have one request." I didn't look at Damon when I said it.

Across the room, Damon crossed his arms. He hadn't said

syringes, a three-carat princess-cut diamond, makeup, and two rectangular objects.

"I assume the syringes will put someone out, but what are these things?" I asked.

"Correct about syringes. The solution also gives temporary memory loss. Those other things are state-of-the-art tech developed by some friends at a security firm. You clamp this to a video line, and it'll loop the last ten minutes of a video feed. It will also essentially stop recording all technical movements in a given system by giving it a little virus."

He turned one of the small rectangular objects and showed me the button on the bottom. "You press this, and it takes out security on that system line for one minute and spreads the virus through the system. By the time it comes back online, the system is already infected. It's called a Reaser698."

I lifted my brow. "Are you shitting me?"

"Not at all."

"So some *Mission Impossible*, James Bond shenanigans?"

His grin told me this was what he was most excited about. "Yep, *Mission Impossible*. Thanks to friends at a security company here in New York, we're able to get someone undercover to work the event. Larger items can be smuggled in and hidden. Penny will be given the locations. But smaller items, like little explosives, personal Tasers, we can smuggle in."

Damon whistled. "No way."

Damon picked up a lipstick, and Penny shrugged at him.

"That's a Taser. It has one charge. You have to be close to use it, and it needs to make contact with the skin," Penny said.

"And what's our egress route?"

Lucas pointed it out on the map. "Right here. If you both make it to this drain, it'll take you out under the moat to the edge of the woods. There'll be a vehicle waiting, and you'll be in the clear. Change of clothes, the whole thing."

I chewed on the end of my pinky nail. "What's the plan B?"

Damon rubbed at the back of his neck. "Ari—"

Lucas interjected though. "No she's right. In case something happens and you can't get access to the car. There is a boat at the boathouse. It'll take you to the other side of the lake. About half a mile in, there will be another car. Camouflaged and everything. I have thought about this. It'll be okay."

I swallowed and gave him a small nod, appreciating that he was at least taking my concerns seriously. "Where will you be?"

It needed to be asked because I was risking my neck. This was still a recovery mission. I knew that. But the people who were going to be inside were extremely dangerous.

"Penny and I will be inside. We need to stay the whole weekend. And remember, you'll be watched the whole time. We still don't know if the rooms will be surveilled, so we'll provide you with a couple of jammers."

I lifted a brow. "Won't Reaper's goons notice expensive tech we're dragging in?"

Lucas grinned. "Nope. Because to the regular world, the dual-purpose jammer and decryption device will look like your phone."

He pointed at the phones over on the side table. Next to them sat a glittering diamond pendant, two signet rings, several

Lucas pulled out the blueprints, and I knew it was time to get back to work, but all I wanted to do was talk to Penny. She fascinated me. I was drawn by her wit and especially her humor, considering the situation. Not to mention her willingness to help her future brother-in-law. It completely endeared her to me.

I was almost having fun until I lifted my gaze to find Damon watching me. But I refused to let him get under my skin today. I plastered a neutral expression on my face and turned my back on him.

Penny lifted a brow. "Problems?"

"You mean other than the fact I don't trust him and he's a renowned thief? No, no problems at all."

Penny laughed. "I have a feeling there's a long story in there somewhere. And, well, thieves aren't so bad."

"There *is* a long complicated story in there."

She eyed me. "Mm-hmm. Well, maybe when we're done here, we'll grab a drink, and you can tell me all about it. And I'll tell you all about how I ended up in love with a royal."

"Deal."

Damon was all business today. His brows knitted as he stared at the blueprints over Lucas's shoulder.

When I strolled over, I also frowned at the layout. "Okay, so there's a lake. Is that to scale? It looks enormous. Is the location that remote?"

Lucas nodded. "Yeah, completely. Upstate New York. Big fuck-off compound and gothic mansion. The property is dotted with guest cottages here," he said as he passed a finger over the plans.

developed a friendship over the last year, and I understand where he's coming from. I think he should just tell Sebastian, but, as a former prodigal daughter, I get it. And I know he's a little worried about his past. Sebastian has a lot on his plate, so I'm going to help Lucas make sure nothing goes wrong. Besides, it's currently still sort of my job."

I cocked my head. "What do you mean?"

"Oh, I'm a royal guard. I've been assigned to Lucas while he's traveling before he comes to the Winston Isles officially."

I chuckled low. "*You're* a royal guard?"

"Yes, I know it's confusing. But it is what it is."

"And the king just lets you run around after his brother? Isn't he worried about *your* protection?"

"He's always worried about my protection, but considering I was his royal guard first and this is only temporary, he can't say much. Besides, Lucas will be assigned a new guard once I get married."

I liked her. She had one of those smiles that made you want to pull up a chair and gossip about trashy television. "So you're down for this heist?"

She pressed her lips together. "I'm down for Sebastian not being embarrassed. And I'm down for the media not having a field day. I'm in a precarious position, so the less negative press the better. So right now, whatever Lucas needs, I'll assist. And if it means helping him steal the Royal Heart, then that's what I'll do."

"Oddest family I have ever met. I think I like you."

Having her there had me feeling infinitely more comfortable.

## ARI

This already felt like a mistake.

I prowled around the prince's hotel suite, then stared at the rolling bar with the gowns hung on it. "This is my wardrobe?"

Lucas nodded. "Yes. Penny is here, and she can help you with anything you need. If you don't like something, we'll get some alternatives."

The door to one of the bedrooms opened, and out walked a stunning woman with nut-brown skin and a shock of curly hair cut stylishly in a bob. "Hi," she said with a grin. "You must be Ari." A dimple peeked out, and I couldn't help but return the smile.

"Penny, I presume?"

"That I am. And apparently, my future brother-in-law is in a bit of a bind."

I blinked in surprise. "This happen often?"

She bit back a smile. "Let's say Lucas is—colorful. We've

couple madly in love. Inside the hotel room, you should be okay, but remember that outside your room, you must sell the act."

I rolled my shoulders. "In terms of safety, can we get some of Galen's people in there too?"

He shook his head. "No, invites are already out. You'll have me and Penny. Penny has a piece of her work up for auction, and she's pretty badass in the field. Galen, you can have as many people as you want watching them before, and you can have your people outside the perimeter of the location, but no men inside. Even the staff members are heavily vetted."

Galen nodded and turned his gaze to Ari. "I have full faith in my people. As long as you can hold up your end, Damon, Ari will be ready."

I lifted my gaze to hers, knowing full well we were going to have a hell of a time establishing trust. In a week and a half, we were either going to be on this mission together as a unit, or one of us would be dead. And I would be the one in need of a body bag.

Lucas slid his gaze to Ari and continued. "The cover story is the other piece I've been working on. Since you're going in together as a couple, I'm going to need you to *be* a couple. You'll get fake names and a background to go along with them. The IDs have been backstopped by the best in the business. They'll come complete with employment history, tax records, and prior dating and social media profiles too. It won't get you security clearance or anything, but it's enough to make you real. But I can't stress this enough: Reaper thinks anything is suspicious, and it's game over, so you need to sell the covers."

Ari just chuckled. "And let me guess, there's only one bed?"

Lucas smiled sheepishly. "The good news is the two of you are already acquainted with each other. You'll work it out. The other component is you will need to meet with the Concierge in person. Also, you need to move in together to establish your cover. Once you send in your RSVP, you will be watched. Sometimes there are people who don't want to wait for the auction to begin, so they try and either influence buyers to drop out or participants not to take part, that sort of thing. To make sure everyone is following the rules, they will have you followed."

Even Galen groaned at that one. "Is there no good news here? You're telling us that not only will they be surveilled at the auction but before it as well?"

Lucas shrugged. "Yup, that's the gist."

Ari groaned. "The good news just keeps coming, doesn't it?"

Lucas nodded. "The auction is in a week and a half. As soon as they receive your RSVP, we need to assume you're being watched. So you will be staying at a hotel together, acting like a

I pushed away from the wall. "It won't come to that, Ari. I will get you out of there before anything goes wrong. If anything goes the least bit sideways, I will abandon this job in a minute if it means your safety. But just so you know, we're all risking something on this job."

Galen scowled. "Like Lucas said, if you use the safe word, *I* will send men in. I don't give a fuck who will be pissed off."

Her brow furrowed. "So we've got our backup exfil in place. Tell me we've got more than one. I'll need us to know them all backward and forward."

Lucas sighed. "We do. You will be safe. I'm telling you what you're dealing with so you can walk in with eyes wide-open, so that nothing scares you or concerns you in the moment. That's how you walk into a field assignment."

I crossed my arms. "Lucas, when was the last time you were on a field assignment? From what I understand, you preferred to do things when people weren't at home."

He chuckled low. "Let's just say I've had my fair share of too much adventure, okay? In my misspent youth, I learned to watch my back, trust my instincts, and be prepared. I'm only trying to prepare you, Ari, not scare you." He turned to Galen. "She's on your team, so I know how much you value her. I won't let anything happen to her."

"No, Galen. I'm the one who'll make sure Ari doesn't leave my side," I assured him.

Ari sat back down and grumbled, "That's what I'm worried about."

Galen nodded at Lucas. "What else will we be dealing with?"

been doing God knows what until now, and now you're telling me the auction has a sexy component."

Lucas shook his head. "None of that has anything to do with us. We won't be participating in the auction at all. We will be switching out the Royal Heart after it's shown."

Ari sighed. "Look, I don't care how consenting adults get their rocks off. If this Reaper guy runs kink clubs, I can only imagine what the auction is like. But as long as everyone is of age, consenting, and there willingly, whatever. My concern is the legality of the exchanges. If deals will be honored. These aren't refined collectors. Some of these people will be carrying weapons and be used to getting their own way. This is dangerous, and I don't know what to expect. How can I plan for the unpredictable?"

Lucas was completely unfazed. "Reaper runs a tight ship. No violence will be tolerated. I have no word on if they'll be confiscating weapons or not. Usually the fear of his retribution is enough to keep people in line. But he won't risk it. We'll need to get weapons in another way."

"And you think he's not going to notice when we slip a priceless necklace out from under his nose?" she asked.

Lucas shook his head. "He'll never know. We'll be replacing it with a stellar replica. But we need to be careful. If we're not, it could mean our lives."

Ari glowered at Galen. "You want me to walk in there when not one of you can guarantee my safety?"

Lucas sighed. "*I* will guarantee your safety. If you use the safe word on comms, I will walk you out that front door myself. No one will touch me. I'm royalty."

We were walking right into the lion's den. Basically a den of thieves, murderers, and God knew what else, all dressed in bespoke suits. The wealthiest people in the world would be buying and selling anything they wanted. She should be afraid.

Lucas clicked a button on the remote, and a screen came down, showing a list of all the major players. "The Black Rose Auction is put on every year." Lucas clicked to the next slide. "From the moment you arrive, you'll have a concierge. They'll take care of all your needs while you're there. I cannot stress this enough: this auction is unlike any you've ever seen. It's not going to be some nice refined affair with everyone silently raising their paddles while bidding on artwork and jewelry. Trust nothing and nobody, and know there is always another game being played. Oh, and stay the fuck away from Reaper if you can. He has a way of seeing through people. It can be... discomfiting."

Ari's brows furrowed. "He owns some really famous high-end sex clubs, right? How do you go from sex clubs to an underground auction?"

Lucas shook his head. "He's a man of many talents. I'm serious. Stay away from him. We don't want to be on his radar. In and out. No muss. No fuss. And no matter what you see or hear, just think, *None of my business*."

I knew what Lucas was thinking of. Reaper was a master and connoisseur of kink. "Think of the Black Rose Auction as part auction, part fantasy playground, with a very sexy component."

Ari very calmly turned to Galen. "Everything has been a mess, from the prince's murky background, to Damon, who has

# DAMON

I couldn't take my eyes off her.

Good old Ari. Always the perfect student. She even had her glasses on, which was adding to the allure.

We'd all agreed to meet Lucas in his hotel suite. Though *suite* hardly covered it. He had the whole damned floor.

Plenty of room. Snacks were laid out. I'd already eaten half my weight in them.

Galen had forced Ari to eat something, and I was grateful for that because I knew her. When she was tense, she didn't eat.

Lucas shoved his hands in his jeans. "Since we're all on board, we might as well get to the important things."

"What important things?" Ari muttered the question softly as she picked at the grapes on her plate. Galen frowned at her. This was not the picture of a woman who wanted to be here.

*Of course not, you idiot. She's an analyst. She doesn't go in the field. She's scared.*

"I'm good, Galen. I can stay on task."

"I believe in you, Ari. Just make sure you don't let your past interfere with this job. Got it?"

"Of course. Nothing will interfere."

*And you will never, ever give in to what Damon wants.*

much I begged and pleaded. So I don't trust him. My father did, and look where it got him."

He nodded slowly. "Okay. Because you know going into these kinds of jobs with someone you're attracted to can make you complacent."

"You don't have to worry about me, Galen. I attach to no one, remember?"

His grin was quick. "And that's why I hired you." My gut knotted as he said that.

I eased myself into my chair to get things ready. "I have always wondered that. Hiring me was a risk."

He stopped. "Well, not really. I'm a good businessman. A kid with daddy issues whose daddy was a thief is generally on the exact *opposite* side of the law. It's kind of how it works. So you are undoubtedly more trustworthy than anyone else who works for me. I know your motivation. That's why seeing you with Damon worries me. I don't like it."

"I don't like it either. So why are you making me work with him?"

"Because having the royal family as a client is good for us. So you play nice now, you hear?"

I rolled my eyes. "Don't I always?"

He chuckled low. "You are professional to a fault. You take no shit, you are always on the ball, and you always have the right answer. But you can be fucked with."

"Excuse me?"

"Hey, I can be fucked with too. You are all about outcomes, but it means certain frustrations may get to you."

hurt seeing Damon again and reliving all the baggage he brought with him, and that pang in my chest wouldn't go away. Eight years, and I was no closer to understanding what the hell had happened with my father, what had gone wrong. All I knew was that he'd been on a job with Damon and then died, leaving me with this hole in my chest that I couldn't fill, one made worse and more complicated by the fact that my father had chosen *Damon* to be his protégé.

Dad loved him like a son. Showed him things he wouldn't show me. I had to sneak around to gain my knowledge. I had to hide, listen when I shouldn't, and pore over Dad's notes while he slept.

My father said he did it out of love, wanting a different life for me. But all I'd wanted was his time, and Damon Hunt had robbed me of that.

*And now look at you. The perfect good girl who hides away from the world, even though you want to take part.*

That was what stung. There was a part of me that wanted to do this so I could prove myself to someone who was long gone.

*He didn't want this for you.*

Galen cleared his throat. "As a precaution, there's one more thing I need to ask."

"Then stop beating around the bush." He knew me too well. I could only hold my shit together for so long. And right about now, I needed to collapse in a heap and curl up in the dark with a blanket over my head while I processed all this.

"You and Hunt, is something romantic going on there?"

I snickered at that. "With him? No. He's responsible for my father being gone. He might not have been the shooter, but he knows what happened, and he's never told me. No matter how

I frowned at him. "No. Of course not. I haven't seen him in years, but he was there the night my father died."

Galen cursed. "Oh, for fuck's sake." His brows knitted, and I could see he was trying to work out what to say, what to do, how to make sure I could still do my job.

"Galen, can I ask you a question?"

"Yeah, what is it?"

"Would you still be here if I were one of the male agents?"

He frowned. "Honestly, yes. But for a different reason."

"Oh yeah?" I lifted a brow. "What would the different reason be?"

"I'd be worried one of them was going to kill him, punch him, or find a way to sabotage the job. Sometimes the lads can get a bit territorial, but with you, I don't foresee you actually murdering him. Maybe some light torture. As long as you're not going to go all stabby, you'll be all right."

"You have a lot of faith," I groused.

"I know you. You're a great analyst. An out-of-the-box thinker. Quick on your feet, levelheaded, and steady. I have never seen you this shaken before."

He was right. I'd become very good at locking away all my emotions. It was easier. I never let anything touch me. But then that asshole Damon had walked in yesterday, and all that was gone. I was suddenly back to being that little girl, holding my father's bleeding body as his breathing labored, begging someone to answer me and tell me what the hell had happened. And no one would.

It hurt knowing that was who I still was after all these years. It

are hopelessly in love. The sooner you get on board with that, the happier and safer we'll be."

"I'm not pretending to be in love with you."

"Sure you are." I marched over to her, stepping into her space.

She smelled the same as she always did. Faintly of strawberries and something else that I couldn't quite place. She smelled sweet. Intoxicating. Tempting.

"You and I will have to be closer than this. Get used to it." I twined our fingers together.

"Then one of us is going to be missing their left nut. Don't touch me."

"Whatever you say, Ari Sari. But the next time I touch you, you'll be begging me to."

## ARI

When he left, I was shaking. How dare he?

I marched to my office just down the hall from the conference room I'd escaped, desperate to close the door and block it all out and pretend that I didn't have to do this.

But sure enough, Galen was not going to let me get away with that. He knocked at my door, opened it a crack, and lifted a brow. "You look like you've been put through the wringer. Are you okay? Damon is just doing his job."

"I've never needed you to coddle me, Galen. Don't start now."

"Are we going to talk about the history there? Is he your ex or something?"

That's good. It means you've learned something. I mean, you *are* hurting my feelings. Oh wait, that's right—I don't have any. So put your claws away. This is just for the job."

"You think I believe that? You're here to torture me. The problem is, I don't know why. I've never done anything to you. I didn't snitch. I said nothing. Why are you torturing me?"

"You think this is torture? You haven't seen anything yet. You and I, together again. Think how proud your father would be."

"Fuck you."

The grin I gave her was cold and full of smug satisfaction. "That's a good girl."

"Look, I'm in charge of this job. I know that doesn't mean much to you, but we do things my way, and *nobody* dies. I know you're used to people being murdered on jobs when they deal with you, but there will be no dead bodies on my watch, understood?"

"I didn't kill your father, Ari."

"Just because you didn't pull the trigger doesn't mean you weren't responsible."

I didn't know why it was so important to me that she believed I would have done anything to protect my mentor, but the truth of her words stung. "Ari, if we walk into this thing at odds with each other, someone *is* going to die."

"Get me the specs, and stay out of my way."

"Princess, I'm pretty certain I mentioned that we have to do this *together*. The cover Lucas has for us spells it out. We have to *act* like a married couple. There are things we're going to have to do before we go into rooms with criminals and murderers. Like it or not, you're stuck with me while we convince people that we

I winced at that. And to be honest, I knew her father would have wanted her to stay far away from the likes of me.

It didn't matter that he'd trained me or that I had become one of the best-known thieves in the world. Because it was my fault he was dead, and she had every right to hold me responsible for that.

"Ari, let's not do this. How about we figure out how to work together? Because for the foreseeable future, you and I are going to be tied to each other."

She gave me a saccharine smirk. "Except I don't trust you. I don't have to like you to work with you."

I sighed. "Galen Trent is smarter than you're giving him credit for. If I were him and the lost prince of the Winston Isles came to me for help, I would fucking help him. You're not seeing the future as it's playing out."

"Why me, after all this time?"

She knew why.*

Hell, *I* knew why. "Would you believe me if I told you I couldn't forget you?"

"Would you believe me if I told you I can spot a con man from a mile away?"

"Ari, just let me—"

"No. Here's how this is going to work. We follow Galen's lead. Do the job. No funny business, no games. I don't work for you. And let me be very, very clear: if you double-cross us, I will hunt you down. I know exactly who you are. Trusting you is how people get dead."

*Ouch*. That one hurt. "Okay, angel has got her claws out.

---

\* KISS–Prince and the Revolution

## DAMON

The next morning, after getting a call from Galen, I was back at GT and could feel every single prick and dart of Ari's angry gaze.

It seemed that Galen had forced her hand, and she blamed me. I'd gotten the call from Lucas and headed to see her at work first thing in the morning.

I told myself I didn't care about her response. This was about getting the job done. But still, knowing that she blamed me stung.

*She's right though.*

"This is a job, Ari. Trent clearly wants you to do it, so why don't the two of us just get on with it, yeah?"

"When you care about people, you don't *make* them do things," I mumbled under my breath.

"It's a shame. I liked the old Ari. She was fun. Resourceful. What happened to her?"

"That Ari grew up. She also didn't want to spend her life in jail."

Which is another reason I need you there."

"Why is this so important to you, Galen?"

"Sure, it's a recovery job, and having the royals as clients is great publicity. But the Black Rose Auction is one of those events where true black-market collectors go. I like having one of my people in there to analyze the who's who of it all. All you have to do is take notes and a couple of photos."

"I don't know if I'll be able to sneak a camera in there."

"We'll figure something out. Eyes and ears only. There are people going that we haven't been able to get visual confirmation of in years."

I leveled my gaze on my boss. "So you're telling me I have no choice. I have to work with my archenemy and act like I can tolerate him while taking on a dangerous assignment. And I also need to surreptitiously take photos and surveil while I'm there."

"That's my girl. The analyst in you is waking up."

"I'm not a field agent, Galen."

"Don't worry. By the time we're done with you, you will be. You won't even recognize yourself."

because I care about you and you're one of my people, I will make sure you'll have everything you need. And if it gets too wild and rocky, I will pull you out myself. You have to know that I won't let you be in any actual danger, right?"

"That's easy for you to say. You're not the one going in, Galen. I just don't know if I can do this."

"I have faith in you, Ari."

"You need someone better. An actual freaking field agent. Someone who does this stuff all the time."

"I have lots of people like that, but none of them have any knowledge of this vault. Plus, you actually know your partner. Even though you seemingly hate him, you two have a certain chemistry. Which will be an advantage because, from my understanding, you are going to have to play your roles to the letter at this auction. From what Prince Lucas told me, the kinds of people who will be there are no joke."

"Don't you want someone much more well-versed in fieldwork? Someone who's had combat experience and won't choke?"

"I *am* putting someone like that in the field. *You.* Get on board, Ari. It's happening."

"It really doesn't matter that I don't like this, does it?"

"I'm sorry, no."

*You could tell him everything.*

But would it matter? I knew when Galen had made up his mind. He needed my specific skill set, so he wouldn't take the risk of sending anyone else.

"Damon Hunt is not trustworthy," I said.

He rolled his eyes. "Of course, he's not. He's a thief, right?

"Thanks. I figured if I spend any time here at all, it might as well be cheery and colorful. You know, as much as I would love to give you the tour, there's not much more to see. So what do you need?"

"Ari, you know why I'm here."

I shook my head. "Galen, I'm asking you—no, I'm begging you—please do not make me do this."

"I'm sorry, Ari, but sometimes it comes down to business, okay? A really important potential client is asking for *you*. You specifically. I have weighed all the pros and cons of you doing this job, and it's come down to my gut. And my gut tells me *you* are the one to do this. I could assign someone else, but no one else has your knowledge of a Klenman vault. Your father notoriously cracked one before."

"Do you realize that my father and I aren't the same person?"

"Yes, but I also know that you are self-taught from his notes, and you have a whole boatload of knowledge about this vault."

I shook my head and dragged my hands through my hair. "And if I quit?"

"That's your right. And I will write you one hell of a recommendation letter. Because I do understand your hesitance, but the Ari Denton I know isn't a coward."

"The Ari Denton you know is an *analyst*, Galen. I don't go into the field. You don't know if I'll lock up or freak out. You don't know what will happen, and neither do I. God, I just don't want to do this job."

"I'm sorry I have to twist your arm, Ari. The client is important, and I don't owe you any more explanation than that. But

## ARI

After the day from hell, I couldn't get home fast enough.

But before I even put my bag down, there was a knock on my front door. When I checked the security monitor, I sighed.

I opened the door with crossed arms and an attitude. "Galen, what are you doing here?"

"It felt kind of important, and you didn't stay late like you normally do."

"Yeah, well, I had a shitty day. I needed a break."

"I don't require you to stay late. You don't have to prove your worth. I know how good you are."

I still didn't let him inside because I knew what he was doing here. "What do you need, Galen?"

He leaned on the doorjamb, not even asking to come in, forcing me to stand there. I eventually stepped back, and he followed me inside. He glanced around as he walked through my entryway into the kitchen. "I like what you've done with the place."

behind a mask. "I was clear. I'm not doing this. I'm not *you*. I'm not my father." Her words were punctuated by venom and felt like a jab.

"Ari…" I reached for her, but she stepped back out of range easily.

"No. Don't you *Ari* me. Because of *you*, my father isn't here. A million things I experienced, and he wasn't here," she said, her voice cracking. "He preferred to be with you more than with me."

There was nothing for me to say.

"Good luck to you, Damon, but don't come back. I'll use real bullets next time." Then she turned and walked away from me.

But just before she got out of earshot, I called out, "He'd be proud, Ari Sari. With or without you, his legacy lives on."

I knew what I'd done. I'd just struck a match while holding a gas can, and I needed to make my quick escape. Evoking his connection to me would not endear me to her.

*You are an asshole.*

An odd weight lifted, and relief flooded my veins. Just seeing her again had made my heart ache. Skinny, scrawny Ari, always chasing after her dad, begging to be a part of it all. But her father had wanted her far the hell away from his world. He'd done everything he could to keep her out of it, including pushing her away for her own good.

When he wasn't watching, she was shadowing him and learning. Picking locks with utmost efficiency. All the things her father refused to teach her, she had gone and learned on her own. That was Ari though, always determined.

As Galen walked with Prince Lucas ahead, I stayed back several steps to talk to Ari.* "Meant to tell you last night before you tranquilized me: you look real good, Ari."

She lifted her chin and looked down her nose at me. "I know."

I grinned at her. "You grew up, kid."

"Yeah, well, that's what happens when you don't see someone for years."

"Last time, you threatened to shoot me if I came back. You still feeling those violent tendencies?"

"I am. Lucky for you, I hate blood, so I only tranquilized you." She looked beautiful with her eyes spitting fire.

"Yeah, lucky for me. I can see it in your eyes, Ari. You *want* to do this, but you're saying no because of me. But we need you. You know how good you are. I've seen it with my own two eyes."

"I don't know how many times I have to repeat myself." Her dark eyes were clear and direct. The hints of mischief and longing and rebelliousness I'd seen in them not so long ago were hidden

* MERCY–Duffy

all, from the looks of this card, security will be out of this world, and you won't have access to the security system several days in advance. Second, it's held in a remote, exclusive location. Ingress and egress alone are going to be a challenge. Any way you go in, security is going to see you."

Lucas shrugged. "I didn't say it wasn't difficult. I just thought you'd be up for a challenge."

And for a moment, as Ari leaned forward like that, staring at the photo of the mansion, I could see it: that hint of rebellion, that sliver of fascination that wanted to dare her to try it. But right then, when she was on the cusp of choosing adventure, she pulled back again and buttoned up tight. "I'm sorry, you came to the wrong person. I can't help you."

Despite knowing she'd say no—despite a part of me *wanting* her to say no, to do what her father would have wanted; for her to be safe—without Ari, none of this would be possible.

*And you want her.*

That sliver of weakness was going to be my undoing.

Lucas shrugged and stood. "It was worth a shot. Thank you for taking the time to meet with us."

Ari nodded. Lucas and I strode toward the door, both knowing we'd have to come up with a different plan. Probably a riskier one. I could pull it off solo, maybe, but it was a gamble. If Lucas did it with me and had no alibi, Reaper and his people would come after him. Lucas's reputation preceded him in certain communities. And while his brother's influence could save him, my association with him would not save me. We were running short on time, with a little over two weeks to go. We'd have to try someone else.

Lucas nodded again. "And I'd like to keep it that way while also keeping that heirloom safe for my family, especially for my future sister-in-law. She's had a rough go of it and doesn't deserve an international incident overshadowing her wedding. Unfortunately, to pull this off, we'll need someone who can access a Klenman vault, which is why I reached out to Damon. The key is to let the necklace be shown, and then, before it's packed up and transported, you two will remove it and replace it with a replica."

Ari chuckled. "You mean you trust *him* to pull that off?"

*What does she mean by that?*

I tried to remind myself that she didn't know who I was now.

I frowned and lifted my gaze to hers. "I get paid either way, Ari. Hell, I get paid for making this introduction. If that's all…" I pushed to my feet. "Lucas, I told you it was a long shot. She's not going to help us."

Galen sat forward. "I promised we'd hear you out. Your Highness—sorry—I mean Lucas, we'll discuss it. But right now, it doesn't seem like Ari is interested."

Lucas nodded. "I understand. It's potentially dangerous and complicated. There are very few people in the world who have the skills and the nerve required to pull something like this off. I hoped Ari was one of them, but I wouldn't want her doing anything she's not comfortable with."

My lips almost twitched, but I kept them under control. Oh, Lucas was good. A master of manipulation.

"I'm sorry I couldn't help," Ari said. "But I don't work in the field. And the Black Rose…that's just a death wish. First of

Lucas pulled a card from his chest with a photo of the location on it and handed it to Ari. "As soon as I saw the necklace, I knew, but I discreetly verified it. My brother absolutely cannot know about this, and it will be a disaster if it leaks. At this point, I'm willing to do whatever is necessary to get it back." He slid his gaze to Galen. "As for the auction," he said, with a note of awe in his voice, "think of it as the sexiest secret playground for the wealthy and powerful. Anything and everything will be up for auction. This year's entries include the freaking Noli Oblivisci. It's a gorgeous piece. Gold and silver. Adorned with jewels. Used by popes."

Ari raised a brow. "First question, why don't we just call the FBI or Interpol? Make it their problem."

I rubbed my jaw as I watched her intently. "Because the man who runs the auction has everyone in his pocket. So getting creative is the best option."

"Why do you sound giddy about it? It's obviously illegally obtained. No way they have their hands on that cleanly."

"Obviously not," I muttered. "This isn't that kind of auction. But we will be within sneezing distance of some of the finest art and jewelry in the world."

"You want me to believe you plan to keep your hands to yourself?" Ari asked.

Lucas nodded. "I only want what belongs to the crown. Besides, Reaper is not the kind of man you run afoul of. He's ruthless."

Ari sat forward, and I could see her mind working out how she would do it, what would be important. "Your brother has no idea that your past is coming back to haunt you?" she asked.

muster. "Ari, I know it's a big ask, but you're the only person in the world skilled enough to help us."

I *needed* her. I didn't care how I got her.

Galen sat back, his eyes flicking between Ari and me, then settling back on Prince Lucas. "Your Highness—"

Lucas held up his hand. "Please, just call me *Lucas*. It's already weird enough being a prince. Don't make it awkward."

Galen smirked at him. "Fine, Lucas. Ari has given me a firm answer. We can discuss this further, but perhaps someone else on my team…"

Lucas slid me a glance that basically said, *This isn't going well.*

I'd tried to tell him Ari was a lost cause. But he'd insisted on the best, so this was our Hail Mary.

"Look," Lucas continued, "no one knows this, so I'm counting on your discretion. Before I became a prince, I had an unsavory past. Once my brother found me and brought me back into the fold, someone from my past apparently wormed their way in. The Royal Heart that was in the royal vault has been replaced by a replica. The real deal is up for sale during the Black Rose Auction, and I need it recovered by someone I trust so that it doesn't fall into the wrong hands. You can imagine the embarrassment for my brother and his new bride if that jewel is discovered missing. Especially if it comes out that I might have known the perpetrator, which is what people will assume."

Ari frowned. "You're certain the one in the royal vault is a fake? Also, what is the Black Rose Auction? Can't you just contact them about the dubious provenance of the item they have?"

# DAMON

*What did you really expect?*

Had I really thought she'd welcome me back instead of tranquilizing me in her room and bolting? Okay, I didn't really think she'd pull out the welcome mat, but I didn't think she would be so hostile. And maybe I'd hoped there might be some part of her that was happy to see me.

The moment I'd seen her, with her sleek slim braids and stormy dark eyes, I wanted to hold her tight and pretend too many years hadn't gone by.

*Why would you think that? You abandoned her. Well, you miscalculated. And now you have problems.*

"As I'm sure Ari will tell you, Galen, we have a complicated past. I was her father's protégé, but I have turned over a new leaf and built a respectable life. But when His Royal Highness reached out with something this delicate, I couldn't really say no." I turned to Ari then, really laying on all the sincerity I could

Galen interjected immediately. "What Miss Denton means is that we will hear the proposal, then make a decision."

Lucas gave me a warm smile. "From what Damon tells me, you two have a history. And for this job, we're going to need two safecrackers. The best of the best."

"I don't know what Mr. Hunt has said, but I work in recovery. I don't steal things. Besides, I'm an analyst. I don't work in the field."

The prince glanced between Damon and me, back to Damon, then to Galen, and tried again. "This *is* a recovery job. Please, all I'm asking is for you to hear me out."

I didn't want to. I knew what Galen expected of me, but I just couldn't. Tinnitus pierced my eardrum, and hazy vision had me blinking rapidly as my eyes started to fail me. I couldn't work with Damon Hunt. What was he doing here? Why now? I didn't want to hear anything. Especially not from the man who was responsible for my father's death.

And there it was…the clunking sound of the other shoe dropping. *No. No. Absolutely not.* That sinking feeling escalated to free-falling. My brain buzzed with the same hyperawareness I had the night before. This couldn't be happening.

Years with no contact. Then, suddenly, twice in twenty-four hours. *What the fuck?*

As if on cue, Damon walked in, his swagger on display. My breath caught, rendering me unable to breathe. I felt like someone was squeezing my heart in a vise. Why was he doing this to me? The moment his gaze met mine, he grinned. "What's up, Ari Sari?"

Galen cleared his throat then. "Mr. Hunt, I can't wait to hear how you know Ari."

Damon had the nerve to keep grinning. "Now *that* is a very long story."

Galen's gaze on me was almost apologetic and definitely a little sympathetic.[*]

"What the hell are you doing here?" I bit out.

I should probably have shown some sort of manners or decorum, followed some kind of protocol. After all, I was in the presence of royalty. But my eyes stayed on Damon.

His face was smooth. "Relax, I'm just here for a job. That's it. No need to tranq me again."

Galen lifted a brow. "Tranq you?"

Damon flashed a grin. "Just some fun between old friends."

I turned my attention from him and focused on the two other men. "Your Highness, I'm so sorry you came all this way, but I'm not available."

[*] DON'T HURT YOURSELF–Beyoncé (feat. Jack White)

rest of the women in the city. A prince had been living under our noses, walking the streets for God knew how long, and no one had known. You'd be weird if you weren't interested.

Galen pushed to his feet, stalked over to him, and shook his hand. The prince gave him a charismatic smile. I could see the appeal. I knew *exactly* why he was the most eligible royal in the world.

Galen introduced me. "Meet Ari Denton, the best safecracker I have. She's a legend."

Lucas gave me a wide smile. "It's a pleasure to meet you finally. I have heard a lot about you, Ms. Denton. Your reputation precedes you. I hear you were instrumental in the Phelps jewels recovery."

I cocked my head. "I think my prowess has been exaggerated. You shouldn't even know who I am."

"Let's just say I was aware of your father. And when I discovered that you worked for GT Securities, I knew you were the person I needed."

I lifted my gaze to Galen's as my stomach twisted. He'd known of my father? No one knew of my father. Unless they were in the business of taking things that didn't belong to them.

Who the hell was Lucas exactly?

*Right now, a client.*

A client I was going to learn more about. But for now, I said, "Well, I'm sure I can figure out an action plan for whatever you want to recover." Now that I was sure it wasn't Damon trying to hire me, I relaxed, the tension flowing out of me in waves.

Abruptly, Lucas checked his watch. "I'm waiting for someone else to join us. Actually, he's the reason I even found you."

assumed Damon had come for me. My stomach twisted at the idea that it wasn't him. Who else knew who I was?

Galen cleared his throat and dragged his gaze from Taryn again. When his eyes met mine, he frowned. I grinned at him, letting him know that I had seen the way he was looking at her. He ignored me. *Shocker.* "Show him in."

When Taryn went to bring in the mysterious guest, Galen pinned me with a look. "I'm going to say this once, Ari: Keep an open mind, would you?"

I lifted my brows. I was always open-minded. I never once lost my cool, not even when a client was screaming their head off because they wanted something that couldn't be done. I just had a firm understanding of what I was—and wasn't—willing to do.

Instead of Damon, in walked a man I never thought I'd see in person. I'd seen his face splashed all over gossip rags. Lucas Newsome Winston, the new prince of the Winston Isles. Some long-lost royal or something. His brother, the king, was getting married soon. All the gossip sites talked about how the new prince was now the most eligible royal in the world.

He was undeniably handsome. Gorgeous eyes, a great athletic body. He clearly worked out. He'd been blessed with a sharp jaw, a dimple that was quick to materialize, and what appeared to be perpetually sun-kissed skin. He had dark hair, dark eyes with a mischievous glint, and humor in his cheeky grin.

From what I'd seen, the rags hadn't given much information on his life before the royal revelation...not that I read gossip.

*Oh, sure you don't.*

Okay, fine. I'd been glued to my TMZ and Deuxmoi like the

"You were specifically requested, Ari."

That made my blood run cold. "No. Sorry."

"Don't you want to know by whom?"

I shook my head. "Nope. If someone asked for me by name, they ran in Dad's circles." I wasn't part of that life. My life was stable, boring, predictable. And I had a feeling Damon Hunt was behind this meeting, attempting to mess that up. "Get someone else to do it."

"I think the client would like to speak with you directly. Hear them out; then decide."

"Why are you doing this to me?" It shouldn't have, but it felt like an attack on my orderly life.

He exhaled. "Why won't you hear them out?"

"Galen, you don't understand."

"All I promised them was a meeting. If you have the heebie-jeebies and don't want to do the job, you don't have to. But we do need to hear them out."

"Is there a reason we need to hear them out?"

"Like you predicted, it's a big client."

I shook my head. "I don't like this."

"I figured as much."

Taryn Mulroney, Galen's PA and my best friend, strolled in at two o'clock, and Galen's gaze flickered to her intently before skittering away. I grinned to myself. Taryn had worked for him for a year, and after all that time, he was still trying to pretend he wasn't totally into her.

She smiled at me. "Hey, Ari. Galen, one of the clients is here."

Wait, *clients*, plural? Had my suspicions been wrong? I'd just want to see the look on their faces when they let you down. And I understand that my name could come with baggage, especially in the security industry. If there are people who were aware of him."

He shook his head. "Well, I will say that you are observant. Your name *is* what's at play here."

My palms went clammy, and my emotions churned until I slapped them back into submission. I loved my life.

*Do you?*

I'd worked too hard to have stability.

*But does it excite you?*

"Sometimes we have to do things we don't want to do, Galen. I'm good at what I do. You know that. If you have to fire me, it's obviously because someone is strong-arming you."

He shook his head as he sighed. "Ari, you should have more faith in people."

I cocked my head. "Wasn't it you who told me not to trust anyone?"

He chuckled softly as he lifted a folder from his desk. "It was. But you trust family. Find a circle, Ari—people you trust. I don't have to be in that circle, but I count you in mine. And I protect what's mine."

My nose tingled at that. It had been a long time since I'd been in anyone's circle. Since anyone other than my aunt had cared enough to protect me. "If you're not firing me, then what is this about?"

"I have a job for you."

I ground my teeth together. "Before you say anything, I don't think this is a good idea."

It was the best way to honor him. He'd tried to tell me a million times not to be like him, but it hadn't sunk in until I tried desperately to keep him from bleeding out. I could still feel the slow, sluggish pump of his blood between my fingers.

Lack of desire for fieldwork notwithstanding, I still needed this job, and it was best not to irritate my boss. "What I mean is I can be of much better use in here." And in here I got to be Ari Denton, security specialist. Not Ari Denton, daughter of a thief. I liked this Ari. My father would have been proud of this Ari.

Galen cocked his head, leaned forward, and met my gaze. A small shiver of awareness hit me. Bad news was coming. The hairs on the nape of my neck stood at attention, and I squared my shoulders against the dread trying to weigh me down. What was I going to do now?

"I appreciate what you've done for me, Galen, but if you're going to fire me, just do it."

His brows knitted. "What?"

"You've got your I-don't-want-to-do-this-and-it's-going-to-hurt look on your face. So just do it."

"Why do you think I'm going to fire you?"

Wasn't it obvious? "Probably because one of your clients found out about me. Or knew who my father was. Likely, they're demanding that you fire me, or you won't get some big account. Am I close?"

His brows furrowed then, and he crossed his arms. "And you think I'd sell out my team? My people?"

I had no idea what he would do. "I make it a point not to ask people to choose. It's a little bit easier that way. You don't a shot when I needed it most. Right when I was looking for direction.

Dad had never been caught, but there had been rumors and whispers, and Galen had a past shrouded in shadows. I always wondered if he'd at least been aware of Dad. But he'd never said.

When I strode into his office at 1:45, I found Galen alone. I was dressed for a simulation in the vault later, so I had all my equipment strapped to me.

He lifted a brow and grinned. "I see you came to impress."

I shrugged. "I'm planning to do a simulation for the field agents, and I want to run some timing scenarios. It'll increase performance. What's so urgent? Something wrong with my report on the Kellerman case?"

He shook his head. "Of course not. You were thorough as always. You found several weak spots in our process. Hell, I could use you in the field."

I shook my head.* "I'm never going in the field." Unlike most agents, I had zero desire for fieldwork.

*Hits close to home, doesn't it?*

Too close. All it took to keep me on the straight and narrow was remembering how Dad had died. Those little adrenaline shivers I felt when I opened a difficult safe or figured out the best way in and out of an impenetrable building were the temptation. The illusion.

I liked cold, hard reality. I'd worked hard to be where I was today. Dad had been right not to teach me, not to want a criminal life for me.

* REHAB—Amy Winehouse

# ARI

I didn't usually bristle at getting a summons from my boss, because, after all, he was my boss. But his text sounded like a demand, not a request for a meeting.

My office. 2 p.m. Don't be late.

I was especially annoyed at the implication I might be late. I was never late. That kind of text would leave anyone cranky. Not to mention I hadn't slept a wink after tranquilizing Damon Hunt in the middle of my apartment. I considered calling the police half a dozen times. But I didn't. Instead, I'd grabbed my gear and a change of clothes for today, and gone to a hotel for the night.

Galen Trent, billionaire securities expert, owned GT Securities, one of the premier security and recovery companies on the East Coast. He was a great boss. He was also controlling, uptight, and strong-willed, but I respected him. He'd given me

I didn't hesitate, and there was barely a sound as I easily fired off a round from the tranq gun.

I watched as he staggered back, shock and disbelief crossing his face, and I knew I'd hit my mark.

"What the hell do you want?" I asked, sighing in exasperation.

"I need your help. If there were another way to do this, I would. But I have a safe—"

Before he could finish the sentence, I twisted the hand at my waist, using a pressure point to my advantage.

When he howled and loosened his grip more, I stepped forward, bringing his body with me, then used the momentum to take his body on a proverbial around-the-world journey, twisting his arm up and around, then flipping him over. He groaned as his back hit my rug, but then he was already scrambling back to his feet. I had to be quicker. My heart thumped an erratic rhythm in my chest as I turned to run, but his whiskey eyes locked with mine, bolting me in place, the pale moonlight highlighting the scar on his cheek.

Now that he was all grown up, that scar kept his face from being too pretty. It, along with that sculpted square jaw, only made him more handsome.

I had known he would come back yet again one day. He hadn't been far from my thoughts since that fateful night eight years ago that changed me and my life forever. Despite his presence being unwelcome and making me miss my father, I did wonder what the hell Damon wanted after all this time. Especially what he wanted badly enough to show up here and wait for me in the dark.

Whatever he wanted couldn't be good for me.

*But maybe it could be fun.*

What? No. This was not the time for inappropriate thoughts.

I had no choice. It was either run or fire.

college. I was drinking in an off-campus bar after I'd put my aunt on a flight to Florida. He came to give me more money. To help me start my life, he said. But I didn't want his damned money. And this time I had *plenty* to say. All those years of resentment and complicated feelings poured right out.

I fully unloaded everything I'd ever felt at him. Yes. Even the schoolgirl fantasies. Including the way his laugh at first had irritated me but then started to make my clit throb. Yes. I told him all that.

In my defense, I'd just graduated with no one else watching besides my aunt. I needed someone to unload on. Anger and longing had produced an odd cocktail that day.

He eased his hold on my mouth but didn't release me, instead sliding his hand down to wrap around my neck with the barest hint of pressure, letting me know he wasn't here to hurt me but could if he wanted.

*Excellent.*

"I thought I told you last time I saw you that if you came back, I would shoot you and then hand you over to the police. Didn't you believe me?"

"Oh, I believed you. But this is important. So it was worth risking you shooting me."

I frowned at the change in his tone. Was that—was that idiot *laughing* at me?

I struggled in his hold, but he just held me tighter. "I'm serious, Ari. I came to talk. When you hear me out, I'll be out of your hair."

He waited, his hand poised around my neck, for my answer.

nothing. It wasn't until I inched by the window to the fire escape that a prickling alarm of dread tickled my scalp again.

*Whiskey\*. Tango. Foxtrot.*

Before I could force my body to heed the warning, a rough hand clamped over my mouth. My head swam, and my pulse bucked and kicked under my skin as panic tried to seize me.

"Easy, Ari Sari, I just want to talk."

Though my brain wanted to flood my body with relief, I knew enough to be wary. That voice. It was even deeper than the last time I'd heard it. I was suddenly all too aware of my intruder's size. He was somewhere over six feet tall. I was nearly five foot eight, yet in his hold, I felt petite. Part of that had to do with his broadness too.

With Damon's chest against my back and one of his arms tightly banded around my waist, I knew the scrawny kid from my childhood was most definitely a man now, with tight, corded muscles and big broad hands. And goddamn, he smelled the same. Like something earthy, piney, and a little bit spicy.

To my utter horror, I purposely took a whiff.

*The hell is wrong with you?*

The first time I'd seen him after he left us in that garage, I'd caught him stuffing money in my mailbox at my aunt's place. A huge wad of it. Like now, in the middle of the night. Trying to be sneaky. We didn't speak. But all those same emotions bubbled to the surface. Ones I didn't want. Ones that reminded me of his quick smile and how he smelled.

The next and last time I saw him was when I graduated from

\* EXPRESS YOURSELF–Charles Wright and the Watts

Barefoot, I slowly approached my sitting room, my feet making minuscule sucking sounds as I walked across the hardwood.

Normally I loved the open floor plan of my apartment because it let me see everything at once, but it provided precious little cover if I should need it. It took only a brief stop in the kitchen to peer inside the pantry, and I'd covered the entire living area.

My scan said nothing had been disturbed, but there was something wrong about the air. A charge of electricity. I had two choices. The first was to run downstairs to the doorman and call the police. The second was to keep going on my own.

I deserved to be in my own bed tonight, so I kept going. Because maybe this was nothing. Maybe I was imagining the weirdness I was feeling.

*You know better than that. Someone is here.*

I inched toward the hall bathroom, checked behind the shower curtain, and even knowing it was too small for someone to fit inside, I checked the cabinet too. Might as well be thorough.

I checked the guest room next. The window was small, barely big enough to climb through, although it led onto a small fire escape. I double-checked the lock and found it closed tight. Besides, the security sensor hadn't been tripped. The cleaning service Galen used for all the units had been through today, so the place was tidy. There wasn't anything left out of place, so why did it feel like someone had been here?

That feeling was even worse in my bedroom. I had an en suite and a massive window that also led onto the fire escape. I checked under the bed, in my closet, and in the bathroom, but

GT Securities had several executive apartments all over the city. I had chosen one in Greenwich Village. It was a fourth-floor walk-up, nothing too fancy, but I loved the neighborhood, and the apartment had lots of windows and natural light. Plus, it was at the heart of NYU, and I loved the vibe.

And I'd made it my own, adding hues of red, orange, and yellow to pick up the light from the afternoon sun with pillows, throws, and artwork. In the bedrooms, I'd used more-calming blues and greens.

I hung my keys on the hook in my entryway, then toed off my heels before groaning as I scooped them up and placed them neatly in the shoe cupboard. Just as I did, the hairs on the nape of my neck stood at attention, so much so that I reached my hand up to massage away the prickle of awareness.

When it wouldn't dissipate, I peered around my apartment briefly. My front door locks, all four of them, had been engaged when I came in. I'd had to punch in my keypad code to undo the two dead bolts and the standard locks. No one had come through this way.

*Better safe than sorry.*

I reached under the entryway table and palmed my tranq gun, then eased the tape away from it. I might not like actual guns, but I did know how to shoot, which was a requirement at GT Securities. I had a license to carry.

Considering how my father had died, I knew I could never put a bullet in someone, but I could sure as hell tranq them. And I had loaded enough tranquilizers in this gun to take down an elephant.

I was responsible for the full analysis and breakdown. Our company was contracted by insurance companies and private collectors to recover lost or stolen items.

Last night, our team had recovered a Picasso. Unfortunately, there was also a minor injury due to a shooting. It was a flesh wound that was addressed in the field, but the field agents had to report it and deal with the police. Which had meant paperwork. So. Much. Paperwork. But GT Securities prided itself on expediency, accuracy, and discretion, so I'd stayed late.

Besides, Galen had hired me straight out of an internship that was part of my criminology degree. I'd apparently impressed him with my knowledge of safes and their internal mechanisms. He eventually hired me partly for my unique ability to completely detach from a situation and analyze all angles. To me, it was like a puzzle. And I was good at it.

But tonight had been more complicated. Thanks to having to involve the police.

It meant more paperwork for me, but since taking a bullet had been the only way to walk out with that painting, police were necessary. And the red tape had taken hours to navigate.

At least I hadn't had to come far to crash. Thanks to Galen, I lived in company housing close to the office. Housing in the city was nuts, but Galen had come to the rescue. My rent came straight out of my paycheck. It made things easy, and I would always appreciate Galen for the option, even though he was getting something out of it too. I had expertise he knew he could use, and he was the only person at my job who knew how I'd developed those skills.

I shook my head and dragged my hand down my face. "Fuck, was it you? Is the con man in the room with us right now?"

He rolled his eyes. "No. It was my piece-of-shit stepfather. I warned her and got him out of her life. Doesn't matter. Manganiello owes me a favor now. Hopefully, it's big enough to buy out Max."

"Fucking hell."

"Look, I've already got a meeting with Manganiello on the books. All you've got to do is find me someone as good as you are for the safe. It's a simple job. And for what it's worth, I'm going to get Max out of trouble anyway. You and I go way back."

I cursed under my breath. "I don't want to owe you."

"We're not keeping tabs, remember?"

"Fine. I'll do it. But we need someone else. I have a name, but there's no way it's going to happen."

Lucas didn't seem the least bit concerned. "We don't know until we ask. Time is of the essence, and we have precious little of it. Who's the other person you're thinking of?"

This was such a bad idea for so many reasons. But Lucas and I went way back, and he'd saved my ass once or twice. Besides, after everything he'd been through, the guy deserved a win. I just hoped I wasn't opening a can of worms right now. "Her name is Ari Denton."

---

# ARI

I was dead on my feet. Just plain exhausted. My boss, Galen Trent, had wanted a rundown of our team's last assignment, and

don't like it, you can walk. And I'll sweeten the pot. I know you've been trying to reach your brother, Max. You're not going to find him. But I know where he is."

I stood up straight then. "What the fuck, Lucas?"

He held his hands up. "I didn't do anything to him. I just heard through the grapevine."

"Shit, Malibu?"

He nodded. "Yeah, she had some leverage."

"Why the fuck didn't she call me to come and get him?"

"Well, you know Malibu. She's a fence, so she's still trying to make her coin. I'm sure if it got really drastic, she would have just called you. But she saw an opportunity, so she's taking it."

"Fucking hell. Where is he?"

"Do you remember James Manganiello?"

I stared at him, my heart knocking against my ribs. "No, there's no fucking way."

"Apparently the kid is in trouble. He owes Manganiello a favor."

Fuck, I was going to kill my brother. Manganiello trafficked in favors. *Dangerous* favors. If he had Max on the hook, Max was going to have to do something that would likely get him killed. And Manganiello didn't trade in money. I couldn't just roll up and buy my brother out. Fuck. What the hell was I going to do?

Lucas interrupted my panicked thoughts. "I will deal with your Max problem. Manganiello owes *me* a favor. I'm willing to use that to help Max out."

"How big a favor does he owe you, Lucas?"

"Let's just say I saved his sister from a con man once."

*two* people good enough for that kind of vault, and I only know a handful. I'm not even the highest on that list."

"Obviously, I can fund this little endeavor. I need someone else who's just as good as you are. I figure it'll be a three-person gig. Possibly four."

"Four?"

He rolled his shoulders. "My sister-in-law-to-be, Penny, she's good with her hands and weapons, and she's a royal guard. Well, she was…is. I mean, she's temporarily my personal royal guard until I get my permanent assignment. Anyway, we're going to attend this auction and try to get the necklace back."

"You *told* her?" I stared at him incredulously.

"The thing about Penny is she's astute. She knew right away while we were walking around the jewels that something was wrong. I told her my suspicions. At first she didn't believe me, but I proved it. So here we are."

"You know, I don't even want to know how you proved it, because a part of me sees you carrying around a jeweler's loupe with you everywhere you go."

"You're not far off."

"Lucas, I don't know if I can get involved in this. It's risky. I've survived this long by making calculated moves. I'm putting my livelihood on the line if I do this."

Not to mention Reaper… Well, he was ruthless and not an enemy I wanted. Every inch of that place would be surveilled, no guests would be allowed weapons, and if we were caught, death would be a mercy. It wasn't worth it.

"I knew you'd say that. But listen, the plan is solid. If you underground auction events in the world. Everything from art to jewelry to virginities were up for auction. It was wild. I'd had a piece or two go through there. The man who ran it was known only as Reaper. He owned a string of exclusive sex clubs. And he was known for his ruthlessness.

Not all auction items were necessarily on the open market. Some were black-market items. This was the auction for the world's most exclusive commodities—legal and illegal.

"Man, are you sure they have the Royal Heart? Because there's no way to get into the auction this late."

Lucas grinned. "It's like you don't even know me. I *have* a way to get into the auction and access the vault. *But* it's a Klenman vault. Which means it's a two-person mechanism."

I ran my hands through my hair. "That is a tall order, Lucas. And you are good, but you're not Klenman good. That's insanity."

"I know. But I just found my brother. I can't let him think that I, or possibly someone I know, stole the crown jewels of the Winston Isles. And my future sister-in-law is awesome. You'll really like her. This is how a royal brother shows his love, Damon. I can't let her walk down the aisle with some shit that's not real."

I stared at him. "Man, I really think you should tell him."

"I can't. I need to get it back. If I can't, I'll tell him then. But I should at least try and fix it first."

I sighed. "Look, I'd love to do you a favor, but I've got a lot going on right now, Lucas."

"I know. And you know I wouldn't ask if I weren't desperate."

"I hear you. But you're forgetting one small fact: we need

coronation, so it's a big deal. Sebastian said we're all going to wear the crown jewels for the ceremony. We were talking about the Royal Heart, and I mentioned that I'd never seen the crown jewels. So we went down to the vault, and he was walking me through everything, and I happened to notice that the fucking Royal Heart is made of glass."

"Are you sure it was a fake? I mean, the shit was in the vault, right? Who could have taken it?"

"I don't know, but at some point, someone replaced it. Sebastian said it had been taken for cleaning as soon as he'd announced he was taking a bride. Which was just weeks after he'd let the world know I was his brother. So probably then. Which is honestly how I would have stolen it."

I shook my head. "Oh, for the love of God. You're worried he's going to think it was you, aren't you?"

Lucas gave me a sheepish smile. "Well, you know, I don't exactly have the best reputation. He put his crown on the line to legitimize me. But let's face it, I'm a jewel thief and a con man. He won't believe me."

"Just talk to him. He's your brother. He might understand that you had nothing to do with it."

He winced. "Except it would seem that the *actual* Royal Heart is part of the Black Rose Auction coming up in a few weeks. The plan is to get it at the event and put it back like it was never missing. I'll tell him everything after."

My eyes went wide. "Are you kidding? This has to be a joke."

The Black Rose Auction was one of the most exclusive

When all was said and done, two of us had walked away that day. The other one had been left bloody and bruised in a hotel laundry room for the authorities to find.

"Lucas, what kind of jam are you in that you or your fancy royal brother can't get you out of?"

"That's just it. That whole being-a-prince thing put a big old target on my back. And my brother's. Every idiot who feels wronged or wants to test his mettle wants a go at me."

I handed him a Perrier from the fridge outside, and we both leaned on the balcony railing. "And why do you need the likes of me?"

"There's this necklace. The Royal Heart. Normally, it goes on display when a new monarch is about to be coronated or when a monarch takes a wife."

"Isn't your brother engaged?"

"Exactly. Their wedding is next month."

I could see where this was going. "Do I dare guess?"

"The Royal Heart has gone missing."

I whistled low. "For fuck's sake. I assume he filed the insurance claim."

Lucas winced. "Um, yeah, that's the thing. He can't."

And here was the rub. The real reason he'd come to me instead of Interpol or somebody official. "Why?"

Lucas shoved his hands in his pockets. "He doesn't know it's gone. There's a Royal Heart there. It's just not the real one."

I frowned. "What do you mean?"

"Look, two weeks ago, we were talking about the plans for the wedding, right? It'll be my first official royal gig since his

Lucas shook his head. "I could probably use a scotch to calm my ass down, but I'm not going to ask for that because I need a favor."

I winced. "You're a prince now. What could I possibly do for you? You have the bankroll to hire anyone for a job."

"Like I said, I need a guy who's good with his hands. Not to mention discreet and loyal. Know anyone like that?"

As far as skill went, I was one of the best. But there were others. And these days I was pulling back from fieldwork. When it came to discretion and loyalty, I knew why he'd come to me. That thing they said about no honor among thieves was right. Luckily, Lucas and I were actually friends. "And Malibu told you I was still in business?"

He shrugged. "Are you or aren't you?"

Malibu Law was another friend. I'd been working with her for years. She was an old contact of Paul's, and she'd helped me out when I'd been in a pinch once or twice after his death. In return, I kept bringing her my best scores to fence.

"Fucking hell," I said, "what do you need?"

"You know I wouldn't come asking if it weren't important. You're doing well for yourself, obviously. The art game is lucrative, and your hands are cleaner this way. Plus what happened with Reinhart. I know you're pulling back. But this is urgent."

Nick Reinhart had worked with me for five years or so, then double-crossed me on a job. To make matters worse, Jazz had been on that job. He'd nearly gotten us killed with his antics. It was one thing to double-cross me on a job; it was a whole other thing to nearly get my people killed.

I whistled low as I waved him in. "Jesus Christ, no wonder Jazz didn't tell me. She wanted it to be a surprise."

From her office, she called out, "Hey, Lucas! I'll be right out to say hi." And then to me, she added, "I told you so."

I rolled my eyes. "One of these days, I need to move her out of the shadows. Give her a shot at normal."

Lucas laughed. "Nah, you're never getting rid of Jazz. She runs you."

He was right. I might kid myself sometimes, but she was my right hand. She knew everything, including where the proverbial bodies were buried.

"Man, what brings you to town? Are you just passing through New York? Obviously, I've heard all the stuff about, you know, you being a prince now and shit. I didn't know you were back, or I would have called you."

He rocked back on his heels as he shoved his hands in his pockets. "Yeah, it's been an adjustment," he said. "I've been going back and forth between the islands and here."

"I'm sorry about your dad. Are you okay?"

He shrugged. "It's…a confusing time."

"But, bro, you're a fucking prince."

Lucas rolled his eyes. "Yeah, but a prince with my background comes with some *baggage*."

I studied him closely. "Fuck, this isn't a social call, is it?"

He shook his head. "No, it's not."

"Jazz, we'll be in my office." And by *office*, I meant my balcony, which offered out-of-this-world views of the Upper West Side. "Do you want something to drink?"

"Normally I would. But this is an old friend, and I can't exactly put him on the books," she said.

"Who's the meeting with, Jazz?"

"I told you: an old friend. He's going to be here in two minutes."

I didn't need old friends coming out of the woodwork. I was too preoccupied right now. After several days, I still hadn't been able to get in touch with my brother.

When the security alarm announced someone at the door, I made my way down to the lower floor of the penthouse. Usually, I only took personal appointments here. Never dates or anything like that; I liked hotels for that. But there were a handful of people I knew well enough to trust letting in. When I checked the security panel to see who it was, my heart lurched a little. "For fuck's sake, Jazz," I yelled. "Why couldn't you tell me who it was?"

I opened the door before the buzzer even rang. "Lucas Newsome? Son of a bitch, what are you doing here?"

I clapped him on the back, and he slapped me just as hard, then pulled back and looked at me.

"Check you out. La-di-da," he said in a singsong voice. "Looks like you've come up in the world since that job we did in Vegas."

I groaned. Would he never let that go? I'd been trapped under some high roller's hotel bed for two days while he played a private poker game in his suite and entertained escorts. I shuddered. "Jesus Christ, Vegas was a fucking lifetime ago."

"Yeah. Imagine my surprise when I went looking for a guy who was great with his hands and Malibu sent me to you."

# DAMON

I checked my agenda for the morning, frowning when I saw hours blocked off and no name associated with the appointment. I buzzed Jazz, who had an office downstairs. "Jazz, what the hell is this meeting?"

"Oh, um, about that. Can't say."

I groaned. "Jesus Christ, Jazz, I told you to check with me before you book just anyone. Especially to come here. You know how I feel about my privacy." My penthouse in The Park on the Upper West Side had become a sanctuary. I didn't bring anyone here. With my job, it was better no one ever get too close.

As far as the world was concetrned, I was an art dealer. I found rare pieces all over the world, and it made me rich. People knew my name, but so few saw my face, and I liked it that way. Anonymity was how I stayed breathing.

Only Jazz and a handful of people actually knew my real job. Even fewer knew my face.

day, as I held on tight, I noticed his hands were cold. And just like that, my father was gone.

Like always, I woke up with a start, covered in sweat, my breath shallow and choppy. And I spoke the name of the man I held responsible.

"Damon Hunt."

He yelled that he was too busy to deal with me that day. Told me I'd be underfoot. I immediately hated that boy, the one with the dirty jeans and the ripped T-shirt, whom my father *wanted* to teach.

Three years later, that same boy had his hand over the hole in my father's chest, and I'd been left looking into his grave whiskey-colored eyes and listening to his whispered apologies.

Even though I knew it was a nightmare, I was sucked back into that time, into the shuddery dread where my world swirled around, my only tether to sanity gone. And I never once got to ask my dad what I'd done wrong or why he'd stopped loving me. Never once got to say, *I love you, Daddy. Please come back to me.*

Like the thief in the night that he was, that young boy with the knowing eyes, the too-handsome face, and the scar that made him more interesting, was gone. Out the back door, no doubt, down the back alley.

Then I was in the hospital, holding my father's hand.

My throat hurt from all the begging and pleading. *Daddy, please don't leave me. Please don't go. I need you.* I'd screamed that over and over and over. When I lost my voice and stopped talking, the speech therapists worried I'd permanently damaged my vocal cords by screaming so much.

Aunt Adele made some kind of bargain with the nurses to let me stay with my father because every time they tried to have me removed, I'd start screaming. So they let me have as much time with him as I wanted. And for the three days he lay in that coma, I held his hands alone, crying, bargaining, wishing. But then one

At the end of the day, those two words couldn't staunch my father's blood or bring him back to the land of the living. Those two words didn't fill that empty hole in my heart.

I wasn't quite certain how long I'd known what my father was or what he did. When I was a little kid, all I knew was hanging out with my dad in the garage was my favorite time.

He showed me all kinds of things and let me fiddle with the old safes there. It was my means of distraction and escape. I'd loved it.

After Mom died, he did his best, but we were both grieving, and the open, jovial man I had known became just a bit more distant. But he tried. And I tried to be the perfect daughter, needing to connect to him even more. But then there'd been the art class debacle.

And then, he didn't want me hanging out at the garage anymore unless it was absolutely urgent. He never looked happy to have me there. He never asked me about blueprints again, about entry points or exit points or alarms. Worse, he refused to teach me how to work on safes anymore.

One day, I'd snuck over there anyway. This bully, Miriam McConnell, had insisted she was going to wait at my house to beat me up after school, so I avoided my house like a coward. I thought my dad would understand.

I went to the garage and found a lanky boy a little older than me tinkering with one of the safes*. He looked like he could use a burger. Dad was annoyed that I was there and that I'd disobeyed his orders to go straight home.

* SON OF A PREACHER MAN—Dusty Springfield

He obviously needed me. But when I called him, using our code—calling once, hanging up, and calling back—he didn't answer. I tried three times. As I ran on the treadmill, I frowned, wondering just what the hell my little brother had gotten himself into.

The thing was, it was *Max*. He might be twenty, but he was *still* a kid, and I felt like I'd abandoned him after getting out of my shitty situation.

The problem was that I'd jumped from getting my ass kicked every day to a life of not-so-stable crime that I didn't want Max involved in. For the year after I ditched the Joneses, I was a pickpocket and a thief. Did anything to survive. That was when Paul Denton found me—I tried to pick his pocket, but he caught me, dragged me into his garage, and tied me up. I thought I was going to die. Instead, he'd given me a job. A life. A home.

*And how did you reward him?*

---

# ARI

When I was young, I was told that nightmares weren't real. That they were only dreams, and I should get over them. But the same nightmare that had gripped me since I was fifteen years old tugged at me now, pulling me down under the weight of it all.

The blood oozing through my fingers. My hoarse screams. *Dad. No, Dad, please! No. I can't lose you.*

I was drowning in the whiskey-colored eyes of the man responsible for my biggest trauma as he mouthed the same words to me on repeat: *I'm sorry. I'm sorry. I'm sorry.*

She shrugged. "Well, you said he's prone to getting himself in trouble, right? What if he's *supposed* to contact you but doesn't want to do that, so he's going through the motions? Maybe that's why he's not leaving a message or calling your cell, where he would actually reach you."

I cursed under my breath. "All right, have all calls rerouted to my cell."

"Oh, no. Do you know how many calls you're going to get?"

"Yes, but if he's calling, I need to talk to him."

"How about this: I'll reroute all calls to me, and if it's urgent, I'll forward it to you. That way you won't get inundated with all the business calls and money requests."

"That's fair," I said. Jazz was a godsend. She protected me in a way I didn't know I needed to be protected. She certainly made my life a lot easier. "You got everything else handled?"

"Yup. Have a good workout." Jazz turned to go, her heels making a *click-clack* sound on the marble floor. I told her she didn't need to do the whole professional-PA thing, but she said the routine and the uniform of sorts helped her.

Jazz was loyal and protected me at all costs, often to her own detriment. My plan wasn't to keep her as my PA forever. It was too risky for her. I'd give her another year and then move her to the import-export side of my business. That was the plan B profession. The one I paid taxes on.

As I started a quick warm-up, I did the one thing I knew I shouldn't do: I called Max. It wasn't a secure line. But I figured I could just call and hear his voice and know he was all right. This risk would be worth it.

to run away and had found Paul. Max ran the streets and got into a lot of trouble. In those early years with Paul, I hadn't kept great tabs on him. I'd been so worried about my own survival. But as soon as I had some money and got stable, I looked him and Jazz up.

Jazz was my age, trying to earn enough money to take classes part-time. She'd had a rough go of it after the Joneses, so when I was in a position to help, I did. Just like with Max.

Except she'd taken to the job I'd given her. Unlike my brother.

Max, I'd taken under my wing and pseudo adopted. Hell, he even took my last name. But he was still struggling with exactly what he wanted to do with his life, and I more often than not struggled with the best way to help him. I'd given him money and opportunities, but he didn't seem to want what I was offering outside of booze and partying.

He resented me for not getting him away from the Joneses. And I carried that guilt. But I'd been starving on the street until I met Paul. I would have just gotten him killed.

*You got him out as soon as you could.*

But somehow it never felt early enough.

"Has he left messages?" I asked.

"No, but he's tried your main office number twice and tried Paris as well."

I muttered under my breath, "Shit." Then I added, louder, "He doesn't have my new cell number? I texted it to him as soon as I changed it. Maybe he's in trouble?"

"Maybe. Or maybe he's not *actually* trying to reach you."

I paused and halted right at the opening of my gym. "What do you mean?"

She laughed nervously while pushing her glasses up her nose. "Fine. *Liberate*. But not that one. You can't liberate it unless you hide it or it's for a private client."

I frowned at her. "Fine, leave it be. Let's wait until the Rembolt Gallery puts it up for sale officially and see where it goes."

"I promise you, it will only be higher."

"I hear you. But we'll see."

"Right. Final item on the list… The last payment you sent to the Burmans wasn't deposited. Should I call and follow up to make sure they received it?"

I stalled. *The Burmans*. They'd by far been my best fostering situation. I'd only been with them for a couple of years though.

The woman, Linda Burman, had gotten cancer, which meant the Burmans had to stop taking on foster kids. They were genuinely good people. I'd loved that home and been really disappointed to leave.

I'd been moved to the Joneses' after that, where I'd met Jazz. I'd run away from there as quickly as I could.

"Um, just check in with the Burmans and see if Linda is okay. If she's not, arrange a flight for me."

"Okay, done. And your brother has been calling. For a couple of weeks now."

I paused again.

*Max.*

We'd met at the Burmans', and he'd been five at the time I moved in. God, the kid had followed me everywhere. I could still see his blond curls bouncing happily by my side.

Like me, he'd had a much shittier family next. But I'd been able

# DAMON

"What are you doing with the Picasso?"

I marched down the hallway of my split-level penthouse with my assistant, Jazz, trailing me. "Store that one in Saint-Tropez."

"And the Polygon painting?"

I considered for a moment. "What's the price?"

"Right now, the price is thirteen million."

I frowned as I stepped back. "Do we need to *buy* that one? Depending on the owners, I can always separate them from the painting the old-fashioned way."

Jazz chewed the corner of her lip and considered while tucking her wavy, often-frizzy hair behind her ears. "Well, if you would like to keep it private and never show it, other than maybe in your office in Paris, then fine. But it's way too hot a commodity to steal otherwise."

I frowned at that. "You mean *liberate*, right, Jazz?"

When we pulled in, Ari was right there. Like she had somehow known she needed to be there.

Her face when I opened the back of that van was not one I'd soon forget. I was responsible for it. And now...now I was running.

*No. You are doing what Paul trained you to do. You are going to get somewhere safe, get your go bag. Recover, and make a new plan.* *

That was what he had taught me. He'd spent weeks teaching me how to survive in case shit went wrong. He had a safe house not five miles away from where he actually lived. A little basement apartment. Nothing special. But it had go bags with money, identification, clothes. And it was a place to rest. I guessed he'd always known that something could go wrong and had wanted me to have a way out.

But the idea of continuing without him left a giant gaping hole in my chest—the size of the very real one in my mentor's chest.

I didn't know how I was going to do it. But one day, I was going to make Michael Lane pay.

---

* FORGOT ABOUT DRE–Dr. Dre and Eminem

poster child for there being no honor among thieves. He'd beat Paul out on a couple of jobs before—jobs he hadn't planned or participated in. He'd just waited until Paul and his crew had done all the work, then swooped in and stolen from Paul.

"What the hell was he doing here?"

Paul's weight on my shoulder had been heavy as I'd tried to drag him toward the door. His words in my ear had been barely intelligible, but I'd heard him mutter, "Silent alarm."

And sure enough, as if on cue, I'd seen flashlights and running feet down the right in the other hall. It was time to go.

As I'd dragged him out the side entrance, he'd wheezed. It wasn't until I'd managed to get him back into the van that I saw the problem. Lane had shot him, and if I didn't do something quick, he was going to die.

*It'll be your fault.*

I'd left him alone instead of staying with him like always.

Paul had all these rules. When you went into the field, you followed the rules, or you never got to do another job again.

But that night, he'd broken his own rules, and I had listened to him like a fool. Now Paul was bleeding out, and Michael Lane had almost taken our prize. My only satisfaction was that the overconfident prick had tripped a silent alarm, so he'd walked away without the compass as well.

The compass was part of a private collection. Easy job. Certainly no one was supposed to fucking die.

I'd managed to get Paul into the van and back to the garage. On the way, I called for his doctor friend to meet us there, but Paul was barely hanging on.

Red ran off my hands as I scrubbed at them furiously, trying to get Paul's blood off me.

I had fucked up tonight. This was all my damned fault. I never should have left him. Thank God I had gone back to look for him when he didn't meet me at the rendezvous point.

Tonight's job was supposed to be simple: in and out. Paul was so anal about his plans. The timing had to be perfect. But something happened tonight. Something that made Paul frown and deviate from his usual plan.

The plan where we were supposed to stay *together*.

But he'd sent me the longer way toward the safe and told me he'd meet me there. When I made it and he didn't, I went looking for him. There was a man standing over him. The man took off running as soon as he saw me.

"What the hell?" I rushed to Paul's side, only to find him bleeding. There was no going after the compass now; we wouldn't make it.

The compass was his white whale. He'd been after it for years. I gave not one shit about it. So when he tried to pull himself up and head toward the retreating bastard, I had to stop him and help him to his feet.

"What the hell do you think you're doing?" I asked.

It was then that he whispered the two words that said everything. "Michael Lane."

My heart tripped into a gallop. It couldn't be.

Paul was always so mellow about everything. He wasn't given to overt big emotions, but get him started on Michael Lane, and he would bluster for hours. Apparently, this Lane dude was the

As the sirens drew nearer, Damon paced and cursed. Aunt Adele told him to go, to run, but he stared at my father and said, "No. I'm not leaving."

I lifted my gaze, staring through but not really seeing the boy my father had chosen over me. The boy with the dancing eyes and quick smile, who made me nervous with his presence. I knew what would happen if he stayed.

I knew my father would never want that, so I whispered, "Go. Run. I'll stay with him." Damon tried to shove me out of the way, but I batted his hands away. "Just go!"

He tugged at his hair. "I'm sorry, Ari…" His breathing was choppy as he continued to mutter. "What the hell was he even doing there?"

I was barely listening. My gaze stayed pinned on my father.

"Daddy. Dad, come on, you promised you wouldn't leave me like Mom did." My heart thundered in my chest.

I couldn't let him die. *Please. Please, please, please.*

# DAMON

I was out the door and running along the back alleyway. My heart and my lungs were ready to burst, but I still pumped my legs and my arms furiously as I sprinted away from the screech of sirens.

By the time I crossed over three blocks and two more alleyways, I was panting. I finally stopped at one of the row houses with a hose connected in the backyard, and I turned the water on.

The bottom fell out of my stomach. My knees quivered, but I managed to stay upright and run with them as they pushed him into the back room.

All I heard was Damon cursing as he pressed his hands to Dad's ribs. "Paul. Paul, you look at me. Eyes on me. What the fuck happened? We were supposed to stay together."

I frowned at his back. "You didn't stay together?"

Damon's head whipped around, and he went pale. "What the fuck is she doing here, Adele?"

Adele frowned at him. "This is her father's shop. What, did you guys think she was going to go to bed and wait for you to get back?"

His face was bleak, his eyes cold and flat. The faded scar on his cheek was far more prevalent now that he was so pale.

He turned back to my dad and continued to press on his chest. "Where the fuck is the doc?"

There was so much blood. So much.

Damon was going to let him die. And I'd be all alone.

So I broke the cardinal rule. I pulled out my phone and dialed 911.

My aunt and Damon stared at me, horrified. But I didn't care. I cradled my father's head where he lay and pressed my hand over Damon's on his chest.

"What have you done, Ari?" my aunt asked as she tried to move me, but I wouldn't let her. If I let go, he'd die. It would be my fault. I didn't have time to feel, and I didn't care who was mad at me. He was all I had left.

Even if he didn't want me, I couldn't let him die.

honestly wasn't fair that his jaw looked like it belonged in one of my mom's old fashion magazines. It made it harder to loathe him. But I was committed to my hate-Damon-Hunt-forever cause.

"Please. I have taste. He's not even that cute."

Adele only lifted a brow and chuckled under her breath. "If you say so, honey. Come find me in a few years when you start noticing other things about Damon Hunt."

"Never going to happen."

For another thirty minutes, I tried to pretend I wasn't watching the door for them, but then I gave up. Half past twelve. They should've been back by now. They were more than forty minutes late.

My father would be pissed to see me waiting. For years I'd been begging him to teach me again, to let me learn from him again, but he'd refused, preferring to train his precious protégé instead.

So I'd kept learning on my own.

My gut churned and twisted, sending splashes of bile up my esophagus—not enough to rise but enough to injure.

Finally, the gate opened, and we heard screeching tires. Adele tried to keep her face completely neutral, but we both knew that sound was bad news.

The van blew in past the open rolling metal gate with razor wire on top, and it didn't stop. The tires smoked as the van barreled straight at us. When it squealed to a stop, Damon Hunt jumped out first.

He ran to the back and swung open the van doors before climbing back in and carrying my father out.

I froze as I watched them. Damon screamed at Adele to clear the gurney and bring it out.

Monetarily, he made sure I had the best. I attended Saint Alban's School for Girls, which would have been shocking on the kind of salary he pretended to have. But as far as the outside world knew, I was on a scholarship. And anyone at the school would tell you that a donor had paid my way. What they didn't know was that my dad was the donor. He had found a way to give me everything I needed and deserved. Even without Mom.

Everything except someone to talk to. Someone who made an effort to understand me.

That didn't stop me from trying to repair our connection though. I kept thinking that if I kept at it, he'd eventually *see* me like he used to.

"Honey, I swear. You're driving me to drink more than I already do." Adele adjusted her glasses so they slid down to the tip of her nose. "Or is there another reason you're trying to get your steps in?" Eyeing me shrewdly, she added, "Another reason you're anxious? Maybe someone else you're waiting for?"

I whipped around, my face flaming. "Wh-what?"

With a chuckle, she turned her gaze back to her papers. "Ari, love, I have eyes. And the kid is cute. Going to be a real looker, that one."

Oh God, was it obvious to everyone? "I don't know what you're talking about."

*When in doubt deny, deny, deny.*

So what if Damon Hunt was the most beautiful boy I'd ever seen?

He was annoying. Not to mention he hogged my father's attention. And he wasn't even as good with safes as I was. It

father. He's an expert at planning. He always has a plan B, a plan C, and a plan D. Everything is fine. And if it's not fine, he has a plan for it. So sit down with a book or whatever the hell, and stop with the pacing. You're making me nervous."

I chewed my bottom lip. She was right about Dad. He always had a plan. So why couldn't I ignore the feelings skipping up my spine?

"When it comes to your father's job, you'll learn to deal with the ups and downs. You'll learn to sit with certain things that nobody else has to deal with."

*Like the secrets you all have to keep.*

For a while there, when Mom was in and out of the hospital, my dad had been my best friend. He used to show me blueprints of buildings and ask me how I'd break in. Unconventional, but it kept me distracted from Mom's illness. He was all I had left after she lost her battle with cancer right before my tenth birthday.

But when I'd started building safe schematics in fifth-grade art class, he'd become increasingly distant, started pushing me away, and made it a point to keep me away from the life.

I would sketch schematics out by myself. Make my own plans based on the conversations I'd overheard or the things I'd seen that I shouldn't have. He'd put a stop to that too.

After that point, it seemed there was nothing I could do for him to look at me the same way. Our bonds were frayed.

To the outside world, my dad owned this repair shop. Cars came in, got fixed, and left. It was his *side* business that no one knew about. And the side business was where Dad built his nest egg.

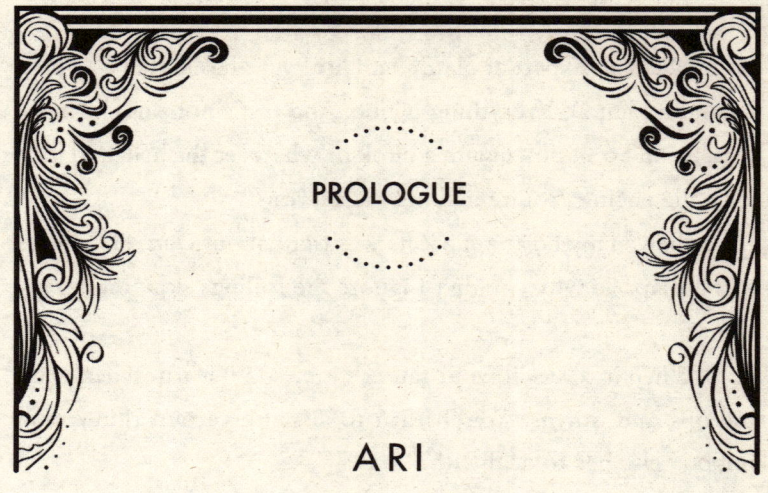

## PROLOGUE

## ARI

I had a bad feeling about this.

They were late. Dad was never late. He hated being even a minute late to *anything*. He was always drilling into me that timing was everything.

But they weren't here.

I paced back and forth in the repair shop, checking the clock. Aunt Adele, my dad's bookkeeper, glowered at me as I moved.

I turned around as soon as I reached the wall to the office and started pacing back the other way.

"Hey, girl, enough is enough. You're going to wear a path into my concrete."

"Sorry, Aunt Adele. It's just… They're late." I played with the ends of two of my box braids like I always did when I was anxious.

Adele rolled her chair from her desk to Dad's, then rifled through a drawer, looking for something. "Ari, you know your

**VEGAS**–Doja Cat

**I WANNA BE YOUR SLAVE**–Måneskin

**GOLDENEYE**–Tina Turner

**NEW RULES**–Dua Lipa

**MONEY ON THE DASH**–Elley Duhé feat. Whethan

**BANG BANG**–K'naan feat. Adam Levine

**WALLS COULD TALK**–Halsey

**LOVE, SEX, MAGIC**–Ciara feat. Justin Timberlake

**MURDER**–Justin Timberlake feat. Jay-Z

**BUBBA SAYS**–Bubba Graham

# PLAYLIST

Throughout *Royal Heart*, you'll find footnotes referring to songs that inspired a scene, might be playing in the background of a scene, or may otherwise enhance your reading experience. We encourage you to cue up these songs so they're ready to play whenever you see them referenced. For a handy Spotify playlist  tailored to each book, go to read.sourcebooks.com /blackroseauction or scan the QR code and search for *Royal Heart*.

**FORGOT ABOUT DRE**–Dr. Dre and Eminem

**SON OF A PREACHER MAN**–Dusty Springfield

**EXPRESS YOURSELF**–Charles Wright and the Watts

**REHAB**–Amy Winehouse

**DON'T HURT YOURSELF**–Beyoncé feat. Jack White

**MERCY**–Duffy

**KISS**–Prince and the Revolution

**TOM'S DINER**–AnnenMayKantereit feat. Giant Rooks

**LOSE CONTROL**–Teddy Swims

**HAVE MERCY**–Chlöe

**PARTITION**–Beyoncé

**BEGGIN'**–Måneskin

**HOLD UP**–Beyoncé

**ME AND THE DEVIL**–Gil Scott-Heron

# CONTENT GUIDANCE

**TROPES:** Heist romance, second-chance romance.

**TAGS:** Good girl gone bad, thief, revenge, bad boy is still bad just with bigger shoulders, I hate you except when you do that thing with your tongue, a little light stalking is fine, antihero, I hate that you've turned me into a bad girl, crush not so unrequited, you killed my father prepare to die, interracial romance.

**CONTENT WARNINGS:** Light stalking, stealing, murder, assault, violence, explicit sex, attempted sexual assault (not the hero), breeding.

*our favorite heist movies! You have the hero and heroine with a complicated history connected to her father/his mentor who have to work together to steal back a necklace called the Royal Heart.*

*We enjoyed this one immensely! This is steamy, sexy spy shit filled with plenty of competence porn! Of course a fake marriage is part of their cover story, giving us delicious forced proximity, tension that's ready to bubble over, and maybe even…a danger bang.*

*Jenny Nordbak and Katee Robert*

# FOREWORD

*When we set out to create the Black Rose Auction series, we knew we wanted it to be luxe and dangerous and sexy! The premise is that there's an annual auction, presided over by the mysterious Reaper, where anything can be purchased for the right price. It's a place to make statements, to auction off the services of some of the world's most exclusive sex workers, to find priceless artifacts that the general public has only heard rumors of. Within these six books, you'll find dangerous men, powerful women, and a heist or two! Be sure to check out read. sourcebooks.com/blackroseauction or scan the QR code to get an introduction to all six authors and their work!*

*When Nana agreed to be part of this project, we desperately hoped that she would write a heist book. What's an illicit auction filled with priceless items if there's not a thief with a heart of gold stealing something from it? This book gives big Italian Job vibes, which is one of*

*To all the girls that want to save the day
and still be called…"Good Girl."*

Copyright © 2024, 2025 by Nana Malone
Cover and internal design © 2025 by Sourcebooks
Cover illustration and Design © Elizabeth Turner Stokes
Internal design by Tara Jaggers/Sourcebooks
Rose frame art © Marek Trawczynski/Getty Images
Header illustration and design © Azura Arts

Sourcebooks and the colophon are registered trademarks of Sourcebooks.

All rights reserved. No part of this book may be reproduced in any form or by any electronic or mechanical means including information storage and retrieval systems—except in the case of brief quotations embodied in critical articles or reviews—without permission in writing from its publisher, Sourcebooks.

No part of this book may be used or reproduced in any manner for the purpose of training artificial intelligence technologies or systems.

The characters and events portrayed in this book are fictitious or are used fictitiously. Any similarity to real persons, living or dead, is purely coincidental and not intended by the author.

All brand names and product names used in this book are trademarks, registered trademarks, or trade names of their respective holders. Sourcebooks is not associated with any product or vendor in this book.

Published by Sourcebooks Casablanca, an imprint of Sourcebooks
1935 Brookdale RD, Naperville, IL 60563-2773
(630) 961-3900
sourcebooks.com

Originally self-published in 2024 by Nana Malone.

Cataloging-in-Publication Data is on file with the Library of Congress.

The authorized representative in the EEA is Dorling Kindersley Verlag GmbH. Arnulfstr. 124, 80636 Munich, Germany

Manufactured in the UK and distributed by Dorling Kindersley Limited, London
001-352804-Oct/25
CPI 10 9 8 7 6 5 4 3 2 1

# ROYAL HEART

# NANA MALONE

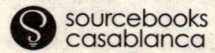

The

# BLACK ROSE AUCTION:

# ROYAL HEART

# ALSO BY NANA MALONE

### WINSTON ISLES ROYALS
*Cheeky Royal*
*Cheeky King*
*Royal Bastard*
*Bastard Prince*
*Royal Tease*
*Teasing the Princess*

### LONDON LORDS
*Big Ben*
*The Benefactor*
*For Her Benefit*
*East End*
*East Bound*
*The Fall of East*
*London Bridge*
*Bridge of Lies*
*Broken Bridge*

### KINGS OF THE BOARDROOM
*Takeover*
*Acquisition*
*Merger*

### GENTLEMEN ROGUES (INTERCONNECTED STANDALONES)
*The King*
*The Saint*
*The Rook*
*The Spy*
*The Villain*

### IN STILETTOS
*Sexy in Stilettos*
*Sultry in Stilettos*
*Sassy in Stilettos*
*Strollers & Stilettos*
*Seductive in Stilettos*
*Stunning in Stilettos*
*Tempting in Stilettos*
*Teasing in Stilettos*
*Tantalizing in Stilettos*

*Welcome to the*

# BLACK ROSE AUCTION

In **SHATTERED INNOCENCE** by Sara Cate, a Cinderella remix, a woman is being auctioned off even though all she wants is her stepsister. Desperate, the two hatch a plan to have an old flame bid on her behalf...only for him to decide he's playing for keeps and wants them both.

In **ROYAL HEART** by Nana Malone, a Beauty and the Beast remix, a woman must work with the thief she blames for her father's death to steal back a priceless royal necklace. But the dark depths of the auction is no place for unwary hearts, and soon she may be the one stolen after all...

# ROYAL
# HEART